THEY WERE SEPARATED
BY TWO CITIES...

There was a hell on earth today and he lived in that City of Fire continually now. He expected to live there forever. It was too late ever to turn back. "All hope abandon, ye who enter here." He had read it and defied it. He had entered knowing what he was about, and thinking, poor fool that he was, that he was doing a wise and noble thing for the sake of another.

Over in the little parsonage, the white-souled girl was walking in an earthly heaven. There was nothing, *nothing* they had in common now anymore. She lived in the City of Hope and he in the City of Fire.

He flung out the book from him and dropped his face into his hands crying softly under his breath. "Oh, Lynn, Lynn—Marilyn!"

Bantam Books by Grace Livingston Hill
Ask your bookseller for the books you have missed

#65 AN UNWILLING GUEST
#66 THE GIRL FROM MONTANA
#67 A DAILY RATE
#68 THE STORY OF A WHIM
#69 ACCORDING TO THE PATTERN
#70 IN THE WAY
#71 EXIT BETTY
#72 THE WHITE LADY
#73 NOT UNDER THE LAW
#74 LO, MICHAEL
#75 THE WITNESS
#76 THE CITY OF FIRE

The City of Fire

Grace Livingston Hill

BANTAM BOOKS

TORONTO · NEW YORK · LONDON · SYDNEY · AUCKLAND

THE CITY OF FIRE

*A Bantam Book / published by arrangement with
Harper & Row, Publishers, Inc.*

PRINTING HISTORY

J.B. Lippincott edition published in 1922

Bantam edition / November 1986

ISBN 0-553-26104-5

Published simultaneously in the United States and Canada

The City of Fire

Chapter 1

Sabbath Valley lay like a green jewel cupped in the hand of the surrounding mountains with the morning sun serene upon it picking out the clean smooth streets, the white houses with their green blinds, the maples with their clear-cut leaves, the cozy brick schoolhouse wide-winged and friendly, the vine-clad stone church, and the little stone bungalow with low spreading roof that was the parsonage. The word manse had not yet reached the atmosphere. There were no affectations in Sabbath Valley.

Billy Gaston, two miles away and a few degrees up the mountainside, standing on the little station platform at Pleasant View, waiting for the morning train, looked down upon the beauty at his feet and felt its loveliness blindly. A passing thrill of wonder and devotion fled through his fourteen-year-old soul as he regarded it idly. Down there was home and all his interests and loyalty. His eyes dwelt affectionately on the pointing spire and bell tower. He loved those bells, and the one who played them, and under their swelling tones had been awakened new thoughts and lofty purposes. He knew they were lofty. He was not yet altogether sure that they were his, but they were there in his mind for him to think about, and there was a strange awesome lure about their contemplation.

Down the platform was the new freight agent, a thickset, rubber-shod individual with a projecting lower jaw and a lowering countenance. He had lately arrived to assist the regular station agent, who lived in a bit of a shack up the mountain and was a thin sallow creature with sad eyes and no muscles. Pleasant View was absolutely what it stated, a pleasant view and nothing else. The station was a well-

1

weathered box that blended into the mountainside unnoticeably, and did not spoil the view. The agent's cabin was hidden by the trees and did not count. But Pleasant View was important as a station because it stood at the intersection of two lines of threadlike tracks that slipped among the mountains in different directions; one, winding among the trees and about a clear mountain lake, carried guests for the summer to and fro, and great quantities of baggage and freight from afar; the other traveled through long tunnels to the world beyond and linked great cities like jewels on a chain. There were heavy bales and boxes and many trunks to be shifted and it was obvious that the sallow station agent could not do it all. The heavy one had been sent to help him through the rush season.

In five minutes more the train would come from around the mountain and bring a swarm of ladies and children for the hotel at the lake. They would have to be helped off with all their luggage, and on again to the lake train, which would back up two minutes later. This was Billy's harvest time. He could sometimes make as much as fifty cents or even seventy-five if he struck a generous party, just being generally useful, carrying bags and marshaling babies. It was important that Billy should earn something, for it was Saturday and the biggest ball game of the season came off at Monopoly that afternoon. Billy could manage the getting there, it was only ten miles away, but money to spend when he arrived was more than a necessity. Saturday was always a good day at the station.

Billy had slipped into the landscape unseen. His rusty, trusty old bicycle was parked in a thick huckleberry growth just below the grade of the tracks, and Billy himself stood in the shelter of several immense packing boxes piled close to the station. It was a niche just big enough for his wiry young length with the open station window close at his ear. From either end of the platform he was hidden, which was as it should be until he got ready to arrive with the incoming train.

The regular station agent was busy checking a high pile of trunks that had come down on the early lake train from the hotel and had to be transferred to the New York train. He was on the other side of the station and some distance down the platform.

Beyond the packing boxes the heavy one worked with brush and paint marking some barrels. If Billy applied an eye to the crack in his hiding place he could watch every stroke of the fat black brush, and see the muscles in the swarthy cheeks move as the man mouthed a big black cigar. But Billy was not interested in the new freight agent, and remained in his retreat, watching the brilliant sunshine shimmer over the blue-green haze of spruce and pine that furred the way down to the valley. He basked in it like a cat blinking its content. The rails were beginning to hum softly, and it would not be long till the train arrived.

Suddenly Billy was aware of a shadow looming.

The heavy one had laid down his brush and was stealing swiftly, furtively to the door of the station with a weather eye to the agent on his knees beside a big trunk writing something on a check. Billy drew back like a turtle to his shell and listened. The rail was beginning to sing decidedly now and the telephone inside the grated window suddenly set up a furious ringing. Billy's eye came round the corner of the window, scanned the empty platform, glimpsed the office desk inside and the weighty figure holding the receiver, then vanished enough to be out of sight, leaving only a wide curious ear to listen:

"That you, Sam? Yep. Nobody about. Train's coming. Hustle up. Anything doing? You *don't say!* Some big guy? *Say,* that's good news at last! Get on the other wire and hold it. I'll come as quick as the train's gone. S'long!"

Billy cocked a curious eye like a flash into the window and back again, ducking behind the boxes just in time to miss the heavy one coming out with an excited air, and a feverish eye on the track where the train was coming into view around the curve.

In a moment all was stir and confusion, seven women wanting attention at once, and imperious men of the world crying out against railroad regulations. Billy hustled everywhere, transferring bags and suitcases with incredible rapidity to the other train, which arrived promptly, securing a double seat for the fat woman with the canary, and the poodle in a big basket, depositing the baggage of a pretty lady on the shady side, making himself generally useful to the opulent-looking man with the jeweled rings; and back again for another lot. A whole dollar and fifteen cents jingled in his grimy pocket as the trains finally moved off in their separate directions and the peace of Pleasant Valley settled down monotonously once more.

Billy gave a hurried glance about him. The station agent was busy with another batch of trunks, but the heavy one was nowhere to be seen. He gave a quick glance through the grated window where the telegraph instrument was clicking away sleepily, but no one was there. Then a stir among the pines below the track attracted his attention, and stepping to the edge of the bank he caught a glimpse of a broad dusty back lumbering hurriedly down among the branches.

With a flirt of his eye back to the absorbed station agent Billy was off down the mountain after the heavy one, walking stealthily as any cat, pausing in alert attention, listening, peering out eerily whenever he came to a break in the undergrowth. Like a young mole burrowing he wove his way under branches the larger man must have turned aside, and so his going was as silent as the air. Now and then he could hear the crash of a broken branch, or the crackle of a twig, or the rolling of a stone set free by a heavy foot, but he went on like a cat, like a little wood shadow, till suddenly he felt he was almost upon his prey. Then he paused and listened.

The man was kneeling just below him. He could hear the labored breathing. There was a curious sound of metal and wood, of a key turning in a lock. Billy drew himself softly into a group of cypress and held his breath. Softly he parted the foliage and peered. The man was down upon his knees before a rough box, holding something in his hand which he put to his ear. Billy could not quite see what it was. And now the man began to talk into the box. Billy ducked and listened:

"Hello, Sam! You there! Couldn't come any quicker, lots of passengers. Lots of freight. What's doing, anyhow?"

Billy could hear a faint murmur of words, now and then one guttural burst out and became distinct, and gradually enough words pieced themselves together to become intelligible.

"... Rich guy! High-power machine.... Great catch.... Tonight!... Got a bet on to get there by sunrise.... Can't miss him!"

Billy lay there puzzled. It sounded shady, but what was the line anyway? Then the man spoke.

"Sounds easy, Sammy, but how we goin' to kidnap a man in a high-power machine? Wreck it of course, but he might get killed and where would be the reward? Besides, he's likely to be a good shot—"

The voice from the ground again growing clearer:

"Put something across the road that he'll have to get out and move, like a fallen tree, or one of you lie in the road beside the car as if you was hurt. I'm sending Short and Link. They'll get there about eight o'clock. Beat him to it by an hour anyway, maybe more. Now it's up to you to look after details. Get anyone you want to help till Shorty and Link get there, and pay 'em so in case anything gets them, or they're late. I'll keep you wise from time to time how the guy gets on. I've got my men on the watch along the line."

"I'd like t' know who I'd get in this godforsaken place!" growled the heavy one. "Not a soul in miles except the agent, and *he'd* run right out and telegraph for the state constab. Say, Sammy, who is this guy anyway? Is there enough in it to pay for the risk? You know kidnapping ain't any juvenile demeanor. I didn't promise no such stuff as this when I said I'd take a hand over here. Now just a common little holdup ain't so bad. That could happen on any lonely mountain road. But this here kidnapping, you never can tell how its going to turn out. Might be murder before you got through, especially if Link is along. *You know Link!*"

"That's all right, Pat, you needn't worry. This'll go through slick as a whistle, and a million in it if we work it right. The house is all ready—you know where—and never a soul in all the world would suspect. It's far enough away and yet not too far. You'll make enough out of this to retire for life if you want to, Pat, and no mistake. All you've got to do is to handle it right, and you know your business."

"Who'd you say he was?"

"Shafton, Laurence Shafton, son of the big Shafton, you know Shafton and Gates."

A heavy whistle blended with the whispering pines.

"You don't say? How much family?"

"Mother living, got separate fortune in her own right. Father just dotes on him. Uncle has a big estate on Long

Island, plenty more millions there. I think a million is real modest of us to ask, don't you?"

"Where's he goin' to? What makes you think he'll come this way 'stead of the valley road?"

" 'Cause he's just started, got all the directions for the way, went over it carefully with his valet. Valet gave me the tip you understand, and has to be in on the rake-off. It's his part to keep close to the family, see? Guy's goin' down to Beechwood to a house party, got a bet on that he'll make it before daylight. He's bound to pass your mountain soon after midnight, see? Are you goin' to do your part, or ain't you? Or have I got to get a new agent down there? And say! I want a message on this wire as soon as the job is completed. Now, you understand? Can you pull it off?"

It was some time after the key clicked in the lock and the bulky form of the freight agent lumbered up through the pines again before Billy stirred. Then he wriggled around through the undergrowth until he found himself in front of the innocent-looking little box covered over with dried grass and branches. He examined it all very carefully, pried underneath with his jackknife, discovered the spot where the wire connected, speculated as to where it tapped the main line, prospected a bit about the place and then on hands and knees wormed himself through the thick growth of the mountain till he came out to the huckleberry clump, and recovering his bicycle walked innocently up to the station as if it were the first time that day and inquired of the surly freight man whether a box had come for his mother.

In the first place Billy hadn't any mother, only an aunt who went out washing and had hard times to keep a decent place for Billy to sleep and eat, and she never had a box come by freight in her life. But the burly one did not know that. Just what Billy Gaston did it for, perhaps he did not quite know himself, save that the lure of hanging round a mystery was always great. Moreover it gave him deep joy to know that he knew something about this man that the man did not know he knew. It was always good to know things. It was always wise to keep your mouth shut about them when you knew them. Those were the two most prominent planks in Billy Gaston's present platform and he stood upon them firmly.

The burly one gave Billy a brief and gruff negative to his

query and went on painting barrel labels. He was thinking of other matters, but Billy still hung around. He had a hunch that he might be going to make merchandise in some way of the knowledge that he had gained, so he hung around, silently, observantly, leaning on old rusty trusty.

The man looked up and frowned suspiciously:

"I told you NO!" he snapped threateningly. "What you standin' there for?"

Billy regarded him amusedly as from a superior height.

"Don't happen to know of any odd jobs I could get," he finally condescended.

"Where would you expect a job around this dump?" sneered the man with an eloquent wave toward the majestic mountain. "Busy little hive right here now, ain't it?"

He subsided and Billy, slowly, thoughtfully, mounted his wheel and rode around the station, with the air of one who enjoys the scenery. The third time he rounded the curve by the freight agent the man looked up with a speculative squint and eyed the boy. The fourth time he called out, straightening up and laying down his brush.

"Say, kid, do you know how to keep yer mouth shut?"

The boy regarded him with infinite contempt.

"Well, that depends!" he said at last. "If anybody'd make it worth my while."

The man looked at him narrowly, the tone was at once so casual and yet so full of possible meaning. The keenest searching revealed nothing in the immobile face of the boy. A cunning grew in the eyes of the man.

"How would a five look to you?"

"Not enough," said the boy promptly. "I need twenty-five."

"Well, ten then."

The boy rode off down the platform and circled the station again while the man stood puzzled, half troubled, and watched him:

"I'll make it fifteen. What you want, the earth with a gold fence around it?"

"I said I needed twenty-five," said Billy doggedly, lowering his eyes to cover the glitter of coming triumph.

The thick one stood squinting off at the distant mountain thoughtfully, then he turned and eyed Billy again.

"How'm I gonta know you're efficient?" he challenged.

"Guess you c'n take me er leave me," came back the boy quickly. "Course if you've got plenty help—"

The man gave him a quick bitter glance. The kid was sharp. He knew there was no one else. Besides, how much had he overheard? Had he been around when the station telephone rang? Kids like that were deep. You could always count of them to do a thing well if they undertook it.

"Well, mebbe I'll try you. You gotta be on hand t'night at eight o'clock sharp. It's mebbe an all-night job, but you may be through by midnight."

"What doing?"

"Nothing much. Just lay in the road with your wheel by your side and act like you had a fall an' was hurt. I wanta stop a man who's in a hurry, see?"

Billy regarded him coolly.

"Any shooting?"

"Oh, no!" said the other. "Just a little evening up of cash. You see that man's got some money that oughtta be mine by good rights, and I wantta get it."

"*I* see!" said Billy nonchalantly. "An' whatcha gonta do if he don't come across?"

The man gave him a scared look.

"Oh, nothin' sinful, son; just give him a rest fer a few days where he won't see his friends, until he gets ready to see it the way I do."

"H'm!" said Billy, narrowing his gray eyes to two slits. "An' how much did ya say ya paid down?"

The man looked up angrily.

"I don't say I pay nothing down. If you do the work right you get the cash, t'night, a round twenty-five, and it's twenty bucks more'n you deserve. Why off in this deserted place you oughtta be glad to get twenty-five cents fer doin' nothin' but lay in the road."

The boy with one foot on the pedal mounted sideways and slid along the platform slowly, indifferently.

"Guess I gotta date t'night," he called over his shoulder as he swung the other leg over the crossbar.

The heavy man made a dive after him and caught him by the arm.

"Look here, kid, I ain't in no mood to be toyed with," he

said gruffly. "You said you wanted a job an' I'm being square with you. Just to show I'm being square here's five down.'"

Billy looked at the ragged green bill with a slight lift of his shoulders.

"Make it ten down and it's a go," he said at last with a take-it-or-leave-it air. "I hadn't oughtta let you off'n less'n half, such a shady job as this looks, but make it a ten an' I'll close with ya. If ya don't like it ask the station agent to help ya. I guess he wouldn't object. He's right here handy, too. I live off quite a piece."

But the man had pulled out another five and was crowding the bills upon him. He had seen a alight in that boy's eyes that was dangerous. What was five in a case of a million anyway?

Billy received the boodle as if it had been chewing gum or a soiled handkerchief, and stuffed it indifferently into his already bulging pocket in a crumple as if it were not worth the effort.

"Aw'right. I'll be here!" he declared, and mounting his wheel with an air of finality, sailed away down the platform, curved off the high step with a bump into the road and coasted down the road below the tunnel toward Monopoly, leaving Sabbath Valley glistening in the sunshine off to the right. With all that money in his pocket what was the use of going back to Sabbath Valley for his lunch and making his trip a good two miles farther? He would beat the baseball team to it.

The thick one stood disconsolately, his grimy cap in his hand, and scratched his dusty head of curls in a troubled way.

"Gosh!" he said wrathfully. "The little devil! Now I don't know what he'll do. I wonder— But what else could I do?"

Chapter 2

Over in Sabbath Valley quiet sweetness brooded, broken now and again by the bell-like sound of childish laughter here and

there. The birds were holding high carnival in the trees, and
the bees humming drowsy little tunes to pretend they were
not working.

Most of the men were away at work, some in Monopoly or
Economy, whither they went in the early morning in their tin
lizzies to a little store or a country bank, or a dusty law office;
some in the fields of the fertile valley; and others off behind
the thick willow fringe where lurked the home industries of
tanning and canning and knitting, with a plush mill higher up
the slope behind a group of alders and beeches, its ugly stone
chimneys picturesque against the mountains, but doing its
best to spoil the little stream at its feet with all colors of the
rainbow, at intervals dyeing its bright waters.

The minister sat in his study with his window open across
the lawn between the parsonage and the church, a lovely
velvet view with the old graveyard beyond and the wooded
hill behind. He was faintly aware of the shouting of the birds
in glad carnival in the trees, and the busy droning of the
bees, as he wrote an article on modern atheism for a magazine in the distant world; but more keenly alive to the song
on the lips of his child, but lately returned from college life in
one of the great universities for women. He smiled as he
wrote, and a light came in his deep thoughtful eyes. She had
gone and come, and she was still unspoiled, mentally, physically or spiritually. That was a great deal to have kept out of
life in these days of unbelief. He had been almost afraid to
hope that she would come back the same.

In the cool sitting room his wife was moving about, putting
the house in order for the day, and he knew that on her lips
also was the smile of the same content as well as if he were
looking at her beloved face.

On the front veranda Marilyn Severn swept the rugs and
sang her happy song. She was glad, glad to be home again,
and her soul bubbled over with the joy of it. There was
happiness in the curve of her red lips, in the softly rounded
freshness of her cheek and brow, in the eyes that held
dancing lights like stars, and in every gleaming tendril of her
wonderful bright hair that burst forth from under the naive
little sweeping cap that sat on her head like a crown. She was
small, lithe, graceful, and she vibrated joy, health, eagerness
in every glance of her eye, every motion of her lovely hands.

Down the street suddenly sounded a car. Not the rattling, cheap affairs that were commonly used in those parts for hard work and dress affairs, with a tramp snuffle and bark as they bounced along beneath the maples like house dogs that knew their business and made as much noise about it as they could; but a car with a purr like a soft petted cat by the fire, yet a power behind that purr that might have belonged to a lion if the need for power arose. It stole down the street like a thing of the world, well oiled and perfect in its way, and not needing to make any clatter about its going. The very quietness of it made the minister look up, sent the minister's wife to raise the shade of the sitting room window, and caused the girl to look up from her task.

The morning flooded her face, the song was stayed, a great light came into her eyes.

The man who was driving the car had the air of not expecting to stop at the parsonage. Even when he saw the girl on the porch he held to his way, and something hard and cold and infinitely sad settled down over his face. It even looked as though he did not intend to recognize her, or perhaps wasn't sure whether she would recognize him. There was a moment's breathless suspense and the car slid just the fraction past the gate in the hedge, without a sign of stopping, only a lifting of a correct looking straw hat that somehow seemed a bit out of place in Sabbath Valley. But Lynn left no doubt in his mind whether she would recognize him. She dropped her broom and sped down the path, and the car came to an abrupt halt, only a hairbreadth past the gate—but still—that hairbreadth.

"Oh, Mark, I'm so glad to see you!" she cried genuinely with her hand out in welcome. "They said you were not at home."

The boy's voice—he had been a boy when she left him, though now he looked strangely hard and old like a man of the world—was husky as he answered gravely, swinging himself down on the walk beside her.

"I just got in late last night. How are you, Lynn? You're looking fine."

He took her offered hand, and clasped it for a brief instant in a warm strong pressure, but dropped it again and there was a quick cold withdrawing of his eyes that she did not understand. The old Mark Carter would never have looked at her coolly, impersonally like that. What was it, was he shy of her after the long separation? Four years was a long time, of course, but there had been occasional letters. He had always been away when she was at home, and she had been home very little between her school years. There had been summer sessions twice and once Father and Mother had come to her and they had taken a wonderful trip together. But always there had seemed to be Mark Carter, her old friend and playmate, in the background. Now, suddenly he seemed to be removed to indefinite distances. It was as if she were looking at a picture that purported to be her friend, yet seemed a travesty, like one wearing a mask. She stood in the sunlight looking at him, in her quaint little cap and a long white enveloping house apron, and she seemed to him like a haloed saint. Something like worship shone in his eyes, but he kept the mask down, and looked at her with the eyes of a stranger while he talked, and smiled a stiff conventional smile. But a look of anguish grew in his young face, like the sorrow of something primeval, such as a great rock in a desert.

The minister had forgotten his article and was watching them through the window, the tall handsome youth, his head bared with the glint of the sun on his short-cropped gold curls making one think of a young prince, yet a prince bound under a spell and frozen in a block of ice. He was handsome as Adonis, every feature perfect, and striking in its manly beauty, yet there was nothing feminine about him. The minister was conscious of all this as he watched—this boy whom he had seen grow up, and this girl of his heart. A great still question came into the father's look as he watched.

The minister was conscious of Lynn's mother standing in the doorway just behind him, although she had made no noise in entering. And at once she knew he was aware of her presence.

"Isn't that Mark Carter?" she asked just above a breath. He nodded.

"And she doesn't know! You haven't told her?"

The minister shook his head.

"He will tell her. See, he is telling her now!"

The mother drew a shade nearer.

"But how do you know? See, she is doing the talking. You think he will tell her? *What* will he tell her, Graham?"

"Oh, he will not tell her in words, but every atom of his being is telling her now. Can't you see? He is telling her that he is no longer worthy to be her equal. He is telling her that something has gone wrong."

"Graham, what do you *think* is the matter with him? Do you think he is—BAD?" She lifted frightened eyes to his as she dropped into her low chair that always stood conveniently near his desk.

A wordless sorrow overspread the minister's face, yet there was something valiant in his eyes.

"No, I can't think that. I must believe in him in spite of everything. It looks to me somehow as if he was trying to be bad and couldn't."

"Well, but—Graham, isn't that the same thing? If he wants to be?"

The minister shook his head.

"He doesn't want to be. But he has some purpose in it. He is doing it—perhaps—well—it might be for *her* sake you know."

The mother looked perplexed, and hesitated, then shook her head.

"That would be—preposterous! How could he hurt her so—if he cared. It must be—he does not care!"

"He cares!" said the man.

"Then how do you explain it?"

"I don't explain it."

"Are you going to let it go on?"

"What can be done?"

"I'd do something."

"No, Mary. That's something he's got to work out himself. If he isn't big enough to get over his pride. His self-consciousness. His—whatever he calls it— If he isn't big enough— Then he isn't *big* enough!" The man sighed with a faraway patient look. The woman stirred uneasily.

"Graham," she said suddenly lifting her eyes in troubled question, "when your cousin Eugenie was here, you remember, she talked about it one day. She said we had no right to let Lynn become so attached to a mere country boy who would grow up a boor. She said he had no education, no

breeding, no family, and that Lynn had the right to the best
social advantages to be had in the world. She said Lynn was a
natural born aristocrat, and that we had a great responsibility
bringing up a child with a face like hers, and a mind like
hers, and an inheritance like hers, in this little antiquated
country place. She said it was one thing for you with your
culture and your fine education and your years of travel and
experience, to hide yourself here if you choose for a few
years, pleasing yourself at playing with souls and uplifting a
little corner of the universe while you were writing a great
book; but it was quite another for us to allow our gifted young
daughter to know no other life. And especially she harped on
Lynn's friendship with Mark. She called him a hobbledehoy,
said his mother was 'common,' and that coming from a home
like that, he would never amount to anything or have an
education. He would always be common and loaferish, and it
wouldn't make any difference if he did, he would never be
cultured no matter how much education he had. He was not
in her *class*. She kept saying that over. She said a lot of
things, and always ended up with that. And finally she said
that we were perfectly crazy, both of us. That she supposed
Lynn thought she was Christianizing the boy or something,
but it was dangerous business, and we ought to be warned.
And Graham, *I'm afraid Mark heard it!* He was just coming
up on the porch as she finished and I'm almost sure he heard it!"

The eyes of the minister gave a startled flicker and then
grew comprehending. "I wondered why he gave up college
after he had worked so hard to get in."

"But, Graham! Surely, if he had heard he would have
wanted to show her that she was wrong."

"No, Mary. He is not built that way. It's his one big fault.
Always to be what he thinks people have labeled him, or to
seem to be. To be that in defiance, knowing in his heart he
really isn't that at all. It's a curious psychological study. It
makes me think of nothing else but when the prince of the
power of the air wanted to be God. Mark wants to be a young
God. When he finds he's not taken that way he makes himself
look like the devil in defiance. Don't you remember, Mary,
how when Bob Bliss broke that memorial window in the
church and said it was Mark did it, how Mark stood looking
defiantly from one to another of us to see if we would believe

it, and when he found the elders were all against him and had begun to get ready for punishment, he lifted his fine young shoulders, and folded his arms, and just bowed in acquiescence, as if to say yes, he had done it? Don't you remember, Mary? He nearly broke my heart that day, the hurt look in his eyes; the game, mistaken, little devil! He was only ten, and yet for four long months he bore the blame in the eyes of the whole village for breaking that window, till Bob told the truth and cleared him. Not because he wanted to save Bob Bliss, for everybody knew he was a little scamp, and needed punishment, but because he was *hurt*—hurt way down into the soul of him to think anybody had *thought* he would want to break the window we had all worked so hard to buy. And he actually broke three cellar windows in that vacant store by the post office, yes, and paid for them, just to keep up his character and give us some reason for our belief against him."

The wife with a cloud of anxiety in her eyes, and disapproval in her voice, answered slowly:

"That's a bad trait, Graham. I can't understand it. It is something wrong in his nature."

"Yes, Mary, it is sin, original sin, but it comes at him from a different direction from most of us, that's all. It comes through sensitiveness. It is his reaction to a deep and mortal hurt. Some men would be stimulated to finer action by criticism, he is stimulated to defy, and he does not know that he is trying to defy God and all the laws of the universe. Someday he will find it out, and know that only through humility can he make good."

"But he is letting all his opportunities go by."

"I'm not so sure. You can't tell what he may be doing out in the world where he is gone."

"But they say he is very wild."

"They were always saying things about him when he was here, and most of them were not true. You and I knew him, Mary. Was there ever a finer young soul on earth than he with his clear true eyes, his eager tender heart, his brave fearlessness and strength. I can not think he has sold his soul to sin—not yet. It may be. It may be that only in the far country will he realize it is God he wants and be ready to say, 'I have sinned' and 'I will arise.'"

"But, Graham, I should think that just because you believe in him you could talk to him."

"No, Mary. I can't probe into the depths of that sensitive soul and dig out his confidence. He would never give it that way. It is a matter between himself and God."

"But Lynn—"

"Lynn has God too, my dear. We must not forget that. Life is not all for this world, either. Thank God Lynn believes that!"

The mother sighed with troubled eyes, and rose. The purring of the engine was heard. Lynn would be coming in. They watched the young man swing his car out into the road and glide away like a comet with a wild sophisticated snort of his engine that sent him so far away in a flash. They watched the girl standing where he had left her, a stricken look upon her face, and saw her turn slowly back to the house with eyes down—troubled. The mother moved away. The father bent his head upon his hand with closed eyes. The girl came back to her work, but the song on her lips had died. She worked silently with a far look in her eyes, trying to fathom it.

The eyes of her father and mother followed her tenderly all that day, and it was as if the souls of the three had clasped hands, and understood, so mistily they smiled at one another.

Billy Gaston, refreshed by a couple of chocolate fudge sundaes, a banana whip, and a lemon ice-cream soda, was seated on the bench with the heroes of the day at the Monopoly baseball grounds. He wore his most nonchalant air, chewed gum with his usual vigor, shouted himself hoarse at the proper places, and made casual grown-up responses to the condescension of the team, wrapping them tenderly in ancient sweaters when they were disabled, and watching every move of the game with a practiced eye and an immobile countenance. But though to the eyes of the small fry on the grass at his feet he was as self-sufficient as ever, somehow he kept having strange qualms, and his mind kept reverting to the swart fat face of Pat at the junction, as it ducked behind the cypress and talked into the crude telephone on the mountain. Somehow he couldn't forget the gloat in his eyes as he spoke of the "rich guy." More and more uneasy he grew, more sure that the expedition to which he was pledged was not strictly "on the square."

Not that Billy Gaston was afraid. The thrill of excitement

burned along his veins and filled him with a fine elation whenever he thought of the great adventure, and he gave his pocket a protective slap where the ten bucks still reposed intact. He felt well pleased with himself to have made sure of those. Whatever happened he had that, and if the man wasn't on the square Pat deserved to lose that much. Not that Billy Gaston meant to turn yellow after promising, but there was no telling whether the rest of the twenty-five would be forthcoming or not. He fell to calculating its worth in terms of new sweaters and baseball bats. If worse came to worst he could threaten to expose Pat and his scheme.

During the first and second innings these reflections soothed his soul and made him sit immovable with jaws grinding in rhythmic harmony with the day. But at the beginning of the third inning one of the boys from his Sunday school class strolled by and flung himself full length on the grass at his feet where he could see his profile just as he had seen it on Sunday while he was listening to the story that the teacher always told to introduce the lesson. He could see the blue of Lynn Severn's eyes as she told it, and strangely enough portions of the tale came floating back in trailing mist across the dusty baseball diamond and obscured the sight of Sloppy Hedrick sliding to his base. It was a tale of one, Judas, who betrayed his best Friend with a kiss. It came with strange illogical persistence, and seemed curiously incongruous with the sweet air of summer blowing over the hard young faces and dusty diamond. What had Judas to do with a baseball game, or with Billy Gaston and what he meant to do on the mountain that night? And earn good money! Ah! That was it. Make good money! But who was he betraying he would like to know? Well if it wasn't on the square perhaps he was betraying that same *One*— Aw— Rats! He wasn't under anybody's thumb and Judas lived centuries ago. He wasn't doing any harm helping a man do something he wasn't supposed to know what. Hang it all! Where was Mark Carter anyway? Somehow Cart always seemed to set a fella straight. He was like Miss Lynn. He saw through things you hadn't even told him about. But this was a man's affair, not a woman's.

Of course there was another side to it. He *could* give some of the money to Aunt Saxon to buy coal—instead of the sweater—well, maybe it would do both. And he *could* give

some to that fund for the Chinese mission, Miss Lynn was
getting up in the class. He would stop on the way back and
give her a whole dollar. He sat, chin in hand, gazing out on
the field, quite satisfied with himself, and suddenly someone
back by the plate struck a fine clean ball with a click and
threw the bat with a resounding ring on the hard ground as
he made for a home run. Billy started and looked keenly at
the bat, for somehow the ring of it as it fell sounded curiously
like the tinkle of silver. Who said thirty pieces of silver? Billy
threw a furtive look about and a cold perspiration broke out
on his forehead. Strange that old Bible story had to stick itself
in. He could see the grieving in the Master's eyes as Judas
gave Him that kiss. She had made the story real. She could
do that, and made the boy long somehow to make it up to that
betrayed Master, and he couldn't get away from the feeling
that he was falling short. Of course, old Pat had *said* the man
had money *belonging* to *him*, and you had to go mostly by
what folks *said*, but it did look shady.

The game seemed slow after that. The two captains were
wrangling over some point of rule, and the umpire was trying
to pacify them both. Billy arose with well feigned languor and
remarked, "Well, I gotta beat it. Guess we're gonta win all
right. So long!" and lounged away to his wheel.

He purchased another soda at the drugstore to get one of
his fives changed into ones, one of which he stowed away in
his breast pocket, while the remainder was stuffed in his
trousers after the manner of a man. He bent low over his
handlebars, chewing rhythmically and pedaled away rapidly
in the direction of Sabbath Valley.

Chapter 3

The bells of the little stone church were playing tender
melodies as he shot briskly down the maple-lined street at a

breakneck pace, and the sun was just hovering on the rim of the mountains. The bells often played at sunset, especially Saturday evenings, when Marilyn Severn was at home, and the village loved to hear them. Billy wouldn't have owned it, but he loved to hear those bells play better than anything else in his young life, and he generally managed to be around when they were being played. He loved to watch the slim young fingers manipulating the glad sounds. A genius who had come to the quiet hill village to die of an incurable disease had trained her and had left the wonderful little pipe organ with its fine chime of bells attached as his memorial to the peace the village had given him in his last days. Something of his skill and yearning had fallen upon the young girl whom he had taught. Billy always felt as if an angel had come and was ringing the bells of heaven when Marilyn sat at the organ playing the bells.

This night a ray of the setting sun slanting through the memorial window on her bronze-gold hair gave her the look of Saint Cecilia sitting there in the dimness of the church. Billy sidled into a backseat still chewing and watched her. He could almost see a halo in yellow-gold sun dust circling above her hair. Then a sudden revulsion came with the thought of that guy Judas and the possibility that he and the old fellow had much in common. But bah! He would go to the mountain just to prove to himself that there was nothing crooked in it.

The music was tender that night and Billy felt a strange constriction in his throat. But you never would have guessed, as Lynn Severn turned at the end of her melody to search the dimness for the presence she felt had entered, that he had been under any stress of emotion, the way he grinned at her and sidled up the aisle.

"Yeah, we won aw'right," in answer to her question. "Red Rodge and Sloppy had 'em beat from the start. Those other guys can't play ball anyway."

Then quite casually he brought forth the dollar from his breast pocket.

"Fer the Chinese fund," he stated indifferently.

The look in her face was beautiful to see, almost as if there were tears behind the sapphire lights in her eyes.

"Billy! All this?"

He felt as if she had knighted him. He turned red and hot with shame and pleasure.

"Aw, that ain't much. I earned sommore too, fer m'yant." He twisted his cap around on his other hand roughly and then blurted out the last thing he had meant to say:

"Miss Lynn, it ain't wrong to do a thing you don't know ain't wrong, is it?"

Marilyn looked at him keenly an laughed.

"It generally is, Billy, if you think it *might* be. Don't ever try to fool your conscience, Billy, it's too smart for that."

He grinned sheepishly and then quite irrelevantly remarked:

"I saw Cart last night."

But she seemed to understand the connection and nodded gravely:

"Yes, I saw him a moment this morning. He said he might come back again this evening."

The boy grunted contentedly and watched the warm color of her cheek under the glow of the ruddy sunset. She always seemed to him a little bit unearthly in the starriness of her beauty. Of course he never put it to himself that way. In fact he never put it at all. It was just a fact in his life. He had two idols whom he worshiped from afar, two idols who understood him equally well and were understood by him, and for whom he would have gladly laid down his young life. This girl was one, and Mark Carter was the other. It was the sorrow of his young life that Mark Carter had left Sabbath Valley indefinitely. The stories that floated back of his career made no difference to Billy. He adored him but the more in his fierce young soul, and gloried in his hero's need of faithful friends. He would not have owned it to himself, perhaps, but he had spoken of Mark just to find out if this other idol believed those tales and was affected by them. He drew a sigh of deep content as he heard the steady voice and knew that she was still the young man's friend.

They passed out of the church silently together and parted in the glow of red that seemed flooding the quiet village like a painting. She went across the stretch of lawn to the low spreading veranda where her mother sat talking with her father. Some crude idea of her beauty and grace stole through his soul, but he only said to himself:

"How—kind of—*little* she is!" and then made a dash for his rusty old wheel lying flat at the side of the church step. He gathered it up and wheeled it around the side of the church to the old graveyard, threading his way among the graves and sitting down on a broad flat stone where he had often thought out his problems of life. The shadow of the church cut off the glow of sunset and made it seem silent and dark. Ahead of him the valley lay. Across at the right it stretched toward the junction, and he could see the evening train just puffing in with a wee wisp of white misty smoke trailing against the mountain green. The people for the hotels would be swarming off, for it was Saturday night. The fat one would be there rolling trunks across and the station agent would presently close up. It would be dark over there at eight o'clock. The mountains loomed silently, purpling and steep and hazy already with sleep.

To the left lay the road that curved up to the forks where one went across to the highway and at right angles the highway went straight across the ridge in front of him and sloped down to the spot where the fat one expected him to play his part at eight o'clock tonight. The highway was the way down which the "rich guy" was expected to come speeding in a high-power car from New York, and had to be stopped and relieved of money that "did not belong to him."

Billy thought it all over. Somehow things seemed different now. He had, by some queer psychological process of his own, brought Lynn Severn's mind and Mark Carter's mind together to bear upon the matter and gained a new perspective. He was pretty well satisfied in his own soul that the thing he had set out to do was not on the level. It began to be pretty plain to him that that rich guy might be in the way of getting hurt or perhaps still worse, and he had no wish to be tangled up in a mess like that. At the same time he did not often get a chance to make twenty-five dollars, and he had no mind to give it up. It was not in his unyellow soul to go back on his word without refunding the money, and a dollar of it was already spent to the Chinese fund, to say nothing of sundaes and sodas and whips. So he sat and studied the mountain ahead of him.

Suddenly, as the sun, which had been for a long time

slipping down behind the mountains at his back, finally disappeared, his face cleared. He had found a solution.

He sprang up from the cold stone, where his fingers had been mechanically feeling out the familiar letters of the inscription: "Blessed are the dead—" and catching up the prone wheel, strode upon it and dashed down the darkening street toward the little cottage near the willows belonging to his Aunt Saxon. He was whistling as he went, for he was happy. He had found a way to keep his cake and eat it too. It would not have been Billy if he had not found a way out.

Aunt Saxon turned a drawn and anxious face away from the window at his approach and drew a sigh of momentary relief. This bringing up boys was a terrible ordeal. But thanks be this immediate terror was past and her sister's orphaned child still lived! She hurried to the stove where the waiting supper gave forth a pleasant odor.

"Been down to the game at M'nop'ly," he explained happily as he flung breezily into the kitchen and dashed his cap on a chair. "Gee! That ham smells good! Say, Saxy, whadya do with that can of black paint I left on the doorstep last Saturday?"

"It's in a wooden box in the corner of the shed, Willie," answered his aunt. "Come to supper now. It'll get cold. I'm been waiting most an hour."

"Oh, hang it! I don't s'pose you know where the brush is— Yes, I'm coming. Oh, here 'tis!"

He ate ravenously and briefly. His aunt watched him with a kind of breathless terror waiting for the inevitable remark at the close: "Well, I gotta beat it! I gotta date with the fellas!"

She had ceased to argue. She merely looked distressed. It seemed a part of his masculinity that was inevitable.

At the door he was visited with an unusual thoughtfulness. He stuck his head back in the room to say:

"Oh, yes, Saxy, I *might* not be home till morning. I *might* stay all night some place."

He was going without further explanation, but her dismay as she murmured pathetically:

"But tomorrow is the Sabbath, Willie!" halted him once more.

"Oh, I'll be home time fer Sunday school," he promised gaily, and was off down the road in the darkness, his old wheel squeaking rheumatically with each revolution growing fainter and fainter in the night.

But Billy did not take the road to the junction in his rapid flight. Instead he climbed the left-hand mountain road that met the forks and led to the great highway. Slower and slower the old wheel went, Billy puffing and bending low, till finally he had to dismount and put a drop of oil in a well known spot which his finger found in the dark, from the little can he carried in his pocket for such a time of need. He did not care to proclaim his coming as he crept up the rough steep way. And once when a tin lizzie swept down upon him, he ducked and dropped into the fringe of alders at the wayside until it was past. Was that, could it have been Cart? It didn't look like Cart's car, but it was very dark, and the man had not dimmed his lights. It was blinding. He hoped it was Cart, and that he had gone to the parsonage. Somehow he liked to think of those two together. It made his own view of life seem stronger. So he slunk quietly up to the fork where the highway swept down round a curve, and turned to go down across the ridge. Here was the spot where the rich guy would presently come. He looked the ground over, with his bike safely hidden below road level. With a sturdy set of satisfaction to his shoulders, and a twinkle of fun in his eye, he began to burrow into the undergrowth and find branches, a fallen log, stones, anything, and drag them up across the great state highway till he had a complete barricade.

There had come a silverness in the sky over the next eastern mountain, and he could see the better what he was doing. Now and again he stopped cautiously and listened, his heart beating high with fear lest after all the rich guy might arrive before he was ready for him. When the obstruction was finished he got out a large piece of cardboard which had been fastened to the handlebars of his wheel, and from a box also fastened on behind his saddle he produced his can of paint and a brush. The moon was beginning to show off at his right, and gave a faint luminous gleam, as he daubed his letters in crudely.

DETOUR to SABBATH VALLEY
Rode flooded. Brige down.

His card was large, but so were his letters. Nevertheless in spite of their irregularity he got them all on, and fastened the

card firmly to the most obvious spot in the barricade. Then
with a wicked gleam of mischief in his eye he looked off down
the highway across the ridge to where some two miles away
one Pat must be awaiting his coming, and gave a single
mocking gesture common to boys of his age. Springing on his
wheel he coasted down the humps and into the darkness
again.

He reflected as he rode that no harm could possibly be
done. The road inspector would not be along for a couple of
days. It would simply mean that a number of cars would go
around by the way of Sabbath Valley for a day or so. It might
break up a little of the quiet of the Sabbath day at home, but
Billy did not feel that that would permanently injure Sabbath
Valley for home purposes, and he felt sure that no one could
possibly ever detect his hand in the matter.

The road at the forks led four ways, highway coming from
New York and the greater Northeast, running north and
south, and the crossroad coming from Economy and running
through Sabbath Valley to Monopoly. He had made the
detour below the crossroad, so that people coming from
Economy would find no hindrance to their progress. He felt
great satisfaction in the whole matter. And now there remained
but to do his part and get his money. He thought he saw a
way to make sure of that money, and his conscience had
no qualms for extracting it from so crooked a thief as
Pat.

The clock on the church tower at Sabbath Valley was
finishing the last stroke of eleven when Billy came slickly up
the slope of the road from Sabbath Valley, and arrived on the
station platform nonchalantly.

By the light of the moon he could dimly see Pat standing
uneasily off by the tracks, and the heads of two men down
below in the bushes near the lower end of the highway where
it crossed the tracks and swept on south between two mountains.

Pat held his watch in his hand and looked very ugly, but
nothing fazed Billy. He didn't have to carry this thing out if
he didn't want to, and the man knew he knew too much to be
ugly to him.

"There you are, you young whippersnapper you!" was Pat's

greeting. "What kinduva time is this 'ere to be coming along to your expensive job? I said *eight!*"

"Oh," said Billy with a shrug and jumped to his wheel again, "then I guess I'll be going back. Good night!"

"Here! Wait up there, you young devil! You come mighty nigh dishing the whole outfit, but now you're here, you'll earn your ten bucks I was fool enough to give you, but nothing more, do you hear that?" and the man leered into his freckled young face with an ugly gun in his hand.

Billy eyed the gun calmly. He had seen guns before. Moreover he didn't believe the man had the nerve to shoot. He wasn't quite so sure of the two dark shadows in the bushes below, but it was well to be on the safe side.

"Keep yer shirt on," said Billy impertinently, "and save yer powder. You don't want the whole nation to know about this little affair of ours do you, *Pat?*"

The wide one glared.

"Well, you better not have anything like shooting going on, fer I've got some friends back here a little way waiting to joy ride back with me when my work's over. They might get funny if they heard a gun and come too soon."

"You little devil, you! I mighta known you'd give it away!" he began, but he lowered the gun perceptibly. "Every little skunk like you is yella—yella as the devil—"

But Pat did not finish his sentence, for Billy, with a blaze in his eyes like the lamps of a tiger, and a fierce young catlike leap, flew at the flabby creature, wrenched the gun out of his astonished hand, and before he could make any outcry held it tantalizingly in his face. Billy had never had any experience before with bullies and bandits except in his dreams; but he had played football, and tackled every team in the valley, and he had no fear of anything. Moreover, he had spent long hours boxing and wrestling with Mark Carter, and he was hard as nails and wiry as a cat. The fat one was completely in his hands. Of course those other two down across the tracks might have made trouble if Pat had cried out, but they were too far away to see or hear the silent scuffle on the platform. But Billy was taking no chances.

"Now, keep on yer shirt, Pat, and don't make no outcry. My friends can get here's easy as yours, so just take it quiet. All you gotta do is take that remark back you just uttered. I ain't yella, and you gotta say so. Then you hand over those fifteen bones, and I'm yer man."

It was incredible that Pat should have succumbed, but he did. Perhaps he was none too sure of his friends in the bushes. Certainly the time was getting short and he was in a hurry to get to his job on the highway. Also he had no mind for being discovered or interrupted. At any rate with a hoarse little laugh of pretended courage he put his hand in his baggy pocket and pulled out the bills.

"You win, kid," he admitted, "I guess you're okay. Anything to please the baby and get down to biz. Now, sonny, put that gun away, it don't look well. Besides, I—got another." He put his hand insinuatingly to his hip pocket with a grin, but Billy's grin answered back:

"That's all right, pard. I'll just keep this one awhile then. You don't need two. Now, what's wanted?"

Pat edged away from the boy and measured him with his eye. The moon was coming up and Billy loomed large in the darkness. There was a determined set to his firm young shoulders, a lithe alertness about his build, and a fine glint in his eye. Pat was really a coward. Besides, Pat was getting nervous. The hidden telephone had called him several times already. He could hear even now in imagination its faint click in the moss. The last message had said that the car had passed the state line and would soon be coming to the last point of communication. After that it was the mountain highway straight to Pleasant View, nothing to hinder. It was not a time to waste in discussion. Pat dropped to an ingratiating whine.

"Come along then, kid. Yes, bring your wheel. We'll want it. Down this way, just over the tracks, so, see? We want you to fall off that there wheel an' sprawl in the road like you had caught yer wheel on the track an' it had skidded, see? Try her now, and just lay there like you was off your feed."

Billy slung himself across his wheel, gave a cursory glance at the landscape, took a running slide over the tracks with a swift pedal or two and slumped in a heap, lying motionless as the dead. He couldn't have done it more effectively if he had practiced for a week. Pat caught his breath and stooped over anxiously. He didn't want a death at the start. He wouldn't care to be responsible for a concussion of the brain or

anything like that. Besides, he couldn't waste time fooling
with a fool kid when the real thing might be along any
minute. He glanced anxiously up the broad white ribbon of a
road that gleamed now in the moonlight, and then pulling out
his pocket flash, flooded it swiftly over Billy's upturned
freckled face that lay there still as death without the flicker of
an eyelash. The man was panic-stricken. He stopped lower,
put out a tentative, turned his flash full in the boy's face
again, and was just about to call to his helpers for aid when
Billy opened a large eye and solemnly winked.

Pat shut off his flash quickly, stuck it in his pocket, backed
off with a low relieved, "All right, kid, you'll do. I guess
you're all right after all, now you jest lay—" and slid away
down the slope into the cypress clump.

Billy with upturned face eyed the moon and winked again,
as if to a friend up there in the sky. He was thinking of the
detour two miles up the road.

It was very pleasant lying there in the cool moonlight with
the evening breeze blowing his rough hair and playing over
his freckles, and with the knowledge of those twenty-four
bucks safely buttoned inside his sweater, and that neat little
gun in his pocket where he could easily close his fingers
about it. The only thing he regretted was that for conscience'
sake he had had to put up that detour. It would have been so
much more exciting than to have put up this all-night camouflage and wait here till dawn for a guy that wasn't coming at
all. He began to think about the guy and wonder if he would
take the detour to Sabbath Valley, or turn back, or perhaps
try Economy. That would be disappointing. He would stand
no chance of even hearing what he was like. Now if he went
through Sabbath Valley, Red or Sloppy or Rube would be
sure to sight a strange car, particularly if it was a *high-power*
racer or something of that sort, and they could discuss it, and
he might be able to find out a few points about this unknown
whom he was so nobly delivering for conscience' sake—or
Lynn Severn's—from an unknown fate. Of course he wouldn't
let the fellows know he knew anything about the guy.

He had lain there fifteen minutes and was beginning to
grow drowsy after his full day in the open air. If it were not
for the joke of the thing he couldn't keep awake.

Pat stole out from the weeds at the slope of the road and whispered sepulchrally:

"That's all right, kid, jest you lay there and hold that pose. You couldn't do better. Yer wheel finishes the blockade. Nobody couldn't get by if he tried. That's the kid! 'Clare if I don't give you another five bucks t'morrer if you carry this thing through. Don't you get cold feet now!"

Billy uttered a guttural of contempt in his throat and Pat slid away to hiding once more. The distant bells struck the midnight hour. Billy thrilled at their sweetness, with the fact that they belonged to him, that he had sat that very evening watching those white fingers among the keys, manipulating them. He thought of the glint on her hair—the halo of dusty gold in the sunshine above—the light in her eyes—the glow of her cheek—her delicate profile against the memorial window—the glint of her hair—it came back, not in those words, but the vision of it—what was it like? Oh—of course. Cart's hair. The same color. They were alike, those two, and yet very different. When he had grown a man he would like to be like Cart. Cart was kind and always understood when you were not feeling right. Cart smoothed the way for people in trouble—old women and animals, and well—girls sometimes. He had seen him do it. Other people didn't always understand, but he did. Cart always had a reason. It took men to understand men. That thought had a good sound to the boy on his back in the moonlight. Although he felt somewhat a fool lying there waiting in the road when all the time there was that detour. It would have been more a man's job if there hadn't had to be that detour, but he couldn't run risks with strange guys, and men who carried guns, not even for—well, thirty pieces of silver! But hark! What was that?

There seemed to be a singing along the ground. Was he losing his nerve lying here so long? No, there it was again! It couldn't be possible that he could hear so far as two miles up that road. It was hard and smooth macadam of course, that highway, but it couldn't be that—what was it they called it—vibrations?—would reach so far! It must be. He would ask Cart about that.

The humming continued and grew more distinct, followed by a sort of throbbing roar that seemed coming toward him and yet was still very far away. It must be a car at the detour.

In a moment it would turn down the bumpy road toward Sabbath Valley, and very likely some of those old broken whiskey bottles along the way would puncture a tire and the guy would take till morning getting anywhere. Perhaps he could even get away in time to come up innocently enough and help him out. A guy like that might not know how to patch a puncture.

But the sound was distinctly coming on. Billy opened one eye, then the other, and hastily scanned the sky in either direction for an airplane, but the sky was as clear as crystal without a speck, and the sound was distinctly drawing nearer.

A voice from the roadside hurtled sharply across:

"Hist! There! He's coming! Lay still! Remember you get five more bucks if you pull this off!"

A cold chill crept down Billy's back on tiny needle-pointed fringe of feet like a centipede. There was a sudden constriction in his throat and a leaden weight on each eye. He could not have opened them if he had tried, for a great white light stabbed across them and seemed to be holding them down for inspection. The thing he had wanted to have happen had come, and he was frightened; frightened cold clear to the soul of him—not at the thing that was about to come, but at the fact that he had broken faith with himself after all; broken faith with the haloed girl at the organ in the golden light; broken faith—for thirty pieces of silver! In that awful moment he was keenly conscious of the fact that when he got the other five there would be just thirty dollars for the whole! Thirty pieces of silver and the judgment day already coming on!

Chapter 4

Lynn Severn was restless as she sat on the porch in the cool dark evening and heard unheeding the small village sounds that stole to her ears. The laughter of two children playing hide-and-seek behind the bushes across the way; the call of their mother summoning them to bed. The tinkle of a piano down the street; the whine of a Victrola in another home; the cry of a baby in pain; the murmur of talk on the porch next door; the slamming of a door; the creak of a gate; footsteps going down the brick pavement; the swinging to and fro of a hammock holding happy lovers under the rose pergola at Joneses'. She could identify them all, and found her heart was listening for another sound, a smooth running cat that purred, coming down the street. But it did not come!

By and by she slipped out and into the church, opening one window to let in the moonlight, and unlocking the organ by the sense of feeling. Her fingers strayed along the keys in tender wandering melodies, but she did not pull the stop that controlled the bells. She would have liked to play those bells and call through them to Mark across the mountains, where he might be riding, call to tell him that she was waiting, call to ask him why he was so strangely aloof, so silent, and pale in his dignity; what had come between them, old friends of the years? She felt she could say with the bells what her lips could never speak. But the bells would cry her trouble to the villagers also, and she could not let *them* hear. So she played soft melodies of trust and hope and patience, until her father came to find her, and linking his arm in hers walked back with her through the moonlight, not asking anything, only seeming to understand her mood. He was that way always. He could understand without being told. Somehow she felt it and was comforted. He was that way with everybody. It was what made him so beloved in his parish, which comprised the whole valley, that and his great sincerity and courage. But always his sense of understanding seemed keenest with this flower-faced girl of his. He seemed to have gone ahead of her always to see that all was right—or wrong—and then walked with her to be sure she did not stumble or miss her way. He never attempted to reason her out of herself, nor to minimize her trials, but was just there, a stronghold when she needed it. She looked up with a smile and slipped her hand in his. She understood his perfect sympathy, as if his own past youth were touching hers and making her know that whatever it was she had to face she would come through. He was like a

symbol of God's strength to her. Somehow the weight was
lifted from her heart. They lingered on the piazza together in
the moonlight a few minutes, speaking quietly of the morrow
and its duties, then they went into the wide pleasant living
room, and sat down, mother and daughter near together,
while the father read a portion:

"He that dwelleth in the secret place of the most High
shall abide under the shadow of the Almighty.

"I will say of the Lord, He is my refuge and my
fortress; my God; in him will I trust.

"Surely he shall deliver thee from the snare of the
fowler, and from the noisome pestilence.

"He shall cover thee with his feathers, and under his
wings shalt thou trust."

The words seemed to fill the room with a sweet peace, and to
draw the hearts of the listeners as a voice that is dear draws
and soothes after a day of separation and turmoil and distress.

They knelt and the minister's voice spoke familiarly to the
Unseen Presence, giving thanks for mercies received,
mentioning little throbbing personalities that belonged to
them as a family and as individuals, reminding one of what it
must have been in the days before sin had come and Adam
walked and talked with God in the cool of the evening, and
received instruction and strengthening straight from the Source.
One listening would instinctively have felt that here was the
secret of the great strength of Lynn Severn's life; the reason
why neither college nor the world had been able to lure her
one iota from her great and simple faith which she had
brought with her from her valley home and taken back again
unsullied. This family altar was the heart of her home, and
had brought her so near to God that she *knew* what she had
believed and could not be shaken from it by any flippant
words from lovely or wise lips that only knew the theory of
her belief and nothing of its spirit and tried to argue it away
with a fine phrase and a laugh.

So Lynn went up to her little white chamber that looked
out upon the quiet hills, knelt awhile beside the white bed in
the moonlight, then lay down and slept.

* * *

Out among the hills on the long smooth road in the white moonlight there shot a car like a living thing gone crazy, blaring a whiter light than the moonlight down the way, roaring and thundering as only a costly and well-groomed beast of a machine can roar and thunder when it is driven by hot blood and a mad desire, stimulated by frequent applications from a handy flask, and a will that has never known a curb.

He knew it was a mad thing he was doing, rushing across space through the dark at the beck of a woman's smile, a woman who was another man's wife, but a woman who had set on fire a whole circle of men of which he was a part. He was riding against all caution to win a bet, riding against time to get there before two other men who were riding as hard from other directions to win the woman who belonged to an absent husband, win her and run away with her if he could. It was the culmination of a year of extravagances, the last cry in sensations, and the telephone wires had been hot with daring, wild allurement, and mad threat in several directions since late the night before.

The woman was in a great summer hotel where extravagances of all sorts were in vogue, and it had been her latest game to call with her lutelike voice over the phone to three of her men friends who had wooed her the strongest, daring them all to come to her at once, promising to fly with the one who reached her first, but if none reached her before morning dawned she remained as she was and laughed at them all.

Laurence Shafton had closed with the challenge at once and given orders for his car to be ready to start in ten minutes. From a southern city about an equal distance from the lady, one Percy Emerson, of the Wellington Emersons, started about the same time, leaving a trail of telegrams and phone messages to be sent after his departure. The third man, Mortimer McMarter, a hot-headed, hot-blooded Scot, had started with the rest, for the lady knew her lovers well, and not one would refuse; but he was lying dead at a wayside inn with his car a heap of litter outside from having collided with a truck that was minding its own business and giving plenty of room to any sane man. This one was not sane. But of this happening not even the lady knew as yet, for Mortimer

McMarter was not one to leave tales behind him when he went out of life, and the servants who had sent his messages were far away.

The clock in the car showed nearly twelve and the way was long ahead. But he would make it before the dawn. He must. He stepped on the accelerator and shot round a curve. A dizzy precipice yawned at his side. He took another pull at the flask he carried and shot on wildly through the night. Then suddenly he ground on his brakes, the machine twisted and snarled like an angry beast and came to a stand almost into the arms of a barricade across the road. The young man hurled out an oath, and leaned forward to look, his eyes almost too bloodshot and blurred to read:

DETOUR to SABBATH VALLEY

He laughed aloud. "Sabbath Valley!" He swore and laughed again, then looked down the way the rude arrow pointed, "Well, I like that! Sabbath Valley. That'll be a good joke to tell, but I'll make it yet or land in hell!" He started his car and twisted it round to the rougher road, feeling the grind of the broken glass that strewed the way. Billy had done his work thoroughly, and anticipated well what would happen. But those tires were costly affairs. They did not yield to the first cut that came, and the expensive car built for racing on roads as smooth as glass bumped and jogged down into the ruts and started toward Sabbath Valley, with the driver pulling again at his almost empty flask, and swaying giddily in his seat. Half a mile farther down the mountain, the car gave a gasp, like the flitting soul of a dying lion, and came with sudden grinding brakes to a dead stop in the heart of a deep wood.

Five minutes later another car, with a soft purring engine, came up to the crossroads from Economy, slowed just a fraction as it crossed the highway, the driver looking keenly at the barricade, then stopping his car with a sudden jerk and swinging out. He turned a pocket flash on the big cardboard Billy had erected, its daubed letters still wet and blurring into the pasteboard. He looked a bit quizzical over the statement, "RODE FLOODED, BRIGE DOWN," because he happened to know there was no bridge and nothing to flood the road for several miles ahead. He examined the barricade carefully, even down to the broken glass in the road, then deliberately, swiftly, with his foot kicked away the glass, cleared a width for his car, and jumping in backed up, turned and started slowly down the condemned road to investigate. Something was wrong down the highway, and the sooner it was set right the better. There was one thing, he wished he had his gun with him, but then— And he swung on down for two miles, going faster and faster, seeing nothing but white still road, and quiet sleeping trees, with looming mountains against the sky everywhere. Then, suddenly, across the way in the blare of his lights a white face flashed into view, and a body, lying full across the road, with a bicycle flung to one side completing the block. He brought his car to a quick stand and jumped out, but before he could take one step or even stoop, someone caught him from behind, and something big and dark and smothering was flung over his head. A heavy blow seemed to send him whirling, whirling down into infinite space, with a long tongue of living fire leaping up to greet him.

"Beat it, kid, and keep yer face shut!" hissed Pat into Billy's ear, at the same time stuffing a bill into his hand.

Billy had just sense enough left to follow the assisting kick and roll himself out of the road, with a snatch at his machine which pulled it down out of sight. He had a secret feeling that he was yellow after all in spite of his efforts, letting a guy get taken this way without even a chance to put up a fight. Where was that gun? He reached his hand into his pocket and was steadied by the feeling of the cold steel. Then he knew that the men were in the car and about to start. They had dumped the owner into the backseat and were going to carry him off somewhere. What were they going to do? He must find out. He was responsible. He hadn't meant to let anything like this happen. If everything wasn't going to be on the square he might have to get into it yet. He must stick around and see.

The men were having a whispered consultation over the car. They were not used to that kind, but a car was a car. They tried to start it with nervous glances down the road. It jerked and hissed and complained but began to obey. The wheels were beginning to move. In a flash it would be gone!

Billy scrambled noiselessly up the bank behind the car, his move well covered by the noise of the engine. With a quick survey of the situation he tucked himself hastily into the spare tire on the back, just as the car gave a lurch and shot forward down across the tracks. He had all he could do to maintain his position and worm himself into a firmer holding for the first minute or two, and when he began to realize what he was doing he found his heart beating like a young trip-hammer. He slid a groping hand into his pocket once more for reassurance. If anything really happened he had the gun.

But his heart was heavy. Things had not gone right. He had planned to carry this thing through as a large joke, and here he was mixed up in a crooked deal if ever there was one. The worst of it was he wasn't out of it yet. He wished he knew whose car this was and where they were bound for. How about the license tag? Gripping his unstable seat he swayed forward and tried to see it just below him. In the dim light it looked like a New York license. It must be the guy they were after all right—they had telephoned about a New York man— yet—*Cart* had a New York license on his car! He was living in New York now—and there must be lots of other guys!

A kind of sickening thud seemed to drop through his mind down to the pit of his stomach as he tried to think it out. His eyes peered into the night watching every familiar landmark— there was the old pine where they always turned off to go fishing; and yes, they were turning *away* from Economy Road. Yes, they were going through Hackett's Pass. A chill crept through his thin old sweater as the damp breath of ferns and rocks struck against his face. His eyes shone grim and hard in the night, suddenly grown old and stern. This was the kind of thing you read about in novels. In spite of pricks of conscience his spirits rose. It was great to be in it if it had to be. The consciousness of Sabbath Valley bathed in peaceful moonlight, all asleep, of the minister and his daughter, and Aunt Saxon, fell away; even the memory of bells that called to righteousness—he was out in the night on a wild ride and his soul thrilled to the measure of it. He fairly exulted as he reflected that he might be called upon to do some great deed of valor—in fact he felt he *must* do a great deed of valor to retrieve his self-respect after having made that balk about the detour. How did that guy get around the detour anyway? *Some guy!*

Hackett's Pass was far behind and the moon was going low when the car stopped for a moment and a hurried consultation took place inside. Billy couldn't hear all that was said, but he gathered that time was short and the conspirators must be back at a certain place before morning. They seemed somehow to have missed a trail that was to have cut the distance greatly. Billy clung breathlessly to his cramped position and waited. He hoped they wouldn't get out and try to find the way, for then some of them might see him, and he was so stiff he was sure he would bungle getting out of the way. But after a breathless moment the car started on more slowly, and finally turned down a steep rough place, scarcely a trail, into the deeper woods. For a long time they went along, slower and slower, into the blackness of the night it seemed. There was no moon, and the men had turned off the lights. There was nothing but a pocket flash which one of them carried, and turned on now and again to show them the way. The engine, too, was muffled and went snuffing along through the night like a blind thing that had been gagged. Billy began to wonder if he would ever find his legs useful again. Sharp pains shot through his joints, and he became aware of sleep dropping upon his straining eyes like a sickening cloud. Yet he must keep awake.

He squirmed about and changed his position, staring into the darkness and wondering if this journey was ever to end. Now they were bumping down a bank, and slopping through water, not very deep, a small mountain stream on one of the levels. He tried to think where it must be, but was puzzled. They seemed to have traveled part of the way in curves. Twice they stopped and backed up and seemed to be returning on their tracks. They crossed and recrossed the little stream, and the driver was cursing, and insisting on more light. At last they began climbing again and the boy drew a breath of relief. He could tell better where he was on the heights. He began to think of morning and Sabbath Valley bathed in its Sabbath peace, with the bells chiming a call to worship—and *he not there!* Aunt Saxon would be *crazy!* She would bawl him out! *He should worry!* And she would weep, pink weak tears from her old thin eyes, that seemed to have never done much

else but weep. The thought turned and twisted his soul like
an ugly curved knife and made him angry. Tears always made
him angry. And Miss Lynn—she would watch for him! He
had promised to be there! And she would not understand—
and there would come that grieved look in her eyes. She
would think— Oh, she would think he did not *want* to come,
and did not *mean* to keep his promise, and things like
that—and she would have to think them! He couldn't help it,
could he? He *had* to come along, didn't he?

In the midst of his miserable reflections the car stopped
dead on a level place, and with a cold perspiration on his
forehead Billy peered around him. They must have reached
the top of a ridge, for the sky was visible with the morning
star pinned against a luminous black. Against it a blacker
shape was visible, half hid in trees, a building of some sort,
solid, substantial, but deserted.

The men were getting out of the car. Billy gripped the gun
and dropped silently to the ground, sliding as stealthily into
the shadows of the trees as if he had been a snake.

Pat stepped heavily to the ground and began to give
directions in a low growl. Billy crouched and listened.

"Let's get him shifted quick! We gotta beat it outta here!
Link, it's up to you an' Shorty to get this car over the state
line before light, an' you'll have to run me back to the
crossing first, so I can be at the station in time for the early
train. That'll be *going some!*"

"Well, I guess *anyhow not*," said Link sullenly. "Whadda
ya think we are? Fools? Run you back to the crossing in a
pig's eye. You'll foot it back if you get there, er come with us.
We ain't gonna get caught with this car on our hands. What
we gonta do with it anyhow, when we get crost the state
line?"

"Why, you run it into the field off behind that row of
alders. Sam's got a man on the lookout. They'll have that
little old car so she won't recognize her best friend before you
can count three, so you should worry. And you'll run me back
or you won't get the dough. See? *I'll* see to that. Sam said I
wasn't to run no risks fer not bein' back in time. Now, shift
that guy's feet out on my shoulder. Handle him quick. Nope,
he won't wake up fer two hours yet. I give him plenty of

dope. Got them bracelets tight on his feet? All right now. He's some hefty bird, ain't he?"

They moved away in the direction of the building, carrying a long dark shape between them, and Billy breathless in the bushes, watched, turning rapid plans in his mind. Here he was in the midst of an automobile getaway! Many the time he had gone with Mark and the chief of police on a still hunt for car thieves, but this time he was of the party. His loyal young heart boiled hot with rage, and he determined to do what he could single-handed to stem the tide of crime. Just what he was going to do he was undetermined. One thing was certain, he must get the number of that license tag. He looked toward the house.

The group had paused with their burden at the door and Pat had turned on his pocket flashlight for just an instant as they fumbled with an ancient lock. In that instant the whole front of the old stone house was lit up clearly, and Billy gasped. The *haunted house!* The house on the far mountain where a man had murdered his brother and then hanged himself. It had stood empty and closed for years, ever since Billy could remember, and was shunned and regarded with awe, and pointed out by hunters as a local point of interest.

Billy regarded with contempt the superstition that hung around the place, but he gasped when he saw where he was, for they must have come twenty miles round about and it was at least ten across the mountains by the shortcut. Ten miles from home, and he had to foot it! If he had only brought old trusty! No telling now whether he would ever see it again. But what were bicycles at such a time as this?

The flash had gone out and the house was in darkness again, but he could hear the grating of a rusty hinge as the door opened, and faint footfalls of rubbered feet shuffled on the dusty floor. Now was his time! He darted out to the back of the car, and stooping down with his face close to the license, holding his own old cap in one hand to shelter it, drew out his own pocket flash and turned it on the sign, registering the number clearly on his alert young mind. The flashlight was on its last breath of battery, and blinked asthmatically, winking out into a thread of red as the boy pressed it eagerly for one more look. He had been so intent that he had not heard the rubbered feet till they were almost upon him, and he had barely time to spring back into the bushes.

"Hist! What was that?" whispered Pat, and the three stopped motionless in their tracks. Billy held his breath and touched the cold steel in his pocket. Of course there was always the gun, but what was one gun against three?

Chapter 5

The whistle of the cannery at Sabbath Valley blew a relief blast five minutes ahead of midnight in deference to the church chimes, and the night shift which had been working overtime on account of a consignment of tomatoes that would not keep till Monday, poured joyously out into the road and scattered to their various homes.

The outmost of these homegoers, Tom McMertrie and Jim Rafferty, who lived at the other extreme of the village, came upon a crippled car, coughing and crawling toward them in front of the graveyard. Its driver, much sobered by lack of stimulant, and frequent necessity for getting out and pushing his car over hard bits of road, called to them noisily.

The two workmen, pleasant of mood, ready for a joke, not altogether averse to helping if this proved to be the right guy, halted and stepped into the road just to look the poor noble car over. It was the lure of the fine machine.

"Met with an accident?" Jim remarked affably, as if it were something to enjoy.

"Had toire thrubble?" added Tom, punching the collapsed tires.

The questions seemed to anger the driver who demanded loftily:

"Where's your garage?"

"Garage? Oh, we haven't any garage," said Jim pleasantly, with a mute twinkle in his Irish eye.

"No garage? Haven't any garage! What town is this—if you call it a town?"

"Why, mon, this is Sawbeth Volley! Shorely ye've heard of Sawbeth Volley!"

"No, I never heard of it!" said the stranger contemptuously, "but from what I've seen of it so far I should say it ought to be called Hell's Pit! Well, what do you do when you want your car fixed?"

"Well, we don't hoppen to hove a cyar," said Tom with a meditative air, stooping to examine the spokes of a wheel. "Boot, ef we hod, mon, I'm thenkin' we'd *fix* it!"

Jim gave a flicker of a chuckle in his throat, but kept his outward gravity. The stranger eyed the two malevolently, helplessly, and began once more, holding his rage with a cold voice.

"Well, how much do you want to fix my car?" he asked, thrusting his hand into his pocket and bring out out an affluent wallet.

The men straightened up and eyed him coldly. Jim turned indifferently away and stepped back to the sidewalk. Tom lifted his chin and replied kindly:

"Why, mon, it's the *Sawbeth*, didn't ye know? I'm s'proised at ye! It's the Sawbeth, an' this is Sawbeth Volley! We don't wurruk on the Sawbeth day in Sawbeth Volley. Whist! Hear thot, mon?"

He lifted his hand and from the stone belfry nearby came the solemn tone of the chime, pealing out a full round of melody, and then tolling solemnly twelve slow strokes. There was something almost uncanny about it that held the stranger still, as if an unseen presence with a convincing voice had been invoked. The young man sat under the spell till the full complement of the ringing was finished, the workman with his hand up holding attention, and Jim Rafferty quietly enjoying it all from the curbstone.

When the last sweet resonance had died out, the Scotchman's hand went slowly down, and the stranger burst forth with an oath:

"Well, can you tell me where I can go to get fixed up? I've wasted enough time already."

"I should say from whut I've seen of ye, mon, that yer roight in thot statement, and if I was to advoise I'd say go right up to the parson. His loight's still burnin' in the windo next beyant the tchurtch, so ye'll not be disturbin' him. Not that he'd moind. He'll fix ye up ef anybody cun; though I'm doubtin' yer in a bad wy, only wy ye take it. Good night to ye, the windo wi' the loight, mon, roight next beyant the tchurtch!"

The car began its coughing and spluttering, and slowly jerked itself into motion, its driver going angrily on his unthankful way. The two workmen, watching him with amused expressions, waited in the shadow of a tree till the car came to a stop again in front of the parsonage, and a tall young fellow got out and looked toward the lighted window.

"Oh, boy! He's going in!" gasped Jim, slapping his companion silently on the back. "What'll Mr. Severn think, Tommy?"

"It'll do the fresh laddie gude," quoth Tom, a trifle abashed but ready to stand by his guns. "I'm thenkin' he's one of them what feels they own the airth, an' is bound to step on all worms of the dust whut comes in thur wy. But, Jim, mon, we better be steppin' on, fer tomorra's the Sawbeth ya ken, an' it wuddent be gude for our souls if the parson shud cum out to investigate." Chuckling away into the silent street they disappeared, while Laurence Shafton stalked angrily up the little path and pounded loudly on the quaint knocker of the parsonage.

The minister was on his knees, beside his desk, praying for the soul of the wandering lad who had been dear to him for years. He had finished his preparation for the coming day, and his heart was full of a great longing. As he poured out his desire he forgot the hour and his need for rest. It was often in such companionship he forgot all else. He was that kind of a man.

But he came to his feet on the instant with the knock, and was ready to go out on any errand of mercy that was needing him. It was not an unusual thing for a knock to come interrupting his midnight devotions. Sometimes the call would be to go far out on the mountain to someone who was in distress, or dying.

The minister swung the door wide and peered into the

night pleasantly almost as if to welcome an unexpected guest. In the sudden flood of the porch light his face was illumined, and behind the pretty living room gave a sweet homely setting. The stranger stood for an instant blinking, half astonished; then the memory of his rendezvous at break of day brought back his irritation at the delay.

"Are you Parsons?" he demanded, just as if "Parsons" were at fault that he had not been on hand before.

"Parsons?" said Mr. Severn reflectively. "I don't recall anyone of that name hereabouts. Perhaps you are on the wrong road. There is a Parsons at Monopoly."

"Parsons is the name. Aren't you Parsons? A couple of men down the road said you were, and that you could fix me up. They said right next the church and that your light was still burning." The visitor's tone was belligerent.

Severn's face cleared with a smile.

"Oh, they must have said 'Parson,' they often call me that. Come in. What can I do for you?"

The young man eyed him coldly and made no move to enter.

"Parson or Parsons, it makes no difference, does it? Mr. Parson, if you're so particular then, come out and look at my car. It seems to be in bad shape, and be quick about it. I've got over two hundred miles to make before daybreak, so get a hustle on. I'll pay you well if you don't waste any time."

A queer look descended upon the minister in twinkles of amusement around his eyes and lips much like the smile that Tom McMertrie had worn, only there was not a rag of hurt pride about it. With entire pleasantness he said:

"Just wait a moment till I get a light."

As he turned to go Shafton called after him:

"Oh, by the way, got anything to drink? I'm thirsty as the devil."

Severn turned, instant hospitality in his face.

"What will you have? Water or milk? Plenty of both."

He smiled and Shafton looked at him in haughty amazement.

"Man! I said I wanted something to *drink!*" he thundered. "But don't stand there all night doddering. I've got to get started!"

A slight lifting of the chin, a trifle of steel in the kind eyes, a shade of coolness in the voice, as the clear comprehension of heaven had sifted the visitor, and the minister said, almost sternly:

"Oh, I see," and disappeared through a swinging door into the pantry.

It was about this time that Lynn Severn awoke to near consciousness and wondered what kind of noisy guest her father had now.

The minister was gone some time and the guest grew impatient, stamping up and down the piazza and kicking a porch rocker out of his path. He looked at his watch and frowned, wondering how near he was to the end of his detour, and then he started in pursuit of his man, tramping through the Severn house as if it were a public garage, and almost running into the minister as he swung the door open. Severn was approaching with a lighted lantern in one hand and a plate of brown bread and butter, with a cup of steaming coffee in his other hand.

Laurence Shafton stopped abruptly, a curse on his lips, but something, either the genial face of the minister, or the aroma of the coffee, silenced him. And indeed there was something about Graham Severn that was worth looking at. Tall and well built, with a face at once strong and sweet, and with a certain luminousness about it that almost seemed like transparency to let the spirit shine through, although there was nothing frail about his well-cut features.

Laurence Shafton, looking into the frank kind eyes of the minister, suddenly became aware that this man had taken a great deal of trouble for him. He hadn't brought any liquor, probably because he did not know enough of the world to understand what it was he wanted, or because he was playing a joke. As he looked into those eyes and noted with his half-befuddled senses the twinkle playing at the corners he was not quite sure but the joke was on himself. But, however it was, the coffee smelled good and he took it and blundered out a brief "Thanks."

Eating his brown bread and butter, the like of which had never entered his pampered lips before, and taking great swoops of the hot strong coffee, he followed this strange new kind of a man out to the car in the moonlight, paying little heed to the careful examination that ensued, being so accustomed to ordering all his needs supplied and finding them forthcoming without delay.

Finally the minister straightened up:

"I'm afraid you won't go many miles tonight. You've burned out your bearings!"

"Hell!" remarked the young gentleman pausing before the last swallow of coffee.

"Oh, you won't find it so bad as that, I imagine," answered the steady voice of the minister. "I can give you a bed and take care of you over tomorrow, and perhaps Sandy McPherson can fix you up Monday, although I doubt it. He'd have to make new bearings, or you'd have to send for some to the factory."

But Laurence Shafton did not wait to hear the suggestions. He stormed up and down the sidewalk in front of the parsonage and let forth such a stream of choice language as had not been heard in that locality in many a long year. The minister's voice, cool, stern, commanding, broke in upon his ravings.

"I think that will be about all, sir!"

Laurence Shafton stopped and stared at the minister's lifted hand, not because he was overawed, simply because never before in the whole of his twenty-four years had anyone dared lift voice to him in a tone of command or reproof. He could not believe his ears, and his anger rose hotly. He opened his mouth to tell this insignificant person who he was and where to get off, and a few other common arguments of gentlemen of his class, but the minister had a surprising height as he stood in the moonlight, and there was that something strange and spiritual about him that seemed to meet the intention and disarm it. His jaw dropped, and he could not utter the words he had been about to speak. This was insufferable! But there was that raised hand. It seemed like someone not of this world quite. He wasn't afraid, because it wasn't in him to be afraid. This was his pose, not afraid of those he considered his inferiors, and he did not consider that anyone was his superior. But somehow this was something new in his experience. A man like this! It was almost as if his mere being there demanded a certain homage. It was queer. The young man passed a hand over his hot forehead and tried to think. Then the minister's voice went

almly on. It was almost as if he had not said that other at all.
Perhaps he had not. Perhaps he dreamed it or imagined it.
Perhaps he had been taking too much liquor and this was one
of the symptoms! Yet there still ringing in his ears—well his
oul anyway—were those quite words, "That will be about
ll, sir!" Sternly. As if he had a *right* to speak that way to *him!*
To Laurence Shafton, son of the great Wilson J. Shafton, of
New York! He looked up at the man again and found a sort of
respect for him dawning in himself. It was queer, but the man
was—well, interesting. What was this he was saying?

"I am sorry"—just as if he had never rebuked him at all, "I
am sorry that there seems to be no other way. If I had a car I
would take you to the nearest railway station, but there are
no trains tonight, not even twenty miles away, until six in the
morning. There are only four cars owned in the village. Two
are gone off on a summer trip, the third is out of commission
being repaired, and the fourth belongs to the doctor, who
happens to be away on the mountain tonight attending a
dying man. You see how it is."

The young man opened his mouth to curse once more, and
strangely enough closed it again. Somehow cursing seemed to
have lost its force.

"There is just once chance," went on the minister thoughtfully, "that a young man who was visiting his mother today
may still be here. I can call up and find out. He would take
you I know."

Almost humbly the great man's son followed the minister
back to the house and listened anxiously while he called a
number on the telephone.

"Is that you, Mrs. Carter? I'm sorry if I have disturbed
you. What? You hadn't gone to bed yet? Oh, waiting for
Mark? Then he isn't there? That's what I called up for. There
is someone here in trouble, needing to be taken to Monopoly.
I was sure Mark would help him out if possible. Yes, please,
if he comes soon, ask him to call me. Just leave a note for
him, can't you? I wouldn't sit up. Mark will take good care of
himself. Yes, of course, that's the mother of it. Well, good
night, Mrs. Carter."

The young man strode angrily out to the door, muttering—
but no words were distinct. He wanted to be away from the
compelling calmness of those eyes that seemed to search him

through. He dashed out the screen door, letting it slam
behind him, and down the steps, intending to *make* his car go
on at all odds until he reached another town somewhere. It
had gone so far, it could go on a little farther perhaps. This
country fellow did not know about cars, how should he?

And then somewhere right on the top step he made a false
step and slipped, or was it his blindness of rage? He caught at
the vines with frantic hands, but as if they laughed at him
they slipped from his grasp. His feet clattered against the
step trying for footing, but he was too near the edge, and he
went down straight into a little rocky nook where ferns and
violets were growing, and a sharp jagged rock stuck up and
hit him viciously as he slid and struggled for a firm footing
again. Then an ugly twist of his ankle, and he lay in a
humiliating heap in the shadow of the vines on the lawn,
crying out and beginning to curse with the pain that gripped
him in sharp teeth, and stung through his whole excitable
inflamed being.

The minister was there almost at once, bending over him.
Somehow he felt as if he were in the power of somebody
greater than he had ever met before. It was almost like
meeting God out on the road somewhere. The minister
stooped and picked him up, lightly, as if he had been a
feather, and carried him like a baby, thrown partly over his
shoulder; up the steps, and into that blasted house again.
Into the bright light that sickened him and made the pain
leap up and bring a mighty faintness.

He laid him almost tenderly upon a soft couch, and straightened the pillows about him, seeming to know just how every
bone felt, and how every nerve quivered, and then he asked
a few questions in a quiet voice. "What happened? Was it
your ankle? Here? Or *here?* All right. Just be patient a
minute, I'll have you all fixed up. This was my job over in
France, you know. No, don't move. It won't hurt long. It was
right here you said. Now, wait till I get my bottle of lotion."

He was back in an instant with bandages, and bottle, and
seemed to know just how to get off a shoe with the least
trouble.

An hour later the scion of a great New York family lay
sleeping in the minister's study, the old couch made up with
cool sheets, and the swollen ankle comfortably bandaged with

cool wet cloths. Outside in the moonlight the crippled car stood alone, and Sabbath Valley slept, while the bells chimed out a single solemn stroke.

Chapter 6

Billy was doing some rapid thinking while he stood motionless in the bushes. It seemed a half hour, but in reality it was but a few seconds before he heard a low whistle. The men piled rapidly into the car with furtive looks on either side into the dark.

Billy gave a wavering glance toward the looming house in the darkness where the motionless figure had been left. Was it a dead man lying there alone, or was he only doped? But what could he do in the dark without tools or flash? He decided to stick with the machine, for he had no desire to foot it home, and anyway, with his bicycle he would be far more independent. Besides, there was the perfectly good automobile to think about. If the man was dead he couldn't be any deader. If he was only doped it would be some time before he came to, and before these keepers could get back he would have time to do something. Billy never doubted his responsibility in the matter. It was only a question of expediency. If he could just get these guys with the goods on them, he would be perfectly satisfied.

He made a dash for his seat at the back while the car was turning, and they were off at a brisk pace down the mountain, not waiting this time to double on their tracks, but splashing through the creek only once and on up to the road again.

Like an uneasy fever in his veins meantime, went and came a vision of that limp inert figure of the man being carried into the haunted house as it stood out in the flare of the flashlight, one arm hanging heavily. What did that hand

and arm remind him of? Oh—h! The time when Mark was
knocked cold at the Thanksgiving Day football game last year.
Mark's hand and arm had looked like that—he had held his
fingers like that—when they picked him up. Mark had the
baseball hand! Of course that rich guy might have been an
athlete too, they were sometimes. And of course Mark was
right now at home and in bed, where Billy wished he was
also, but somehow the memory of that still, dark, knocked-
cold attitude, and that hanging hand and arm would not leave
him. He frowned in the dark and wished this business was
over. Mark was the only living soul Billy felt he could ever
tell about this night's escapade, and he wasn't sure he could
tell him, but he knew if he did that Mark would understand.

Billy watched anxiously for a streak of light in the east, but
none had come as yet. The moon had left the earth darker
than darkness when it went.

He tried to think what he should do. His bicycle was lying
in the bushes and he ought to get it before daylight. If they
went near the station he would drop off and pick it up. Then
he would scuttle through the woods and get to the crossroads, and beat it down to the Blue Duck Tavern. That was
the only place open all night where he could telephone. He
didn't like to go to the Blue Duck Tavern on account of his
aunt. She had once made him promise most solemnly, bringing in something about his dead mother, that he would never
go to the Blue Duck Tavern. But this was a case of necessity,
and dead mothers, if they cared at all, ought to understand.
He had a deep underlying faith in the principle of what a
mother—at any rate a dead mother—would be like. And
anyhow, this wasn't the kind of *going* to the tavern his aunt
had meant. He was keeping the spirit of the promise if not
the letter. In his code the spirit meant much more than the
letter—at least on this occasion. There were often times
when he rigidly adhered to the letter and let the spirit take
care of itself, but this was not one.

But if, on the other hand they did not take Pat all the way
back to the crossing by the station it would be even better for
him, for the road on which they now were passed within a
quarter of a mile of the Blue Duck Tavern, and he could
easily beat the car to the state line, by dropping off and
running.

But suddenly and without warning it became apparent that
Pat was to be let out to walk to the station crossing, and Billy
had only a second to decide what to do, while Pat lumbered
swearing down from the car. If he got off now he would have
to wait till Pat was far ahead before he dared go after his
wheel, and he would lose so much time there would be no
use in trying to save the car. On the other hand if he stayed
on the car he was liable to be seen by Pat, and perhaps
caught. However, this seemed the only possible way to keep
the car from destruction and loss, so he wriggled himself into
his seat more firmly, tucked his legs painfully up under him,
covered his face with his cap, and hid his hands in his
pockets.

"You've plenty of time," raged Pat. "You've only a little
five-mile-run left. It's a good half hour before light. You're a
pair of cowards, that's whut ye are, and so I'll tell Sam. If I
get fired fer not being there fer the early milk train, there'll
be no more fat jobs fer youse. Now be sure ye do as you're
told. Leave the car in the first field beyond the woods after
ye cross the state line, lift yer flashlight and wink three times,
count three slow, and wink three times more. *Then beat it!*
And doncha ferget to go feed that guy! We don't want he
should die on us."

The engine began to mutter. Pat with a farewell string of
oaths rolled off down the road, too sleepy to look behind, and
Billy held his breath and ducked low till the rolling Pat was
one with the deep gray of the morning.

The first streak of light was beginning to show in the east,
and the all-night revelers at the Blue Duck were in the last
stages of going home after a more than usually exciting
season, when Billy like the hardened promise-breaker he felt
himself to be, boldly slid in at the door and disappeared
inside the telephone booth behind the last row of tables in
the corner. For leave it to a boy, even though he be not a
frequenter of a place, to know where everything needful is to
be found!

He had to wait several minutes to get the chief of police in
Economy, and while he waited two gaunt habitues of the
tavern slid into seats at the table to the left of the booth,
ordered drinks, and began to discuss something in a low

tone. Billy paid no heed till he happened to hear his friend's
name:

"Yep, I seen Mark come in with Cherry early in the
evening. He set right over there and gotter some drink. The
girl was mad because he wouldn't get her what she wanted to
drink. I happened to be settin' directly in front and I heard
her gassin' about it. She tossed her head and made her eyes
look little and ugly like a pig, and once she got up to go, and
he grabbed her hands and made her set down; and just set
there fer some time alookin' at her hard an' holdin' her han's
and chewin' the rag at her. I don't know what all they was
sayin', fer he talked mighty low, an' Ike called me to take a
hand in the game over tother side the room, so I didn't know
no more till I see him an' Cherry beatin' it out the side door,
an' Dolphin standin' over acrost by the desk lampin' 'em with
his ugly look, an' pretty quick, Dolph he slid out the other
door an' was gone quite some time. When he come back
Cherry was with him, laughin' and makin' eyes, and vampin'
away like she always does, an' him an' her danced a lot after
that—"

A voice on the end of the wire broke in upon this amazing
conversation, and Billy with difficulty adjusted his jaded
mind to the matter in hand:

"'Zis the chief? Say, Chief, a coupla guys stole a machine—
Holes-Mowbrays—license number 6362656-W— Got that?
New York tag. Theyre on their way over to the state line beyond
the crossroads. They're gonta run her in the field just beyond
the woods, you know. They're gonta give a flashlight signal to
their pal, three winks, count three slow, and three winks
more, and then beat it. Then some guy is gonta wreck the
machine. It's up to you and your men to hold the machine till
I get the owner there. He don't know it's pinched yet, but I
know where to find him, an' he'll have the license and can
identify it. Where'll I find you? Station house? 'Conomy?
Sure! I'll be there soon's I get 'im. What's that? I? Oh, I'm
just a kid that happened to get wise. My name? Oh, rats!
That don't cut any ice now! You get on yer job! They must be
almost there by now. I gotta beat it! Gub-bye!"

Billy was all there even if he had been up all night. He
hung up with a click, for he was anxious to hear what the men
were saying. They had finished their glasses and were prepar-

ing to leave. The old one was gabbling on in a querulous gossipy tone:

"Well, it'll go hard with Mark Carter if the man dies. Everybody knows he was here, and unless he can prove an alibi—"

They were crawling reluctantly out of their haunts now, and Billy could catch but one more sentence:

"Well, I'm sorry fer his ma. I used to go to school with Mrs. Carter when we were kids."

They were gone out and the room suddenly showed empty. The waiter was fastening the shutters. In a moment more he would be locked in. Billy made a silent dash among the tables and slid out the door while the waiter's back was turned. The two men were ambling slowly down the road toward Economy. Billy started on a dead run. His rubber-soled shoes made no echo and he was too light on his feet to make a thud. He disappeared into the grayness like a spirit. He had more cause than ever now for hurry. Mark! Mark! His beloved Mark Carter! What must he do about it? Must he tell Mark? Or did Mark perhaps know? What had happened anyway? There had evidently been a shooting. That Cherry Fenner was mixed up in it. Billy knew her only by sight. She always grinned at him and said: "Hello, Billee!" in her pretty dimpled way. He didn't care for her himself. He had accepted her as a part of life, a necessary evil. She wore her hair queer, and had very short tight skirts, and high heels. She painted her face and vamped, but that was her affair. He had therefore tolerated her because she seemed in some way to be under Mark Carter's recent protection. Therefore he had growled "Ello!" grimly whenever she accosted him and let it go at that. If it had come to a showdown he would have stood up for her because he knew that Mark would, that was all. Mark knew his own business. Far be it from Billy to criticize his hero's reasons. Perhaps it was one of Mark's weaknesses. It was up to him.

But this was a different matter. This involved Mark's honor. It was up to him to find Mark!

Billy did not take the highroad down from his detour. He cut across below the crossroads, over rough ground, among the underbrush, and parting the low growing trees, was lost in the gloom of the woods. But he knew every inch of ground

within twenty miles around, and darkness did not take away
his sense of direction. He crashed along among the branches,
making steady headway toward the spot where he had left his
bicycle, puffing and panting, his face streaked with dirt, his
eyes bleared and haggard, his whole lithe young body straining
forward and fighting against the dire weariness that was upon
him, for it was not often that he stayed up all night. Aunt
Saxon saw to that much at least.

The sky was growing rosy now, and he could hear the
rumbling of the milk train. It was late. Pat would not lose his
job this time, for he must have had plenty of time to get back
to the station. Billy wormed himself under cover as the train
approached, and bided his time. Cautiously, peering from
behind the huckleberry growth, he watched Pat slamming
the milk cans around. He could see his bicycle lying like a
dark skeleton of a thing against the gravel bank. It was lucky
he got there before day, for Pat would have been sure to see
it, and it might have given him an idea that Billy had gone
with the automobile.

The milk train came suddenly in sight through the tunnel,
like a lighted thread going through a needle. It rumbled up
to the station. There was a rattling of milk cans, empty ones
being put on, full cans being put off, grumbling of Pat at the
train hands, loud retorts of the train hands. The engine
puffed and wheezed like a fat old lady going upstairs and
stopping on every landing to rest. Then slamming of car
doors, a whistle, the snort of the engine as it took up its way
again out toward the rosy sky, its headlight weird like a sick
candle against the dawn, its taillight winking with a leer and
mocking at the mountains as it clattered away like a row of
gray ducks lifting webbed feet and flinging back space to the
station.

Pat rolled the loaded truck to the other platform ready for
the lake train at seven, and went in to a much needed rest.
He slammed the door with a finality that gave Billy relief.
The boy waited a moment more in the gathering dawn, and
then made a dash for the open, salvaging his bicycle, and
diving back into the undergrowth.

For a quarter of a mile he and the wheel like two comrades
raced under branches, and threaded their way between trees.
Then he came out into the highroad and mounting his wheel

rode into the world just as the sun shot up and touched the day with wonder.

He rode into the silent sleeping village of Sabbath Valley just as the bells from the church chimed out gently, as bells should do on a Sabbath morning when people are at rest, One! Two! Three! Four! Five!

Sabbath Valley looked great as he pedaled silently down the street. Even the old squeak of the back wheel seemed to be holding its breath for the occasion.

He coasted past the church and down the gentle incline in front of the parsonage and Joneses, and the Littles and Browns, and Gibsons. Like a shadow of the night passing he slid past the Fowlers and Tiptons and Duncannons, and fastened his eyes on the little white fence with the white-pillared gate where Mrs. Carter lived. Was that a light in the kitchen window? And the barn that Mark used for his garage when he was at home, was the door open? He couldn't quite see for the syringa bush hid it from the road. With a furtive glance up and down the street he wheeled in at the driveway, and rode up under the shadow of the green-shuttered white house.

He dismounted silently, stealthily, rested his wheel against the trunk of a cherry tree, and with keen eyes for every window, glanced up to the open one above which he knew belonged to Mark's room. Strong grimy fingers went to his lips and a low cautious whistle, more like a birdcall issued forth, musical as any wild note.

The white muslin curtains wavered back and forth in the summer breeze, and for a moment he thought a head was about to appear for a soft stirring noise had seemed to move within the house somewhere, but the curtains swayed on and no Mark appeared. Then he suddenly was aware of a white face confronting him at the downstairs window directly opposite to him, white and scared and—was it accusing? And suddenly he began to tremble. Not all the events of the night had made him tremble, but now he trembled, it was Mark's mother, and she had pink rims to her eyes, and little damp crimples around her mouth and eyes for all the world like Aunt Saxon's. She looked—she looked exactly as though she had not slept all night. Her nose was thin and red, and her eyes had that awful blue that eyes get that have been much washed with tears. The soft waves of her hair drooped thinly, and the coil behind showed more threads of silver than of brown in the morning sun that shot through the branches of the cherry tree. She had a frightened look, as if Billy had brought some awful news, or as if it was his fault, he could not tell which, and he began to feel that choking sensation and that goneness in the pit of his stomach that Aunt Saxon always gave him when she looked frightened at something he had done or was going to do. Added to this was that sudden premonition, and a memory of that drooping still figure in the dark up on the mountain.

Mrs. Carter set down the candle on a shelf and raised the window:

"Is that you, Billy?" she asked, and there were tears in her voice.

Billy had a brief appalling revelation of mothers the world over. Did all mothers—women—act like that when they were *fools?* Fools is what he called them in his mind. Yet in spite of himself and his rage and trembling he felt a sudden tenderness for this crumply, tired, ghastly little pink-rimmed mother, apprehensive of the worst as was plain to see. Billy recalled like a flash the old man at the Blue Duck saying, "I'm sorry for his ma. I used to go to school with her." He looked at the faded face with the pink rims and trembling lips and had a vision of a brown-haired little girl at a desk, and old Si Appleby, a teasing boy in the desk opposite. It came over him that someday he would be an old man somewhere telling how he went to school— And then he asked:

"Where's Mark? Up yet?"

She shook her head apprehensively, withholdingly.

Billy had a thought that perhaps someone had beat him to it with news from the Blue Duck, and he put it from him. There were tears in her eyes and one was straggling down between the crimples of her cheeks where it looked as if she had lain on the folds of her handkerchief all night. There came a new tenderness in his voice. This was *Mark's* mother, and this was the way she felt. Well, of course it was silly, but she was Mark's *mother.*

"Man up the mountain had n'accident. I thought Mark ud he'p. He always does," explained Billy awkwardly with a feeling that he ought to account for his early visit.

"Yes, of course, Mark would like to help!" purred his mother comforted at the very thought of everyday life and Mark going about as usual. "But," and the apprehension flew into her eyes again, "he isn't home. Billy, he hasn't come home at all last night! I'm frightened to death! I've sat up all night! I can't think what's happened! There's so many holdups and Mark will carry his money loose in his trousers' pocket!"

Billy blanched but lied beautifully up to the occasion even as he would have liked to have somebody lie for him to Aunt Saxon:

"Aw! That's nothing! Doncha worry. He tol' me he might have t'stay down t'Unity all night. There's a fella down there that likes him a lot, an' they had somekinduva blowout in their church last night. He mightuv had ta take some girl home out of town, ya know, and stayed over with the fella."

Mrs. Carter's face relaxed a shade:

"Yes, I've tried to think that!"

"Well, doncha worry, Mizz Carter, I'll lookim up fer ya, I know 'bout where he might be."

"Oh, thank you, Billy," her face wreathed in wavering smiles brought another thought of school days and life and how queer it was that grown folks had been children sometime and children had to be grown folks.

"Billy, Mark likes you very much. I'm sure he won't mind your knowing that I'm worried, but you know how boys don't like to have their mothers worry, so you needn't say anything to Mark that I said I was worried, need you? You understand, Billy. I'm not *really* worried, you know. Mark was always a good boy."

"Aw, sure!" said Billy with a knowing wink. "He's a prince! You leave it t'me, Mizz Carter!"

"Thank you, Billy. I'll do something for you sometime. But how's it come you're up so early? You haven't had your breakfast yet have you?"

She eyed his weary young face with a motherly anxiety:

"Naw, I didn't have no time to stop fer breakfast." Billy spoke importantly. "Got this call about the sick guy and had to beat it. Say, you don't happen to know Mark's license number, do you? It might help a lot, savin' time 'f I could tell his car at sight. Save stoppin' to ast."

"Well, now, I don't really—" said the woman ruminatively.

"Let me see. There was six and six, there were a lot of sixes if I remember—"

"Oh, well, it don't matter—" Billy grasped his wheel and prepared to leave.

"Wait, Billy, you must have something to eat—"

"Aw, naw, I can't wait! Gotta beat it! Might miss 'im!"

"Well, just a bite. Here, I'll get you some cookies!"

She vanished, and he realized for the first time that he was hungry. Cookies sounded good.

She returned with a brimming glass of milk and a plate of cookies. She stuffed the cookies in his pockets, while he drank the milk.

"Say," said he after a long sweet draught of the foaming milk, "ya, ain't got enny more you cud spare fer that sick guy, have ya? Wait, I'll save this. Got a bottle?"

"Indeed you won't, Billy Gaston. You just drink that every drop. I'll get you another bottle to take with you. I got extra last night 'count of Mark being home, and then he didn't drink it. He always likes a drink of milk last thing before he goes to bed."

She vanished and returned with a quart of milk cold off the ice. She wrapped it well with newspapers, and Billy packed it safely into the little basket on his wheel. Then he bethought him of another need.

"Say, m'y I go inta the g'rage an' get a screwdriver? Screw loose on m'wheel."

She nodded and he vanished into the open barn door. Well, he knew where Mark kept his tools. He picked out a small pointed saw, a neat little auger, and a file and stowed them hurriedly under the milk bottle. Thus reinforced without and within, he mounted his faithful steed and sped away to the hills.

The morning sun had shot up several degrees during his delay, and Sabbath Valley lay like a thing newborn in its glory. On the belfry a purple dove sat glistening, green and gold ripples on her neck, turning her head proudly from side to side as Billy rode by, and when he topped the first hill across the valley the bells rang out six sweet strokes as if to remind him that Sunday school was not far off and he must hurry back. But Billy was trying to think how he should get into that locked house, and wondering whether the kidnappers would have returned to feed their captive yet. He realized that he must be wary, although his instinct told him that they would wait for dark; besides, he had hopes that they might have been pinched.

Nevertheless he approached the old house cautiously, skirting the mountain to avoid Pleasant Valley, and walking a mile or two through thick undergrowth, sometimes with difficulty propelling the faithful machine.

Arrived in sight he studied the surroundings carefully, harbored his wheel where it would not be discovered and was yet easily available, and after reconnoitering stole out of covert.

The house stood gaunt and grim against the smiling morning, its shuttered windows giving an expression of blindness or the repellant mask of death. A dead house, that was what it was. Its doors and windows closed on the tragedy that had been enacted within its massive stone walls. It seemed more like a fortress than a house where warm human faces had once sounded out. To pass it had always stirred a sense of mystery and weirdness. To approach it thus with the intention of entering to find that still limp figure of a man gave a most overpowering sense of awe. Billy looked up with wide eyes, the deep shadows under them standing out in the clear light of the morning and giving him a strangely old aspect as if he had jumped over at least ten years during the night. Warily he circled the house, keeping close to the shrubbery at first and listening as a squirrel might have done, then gradually drawing nearer. He noticed that the downstairs shutters were solid iron with a little half-moon peephole at the top. Those upstairs were solid below and fitted with slats above, but the slats were closed on all the front windows, and all but two of the back ones, which were turned upward so that one could not see the glass. The doors, both back and front, were locked, and unshakable, of solid oak and very thick. A Yale lock with a new look gave all entrance at the front an impossible look. The back door was equally impregnable unless he set to work with his auger and saw and took out a heavy oak panel.

He got down to the ground and began to examine the cellar windows. They seemed to be fitted with iron bars set into the solid masonry. He went all around the house and

found each one unshakable, until he reached the last at the
back. There he found a bit of stone cracked and loosened,
and it gave him an idea. He set to work with his few tools and
finally succeeded in loosening one rusted bar. He was much
hindered in his work by the necessity of keeping a constant
watch out, and by his attempts to be quiet. There was no
telling when Link and Shorty might come to feed their
captive and he must not be discovered.

It was slow work picking away at the stone, filing away at
the rusty iron, but the bars were so close together that three
must be removed before he could hope to crawl through, and
even then he might be able to get no further than the cellar.
The guy that fixed this house up for a prison knew what he
was about.

Faintly across the mountains came the echo of bells, or
were they in the boy's own soul? He worked away in the hot
sun, the perspiration rolling down his weary dirty face, and
sometimes his soul fainted within him. Bells and the sweet
quiet church with the pleasant daily faces about and the hum
of Sunday school beginning! How far away that all seemed to
him now as he filed and picked, and sweated, and kept up a
strange something in his soul half yearning, half fierce dread,
that might have been like praying, only the burden of its
yearning seemed to be expressed in but a single word,
"Mark! Mark!"

At last the third bar came loose and with a great sigh that
was almost like a sob, the boy tore it out and cleared the way.
Then carefully gathering his effects, tools, milk bottle, and
cap together, he let them down into the dungeonlike blackness
of the cellar, and crept in after them, taking the precaution to
set up in place the iron bars once more and leave no trace of
his entrance.

Pausing cautiously to listen he ventured to strike a match,
mentally belaboring himself at the wasteful way in which he
had always used his flashlight which was now so much needed
and out of commission. The cellar was large, running under
the whole house, with heavy rafters and looming coal pits. A
scurrying rat started a few lumps of coal in the slide, and a
cobwebby rope hung ominously from one cross beam, giving
him a passing shudder. It seemed as if the spirit of the past
had arisen to challenge his entrance thus. He took a few steps

forward toward a dim staircase he sighted at the farther end,
and then a sudden noise sent his heart beating fast. He
extinguished the match and stood in the darkness listening
with straining ears. That was surely a step he heard on the
floor above!

Chapter 7

Laurence Shafton awoke late to the sound of church bells
come alive and singing hymn tunes. There was something
strangely unreal in the sound, in the utter stillness of the
background of Sabbath Valley atmosphere that made him
think, almost, just for an instant, that he had stumbled
somehow into the wrong end of the other world, and come
into the fields of the blessed. Not that he had any very
definite idea about what the fields of the blessed would
look like or what would be going on there, but there was
something still and holy between the voices of the bells
that fairly compelled his jaded young soul to sit up and
listen.

But at the first attempt to sit up a very sharp, very decided
twinge of pain caught him, and brought an assorted list of
words which he kept for such occasions to his lips. Then he
looked around and tried to take in the situation. It was almost
as if he had been caught out of his own world and dropped
into another universe, so different was everything here, and
so little did he remember the happenings of the night before.
He had had trouble with his car, something infernal that had
prevented his going farther—he recalled having to get out
and push the thing along the road, and then two loutish men
who made game of him and sent him here to get his car fixed.
There had been a man, a different sort of man who gave him
bread and butter instead of wine—he remembered that—and
he had failed to get his car fixed, but how the deuce did he

get landed on this couch with a world of books about him and a thin muslin curtain blowing into the room, and fanning the petals of a lovely rose in a long-stemmed clear glass vase? Did he try to start and have a smashup? No, he remembered going down the steps with the intention of starting, but stay! Now it was coming to him. He fell off the porch! He must have had a jag on or he never would have fallen. He did things to his ankle in falling. He remembered the gentle giant picking him up as if he had been a baby and putting him here, but where was *here*? Ah! Now he remembered! He was on his way to Opal Verrons's. A bet. An elopement for the prize! Great stakes. He had lost of course. What a fool! If it hadn't been for his ankle he might have got to a trolley car or train somehow and made a garage. Money would have taken him there in time. He was vexed that he had lost. It would have been great fun, and he had the name of always winning when he set out to do so. But then, perhaps it was just as well—Verrons was a good fellow as men went—he liked him, and he was plain out and out fond of Opal just at present. It would have been a dirty shame to play the trick behind his back. Still, if Opal wanted to run away with him it was up to him to run of course. Opal was rare sport and he couldn't stand the idea of smart aleck McMarter or that conceited Percy Emerson getting there first. He wondered which had won. It made his fury rise to think of either, and he had promised the lady neither of them should. What was she thinking of him by now that he had sent her no word of his delay? That was inexcusable. He must attend to it at once.

He glanced around the pleasant room. Yes, there on the desk was a telephone! Could he get to it? He sat up and painfully edged his way over to the desk.

> Safely through another week,
> God has brought us on our way—

chimed the bells,

> Let us now a blessing seek,
> Waiting in His courts today—

But Laurie Shafton had never sung those words in his life

and had no idea what the bells were seeking to get across to him. He took down the receiver and called for Long Distance.

> O day of rest and gladness!

pealed out the bells joyously,

> O day of joy and light!
> O balm of care and sadness,
> Most beautiful, most bright—!

But it meant nothing to Laurie Shafton seeking a hotel in a fashionable resort. And when he finally got his number it was only Opal's maid who answered.

"Yes, Mrs. Verrons was up. She was out walking on the beach with a gentleman. No, it was not Mr. Emerson, nor yet Mr. McMarter. Neither of those gentlemen had arrived. No, it was not Mr. Verrons. He had just telegraphed that he would not be at the hotel until tomorrow night. Yes, she would tell Mrs. Verrons that he had met with an accident. Mrs. Verrons would be very sorry. Number one-W Sabbath Valley. Yes, she would write it down. What? Oh! The gentleman Mrs. Verrons was walking with? No, it was not anybody that had been stopping at the hotel for long, it was a new gentleman who had just come the night before. She hadn't heard his name yet. Yes, she would be sure to tell Mrs. Verrons at once when she came in, and Mrs. Verrons would be likely to call him up!"

He hung up the receiver and looked around the room discontentedly. A stinging twinge of his ankle added to his discomfort. He gave an angry snarl and pushed the wavering curtain aside, wishing those everlasting bells would stop their banging.

Across the velvet stretch of lawn the stone church nestled among the trees, with a background of mountains, and a studding of white gravestones beyond its wide front steps. It was astonishingly beautiful, and startlingly close for a church. He had not been so near to a church except for a wedding in all his young life. Dandy place for a wedding that would be, canopy over the broad walk from the street, charming architecture, he liked the line of the arched belfry and the slender

spire above. The rough stone fitted well into the scenery. The
church seemed to be a thing of the ages placed there by
Nature. His mind trained to detect a sense of beauty in
garments, rugs, pictures, and women, appreciated the picture on which he was gazing. Where was this anyway? Surely
not the place with the absurd name that he remembered now
on the mountain detour. Sabbath Valley! How ridiculous! It
must be the home of some wealthy estate, and yet there
seemed a rustic loveliness about it that scarcely established
that theory.

The bells had ceased. He heard the roll of a deep throated
organ skillfully played.

And now, his attention was suddenly attracted to the open
window of the church where framed in English ivy a lovely
girl sat at the organ. She was dressed in white with hair of
gold, and a golden window somewhere back of her across the
church, made a background of beaten gold against which her
delicate profile was set like some young saint. Her white
fingers moved among the keys, and gradually he came to
realize that it was she who had been playing the bells.

He stared and stared, filled with admiration, thrilled with
this new experience in his blasé existence. Who would have
expected to find a beauty like that in a little out-of-the-way
place like this? His theory of a great estate and a rich man's
daughter with a fad for music instantly came to the front.
What a lucky happening that he should have broken down
close to this church. He would find out who the girl was and
work it to get invited up to her house. Perhaps he was a
fortunate loser of his bet after all.

As he watched the girl playing, gradually the music entered
his consciousness. He was fond of music, and had heard the
best of the world of course. This was meltingly lovely. The
girl had fine appreciation and much expression, even when
the medium of her melody was clumsy things like bells. She
had seemed to make them glad as they pealed out their
melodies. He had not known bells could sound like happy
children, or like birds.

His meditations were interrupted by a tap on the door,
followed by the entrance of his host bearing a tray:

"Good morning," he said pleasantly, "I see you're up. How
is the sprain? Better? Would you like me to dress it again?"

He came over to the desk and set down the tray on which was beautifully brown buttered toast, eggs and coffee:

"I've brought you just a bite. It's so late you won't want much, for we have dinner immediately after church. I suppose you wouldn't feel like going over to the service?"

"Service?" the young man drawled almost insolently.

"Yes, service is at eleven. Would you care to go over? I could assist you."

"Naw, I shouldn't care to go," he answered rudely, "I'm pulling out of here as soon as I can get that machine of mine running. By the way, I've been doing some telephoning"—he slung a ten-dollar note on the desk. "I didn't ask how much it was, guess that'll cover it. Now, help me to the big chair and I'll sample your breakfast."

The minister picked up the young man easily and placed him in the big chair before the guest realized what he was doing, and then turned and took the ten-dollar bill between his thumb and finger and flipped it down in the young man's lap.

"Keep it," he said briefly. "It's of no consequence."

"But it was long distance," explained the guest loftily. "It'll be quite a sum. I talked overtime."

"No matter," said the minister pulling out a drawer of the desk and gathering a few papers and his Bible. "Now, would you like me to look at that ankle before I go, or will you wait for the doctor? He's likely to be back before long, and I've left a call for him."

"I'll wait for the doctor," the young man's tone approached the insolent note again, "and, by the way, I wish you'd sent for a mechanic. I've got to get that car running."

"I'm sorry," said Severn, "I'm afraid you'll have to wait. The only one in this region that would be at all likely to help you out with those bearings is Carter. He has a car, or had one, of that make. He might happen to have some bearings, but it is not at all likely. Or, he could tow you ten miles to Monopoly. But Carter is not at home yet."

The young man fairly frothed at the mouth:

"Do you mean to tell me that there is no one can mend a broken machine around this forsaken dump? Where's your nearest garage? Send for a man to come at once. I'm willing to pay anything." He flourished a handful of bills.

The minister looked at his watch anxiously:

"I'm sorry," he said again. "I've got to go to the service now. There is a garage at Monopoly and their number is ninety-seven-M. You can phone them if you are not satisfied. I tried them quite early this morning while you were still sleeping, but there was nothing doing. The truth is the people around this region are a little prejudiced against working seven days out of the week, although they will help a man out in a case like yours when they can, but it seems the repairman, the only one who knows about bearings, had gone fifty miles in another direction to a funeral and won't be back till tomorrow morning. Now, if you're quite comfortable I'll have to leave you for a little while. It is time for my service to begin."

The young man looked at his host with astonishment. He was not used to being treated in this offhand way. He could hardly believe his ears. Throw back his money and lay down the law that way!

"Wait!" he thundered as the door was about to close upon the departing minister.

Severn turned and regarded his guest quietly, questioningly:

"Who's that girl over there in the window playing the organ?" He pulled the curtain aside and revealed a glimpse of the white and gold saint framed in the ivy. Severn gave a swift cold glance at the insolent youth and then answered with a slightly haughty note in his courteous voice, albeit a quiver of amusement on his lip:

"That is my daughter."

Laurence Shafton dropped the curtain and turned to stare at his host, but the minister had closed the door and was already on his way to church. Then the youth pulled back the curtain again and regarded the lady. The man's daughter! And playing like that!

The rich notes of the organ were rolling out into the summer day, a wonderful theme from an old master, grandly played. Yes, she could play. She had been well taught. And the looks of her! She was wonderful at this distance. Were these then wealthy people perhaps summering in this quiet resort? He glanced about at the simple furnishings. That was a good rug at his feet, worn in places, but soft in tone and unmistakably of the Orient. The desk was of fumed oak, somewhat massive and dignified with a touch of hand carving. The chairs were of the same dark oak with leather cushions, and the couch so covered by his bed drapery that he could not see it, but he remembered its comfort. There was nothing showy or expensive looking but everything simple and good. One or two fine old pictures on the wall gave evidence of good taste. The only luxury seemed books, rows and rows of them behind glass doors in cases built into the wall. They lined each space between windows and doors, and in several spots reached to the ceiling. He decided that these people must have had money and lost it. These things were old and had perhaps been inherited. But the girl! She teased his curiosity. She seemed of a type entirely new, and most attractive. Well, here was good luck again! He would stay till church was out and see what she might be like at nearer view. It might amuse him to play the invalid for a day or two and investigate her. Meantime, he must call up that garage and see what could be done for the car. If he could get it patched up by noon he might take the girl out for a spin in the afternoon. One could judge a girl much better getting her off by herself that way. He didn't seem to relish the memory of that father's smile and haughty tone as he said "My daughter." Probably was all kinds of fussy about her. But if the girl had any pep at all she surely would enjoy getting away from oversight for a few hours. He hoped Opal would call before they got back from their service. It might be awkward talking with them all around.

But the organ was suddenly drowned in a burst of song:

Glory be to the Father, and to the Son, and to the Holy Ghost, As it was in the beginning, is now and ever shall be—world without end, Amen!

Somehow the words struck him with a strange awe, they were so distinct, and almost in the room with him. He looked about half feeling that the room was filled with people, and felt curiously alone. There was an atmosphere in the little house of everybody being gone to church. They had all gone and left him alone. It amused him. He wondered about this odd family who seemed to be under the domination of a church service. They had left him a stranger alone in their house. The doors and windows were all open. How did they know but he was a burglar?

Someone was talking now. It sounded like the voice of his host. It might be a prayer. How peculiar! He must be a preacher. Yet he had been sent to him to fix his car. He did not look like a laboring man. He looked as if he might be—well almost anything—even a gentleman. But if he was a clergyman, why, that of course explained the ascetic type, the nunlike profile of the girl, the skilled musician. Clergymen were apt to educate their children, even without much money. The girl would probably be a prude and bore, but there was a chance that she might be a princess in disguise and need a prince to show her a good time. He would take the chance at least until after dinner.

So he ate his delicate toast, and drank his delicious coffee, and wished he had asked that quiet man to have his flask filled at the drugstore before he went to his old service, but consoled himself with numerous cigarettes, while he watched the face of the musician, and listened idly to the music.

It was plain that the young organist was also the choir leader, for her expressive face was turned toward the singers, and her lovely head kept time. Now and then a motion of the hand seemed to give a direction or warning. And the choir too sang with great sweetness and expression. They were well trained. But what a bore such a life must be to a girl. Still, if she had never known anything else! Well, he would like to see her at closer range. He lit another cigarette and studied her profile as she slipped out of the organ bench and settled herself nearer the window. He could hear the man's voice reading now. Some of the words drew his idle attention:

"All the ways of a man are clean in his own eyes; but the Lord weigheth the spirits."

Curious sentence that! It caught in his brain. It seemed rather true. From the Bible probably, of course, though he was not very familiar with that volume, never having been obliged to go to Sunday school in his childhood days. But was it true? Were all a man's ways clean in his own eyes? Take, for instance, his own ways? He always did about as he pleased, and he had never asked himself whether his ways were clean or not. He hadn't particularly cared. He supposed some people would think they were not—but in his own eyes, well—was he clean? Take for instance this expedition of his? Running a race to get another man's wife—an alleged friend's wife, too? It did seem rather despicable when one thought of it after the jag was off. But then one was not quite responsible for what one did with a jag on, and what the deuce did the Lord have to do with it anyway? How could the Lord weigh the spirit? That meant of course that He saw through all subterfuges. Well, what of it?

Another sentence caught his ear:

"When a man's ways please the Lord, he maketh even
his enemies to be at peace with him."

How odd, the Lord—if there was a Lord, he had never thought much about it—but how odd, if there was a Lord for Him to care about a man's ways. If he were Lord he wouldn't care, he'd only want them to keep out of his way. He would probably crush them like ants, if he were Lord. But the Lord—taking any notice of men's ways, and being pleased by them and looking out to protect them from enemies! It certainly was quaint—a quaint idea! He glanced again at the reverent face of the girl, the down-drooped eyes, the lovely sensitive mouth. Quaint, that was the word for her, quaint and unusual. He certainly was going to enjoy meeting her.

"Ting-aling-ling-ling!" burst out the telephone bell on the desk. He frowned and dropped the curtain. Was that Opal? He hobbled to the desk painfully, half annoyed that she had called him from the contemplation of this novel scene, not so sure that he would bother to call up that garage yet. Let it go till he had sampled the girl.

He took down the receiver and Opal's voice greeted him, mockingly, tauntingly from his own world. The little ivy-leaved church with its Saint Cecilia at the organ, and its strange weird message about a God that cared for man's ways, dropped away like a dream that was past.

When he hung up the receiver and turned back to his couch again the girl had closed the window. It annoyed him. He did not know how his giddy badinage had clashed in upon the last words of the sermon.

It seemed a long time after the closing hymn before the little throng melted away down the maple-lined street. The young man watched them curiously from behind his curtain, finding only food for amusement in most of them. And then came the minister, lingering to talk to one here and there, and his wife—it was undoubtedly his wife, even the hare-brained Laurie knew her, in the gray organdy, with the white at her neck, and the soft white hat. She had a pleasant light in her eyes, and one saw at once that she was a lady. There was a grace about her that made the girl seem possible. And lastly, came the girl.

She stepped from the church door in her white dress and simple white hat, white even to her little shoes, and correct in every way, he could see that. She was no country gawk! She came forth lightly into the sunshine which caught her hair in golden tendrils around her face as if it loved to hide therein, and she was immediately surrounded by half a dozen urchins. One had brought her some lilies, great white starry things with golden hearts, and she gathered them into her arms as if she loved them, and smiled at the boys. One could see how they adored her. She lingered talking to them, and laid her hand on one boy's shoulder, he walking like a knight beside her trying to act as if he did not know her hand was there. His head was drooped, but he lifted it with a grin at last and gave her a nod which seemed to make her glad, for her face broke forth in another smile:

"Well, don't forget, tonight," she called as they turned to go, "and remember to tell Billy!"

Then she came trippingly across the grass, a song on her lips. Some girl! Say! She certainly was a stunner!

Chapter 8

Opal Verrons was small and slight with large childlike eyes that could look like a baby's, but that could hold the very devil on occasions. The eyes were dark and lustrous with long curling black lashes framing them in a face that might have been modeled for an angel, so round the curves, so enchanting the lips, so lofty the white brow. Angelé Potocka had no lovelier set to her head, no more limpal fire in her eye, than had Opal Verrons. Indeed her lovers often called her the Fire Opal. The only difference was that Angelé Potocka developed her brains, of which she had plenty, while Opal Verrons had placed her entire care upon developing her lovely little body, though she too had plenty of brains on occasion.

And she knew how to dress! So simply, so slightly sometimes, so perfectly to give a setting—the right setting—to her little self. She wore her heavy dark hair bobbed, and it curled about her small head exquisitely, giving her the look of a Raphael cherub or a boy page in the court of King Arthur. With a flat band of silver olive leaves about her brow, and the soft hair waving out below, nothing more was necessary for a costume save a brief drapery of silver spangled cloth with a strap of jewels and a wisp of black malines for a scarf. She was always startling and lovely even in her simplest costume. Many people turned to watch her in a simple dark blue serge made like a child's girded with a delicate arrangement of medallions and chains of white metal, her dark rough woollen stockings rolled girlishly below white dimpled knees, and her feet shod in flat-soled white buckskin shoes. She was young enough to get away with it, the older women said cattishly as they watched her stroll away to the beach with a new man each day, and noted her artless grace and indifferent pose. That she had a burly millionaire husband who still was under her spell and watched her jealously only made her more interesting, and they pitied her for being tied to a man twice her age and bulky as a bale of cotton. She who could dance like a sylph and was light on her little feet as a thistle-down. Though wise ones sometimes said that Opal had her young eyes wide open when she married Ed Verrons, and she had him right under her little pink well manicured thumb. And some said she was not nearly so young as she looked.

Her hands were the weakest point in Opal Verron's whole outfit. Not that they were unlovely in form or ungraceful. They were so small they hardly seemed like hands, so undeveloped, so useless, with the dimpling of a baby's, yet the sharp nails of a little beast. They were so plump and well cared for they were fairly sleek, and had an old wise air about them as she patted her puffy curls daintily with a motion all her own that showed her lovely rounded arm, and every needle-pointed, shell-tinted fingernail, sleek and puffy, and never used, not even for a bit of embroidery or knitting. She couldn't, you know, with those sharp transparent little nails, they might break. They were like her little sharp teeth that always reminded one of a mouse's teeth, and made one shudder at how sharp they would be should she ever decide to bite.

But her smile was like the mixing of all smiles, a baby's, a woman of the world, a grieved child's, a spirit who had put aside all moral purpose. Perhaps, like mixed drinks it was for that reason but the more intoxicating. And because she did not hide her charms and was lavish with her smiles, there were more poor victims about her little feet than about any other woman at the shore that summer. Men talked about her in the smoking rooms and billiard rooms and compared her to vamps of other seasons, and decided she had left them all in the shade. She was a perfect production of the modern age, more perfect than others because she knew how to do the boldest things with that cherubic air that bereft sin of its natural ugliness and made it beautiful and delicious, as if degradation had suddenly become an exalted thing, like some of the old rites in a pagan temple, and she a lovely priestess. And when each new folly was over there was she with her innocent baby air, and her pure childlike face that looked dreamily out from its frame of little girl hair, and seemed not to have been soiled at all. And so men who played her games lost their sense of sin and fell that much lower than those who sin and know it and are afraid to look themselves in the face. When a man loses his sense of shame of being among the pigs, he is in a far country indeed.

But Opal Verrons sauntering forth to the hotel piazza in company with three of her quondam admirers suddenly lost her luxurious air of nestling content. The hotel clerk handed her two telegrams as she passed the desk. She tore them open carelessly, but her eyes grew wide with horror as she read.

Percy Emerson had been arrested. He had run over a woman and a baby and both were in a hospital in a critical condition. He would be held without bail until it was seen whether they lived.

She drew in her breath with a frightened gasp and bit at her red lip with her little sharp teeth. A pretty child with floating curls and dainty apparel ran laughing across her way, its hand outstretched to a tiny white dog that was dancing after her, and Opal gave a sharp cry and tore the telegram into small bits. But when she opened the second message her face paled under its delicate rouge as she read: "Mortimer McMarter killed in an accident when his car collided with a truck. His body lies at Saybrook Inn. We find your address on his person, with a request to let you know if anything happens to him. What do you wish done with the body?"

Those who watched her face as she read say that it took on an ashen color and she looked years older. Her real spirit seemed to be looking forth from those wide limpid eyes for an instant, the spirit of a coward who had been fooling the world; the spirit of a lost soul who had grown old in sin; the spirit of a soul who had stepped over the bounds and sinned beyond her depth.

She looked about upon them all, stricken, appalled—not sorry but just afraid—and not for her friends, but for *herself!* And then she gave a horrid little lost laugh and dropping the telegram as if it had burned her, she flung out her voice upon them with a blaze in her big eyes and a snarl in her lute voice:

"Well, I wasn't to blame was I? They all were grown men, weren't they? It was up to them. *I'm* going to get out of here! This is an *awful* place!"

She gave a shudder and turning swiftly fled to the elevator, catching it just as the door was being shut, and they saw her rising behind the black and gold grating and waving a mocking little white hand at them as they watched her amazed. Then one of them stooped and picked up the telegram. And while they still stood at the doorway wondering someone pointed to a brilliant blue car that was sliding down the avenue across the beach road.

"She has gone!" they said looking at one another strangely. Did she really care then?

*   *   *

The dinner at Sabbath Valley parsonage was a good one. It was quite different from any dinner Laurie Shafton had ever eaten before. It had a taste that he hadn't imagined just plain chicken and mashed potatoes and bread and butter and coffee and cherry pie could have. Those were things he seldom picked out from a menu, and he met them as something new and delicious, prepared in this wonderful country way.

Also the atmosphere was queer and interesting.

The minister had helped him into the dining room, a cheery room with a bay window looking toward the church and a window box of nasturtiums in which the bees hummed and buzzed.

The girl came in and acknowledged the casual introduction of her father with a quite sophisticated nod and sat down across from him. And there was a *prayer* at the beginning of the meal! Just as he was about to say something graceful to the girl, there was a *prayer*. It was almost embarrassing. He had never seen one before like this. At a boarding school once he had experienced a thing they called grace which consisted in standing behind their chairs while the entire assembled hungry multitude repeated a poem of a religious nature. He remembered they used to spend their time making up parodies on it—one ran something about "this same old fish upon my plate," and rhymed with "hate." He stared at the lovely bowed hair of the girl across the table while it was going on, and got ready a remark calculated to draw her smiles, but the girl lifted eyes that seemed so far away he felt as though she did not see him, and he contented himself with replying to his host's question something about the part of the chicken he liked best. It was a strange home to him, it seemed to intimate. Even the chicken seemed to be a detail of their life together, perhaps because there was only one chicken, and one breast. Where he dwelt there were countless breasts, and everybody had a whole breast if he wanted it, or a whole chicken for the matter of that. Here they had to stop and ask what others liked before they chose for themselves. This analysis went through his mind while he sat waiting for his plate and wondering over the little things they were talking about. Mrs. Severn said Miss Saxon had been crying all through church, and she told her Billy had been away all night. She was awfully worried about his going with that baseball team.

A fleeting shadow passed over the girl's face:

"Billy promised me he would be there today," she said thoughtfully. "Something must have happened. I don't think Billy was with the baseball team—" then her eyes traveled away out the window to the distant hills, she didn't seem to see Laurence Shafton at all. It was a new experience for him. He was fairly good-looking and knew it.

Who the deuce was this Billy? And what did she care about Miss Saxon crying? Did she care so much for Billy already? Would it be worth his while to make her uncare?

"Mrs. Carter wasn't out," said Mrs. Severn as she poured coffee. "I hope she's not having more trouble with her neuralgia."

The minister suddenly looked up from his carving:

"Did Mark come back yesterday, Marilyn?"

The girl drew a quick breath and brought back her eyes from the hills, but she did not look at the young man:

"No, Father, he didn't come."

Who the deuce was *Mark?* Of course there would be several, but there was always *one.* Billy and Mark! It was growing interesting.

But Billy and Mark were not mentioned again, though a deep gravity seemed to have settled into the eyes of the family since their names had come up. Laurie decided to speak of the weather and the roads:

"Glorious weather we're having," he chirped out condescendingly, "but you certainly have the limit for roads. What's the matter with the highway? Had a detour right in the best part of the road. Bridge down, it said, road flooded! Made the deuce of a time for me!"

"Bridge?" remarked Marilyn looking up thoughtfully.

"Flood?" echoed the minister sharply.

"Yes. About two miles back where the highway crosses this valley. Put me in some fix. Had a bet you know. Date with a lady. Staked a lot of money on winning, too. Hard luck." Then he looked across at Marilyn's attentive face. Ah! He was getting her at last! More on that line.

"But it'll not be all loss," he added gallantly with a gesture of admiration toward her. "You see, I didn't have any idea I was going to meet *you*."

But Marilyn's eyes were regarding him soberly, steadily, analytically, without an answering smile. It was as if she did not like what he had said—if indeed she had heard it at all—as if she were offended at it. Then the eyes took on an impersonal look and wandered thoughtfully to the mountains in the distance. Laurie felt his cheeks burn. He felt almost embarrassed again, like during the prayer. Didn't the girl know he was paying her a compliment? Or was she such a prude that she thought him presuming on so light an acquaintance? Her father was speaking:

"I don't quite understand," he said thoughtfully. "There is no bridge within ten miles, and nothing to flood the road but the creek, which never was known to overflow its banks more than a few feet at most. The highway is far above the valley. You must have been a bit turned around."

The young man laughed lightly:

"Well, perhaps I had a jag on. I'm not surprised. I'd been driving for hours and had to drink to keep my nerve till morning. There were some dandy spilling places around those mountain curves. One doesn't care to look out and see when one is driving at top speed."

Heavens! What had he said now? The girl's eyes came round to look him over again and went through to his soul like a lightning flash and away again, and there was actually scorn on her lips. He must take another line. He couldn't understand this haughty country beauty in the least.

"I certainly did enjoy your music," he flashed forth with a little of his own natural gaiety in his voice that made him so universal a favorite.

The girl turned gravely toward him and surveyed him once more as if she were surprised and perhaps had not done him justice. She looked like one who would always be willing to do one justice. He felt encouraged:

"If it hadn't been for this blamed foot of mine I'd have hobbled over to the—service. I was sorry not to hear the music closer."

"There is another service this evening," she said pleasantly. "Perhaps Father can help you over. It is a rather good organ for so small a one." She was trying to be polite to him. It put him on his mettle. It made him remember how rude he had been to her father the night before.

"Delightful organ, I'm sure," he returned, "but it was the organist that I noticed. One doesn't often hear such playing even on a good organ."

"Oh, I've been well taught," said the girl without self-consciousness. "But the children are to sing this evening. You'll like to hear the children, I'm sure. They are doing fairly well now."

"Charmed, I'm sure," he said, with added flattery of his eyes which she did not take at all because she was passing her mother's plate for more gravy. How odd not to have a servant pass it!

"You come from New York?" the host hazarded.

"Yes," drawled the youth. "Shafton's my name, Laurence Shafton, son of William J., of Shafton and Gates, you know," he added impressively.

The host was polite but unimpressed. It was almost as though he had never heard of William J. Shafton the multi-millionaire. Or was it? Dash the man, he had such a way with him of acting as though he knew everything and *nothing* impressed him; as though he was just as good as the next one! As though his father was something even greater than a millionaire! He didn't seem to be in the least like Laurie's idea of a clergyman. He couldn't seem to get anywhere with him.

The talk drifted on at the table, ebbing and flowing about the two ladies as the tide touches a rising strand and runs away. The girl and her mother answered his questions with direct steady gaze, and polite phrases, but they did not gush nor have the attitude of taking him eagerly into their circle as he was accustomed to being taken in wherever he went. Nothing he said seemed to reach further than kindly hospitality. When that was fulfilled they were done and went back to their own interests.

Marilyn did not seem to consider the young man a guest of hers in any sense personally. After the dinner she moved quietly out to the porch and seated herself in a far chair with a leather-bound book, perhaps a Bible, or prayer book. He wasn't very familiar with such things. She took a little gold pencil from a chain about her neck and made notes on a bit of paper from what she read, and she joined not at all in the conversation unless she was spoken to, and then her thoughts seemed to be elsewhere. It was maddening.

Once when a tough-looking little urchin went by with a grin she flew down off the porch to the gate to talk with him; she stood there sometime in earnest converse. What could a girl like that find to say to a mere kid? When she came back there was a look of trouble in her eyes, and by and by her father asked if Harry had seen *Billy*, and she shook her head with a cloud on her brow. It must be *Billy* then. Billy was the one! Well, dash him! If he couldn't go one better than Billy he would see! Anyhow, Billy didn't have a sprained ankle, and a place in the family! A girl like that was worth a few days' invalidism. His ankle didn't hurt much since the minister had dressed it again. He believed he could get up and walk if he liked, but he did not mean to. He meant to stay here a few days and conquer this young beauty. It was likely only her way of vamping a man, anyway, and a mighty tantalizing one at that. Well, he would show her! And he would show Billy, too, whoever Billy was! A girl like that! Why, a girl like that with a face like that would grace any gathering, any home! He had the fineness of taste to realize that after he got done playing around with Opal and women like her, this would be a lady anyone would be proud to settle down to. And why not? If he chose to fall in love with a country nobody, why couldn't he? What was the use of being Laurie Shafton, son of the great William J. Shafton, if he couldn't marry whom he would? Shafton would be enough to bring any girl up to par in any society in the universe. So Laurie Shafton set himself busily to be agreeable.

And presently his opportunity arrived. Mrs. Severn had gone in the house to take a nap, and the minister had been called away to see a sick man. The girl continued to study her little book:

"I wish you would come and amuse me," he said in the voice of an interesting invalid.

The girl looked up and smiled absently:

"I'm sorry," she said, "but I have to go to my Sunday school class in a few minutes, and I was just getting my lesson ready. Would you like me to get you something to read?"

"No," he answered crossly. He was not used to being

crossed in any desire by a lady, "I want you to talk to me. Bother the Sunday school! Give them a vacation today and let them go fishing. They'll be delighted, I'm sure. You have a wonderful foot. Do you know it? You must be a good dancer. Haven't you a Victrola here? We might dance if only my foot weren't out of commission."

"I don't dance, Mr. Shafton, and it is the Sabbath," she smiled indulgently with her eyes on the book.

"Why don't you dance? I could teach you easily. And what has the Sabbath got to do with it?"

"But I don't care to dance. It doesn't appeal to me in the least. And the Sabbath has everything to do with it. If I did dance I would not do it today."

"But why?" he asked in genuine wonder.

"Because this is the day set apart for enjoying God and not enjoying ourselves."

He stared.

"You certainly are the most extraordinary young woman I ever met," he said admiringly. "Did no one ever tell you that you are very beautiful?"

She gave him the benefit of her beautiful eyes then in a cold amused glance:

"Among my friends, Mr. Shafton, it is not considered good form to say such things to a lady of slight acquaintance." She rose and gathered up her book and hat that lay on the floor beside her chair, and drew herself up till she seemed almost regal.

Laurie Shafton stumbled to his feet. He was ashamed. He felt almost as he had felt once when he was caught with a jag on being rude to a friend of his mother's:

"I beg your pardon," he said gracefully, "I hope you will believe me, I meant no harm."

"It is no matter," said the girl graciously, "only I do not like it. Now you must excuse me. I see my class is gathering."

She put the hat on carelessly, with a push and a pat, and slipped past him down the steps and across the lawn. Her dress brushed against his foot as she went and it seemed like the touch of something ethereal. He never had felt such an experience before.

She walked swiftly to a group of boys, ugly, uncomely, overgrown kids, the same who had followed her after church, and met them with eagerness. He felt a jealous chagrin as he watched them follow her into the church, an anger that she dared to trample upon him that way, a fierce desire to get away and quaff the cup of admiration at the hand of some of his own friends, or to quaff some some cup, *any* cup, for he was thirsty, thirsty, *thirsty,* and this was a dry and barren land. If he did stay and try to win this haughty country beauty he would have to find a secret source of supply somewhere or he never would be able to live through it.

The Sunday school hour wore away while he was planning how to revenge himself, but she did not return. She lingered for a long time on the church steps talking with those everlasting kids again, and after they were gone she went back into the church and began to play low sweet music.

It was growing late. Long red beams slanted down the village street across the lawn, lingered and went out. A single ruby burned on one of the memorial windows like a lamp, and went purple then gray. It was growing dusk, and that girl played on! Dash it all! Why didn't she quit? It was wonderful music, but he wanted to talk to her. If he hobbled slowly could he get across the lawn? He decided to try. And then, just as he rose and steadied himself by the porch pillar, down the street in a whirl of dust and noisy claxon there came a great blue car and drew up sharp in front of the door, while a lutelike voice shouted gaily: "Laurie, Laurie Shafton, is that you?"

Chapter 9

After Billy had listened a long time he took a single step to relieve his cramped toes, which were numb with the tensity of his strained position. Stealthily as he could he moved his shoe, but it seemed to grind loudly upon the cement floor of the cellar, and he stopped frozen in tensity again to listen. After a second he heard a low growl as if someone outside the house were speaking. Then all was still. After a time he heard the steps again, cautiously, walking over his head, and his spine seemed to rise right up and lift him, as he stood trembling. He wasn't a bit superstitious, Billy wasn't. He knew there was no such thing as a ghost, and he wasn't going to be fooled by any noises whatsoever, but anybody would admit it was an unpleasant position to be in, pinned in a dark unfamiliar cellar without a flashlight, and steps coming over head, where only a dead man or a doped man was supposed to be. He cast one swift glance back at the cobwebby window through which he had so recently arrived, and longed to be back again, out in the open with the bells, the good bells sounding a call in his ears. If he were out wouldn't he run? Wouldn't he even leave his old bicycle to any fate and *run?* But, no! He couldn't! He would have to come back inevitably. Whoever was upstairs in that house alone and in peril he must save. Suppose— His heart gave a great dry sob within him and he turned away from the dusty exit that looked so little now and so inadequate for sudden flight.

The steps went on overhead shuffling a little louder, as they seemed further off. They were climbing the stair he believed. They wore rubber heels! *Link* had worn rubber heels! And Shorty's shoes were covered with old overshoes! Had they come back, perhaps to hide from their pursuers? His heart sank. If that were so he must get out somehow and go after the police, but that should be his last resort. He didn't want to get anyone else in this scrape until he knew exactly what sort of a scrape it was. It wasn't square to anybody—not square to the doped man, not square to himself, not even square to Pat and the other two, and—yes, he must own it—not square to *Cart*. That was his first consideration, Cart! He must find Cart. But first he must find out somehow who that man was that had been kidnapped.

It seemed an age that he waited there in the cellar and everything so still. Once he heard a door far up open, and little shuffling noises, and by and by he could not stand it any longer. Getting down softly on all fours, he crept slowly, noiselessly over the cellar stairs, and began climbing, stopping at every step to listen. His efforts were much hampered by the milk bottle which kept dragging down to one side and threatening to hit against the steps. But he felt that milk was essential to his mission. He dared not go without it. The tools were in his other pocket. They too kept catching in his sleeve as he moved cautiously. At last he drew himself to the top step. There was a crack of light under the door. Suppose it should be locked? He could saw out a panel, but that would make a noise, and he still had the feeling that someone was in that house. A cellar was not a nice place in which to be trapped. One bottle of milk wouldn't keep him alive very long. The haunted house was a great way from anywhere. Even the bells couldn't call him from there, once anybody chose to fasten him in the cellar, and find the loose window and fasten it up!

Such thoughts poured a torrent of hot fire through his brain while his cold fingers gripped the doorknob, and slowly, fiercely, compellingly, made it turn in its socket till its rusty old spring whined in complaint, and then he held his breath to listen again. It seemed an age before he dared put any weight upon that unlatched door to see if it would move, and then he did it so cautiously that he was not sure it was opening till a ray of light from a high little window shot into his eyes and blinded him. He held the knob like a vise, and it was another age before he dared slowly release the spring and relax his hand. Then he looked around. He found himself in a kind of narrow butler's pantry with a swinging door opposite him into the room at the back, and a narrow passage leading around the corner next the door. He peeked cautiously, blinkingly round the doorjamb and saw the lower step of what must be back stairs. There were no back stairs in Aunt Saxon's house, but before his mother died Billy Gaston had lived in the city where they always had back stairs. That door before him likely led to the dining room. He took a careful step, pushed the swing door half an inch and satisfied himself that was the kitchen at the back. No one there. Another step or two gave him the same assurance about the dining room and no one there. He surveyed the distance to the foot of the back stairs. It seemed long. What he was afraid of was that light space at the foot of those stairs. He was almost sure there was a hall straight through to the front door, and he had a hunch that that front door was open. If he passed the steps

and anyone was there they would see him, and yet he wanted
to get up those stairs now, right away, before anything happened.
It was too still up there to suit him. With trembling fingers
he untied his shoestrings, and slipped off his shoes, knotting
the strings together and slinging the shoes around his neck.
He was taking no chances. He gripped the revolver with one
hand and stole out cautiously. When he reached the end of
the dining room wall he applied an eye toward the opening of
light, and behold it was as he had suspected, a hall leading
straight through to the front door, and Shorty, with his full
length profile cut clear against the morning, standing on the
upper step keeping lookout! He dodged back and caught his
breath, then made a noiseless dart toward those stairs. If
Shorty heard, or if he turned and saw anything he must have
thought it was the reported ghost walking, so silently and like
a breath passed Billy up the stair. But when he was come to
the top, he held his breath again, for now he could distinctly
hear steps walking about in the room close at hand, and
peering up he saw the door was open partway. He paused
again to reconnoiter and his heart set up an intolerable
pounding in his breast.

He could dimly make out the back of a chair, and further
against a patch of light where the back window must be he
could see the footboard of a bed, the head of which must be
against the opposite wall. The door was open about a third of
the way. There was a key in the lock. Did that mean that they
locked the man in? It would be a great thing to get hold of
that key!

A moan in the direction of the bed startled him, and
prodded his weary mind. He gave a quick silent spring across
in front of the door and flattened himself against the wall. He
knew he had made a slight noise in his going, and he felt the
stillness in the room behind the half open door. Link had
heard him. It was a long time before he dared stir again.

Link seemed to lay down something on the floor that
sounded like a dish and started toward the door. Billy felt the
blood fly to the top of his head. If Link came out he was
caught. Where could he fly? Not downstairs. Shorty was
there, with a gun of course. Would it do to snap that door
shut and lock Link in with the prisoner? No telling what he
might do, and Shorty would come if there was an outcry. He

waited in an agony of suspense, but Link did not come out yet. Instead he tiptoed back to the bed again, and seemed to be arranging some things out of a basket on a little stand by the bed. Billy applied an eye to the crack of the door and got a brief glimpse. Then cautiously he put out his stubby fingers and grasped that key, firmly, gently; turning, slipping, little by little, till he had it safe in his possession. Several times he thought Link turned and looked toward the door. Once he almost dropped the key as he was about to set it free from the lock, but his anxious fingers were true to their trust, and the key was at last drawn back and safely slid into Billy's pocket. Then he looked around for a place to hide. There were rooms on the front, and a door was open. He could slide in there and hide. It was dark, and there might be a closet. He cast one eye through the door crack and beheld in the dim light Link bending over the inert figure on the bed with a cup and spoon in his hand. Perhaps they were giving him more dope! If he only could stop it somehow! The man was doped enough, sleeping all that time! But now was the time for him and the key to make an exit.

Slowly, cautiously he backed away from the door, down the hall and into the next open door, groping his silent way toward a little half-moon in the shutter. He made a quick calculation, glanced about, did some sleight of hand with the door till it swung noiselessly shut, and then slipping back to the window he examined the catches. There was a pane of glass gone, but it was not in the right place. If he only could manage to slide the sash down. He turned the catch and applied a pressure to the upper sash, but like most upper sashes it would not budge. If he strained harder he might be able to move it but that would make a noise and spoil his purpose. He looked wildly round the room, with a feeling that something must help him, and suddenly he discovered that the upper sash of the other window was pulled all the way down, and a sweet breath of wild grape blossoms was being wafted to his heated forehead. With a quick move he placed himself under this window, which he realized must be almost over Shorty's head. It was but the work of an instant to grasp Pat's gun and stick its nose well through the little half-moon of an opening in the shutter, pointed straight over Shorty's head into the woods, and pull the trigger.

The report went rolling, reverberating down the valley from hill to hill like a whole barrage it seemed to Billy; and perhaps to Shorty waiting for his pard below, but at any rate before the echoes had ceased to roll Shorty was no longer on the doorstep. He had vanished and was far away, breaking through the underbrush, stumbling, and cutting himself, getting up to stumble again, he hurled himself away from that haunted spot. Ghosts were nothing to Shorty. He could match himself against a spirit any day, but ghosts that could shoot were another matter, and he made good his going without hesitation or needless waiting for his partner in crime. He was never quite sure where that shot came from, whether from high heaven or down beneath the earth.

As for Link, if he was giving more dope, he did not finish. He dropped a cup in his hurry and darted like a winged thing to the head of the stairs, where he took the flight at a slide and disappeared into the woods without waiting for locks or keys or any such things.

"He seems a little nervous," grinned Billy, who had climbed to the window seat with one eye applied to the half-moon, watching his victims take their hurried leave. And lest they should dare to watch and return before he was ready for them he sent another shot into the blue sky, ricocheting along the hills; and still another, grimly, after an interval.

Then swiftly turning he stole down the front stairs and took the key from the lock, shut the door, pushing a big bolt on the inside. With a hasty examination of the lower floor that satisfied him that he was safely ensconced in his stronghold and would not be open to immediate interruption he hurried upstairs again.

His first act was to open a window and throw back the shutters. The morning sunlight leaped in like a friend, and a bird in a tree caroled out gladly. Something in Billy's heart burst into a tear. A tear! Bah! He brushed it away with his grimy hand and went over to the bed, rolling the inert figure toward him till the face was in plain view. A sudden fit of trembling took possession of him and he dropped nervelessly beside the bed with his hands outstretched and uttered a sob ending in a single syllable.

"Cart!"

For there on the bed still as the dead lay Mark Carter, his beloved idol, and *he had helped to put him there!*

Thirty pieces of silver! And his dearest friend dead, perhaps! A Judas! All his life he would be a Judas. He knew now why Judas hanged himself. If Cart was dead he would have to hang himself! Here in this house of death he must hang himself, like Judas, poor fool. And he would fling that blood money back. Only, *Cart must not be dead!* It would be hell forever for Billy if Cart was dead. He *could not stand it!*

Billy sprang to his feet with tears raining down his cheeks, but his tired dirty face looked beautiful in its anxiety. He tore open Mark Carter's coat and vest, wrenched away collar, necktie, and shirt, and laid his face against the breast. It was warm! He struggled closer and put his ear to the heart. It was beating!

He shook him gently and called,

"Cart! Cart! Oh, *boy!*" with sobs choking in his throat. And all the while the little bird was singing in a tree enough to split his feathered throat, and the sweet air full of wild grape was rushing into the long closed room and driving out the musty air.

Billy laid Mark down gently on the dusty pillow and opened another window. He stumbled over the cup and spoon, and a bottle fell from the table and broke sending out a pungent odor. But Billy crept close to his friend once more and began rubbing his hands and forehead and crooning to him as he had once done to his dog when he suffered from a broken leg. Nobody would have known Billy just then, as he stood crooning over Mark.

Water! He looked around. A broken pitcher stood on the table half filled. He tasted it dubiously. It was water, lukewarm, but water! He soused a towel he found on the washstand into it and slopped it over Mark's face. He went through all the maneuvers they use on the football field when a man is knocked out, and then he bethought him of the milk. Milk was an antidote for poisons. If he could get some down him!

Carefully he rinsed out a glass he found on the bureau and poured some milk in it, crept on the bed and lifted Mark's head in his arms, put the glass to his lips, and begged and pled, and finally succeeded in prying the lips and getting a few drops down. Such joy as thrilled him when Mark finally swallowed. But it was a long time, and Billy began to think he must go for the doctor, leave his friend here at the mercy of who would come and go after all. He had hoped he might keep his shame and Mark's capture from everybody, but what was that verse the teacher had taught them once a while ago? "Be sure your sin will find you out." That was true. He couldn't let Mark die. He must go for the doctor. Doc would come, and he would keep his mouth shut, but Doc would *know*, and Billy liked Doc. Well, he would have to get him! Mark would hate it so, too, but Billy would have to!

It was just then that Mark drew a long deep breath of the sweet air, sighed, and drew another. Billy pressed the glass to his lips and Mark opened his eyes, saw the boy, smiled, and said in a weak voice:

"Hullo, Billy, old boy, got knocked out, didn't I?" Then he closed his eyes and seemed to go away again. But Billy, with wildly beating heart poured some more milk and came closer:

"Drink this, Cart. It's good. Drink it. We gotta get them dirty bums, Cart! Hurry up an' drink it!"

Billy understood his friend. Mark opened his eyes and roused a little. Presently he drank some more, nearly a whole glassful and Billy took heart of hope.

"Do ya think ya could get up now, Cart, ef I he'ped ya?" he asked anxiously. "We gotta get after those guys ur they'll maka a getaway."

"Sure!" said Mark rousing again. "Go to it, kid. I'm with you," and he tried to sit up. But his head reeled and he fell back. Billy's heart sank. He must get him out of this house before the two keepers returned, perhaps with Pat or some other partner in their crime. Patiently he began again, and gradually by degrees he propped Mark up, fed him more milk, and urged him to rise; fairly lifted him with his loving strength, across the room, and finally, inch by inch down the stairs and out the back door.

Billy felt a great thrill when he heard that door shut behind him and knew his friend was out in the open again under God's sky. Nothing ever quite discouraged Billy when he was out of doors. But it was a work of time to get Mark across the clearing and down in the undergrowth out of sight of the house, where the old bicycle lay. Once there Billy felt like holding a Thanksgiving service. But Mark was very white and lay back on the grass looking wholly unlike himself.

"Say, Cart," said Billy after a brief silence of thought, "I gotta get you on my machine. We gotta get down to Unity an' phone."

"All right, old man, just as you say," murmured Mark too dizzy to care.

So Billy with infinite tenderness, and much straining of his young muscles got Mark up and managed to put him astride the wheel; but it was tough going and slow, over rough places, among undergrowth, and sometimes Billy had to stop for breath as he walked and pushed and held his friend.

But Mark was coming to his own again, and by the time they reached a road he was able to keep his balance, and know what he was doing. It was high noon before they reached Unity and betook themselves to the drugstore. While Mark asked for medicine Billy hied him to a telephone booth. His heart was beating wildly. He feared him much that Mark's car was gone.

But the chief's voice answered him after a little waiting, and he explained:

"Say, I'm the kid that phoned you early this morning. Didya get the car aw'right?" Billy held his breath, his jaded eyes dropped shut with anxiety and weariness. But the chief's voice answered promptly, "Yes, we got yer car all right, but didn't get the men. They beat it when they heard us coming. What sort of men were they, do you know?"

"Aw, that's aw'right, Chief, I'll tell ya when I gi'down there. Can't tell ya over the phone. Say, I'm Billy, Billy Gaston. You know me. Over to Sab'th Valley. Yes. You seen me play on the team. Sure. Well, say, Chief, I'm here in Unity with the guy that owns the car. Mark Carter. You know him. Sure! Mark! Well, he's all in, an' he wants his car to get home. He's been up all night and he ain't fit to walk. He wants me to come over and bring his car back to Unity fer him. I got my bike here. See? Now, I ain't got a license of course, but I c'd bring his along. That be aw'right, Chief, just over to Unity? Aw'- right, Chief? Thank ya, Chief. Yas, I'm comin' right away. S'long!"

Billy saw Mark comfortably resting on a couch in the back room of the drugstore, where an old pal of his was clerk, and then stopping only for an invigorating gulp or two of a chocolate ice cream soda, he climbed on his old wheel and pedaled on his happy way to Economy. The winds touched him pleasantly as he passed, the sunshine had a queer reddish look to his feverish eyes, and the birds seemed to be singing in the top of his head, but he was happy. He might go to sleep on the way and roll off his wheel, but he should worry! Mark was safe. He had almost sold him for thirty pieces of silver, but God had somehow been good to him and Mark was alive. Now he would serve him all the rest of his life—Mark or God—it seemed all one to him now somehow, so long had he idealized his friend, so mixed were his ideas of theology.

But Billy did not go to sleep nor fall off his wheel, and in due time he arrived in Economy and satisfied the chief's curiosity with vague answers, a vivid description of Link and Shorty, and the suggestion that they might be found somewhere near the haunted house on Stark Mountain. He had heard them talking about going there, he said. He got away without a mention of the real happening at Pleasant View or a hint that he had had anything to do with the stealing of the car. Billy somehow was gifted that way. He could shut his mouth always just in time, and grin and give a turn to the subject that entirely changed the current of thought, so he kept his own counsel. Not for his own protection would he have kept back any necessary information, but for Mark's sake. Yes—for Mark's sake! Mark would not want it to be known.

It was in the early evening, and the sky was still touched by the afterglow of sunset, beneath the evening star, as Mark and Billy in the reclaimed car, finally started from Unity for home.

In both their hearts was the thought of the bells that would be ringing now in Sabbath Valley for the evening service, and of the one who would be playing them, and each was trying to frame some excuse that would explain his absence to her without really explaining *anything*.

And about this time the minister came forth from the parsonage, much vexed in spirit by the appearance of the outlandish lady in her outlandish car. She seemed to be insisting on remaining at the parsonage as if it were a common hostelry, and he and his wife had much perplexity to know just what to do. And now as he issued quietly forth from a side door he could hear her lutelike voice laughing from his front porch, and looking back furtively he saw to his horror that the lady, as well as the gentleman, was smoking a cigarette!

He paused and tried to think just what would be the best way to meet this situation, and while he hesitated his senior elder, a man of narrow vision, hard judgments, yet staunch sincerity, approached him. The minister had grown to expect something unpleasant whenever this man sought him out, and tonight he shrank from the ordeal; but anything was better than to have him see the visitor upon his front steps, so Severn turned and hurried toward him cordially:

"Good evening, Harricutt. It's been a good day, hasn't it?" he said grasping the wiry old hand:

"Not so pleasant as you'd think, Mr. Severn," responded the hard old voice harshly. "I've come on very unpleasant business. Very unpleasant indeed; but the standard of the church must be kept up, and we must act at once in this matter! It is most serious, most serious! I've just called a meeting of the session to be held after church, and I've sent out for this *Mark Carter* to be present. He must answer for himself the things that are being said about him, or his name must be stricken from our church roll. Do you know what they are saying about him, Brother Severn? Do you know what he's done?"

But the arrow had entered the soul of the minister and his voice was too unsteady to respond, so the senior elder proceeded:

"He has been keeping company with a young woman of dissolute character, and he has been to a place of public amusement with her and been seen drinking with her. He affects dance halls, and is known to live a worldly life. It is time he was cast out from our midst and became anathema. And now, it is quite possible he may be tried for murder! Have you heard what happened last night, Mr. Severn? Did you know that Mark Carter, a member of *our church*, tried to *kill a man* down at the Blue Duck Tavern, and for jealousy about a girl of loose character? And now, Brother Severn, what are we going to do about it?"

Said the minister, answering quietly, calmly:

"Brother Harricutt, we are not going to do anything about it just now. We are going into the church to worship God. We will wait at least until Mark Carter comes back and see what he has to say for himself."

And about that minute, Mark, now thoroughly restored and driving steadily along the road, turned to Billy and said quietly with a twinkle in his eye:

"Kid, what made you put up that detour?"

Chapter 10

The service that evening had been one of peculiar tenderness. The minister prayed so earnestly for the graces of forgiveness, loving kindness, and tender mercy, that several in the congregation began to wonder who had been hard on his neighbor now. It was almost uncanny sometimes how that minister spotted out the faults and petty differences in his flock. Many examined their own hearts fearfully during the prayer, but at its close the face of the senior elder was stern and severe as ever as he lifted his hymnbook and began to turn the leaves to the place.

Then the organ swelled forth joyously:

> Give to the winds thy fears,
>   Trust and be undismayed,
> God hears thy prayers and counts thy tears
>   God shall lift up thy head.

Elder Harricutt would much rather it had been "God the All Terrible." His lips were pursed for battle. He knew the minister was going to be softhearted again, and it would fall to his lot to uphold the spotless righteousness of the church. That had been his attitude ever since he became a Christian.

He had always been trying to find a flaw in Mr. Severn's theology, but much to his astonishment and perhaps disappointment, he had never yet been able to find a point on which they disagreed theologically, when it came right down to old-fashioned religion, but he was always expecting that the next sermon would be the one wherein the minister had broken loose from the old dyed-in-the-wool creeds and joined himself to the new and advanced thinkers, than whom, in his opinion, there were no lower on the face of God's earth. And yet in spite of it all he loved the minister, and was his strong admirer and loyal adherent, self-appointed mentor though he felt himself to be.

Over on the other side of the church Elder Duncannon, tall, gaunt, hairy, with kind gray eyes and a large mouth, reminding slightly of Abraham Lincoln, sang earnestly, through steel-bowed spectacles adjusted far out on the end of his nose. Behind him Lemuel Tipton, also an elder, sandy, with cherry lips, apple cheeks, and a fringe of grizzled red hair under his chin, sang with his head thrown back, looking like a big robin. The minister knew he could depend on those two. He scanned his audience. The elders were all present. Gibson. He had a narrow forehead, near-sighted eyes, and an inclination to take the opposite side from the minister. His lips were thin, and he pursed them often, and believed in efficiency and discipline. He would undoubtedly go with Harricutt. Jones, the short fat one who owned the plush mills and hated boys. He had taken sides against Mark about the memorial window. No hope from him! Fowler, small, thin, gray, with a retreating chin, had once lived next to Mrs. Carter and had a difference about some hens that strayed away to lay. Harricutt likely had him all primed. Jones, Gibson, Harricutt—three against three. Joyce's vote would decide it. Joyce was a new man, owner of the canneries. He was a great stickler for proprieties, yet he seemed to feel that a minister's word was law— Well— God was still above!

The benediction held a tenderness that fairly compelled the waiting congregation to attend with their hearts.

* * * * * * * *

"Let's go over there and hear that girl play," suggested Laurie suddenly. "Church is out and we'll make her play the bells. They're simply *great*. She's some *player!*"

Opal leaned back in her chair and regarded him through the fringes of her eyelashes, laughing a silvery peal that shivered into the reverence of the benediction like a shower of icicles going down the back. Marilyn heard and blended the Amen into the full organ to break the shock as the startled congregation moved restlessly, with half unclosed eyes. Elder Harricutt heard, shut his eyes tighter, and pressed severe lips together with resistance. This doubtless was that woman they called Cherry. That irreverent Mark Carter must be close at hand. And on the rose-vined porch Laurence Shafton felt the sting of the laugh and drew himself together:

"Oh, Laurie, Laurie!" she mocked, "you might as well be dead at Saybrook Inn or imprisoned for killing a family as fall in love with that girl. She isn't at all your kind. How would you look singing psalms? But come on, I'm game! I can see how she'll hate me. Can you walk?"

They sauntered slowly over to the church in the fragrant darkness, he leaning on a cane he had found by the door. The kindly, curious people coming out eyed them interestedly, looking toward the two cars in front of the parsonage, and wondered. It was a neighborhood where everybody took a kindly interest in everybody else, and the minister belonged to them all. Nothing went on at his house that they did not just love and dote on.

"Seems to me that girl has an awful low-necked dress for Sunday night," said Mrs. Little to Mrs. Jones as they walked slowly down the street. "Did you catch the flash of those diamonds on her neck and fingers?"

"Yes," said Mrs. Jones contemptuously, "paint on her face too, thick as piecrust. I saw her come. She drove her own car and her dresses were up to her knees, and such stockings! With stripes like lace in them! And little slippers with heels like knitting needles! I declare, I don't know what this generation is coming to! I'm glad my Nancy never wanted to go away to boarding school. They say it's terrible, the boldness of young girls nowadays."

"Well, if you'd ask me, *I'd* say she wasn't so very *young!*" declared Mrs. Little. "The light from the church door was full in her face when I was coming down the steps, and she looked as if she'd cut her eyeteeth sometime past."

"She had short hair," said Mrs. Jones, "for she pulled off her hat and ran her fingers through it just like a boy. I was cutting bread at the pantry window when she drove up and I couldn't help seeing her."

"Oh, when my sister was up in New York this spring she said she saw several old gray-haired women with bobbed hair. She said it was something terrible to see how the world had run to foolishness."

"Well, I don'no as it's wicked to bob your hair," said Mrs. Jones. "I suppose it does save some time taking care of it if you have curly hair, and it looks good on you, but mercy! It attracts so much attention. Well, I'm glad we don't live in New York! I declare, every time I come to church and hear Mr. Severn preach I just want to thank God that my lines are cast in Sabbath Valley. But speaking of going to boarding school, it didn't hurt Marilyn Severn to go. She's just as sweet and unspoiled as when she went away."

"Oh, *her!* You *couldn't* spoil her. She's all *spirit*. She's got both her father's and mother's souls mixed up in her and you couldn't get a better combination. I declare I often wonder the devil lets two such good people live. I suppose he doesn't mind as long's he can confine 'em to a little place among the hills. But, my soul! If those two visitors didn't need a sermon tonight I never saw folks that did. Do you know, when that man came last night in a broken-down car he swore so he woke us all up, all around the neighborhood. If it had been anybody else in town but Mr. Severn he'd been driven out or tarred and feathered. Well, good night. I guess you aren't afraid to walk the rest of the way alone."

Back in the church Marilyn had lingered at the organ, partly because she dreaded going back to the house while the two strangers were there, partly because it was only at the organ that she could seem to let her soul give voice to the cry of its longing. All day she had prayed while going quietly about her Sabbath duties. All day she steadily held herself to the tasks that were usually her joy and delight, though sometimes it seemed that she could not go on with them. Billy and Mark! Where were they? What had their absence to do with one another? Somehow it comforted her a little to think of them *both* away, and then again it disquieted her. Perhaps, oh, perhaps Mark had really changed as people said he had. Perhaps he had taken Billy to a baseball game somewhere. In New York or many other places that would not seem an unusual thing, she knew, not so much out of the way. Even church members were lenient about these things in the great world. It would not be strange if Mark had grown lax. But here in Sabbath Valley public opinion on the keeping of the Sabbath day was so strong that it meant a great deal. It amounted to public disgrace to disregard the ordinary rules of Sabbath; for in Sabbath Valley working and playing were alike laid aside for the entire twenty-four hours, the housewives prepared their dinner the day before, an unusually good one always, with some delectable dessert that would keep on ice, and everything as in the olden time was prepared in the home for a real keeping of a day of rest and enjoyment of the Lord. Even the children had special pastimes that belonged to that day only, and Marilyn Severn still cherished a box of wonderful stone blocks that had been her most precious possessions as a child, and had been used for Sabbath amusement. With these blocks she built temples, laid out cities, went through mimic battles of the Bible until every story lived as real as if she had been there. There were three tiny blocks, one a quarter of a cube which she always called Saul, and two half the size that were David and Jonathan. So vivid and so happy were those Sunday afternoons with Mother and Father and the blocks. Sabbath devoted to the pursuance of heavenly things had meant real joy to Marilyn. The calm and quiet of it were delight. It had been the hardest thing about her years in the world that there seemed to be so little Sabbath there. Only by going to her own room and fencing herself away from her friends, could she get any semblance of what had been so dear to her, that feeling of leisure to talk to and think about Christ, her dearest Friend. I grant she was an unusual girl. There is now and then an unusual girl. We do not always hear about them. They are not always beautiful nor gifted. It chanced that Marilyn was all three.

So she sat and played at her dear organ, playing sweet and tender hymns. Played gentle, pleading, throbbing themes that almost spoke their words out, as she saw Elder Harricutt leading his file of elders into the session room which was just

behind the organ. She knew that in all probability there was
to be a time of trial for her father, and that some poor soul
would be mauled over and ground up in the mill of criticism,
or else some of her father's dearest plans were to be held up
for an unsympathetic discussion. She thanked God for the
strong homely face of Elder Duncannon as he stalked behind
the rest with a look of uplift on his worn countenance, and
she played on softly through another hymn, until suddenly
somehow, she became aware that the two strangers on the
parsonage porch had left their rockers and were coming
slowly across the lawn. The woman's hard silvery laugh rang
out and jabbed into the tender hymn she was playing, and
she stopped short in the middle of a phrase, as if the poor
thing had been killed instantly. The organ seemed to hold its
breath, and the sudden silence almost made the little church
tremble.

She sat tense, listening, her fingers spread toward the
stops to push them in and close the organ and be gone before
they arrived if they contemplated coming in, for she had no
mind to talk to them just now. Then coldly, harshly out from
the cessation of great sound came Elder Harricutt's voice:

"But, Brother Severn, supposing that it turns out that
Mark Carter is a murderer! You surely would not approve of
keeping his name on the church roll then, would you? It
seems to me that in order to keep the garments of the bride
of Christ clean from soil we should anticipate such a happening and show the world that we recognize the character of
this young man, and that we do not countenance such doings
as he has been guilty of. Now, last night, it is positively stated
that he and this person they call Cherry Fenning were at the
Blue Duck!"

Crash! The bells!

Lynn had heard so much through the open session-room
door, had turned a quick frightened glance and caught the
glimpse of two people coming slowly in at the open door of
the church peering at her, had made one quick motion which
released the bells, and dashed into the first notes that came
to her mind, the old hymn "Rock of Ages, Cleft for Me, Let
Me Hide Myself in Thee!" But instead of playing it tenderly,
grandly, as she usually did, with all the sweetness of the years
in which saints and sinners have sung it and found refuge and

comfort in its noble lines, she plunged into it with a mad rush as if a soul in mortal peril were rushing to the refuge before the gates should be forever closed, or before the enemy should snatch it from the haven. The first note boomed forth so sharply, so suddenly, that Elder Harricutt jumped visibly from his chair, and his gossipy little details were drowned in the great tone that struck. Behind his hand, the troubled minister smiled in spite of his worries, to think of the brave young soul behind those bells defending her own.

Down the aisle just under the tower Opal Verrons paused for an instant, startled, thinking of prison walls, and of the dead man lying at Saybrook Inn that night. Suddenly the words of the telegram flashed across her: "What disposition do you want made of the body?" The body! The *body!* Oh! Her eyes grew wide with horror. She ought to answer that telegram and give them his home address. But why should she? What had she to do with him now? Dead. He was *dead.* He had passed to another world. She shuddered. She looked around and shrank back toward Shafton, but Laurie was rapt in the vision of Saint Cecilia seated at the organ under the single electric light that the janitor had left burning over her head. She resembled a saint with a halo more than ever, and his easily excited senses were off chasing this new flower of fancy.

Behind the organ pipes the session sat with the reputation of a man in their ruthless fingers, tossing it back and forth, and deliberating upon their own damning phrases, while the minister sat with stern white face, and sought to hold them from taking an action that might brand a human soul forever. Marilyn needed no more than those harsh words to know that her friend of the years was being weighed in the balance.

Many a Sabbath afternoon in his childhood had Mark Carter spent with her playing the stone block play of David and Jonathan, and then eaten bread and milk and applesauce and sponge cake with her and heard the evening prayers and songs and said good night with a sweet look of the heavenly Father's child on his handsome little face. Many a time as an older boy had he sung hymns with her and listened to her read the Bible, and talked it over with her afterward. He had not been like that when she went away. Could he so have changed? And Cherry Fenning! The little girl who had been but ten years old when she went away to college, Cherry a precocious little daughter of a tailor in Economy, who came over to take music lessons from her. Cherry at the Blue Duck! And with Mark! Could it be true? It could not be true! Not in the sense that Mr. Harricutt was trying to make out. Mark might have been there, but never to do wrong. The Blue Duck was a dance hall where liquor was sold on the quiet, and where unspeakable things happened every little while. Oh, it was outrageous! Her fingers made the bells crash out her horror and disgust, and her appeal to a higher power to right this dreadful wrong. And then a hopeless sick feeling came over her, a whirling dizzy sensation as if she were going to faint, although she never fainted. She longed to drop down upon the keys and wail her heart out, but she might not. Those awful words or more like them were going on behind the organ there, and the door was open—or even if the door was not open they could be heard, for the room behind the organ was only screened by a heavy curtain! Those two strangers must not hear! At all costs they must not hear a thing like this! They did not know Mark Carter of course, but at any rate they must not hear! It was like having him exposed in the public square for insult. So she played on, growing steadier, and more controlled. If only she could know the rest! Or if only she might steal away then, and lie down and bear it alone for a little! So this was what had given her father such a white drawn look during his sermon! She had seen that hard old man go across the lawn to meet him, and this was what he was bringing her father to bear!

But the music itself and the words of the grand old hymns she was playing gradually crept into her soul and helped her, so that when the lame stranger made at last his slow progress up to the choirloft and stood beside her she was able to be coolly polite and explain briefly to him how the organ controlled the action of the bells.

He listened to her, standing in open admiration, his handsome careless face with its unmistakable look of self-indulgence was lighted up with genuine admiration for the beautiful girl who could play so well, and could talk equally well about her instrument, quite as if it were nothing at all out of the ordinary run of things that she were doing.

Opal, sitting in the front pew, where she had dropped to

wait till her escort should be satisfied, watched him at first discontentedly, turning her eyes to the girl, half wondering, half sneering, till all at once she perceived that the girl was not hearing the hot words of admiration poured upon her, was not impressed in the least by the man, did not even seem to know who he was—or care. How strange. What a very strange girl! And really a beautiful girl, too, she saw, now that her natural jealousy was for the moment averted. How extremely amusing. Laurie Shafton interested in a girl who didn't care a row of pins about him. What a shouting joke! She must take it back to his friends at the shore, who would kid him unmercifully about it. The thing had never been known in his life before. Perhaps, too, she would amuse herself a little, just as a pastime, by opening the eyes of this village maiden to the opportunity she was missing. Why not? Just on the verge of his departure perhaps.

And now, with tender touch, the music grew softer and dropped into the sorrowful melody:

> The mistakes of my life have been many,
>   The sins of my heart have been more,
> But I come as He has bidden,
>   And enter the open door,
> I know I am weak and sinful,
>   It comes to me more and more
> But since the dear Saviour has bid me come in
>   I'll enter the open door.

It was one of the songs they used to sing together, Mark and she, on Sunday afternoons just as the sun was dropping behind the western mountain, and Marilyn played it till the bells seemed to echo out a heart's repentance, and a great forgiveness to one far, far away.

At its first note the song was recognized by Mark Carter as he drove along through the night and it thrilled him to his sad sick soul. It was as if she had spoken to him, had swept his heartstrings with her white fingers, had given him her sweet wistful smile, and was calling to him through the dark. As they came in sight of the church Billy pulled his cap a little lower and tried to keep the choke out of his throat. Somehow, the long hours without sleep or food, the toil, the anxiety, the reaction, had suddenly culminated in a great desire to cry. Yes, *cry* like a baby! Why, even when he was a baby he didn't cry, and now here was this sickening gag in his throat, this smarting in his eyelids, this sinking feeling. He cast an eye at Cart. Why, Cart looked that way too. Cart was feeling it also. Then he wasn't ashamed. He gulped and smudged his dirty hand across his smarting eyes, and got a long streak of wet on the back of his hand which he hastily dried on the side of his sweater, and so they sat, two still dark figures traveling along quietly through the night, for Carter had shut off the engine and let the natural incline of the road carry them down almost in front of the church.

When they reached the church they saw a figure standing with a lifted hand. The janitor, ordered by Harricutt to keep a watch.

The car stopped at once.

"Mark, they're wantin' ye in there," he said with a flirt of his thumb over his shoulder and a furtive glance behind. "Keep yer eyes peeled, fer old Cutter-up is bossin' the job, an' *you know him!*"

Billy sat up and took notice.

Mark got out with a grave old look upon his face, and started up the walk. Billy made a move to follow, hesitated, drew back, held himself in readiness, and watched, all his boy instincts and prejudices keen on the trail again.

And so to the old sad song of his mistakes and sins Mark entered the door of the sessions room where once he and Marilyn had gone one happy summer morning to meet the session and confess their faith in Christ.

As he had passed the window by the organ loft he gave one look up where Lynn's face was framed in the ivy of the window under the light. He drank in the sight hungrily. But the next instant he caught the vision of the young stranger standing with admiring eyes, saw Marilyn turn and look up and answer him, but could not see how far away and sad her eyes.

And with this shadow upon his heart he passed in to that waiting group of hard critical men, with the white-faced minister in their midst, and stood to meet their challenge.

Chapter 11

The janitor had gone in to put the church in order for the
night and hover about to find out what was going on in the
session room. He never told but he liked to know. The moon
had gone under a cloud. Billy slipped out of the car, and slid
up the side path like a wraith, his tired legs seeming to
gather new vigor with the need. He gave a glance of content
up to the window. He was glad the bells were ringing, and
that *she* was there. He wished she knew what peril their
friend had been in last night, and how he was rescued and
safe.

And then *he* sighted the stranger!

Who was that guy! Some sissy, that was sure! Aw,
gee!

He slid into the shadow out of sight and flattened himself
against the wall with an attentive ear to the door of the
session room. He raised himself by chinning up to the
window ledge and got a bird's-eye view of the situation at a
glance. Aw, gee! That old crab! He wished the bells would
stop. That sissy in there with *her*, and all these here with
Cart, and no telling what's up next? Aw, *gee!* Life was jest
one— He slumped his back to the wall and faced the
parsonage. Say, what were those two cars over there in
front of the parsonage? *Say!* That must be the guy, the rich
guy! Aw, gee! In there with *her!* If he only hadn't put up
that detour! Pat knew what he was about after all, a little
sissy guy like that— *Aw, gee!* But *two* cars! What did two cars
mean?

And over on the parsonage piazza, at the far end in the
shelter of the vines sat Aunt Saxon in the dark crying. Beside
her was Mrs. Severn with her hand on the woman's shoulder

talking in her gentle steady voice. Everybody loved the minister's wife just as much as they loved the minister:

"Yes, he went away on his wheel last night just after dark," she sobbed. "Yes! he came home after the baseball game, and he made a great fuss gettin' some paint and brushes and contrapshions fixed on his old bicycle, and then he went off. Oh, he usually goes off awhile every night. I can't seem to stop him. I've tried everything short of lockin' him out. I reckon if I did he'd never come back, an' I can't seem to bring myself to lock out my sister's baby!"

"Of course not!" said Mrs. Severn tenderly.

"Well, he stuck his head back in the door this time, an' he said mebbe he wouldn't be back till mornin', but he'd be back all right for Sunday school. That's one thing, Mrs. Severn," she lifted her tearstained face, "that's one thing he does like—his Sunday school. Billy does, and I'm that glad! Sometimes I just sit down an' cry about it I'm so glad. You know a while back when Miss Lynn was off to college that Mr. Harricutt had the boys' class, an' I couldn't get him to go anyhow. Why, once I offered to pay him so he could save fer a baseball bat if he'd go, but do you know he said he'd rather go without baseball bats fer ever than go listen to that old— Well, Mrs. Severn, I won't repeat what he said. It wasn't respectful, not to an elder, you know. But Miss Lynn, why he just worships, an' anything she says he does. But that's one thing worries me, Mrs. Severn, he *didn't come back for her even!* He said he'd be back fer Sunday school, an' he hasn't come back yet!"

"Who does he go with most, Miss Saxon? Let's try to think where he might be. Perhaps we could call up someone and find out where he is."

"Well, I tell you," wailed the aunt, "that's just it. There's just one person he likes as well, or mebbe better'n Miss Mary Lynn, an' that's Mark Carter! Mrs. Severn, I'm just afraid he's gone off with Mark Carter!" she lowered her voice to a sepulchral whisper, "and, Mrs. Severn, they do say that Mark is real *wild!*"

Mrs. Severn sat up a little straighter and put a trifle of assurance into her voice, or was it aloofness?

"Oh, Miss Saxon!" she said earnestly. "I don't think you ought to feel that way about Mark. I've know him since he

was a mere baby, and I've always loved him. I don't believe
Mark will ever do Billy any harm. He's a boy with a strong
character. He may do things that people don't understand,
but I'd trust him to the limit!"

She was speaking eagerly, earnestly, in the words that her
husband had used to her a few days before, and she knew as
she said it that she believed it was all true. It gave her a
great comfort to know that she believed it was true. She
loved Mark almost as though he were her own.

Miss Saxon looked up with a sigh and mopped her pink wet
face:

"Well, I certainly am relieved to hear you say that! Billy
thinks the sun rises and sets in Cart, as he calls him. I guess
if Cart should call him he'd go to the ends of the earth with
him. I know *I* couldn't stop him. But you see, Mrs. Severn, I
oughtn't to have to bring up children, especially boys. Billy
always was headstrong, and he's getting worse every day."

"I'm sure you do your best, Miss Saxon, and I'm sure Billy
will turn out a fine man someday. My Lynn thinks a great
deal of him. She feels he's growing very thoughtful and manly."

"Does she now?" The tired pink face was lifted damply
with a ray of cheer.

Then the telephone bell rang. Mrs. Severn rose and ex-
cused herself to answer it:

"Yes? Yes, Mrs. Carter. Mrs. Severn is speaking. Is anything the matter? Your voice sounds troubled. Oh, Mrs.
Carter! I'm so sorry, but I'm sure you can trust Mark. He's a
man, you know, and he's always been an unusually depend-
able boy, especially to us who know him well. He'll come
back all right. What? Oh, Mrs. *Carter!* No, I haven't heard
any such reports, but I'm sure they're just gossip. You know
how people will talk. What do you say? They phoned you
from Economy? Who? The police? They asked for Mark?
Well, I wouldn't let that worry you. Mark always was helpful
to the police in finding people, or going with them after a lost
car, you know. I wouldn't worry. Who? Billy? Billy Gaston?
Oh, you saw Billy this morning? Well, that's good. His aunt
has worried all day about him. I'll tell her. Who? A sick man
on the mountain? Well, now Mrs. Carter, don't you know
Mark always was doing things for people in trouble? He'll
come home safely, but of course we'll just turn the earth

upside down to find him for we are not going to let you and
Miss Saxon worry any longer. Just you wait till Mr. Severn
gets back. He's in a session meeting and it oughtn't to last
long, it was just a special meeting called hurriedly. He'll
come right over as soon as it's out and see what he can do to
help. Yes, of course he will. No, don't bother to thank me.
He would want to of course. Good-bye!"

She came hopefully out to the piazza to Miss Saxon. But
just at that instant Billy's aunt jumped to her feet, her eyes
large with excitement, and pointed toward the open session
door, where framed against the light stood Mark Carter,
straight and tall facing the circle of men, and behind him, out
in the dark, with only his swaggy old sweater shoulder and
the visor of his floppy old cap showing around the doorjamb
lurked Billy.

"There! There!" whispered Mrs. Severn, patting her shoulder. "I told you he'd come back all right. Now, don't you
worry about it, and don't you scold him. Just go home and get
him some supper. He'll be likely very hungry, and then get
him to go right to bed. Wait till tomorrow to settle up. Miss
Saxon, it's always better, then we have clearer judgment and
are not nearly so likely to lose our tempers and say the wrong
thing."

The bells had stopped ringing, and Marilyn had closed the
organ and drawn the window shut. The two strangers were
trailing slowly across the lawn, the lady laughing loudly. Miss
Saxon eyed them with the kind of fascination a wild rabbit has
for a strange dog, pressed the hand of the minister's wife with
a fervent little squeeze, and scurried away into the dark
street. Marilyn lingered silently on the front steps after the
janitor had locked the door inside and gone back to the
session room.

In the session room Mark Carter, white with the experiences of the night and day, yet alert, stern, questioning, stood
looking from one man to another, keenly, uncompromisingly.
This was a man whom any would notice in a crowd. Character, physical perfection, strength of will all combined to make
him stand out from other men. And over it all, like a fire from
within there played an overwhelming sadness that had a
transparent kind of refining effect, as if a spirit dwelt there

who by sheer force of will went on in the face of utter hopelessness.

The stillness in the session room was tense as the self-appointed jury faced their victim and tried to look him down; then slowly recognized something that made them uneasy, and one by one each pair of eyes save two were vanquished and turned embarrassedly away, or sought the pattern of the mossy carpet.

Those two pair of eyes that were friendly Mark found out at once, and it was as if he embraced them with his own. His friends—Duncannon and the minister! He shot a grateful glance at them and faced the others down, but opened not his lips.

At last Harricutt, his chief accuser, mustered up his sharp little eyes again from under the overhanging eaves of rough gray brow, and shot out a disagreeable underlip:

"We have sent for you, here, tonight, Mark Carter," he began slowly, impressively, raising a loose-jointed long forefinger accusingly, as he gained courage, "to inquire concerning the incriminating reports that are in circulation with regard to your character."

Mark turned his hard eyes toward the elder, and seemed to congeal into something inflexible, impenetrable, as if he had suddenly let down a cold sheet iron door between his soul and them, against which the words, like shot or pebbles, rattled sharp and unharming and fell in a shower at the feet of the speaker. There was something about his bearing that became a prince or president, and always made a faultfinder feel small and inadequate. The minister felt his heart throb with a thrill of pride in the boy as he stood there just with his presence hurling back the suspicions that had meant to undo him. His stern young face was like a mask of something that had once been beautiful with life, whose utter sorrow and hopelessness pierced one at the sight. And so he stood and looked at Elder Harricutt, who shot him one glance and then looking down began to fiddle with his watch chain, halting in his speech:

"They say—" he began again with a hiss, as he lifted his eyes, strong in the consciousness that he was not alone in his accusation—"They *say*—!"

"Please leave what they say out of the question, Mr.

Harricutt. What do *you* say?" Mark's voice was cold, incisive, there was nothing quailing in his tone.

"Young man, we can't leave what they say out of the question! It plays a very important part in the reputation of the Church of Christ of which you are an unworthy part," shot back the hard old man. "We are here to know what you have to say concerning the things that are being said openly about you."

"A man does not always know what is being said about him, Mr. Harricutt." Still that hard cold voice, still indifferent to the main issue, and ready to fight it.

"A man ought to!" snapped Harricutt impatiently.

Suddenly, without warning, the mask lifted, the curve of the lips drew up at the left corner revealing the row of even white teeth, and a twinkle at the corners of the gray, thoughtful eyes, giving in a flash a vision of the merry mischief-loving boy he had been, and his whole countenance was lit. Mark was never so attractive as when smiling. It brought out the lovingness of his eyes, and took away the hard oldness of his finely cut features.

"Mr. Harricutt, I have often wondered if *you* knew, all that people say about *you?*"

"*WHAT?*"

There was sudden stir in the session room. The elders moved their chairs with a swishing sound, cleared their throats hastily, and put sudden hands up to hide furtive smiles. Elder Duncannon grinned broadly, there was a twinkle in even the minister's eyes, and outside the door Billy manfully stifled a snicker. Elder Harricutt shot his angry little eyes around in the mirthful atmosphere, starting at Mark's quizzical smile, and going around the uneasy group of men, back to Mark again. But the smile was gone! One could hardly be sure it had been there at all. Mark was hard cold steel again, a blank wall, impenetrable. There was no sign that the young man intended to repeat the mocking offense.

"Young man! This is no time for levity!" he roared forth menacingly. "You are on the verge of being arrested for murder! Did you know it?"

The minister watching, thought he saw a quiver go through the steady eyes, a slight contracting of the pupil, a hardening of the sensitive mouth, that was all. The boy stood unflinching, and spoke with steady lips:

"I did not."

"Well, you are!" reiterated the elder. "And even if the man doesn't die, there is plenty else. Answer me this question. It's no use beating around the bush. Where were you at three o'clock this morning?"

The answer came without hesitation, steadily, frankly:

"On Stark Mountain, as nearly as I can make out."

Billy held his breath and wondered what was coming next. He caught his hands on the window ledge and chinned himself again, his eyes and the fringe of his disheveled brown hair appearing above the windowsill, but the startled session was not looking out the window just then. Mr. Harricutt looked slightly put out. Stark Mountain had nothing to do with this matter, and the young man was probably trying to prove an alibi. He sat up jerkily and placed his elbows on the chair arms, touching the tips of his long bony fingers, fitting them together carefully and speaking in aggravated detached syllables in rhythm with the movement of his fingers.

"Young—man! An—swer me! *Ware*—you—or ware you—*not*—at—the—Blue—Duck—Tavern—last—evening?"

Blue and red lights seemed to flicker in the cold steel eyes of the young man.

"I *was!*"

"A—hemmm!" The elder glanced around triumphantly, and went on with the examination:

"Well—young *man!* Ware you—or—ware you *not*—ac-companied—by a young wumman—of—notorious—I may say—infamous character? In other words—a young girl—commonly called—Cherry? Cherry Fenning I believe is her whole name. Ware you with her?"

Mark's face was set, his eyes were glaring. The minister felt that if Harricutt had dared look up he would almost be afraid, now.

But after an instant's hesitation when it almost looked as if Mark were struggling with desire to administer corporal punishment to the little old bigot, he lifted his head defiantly and replied in hard tones as before:

"I *was!*"

"There!" said Elder Harricutt, wetting his lips and smiling fiendishly around the group. "There! Didn't I tell you?"

"May I inquire?" asked Mark startlingly, "what business of yours it is?"

Harricutt bristled.

"What business? What *business?*" he repeated severely. "Why, this business, young man. Your name is on our church roll as a member in good and regular standing! For sometime past you have been dragging the name of our Lord and Saviour in the dust of dishonor by your goings on. It is our responsibility as elders of this church to see that this goes on no longer."

"I see!" said Mark. "I haven't heard from any of the other elders on the subject, but assuming that you are all of one mind—" he swept the room with his glance, omitting the stricken faces of the minister and Mr. Duncannon, "I will relieve you of further responsibility in the matter by asking you to strike my name from the roll at once."

He was turning, his look of white still scorn fell upon them like fire that scorches. Outside the door Billy, forgetful that he might be seen, was peering in, his brows down in deep scowls, his lower jaw protruded, his grimy fists clenched. A fraction of a second longer and Billy would butt into the session like some mad young goat. Respect for the session? Not he! They were bullying his idol, Cart, who had already gone through death and still lived! They should see! Aw, gee!

But a diversion occurred just in the nick of time. It was Joyce, the new member, the owner of the canneries, who had just built a new house with electric appliances, and owned the best car in town. He was a stickler for proprieties, but he was a great admirer of the minister, and he had been watching Mr. Severn's face. Also, he had watched Mark's.

"Now, now, *now,* young brother!" he said soothingly, rising in his nice pleasant gentlemanly way. "Don't be hasty! This can all be adjusted I am sure if we fully understand one another. I am a comparative stranger here I know, but I would suggest taking this thing quietly and giving Mr. Carter a chance to explain himself. You must own, Brother Carter, that we had some reason to be anxious. You know, the Bible tells us to avoid even the appearance of evil."

Mark turned with perfect courtesy to this new voice:

"The Bible also tells us not to judge one another!" he replied quickly. "Mr. Joyce, you are a stranger here, but I am not. They have known me since childhood. Also there are some items that might be of interest to you. Cherry Fenning five years ago was a little girl in this Sunday school. She stood up in that pulpit out there one Children's Sunday and sang in a sweet little voice, 'Jesus loves me this I know, for the Bible tells me so.' She was an innocent little child then, and everybody praised her. Now, because she has been talked about you are all ready to condemn her. And who is going to help her? I tell you if that is the kind of Christ you have, and the kind of Bible you are following, I want no more of it, and I am ready to have my name taken off the roll at once."

Harricutt rose in his excitement pointing his long flapping forefinger:

"You see, gentlemen, you see! He defies us! He goes farther! He defies his God!"

Suddenly the minister rose with uplifted hand, and the voice that never failed to command attention, spoke:

"Let us pray!"

With sudden startled indrawing of breath, and half obedient bowing of heads, the elders paused, standing or sitting as they were, and Mark with high defiant head stood looking straight at his old friend.

"Oh, God, our Father, oh, Jesus Christ our Saviour," prayed the minister in a voice that showed he felt the Presence near, "save us in this trying moment from committing further sin. Give us Thy wisdom, and Thy lovingkindness. Show us that only he that is without sin among us may cast the first stone. Put Thy love about us all. We are *all* Thy children. Amen."

Into the silence that followed this prayer his voice continued quietly:

"I will ask Mr. Harricutt to take the chair for a moment. I would like to make a motion."

The elders looked abashed.

"Why—I—" began Harricutt, and then saw there was nothing else for him to do, and stepped excitedly over to the minister's seat behind the table, and sank reluctantly down, trying to think how he could best make use of his present position to further his side of the question.

The minister was still standing, seeming to hold within his gaze the eyes of everyone in the room including Mark.

"I wish to make a motion," said the minister. "I move that we have a rising vote, expressing out utmost confidence in Mr. Carter, and leaving it to his discretion to explain his conduct or not as he pleases! I have known this dear young brother since he was a boy, and I would trust him always, anywhere, with anything!"

A wonderful shiny look of startled wonder, and deep joy came into the eyes of the young man, followed by a stabbing cloud of anguish, and then the hard controlled face once more, with the exception of a certain tenderness as he looked toward the minister.

"Mr. Duncannon, will you second my motion?" finished Severn.

The long gaunt dark elder was on his feet instantly:

"Sure, Brother Severn, I second that motion. If you hadn't got ahead of me I'd have firsted it myself. I know Mark. He's *all right!*" and he put out a hairy hand and grasped Mark's young strong fingers, that gripped his warmly.

Harricutt was on his feet, tapping on the table with his pencil: "I think this motion is out of order," he cried excitedly. But no one listened, and the minister said calmly, "Will the chair put the question?"

Baffled, angry, bitter, the old stickler went through the hated words: "It is moved and seconded that we express our confidence—"

"Utmost confidence, Brother Harricutt—" broke in the minister's voice. The red came up in the elder's face, but he choked out the words "utmost confidence," on through the whole motion, and by the time it was out four elders were on their feet, Duncannon and Joyce first, thank God, Gibson more slowly, Fowler pulled up by the strong wiry hand of Duncannon who sat next him.

"Stop!" suddenly spoke Mark's clear incisive voice, "I cannot let you do this. I deeply appreciate the confidence of Mr. Severn and Mr. Duncannon," he paused looking straight into the eyes of the new elder and added—"and Mr. Joyce, who does not know me. But I am not worthy of so deep a trust. I ask you to remove my name from your church roll that in future my actions shall not be your responsibility!"

With that he gave one lingering tender look toward the minister, pressed hard the hairy hand of the old Scotch elder, and went out of the room before anyone realized he was going.

Billy, with a gasp, and a look after his beloved idol, hesitated, then pulled himself together and made a dash into the session room, like a catapult landing straight in the spot where Mark had stood, but ignoring all the rest he looked up at the minister and spoke rapidly:

"Mr. Severn, please, sir. Mark was with me last night from twelve o'clock on. Me an' him passed the Pleasant View station in a car going over to Stark Mountain, just as the bells was ringing over here fer midnight, cause I counted 'em, and Mark was over to Stark Mountain till most noon today, and I come home with him!"

The minister's face was blazing with glory, and old Duncannon patted Billy on the shoulder, and beamed, but Harricutt arose with menace in his eye and advanced on the young intruder. However, before anyone could do anything about it a strong firm hand reached out from the doorway and plucked Billy by the collar:

"That'll do, kid. Keep your mouth shut and don't say another word!" It was Mark and he promptly removed Billy from the picture.

"I move we adjourn," said Elder Duncannon, but the minister did not even wait for the motion to be seconded. He followed Mark out into the moonlight, and drew him, Billy and all, across the lawn toward the parsonage, one arm thrown lovingly across Mark's shoulder. He had forgotten entirely the two guests parked on the piazza smoking cigarettes!

Chapter 12

As the shades of evening had drawn down two figures that had been lurking all day in the fastnesses of Lone Valley over

beyond the state highway, stole forth and crept stealthily
under cover to Stark Mountain.

A long time they lingered in the edge of the woods till the
dark was velvet black around them, before the moon arose.
Then slowly, cautiously they drew near the haunted house,
observing it long and silently from every possible angle, till
satisfied that no enemy was about. Yet taking no chances even
then, the taller one crept forth from shelter while the other
watched. So stealthily he went that even his companion
heard no stir.

It was some ten minutes that Shorty waited there in the
bushes scarcely daring to breathe, while Link painfully quiet,
inch by inch encircled the house, and listened, trying the
front door first and finding it fast; softly testing the cellar
windows one by one, beginning from the eastern end, going
toward the front first, and so missing the window by which
Billy had entered. A hundred times his operation was halted
by the sound of a rat scuttling across the floor, or racketing in
the wall, but the hollow echoes assured him over and over
again that the house was not occupied, at least not by anyone
awake and in his senses. Link had been in the business so
long that he "felt" when there was an enemy near. That was
what vexed him now. He had felt that morning that someone
was near, but he had laid it to nerves and the reported ghost,
and had not heeded his trained faculties. He was back now
doubly alert to discover the cause and make good his failure
in the morning. He had undertaken to look after this guy and
see this job through and there was big money in it. He was
heavily armed and prepared for any reasonable surprise. He
meant to get this matter straight before morning. So, feeling
his way along in the blackness, listening, halting at every
moment with bated breath, he came at last to the back door,
and drawing himself up to the steps, took the knob in his
hand and turned it. To his surprise it yielded to his touch,
and the door came open. And yet it was some seconds of
tense listening before he let himself down to the ground
again, and with his hand in the grass let out a tiny winking
flashlight, no more than a firefly would flicker, and out
again.

This was answered by a wink from the bushes, as if the
same firefly or its mate might be glowing, and after an instant

another wink from the ground near the house. Slowly Shorty
arrived without noise, his big bulk muffling in fat the muscles
of velvet. It was incredible how light his step could be—
professionally. It was as if he had been wafted there like
down. Silently still and without communication the two drifted
into the open door, sent a searching glowworm ahead into the
crannies of the dusty, musty kitchen, surprising a mouse that
had stolen forth domestically. The door being shut and fastened cautiously, the key in Link's pocket, they drifted through
the swing door, as air might have circulated, identifying the
mouse's scuttle, the rattle of a cat among the loose coal in
the cellar bin, the throaty chirp of a cricket outside in the
grass, and drifting on.

Thus they searched the lower floor, even as Billy had done,
though more thoroughly, and mounted to the landing above,
here they divided. Shorty at watch in the hall, while Link
went to the front rooms and searched each hastily, not
omitting closets, ending at the back room where the prisoner
had been.

"He's gone!" said Link in a hoarse whisper, speaking for the
first time after a hasty scanning of the shadowy place.

Shorty took the precaution to turn the key of the door
leading to the third story before he entered to investigate.

"Do you think it was him fired that shot?"

Link shook his head.

"Couldn't. I had him lifted up in my arms and was just
handing him some more dope when the sound came. It
seemed it was out front. It must a been somebody in the
front room. Sure! That guy never coulda got them bracelets
off hisself. Looka here! Them was filed off!" They stood with
the flashlight between them examining the handcuffs, and
then turned their attention to the rest of the room, studying
the bed and floors carefully for any traces of the possible
assistant to the runaway but finding none. Then they went in
the front room again, and this time discovered the lowered
window and the little half-moon aperture in the shutter.

"How do you figger it?" asked Shorty turning a ghastly face
toward Link in the plaided darkness of the flashlight.

"Pat!" said Link laconically.

"Pat?"

"Pat. He's yella! I told Sam, but he would have him! I ain't sure but Sam's yella! I think I'm about done with this outfit!"

"But Pat? What would he do it for?"

"Goin' to run the whole game hisself, perhaps, or then again he might be in with Sam, so they won't have to divvy up. He could say we hadn't kept our contrac', you know, runnin' away like that."

"We ain't to blame. How'd we know it want the police? We had a mighty close shave over that state line this A.M."

"Well, that's what he could say, an' refuse to divvy up. But b'lieve me, Shorty! Nobody's goin' to do me dirty like that! Somebody's been doing us dirty, you and me, and it's good and right we beat 'em to it."

"Yes, but how ya goin' to do it?"

"I ain't sure yet, but I'm goin' to do it. The first thing, Shorty, is fer us to get outta here mighty good an' quick. Ef anybody's watchin' round, we better not be here. We'll fade away. See?"

Without flash or noise they faded, going cautiously out by the front door this time and disappearing into the dark of the woods just as the horizon over Lone Valley began to show luminous in the path of the oncoming moon.

They walked several miles, stealthily, and a mile or two more naturally, before they ventured on a word, and then Shorty impatiently:

"I don't see what you can do. Whattirya goin' ta do?"

"Don't get excited. Shorty, I see my way out," said Link affably. "I didn't come off here half-cocked. I investigated before I took on the job."

"Whaddaya mean?"

"Well, I just looked up the parties in the blue book before I come off. Didn't have much time, but I just looked 'em up. Great thing that blue book. Gives ya lots of information. Then I got another thing, a magazine I always buy and keep on hand. It's called *The House Lovely*, an' it has all these grand gentlemen's places, put down in pictures, with plans and everything. It's real handy when you wantta find out how to visit 'em sort of intimate like, and it kind of broadens yer mind. It's a real pity you never learned to read, Shorty. There's nothing like it fer getting valuable information. I read a lot and I always remember anything that's worthwhile."

"I don't see how that's doin' us any good now," growled Shorty.

"Don't get hasty, Shorty, I'm comin' to it. You see these here Shaftons have been on my mind fer some while back. I make it a point to know about guys like that. I read the society columns and keep posted about little details. It pays, Shorty. Now see! I happen to know that these here Shaftons have several summer homes, one in the mountains, one at the seashore, one up at an island out in the ocean, and a farm down in Jersey, where they go at Christmas fer the holidays sometimes. Well, just now I happen to know Mrs. Shafton—that's this guy's mother, is down at the Jersey house all alone with the servants. Real handy fer our purposes, ain't it? Not so far we can't get there by mornin' if we half try, and the old man is off out West on a business trip."

"What you gonta do?" asked Shorty.

"Well, I haven't exactly got it all doped out yet, but I reckon our business is with the old lady. Let's beat it as fast as we can to a trolley and dope it out as we go. You see this here old woman is nuts on her son, and she's lousy with money and don't care how she spends it, so her baby boy is pleased. Now, I figger if we could come off with five thousand apiece, you'n I we'd be doin' a good night's work and no mistake. Whaddayou say?"

"Sure thing," grumped Shorty unbelievingly.

"You see," continued Link, "we're in bad, this guy escaping and all, and like as not Pat swiping all the boodle and layin' the blame onto us. You can't tell what might happen with Pat an' Sam, the dirty devils. They might even let it come to a trial and testify against us. Sam has it in fer me an' you this long time, 'count of that last pretty little safe blowout that didn't materialize. See?"

Shorty growled gloomily.

"Now on the other hand if we can step in before it is too late, or before the news of his havin' escaped gets to his fond parents, and get in our little work, we might at least make expenses out of it and beat it out of the country fer a while. I been thinkin' of South America fer my health fer some time past. How 'bout you?"

"Suits me. But how you gonta work it?"

"Well, you see I know a little bit about wimmen. An' I seen

this woman oncet. If she was one of these here newfangled political kind you couldn't do nothin' with her, she'd be onta you in no time an' have you up before the supreme court 'fore she goddone, but this here woman is one o' them old-fashioned, useless kind that's afraid of everything and cries easy, and gets scairt at her shadder. I seen her on the boardwalk once with her husband, took notice to her, thought I might need it sometime. She has gray hair but she ain't never growed up. She was ridin' in a wheeled chair, an' him walkin' beside her an' a man behind pushin' her, an' a maid comin' along with a fur coat. She never done a thing fer herself, not even think, an' that's the kind you can put anything over on from a teaparty to a blizzard without her suspectin' a thing. Shorty, I'm gonta make up to Mrs. Shafton an' see what I can get out of her. But we gotta get a trolley line down to Unity an' catch that evenin' train. See?"

About half past ten that night, with the moon at full sail, Shorty and Link, keeping the shady side of the street, slunk into a little obscure, and as yet unsuppressed saloon in a back street in a dirty little manufacturing city not many miles from Unity. Just off the side entrance was a back hall in which lurked a dark smelly little telephone booth under a staircase, too far removed from the noisy crowd that frequented the place to be heard. Here Link took instant refuge with Shorty bulking largely in front of the door, smoking a thin black twisted cigar, and looking anything but happy. He had figured greatly on getting his share of a million, and now at a single shot he had let it go through his fingers. There were reasons why he needed that part of a million at once.

Link had all sorts of nerve. He called up the Shafton home in New Jersey and jollied the maid, calling her girlie, and saying he was in the employ of young Laurie Shafton and had a special private message from the young man to his mother. It was not long before a peevish elderly voice in his ear said:

"Well? Mrs. Shafton at the phone."

And Link sailed in:

"Mrs. Shafton, I got a message from your son, a very private message. He said, would you please send your maid out of the room first before I told you?"

She seemed annoyed and hesitant at this, but finally complied:

"Now, Mrs. Shafton, you don't need to get worried at what

I'm tellin' you. Your son ain't dead, nor nothing like that, you know, but he's just met with a little accident. No, now, wait a minute till I tell you. You don't need to get excited ner nothing. If you just keep calm an' do as I tell you it'll all come out right in the end—"

He could tell by her voice that she was much excited and that so far his scheme was working well. If he could only pull the rest off! He winked one eye jauntily at Short who was standing wide-mouthed, bulging-eyed listening, and went on.

"No, he didn't have no collision, ma'am, he just got kidnapped, you see. And not wanting to get found out, natchelly the kidnappers give him a little dope to keep his mouth shut fer a while. What's that? Who'm I? Well, now, Mrs. Shafton, that's tellin', ain't it? I wouldn't want to go so far as that 'thout I was sure of your cooperation. What's that? You'll reward me? Oh, thanks, that's what I was figgering about. You see, I'm in rather of a hole myself. That's what. You see, much against my will I was one of the kidnappers myself, ma'am. Yes, ma'am, much against my will! You see I'm a farmer's son myself, good an' honest and respectable. Never had nothin' to do with such doin's in my life, my word of honor, lady. But I come to town just to look around an' have a bit of fun an' I got in with a bad lot, an' they pract'cally *compelled* me to assist 'em in this here kidnappin'. Oh, I didn't do nothin', jest helped to carry him— Oh, ma'am, it ain't that bad. He's still livin' an' he'll be aw'right if you just he'p me to get him away 'thout their knowin'. Yes, ma'am. I'm honest. I'm offerin' to help you. You see, when I see him layin' there on the bed— Oh, yes, he's on a bed, I ain't sayin' how comfortable it is, but it's a bed, an' he ain't sufferin' now—but of course if they don't get what they want they may put him to the torture jest to get more outta you all— No, ma'am, don't scream that way ur I'll have to hang up. This is on the qt you know. What? You don't understand? Why, I was sayin' you mustn't let a soul know what's happened. Not a *soul*. If it should get out an' his kidnappers should find it out they'd kill him easy as a fly an' no mistake. You gotta go slow on this. Yes, lady, they're desperate characters, *I'm sayin' it!* An' the sooner you get your son outta their han's the better fer his future, lady, fer even if he should escape after they'd been found out they'd probably lame him fer life or put out his eyes or some little old thing like that, so you see, lady, you gotta talk low an' take care you don't let on to no one. If you should turn yella it ud be all up with little Laurie an' no mistake, so keep yer mouth shet an' do as I tell ye, and I'll help ye out. Yes, as I was sayin' when I seen little Laurie layin' there so still an' white, my conscience— There, there, lady, don't you take on—as I was sayin' my conscience troubled me, an' I says, I'm agonta get this fella free! So I figgered out a way. You see, lady, there's two of us, me'n another feller set to watch 'im, an' feed him dope if he tried to wake up, an' when I get feelin' worrid about it I says to the other fella I was agonta tell his folks, an' he says he'll shoot me, but I keeps on tellin' him how sinful 'twas to make a poor mother suffer—I gotta mother myself, ma'am! Yes, ma'am, a good old mother, an' she taught me to be honest, so I says to thother fella, I says what'll you take an' git out, an' he says ten thousand dollars, an' I says, aw'right, I'll get it fer ya, an' so now, lady, 'f I was you I'd pay it right down quick 'fore he changes his mind. Cause the other fellas they was goin' to ast a million, an' kill 'im if you didn't fall fer it right to oncet. No, ma'am, I don't want nothin' fer myself. I just want to go back to the old farm with a clean conscience. What? Oh, yes, I want the money right away, that is before mornin'. If we can't get him out before mornin' it ain't no use, fer the other fellas is comin' back an' move him an' we can't do nothin'. What? Where is he? I couldn't really say, lady, it wouldn't be allowed, an' my mate he's outside the telephone booth with a loaded revolver holdin' it up to my head, and he's listenin' an' ef I give anythin' away he'd shoot me on the spot. So where would your nice lookin' son be then? Mrs. Shafton, hadn't you better— That's right, lady, I knew you'd thank me, an', yes, now I'll tell you what to do. First place, how much money ya got in the house? No, that's not 'nough. That wouldn't do a mite of good, it wouldn't be a drop in the bucket. Ain't ya got any bonds, ur jewels, or papers? Yes, that's the talk! Now yer shoutin'— Yes, lady, that would do. No—not that. You gotta have something that he can't get caught with. I know you're loosin' a lot lady, but you got lots left, and what's money an' jewels compared to your only son, ma'am? Why, think how he used to look when he wore little white dresses an' used to come to have his head kissed when he fell down! Wasn't he sweet, lady, and he had a pair of little blue shoes, didn't he? I thought so. Say, lady, you'r the right sort! I knowed you must be to be a mother of such a handsome son. Now, lady, could you hustle those things together you spoke of an' any more you may happen to come on, and just put 'em in a little box er basket, and tie a string on 'em an' let 'em down outta yer winda? It's all I'll ask. Let 'em down outta yer winda. Then you turn out the lights and turn 'em on again three times real quick, out an' in, an' that'll be the signal. An' after ten minutes you look out yer front winda an' off as fur as ye can see an' I'll flash a signal light to ya jest to let ya know it's all right. An' I'll promise you on my word of honor that you'll hear your own son's voice over the telephone good an' early tomorrow mornin' an' no mistake. But, lady, ye mustn't turn yella an' holler ner nothin or we'll fling yer jewels an' paper back in yer yard an' let your son die. We ain't goin' to run no chances ye know. You ain't got no dogs, have ye? And which side is yer room on? The front? Yes, an' which is the easiest way to get to the house without comin' near the servants' quarters? To the right? Yes, I see. An' you'll play straight? All right, lady. Your son's as good as home now. I'll give you just one hour by the clock to get yer stuff together, but mind ya, if ya weaken an' try to put the p'lice onto me, I got a way to signal my pal, an' he'll have that boy o' yours shot within five minutes after you call fer help. Understand? Oh, yes, I know, lady, you wouldn't do no such thing, but my pal he made me say that. He's a desperate man, lady, an' there ain't no use toyin' with him. All right. One hour. It's just quarter to 'leven. Good-bye!"

Link came lounging out of the booth mopping his wet forehead:

"She fell fer it all right," he said jerking a wan smile, but he looked as though the last of his own nerve had gone into the telephone receiver. "She wanted to put in an extra check, but I told her we'd be generous and let it go at what she could find without her name on it. Gosh, what fools some wimmen are! I thought I got her number all right, a whimperin' fool! A whimperin' little old fool! Now, Shorty, all we gotta do is collect the boodle. It's up to you to watch outside the hedge. I'm takin' all the risks this time m'self, an' I'm goin' to ferret my way under that there madam's winder. You stay outside and gimme the signal. Ef you get cold feet an' leave me in the lurch you don't get no dividends. See?"

Chapter 13

Billy, with that fine inner sense that some boys have, perceived that there was deep emotion of a silent sort between the minister and Mark, and he drifted away from them unnoticed, back toward the car.

"Billy!" whispered Lynn, rising from the upper step in the shadow of the church.

The boy turned with a quick silent stride and was beside her:

"I couldn't help it, Miss Lynn, I really couldn't— There was something very important—Cart— That is—Cart needed me! I knew you'd understand."

"Yes, Billy, I understand. Somehow I knew you were with Mark. It's good to have a friend like you, Billy!" She smiled wanly.

Billy looked up half proud, half ashamed:

"It's nothin'!" said Billy. "I just had to. Cart—well, I had to."

"I know, Billy—Mark needed you. And, Billy, if there's any trouble—any—any—that is if Mark ever needs you, you'll stick by him I know."

"Sure!" said Billy looking up with a sudden searching glance. "Sure, I'll stick by him!"

"And if there's anything—anything that ought to be done— why—I mean anything *we* could do—Billy—you'll let us know?"

"Sure, I will!" There was utmost comprehension in the firm young voice. Billy kicked his heel softly into the grass by the walk, looking down embarrassedly. He half started on toward the car and then turning back he said suddenly, "Why doncha go see Cherry, Miss Lynn?"

"Cherry?" she said startled, her face growing white in the darkness.

The boy nodded, stuffing his hands deep into his pockets and regarding her with sudden boldness. He opened his lips as if he would speak further, then thought better of it and closed them again firmly, dropping his eyes as if he were done with the topic. There was a bit of silence, then Lynn said gravely:

"Perhaps I will," and, "thank you, Billy."

Billy felt as though the balm of Gilead had suddenly been poured over his tired heart.

"G'night!" he murmured, feeling that he had put his troubles into capable hands that would care for them as he would himself.

There had been no word spoken between the minister and Mark as they went together toward the parsonage, but there had seemed to each to be a great clearing of the clouds between them, and a tender love springing anew, with warm understanding and sympathy. Mark felt himself a boy again, with the minister's arm across his shoulder, and a strong yearning to confide in this understanding friend swept over him. If there had been a quiet place with no one about just then there is no telling what might have happened to change the story from that point on, but their silent intercourse was rudely interrupted by the voice of Laurie Shafton breaking in:

"Oh, I say, Mr. Severn, who did you say that man was that could fix cars? I'd like to call him up and see if he doesn't happen to have some bearings now. He surely must have returned by this time, hasn't he? I'd like to take these girls for a spin. The moon is perfectly gorgeous. We could go in the lady's car, only it is smaller and I thought I'd ask your daughter to go along."

"Oh!" said the minister suddenly brought back into the world of trivial things. "Why, *this* is Mr. Carter, Mr. Shafton. He can speak for himself."

Mark stood with lifted head and his princely look regarding the interloper with cold eyes. He acknowledged the introduction almost haughtily, and listened to the story of the burnt out bearings without a change of countenance, then said gravely:

"I think I can fix you up in the morning."

"Not tonight?" asked the spoiled Laurie with a frown of displeasure.

"Not tonight," said Mark with a finality that somehow forbade even a Shafton from further parley.

Opal had regarded Mark from the vine-covered porch as he stood with bared head in the moonlight and clattered down on her tiny patent leather pumps to be introduced. She came and stood hanging pertly on Laurie Shafton's arm as if he were her private property, with her large limpid eyes fixed upon the stranger, this prince of a man that had suddenly turned up in this funny little country dump.

She put her giddy little tongue into the conversation, something about how delicious it would be to take a little ride tonight, implying that Mark might go along if he would fix up the car. She was dressed in a slim, clinging frock of some rich Persian gauzy silk stuff, heavy with beads in dull barbaric patterns, and girt with a rope of jet and jade. Her slim white neck rose like a stem from the transparent neckline, and a beaded band about her forehead held the fluffy hair in place about her pretty dark little head. She wore long jade earrings which nearly touched the white shoulders, and gave her the air of an Egyptian princess. She was very gorgeous, and unusual even in the moonlight, and she knew it, yet this strange young man gave her one cold scrutinizing glance and turned away.

"I'll see you again in the morning, Mr. Severn," he said, and wringing the minister's hand silently, he went back across the lawn. The spell was broken and the minister knew it would be of no use to follow. Mark would say no more of his trouble tonight.

It was so that Lynn, coming swiftly from her shadow, with troubled thoughts, came face to face with Mark:

He stopped suddenly as if something had struck him.

"Oh, Mark!" she breathed softly, and put out her hand.

He made a swift motion away from her, and said quickly: "Don't touch me, Marilyn—I am—not—*worthy!*"

Then quickly turning he sprang into his car and started the engine.

The minister stood in the moonlight looking sadly after the wayward boy whom he had loved for years.

Lynn came swiftly toward her father, scarcely seeing the two strangers. She had a feeling that he needed comforting. But the minister, not noticing her approach, had turned, and was hurrying into the house by the side entrance.

"Come on, girls, let's have a little excitement," cried Laurie Shafton gaily. "How about some music? There's a piano in the house, I see, let's boom her up!"

He made a sudden dive and swooped an arm intimately about each girl's waist, starting them violently toward the steps, forgetting the lame ankle that was supposed to make him somewhat helpless.

The sudden unexpected action took Marilyn unware, and before she could get her footing or do anything about it she caught a swift vision of a white face in the passing car. Mark had seen the whole thing! She drew back quickly, indignantly flinging the offending arm from her waist, and hurried after her father; but it was too late to undo the impression that Mark must have had. He had passed by.

Inside the door she stopped short, stamping her white-shod foot with quick anger, her face white with fury, her eyes fairly blazing. If Laurie had seen her now he would scarcely have compared her to a saint. To think that on this day of trouble and perplexity this insolent stranger should dare to intrude and presume! And before Mark!

But a low-spoken word of her mother's reached her from the dining room, turning aside her anger:

"I hate to ask Lynn to take her into her room. Such a brash girl! It seems like a desecration! Lynn's lovely room!"

"She had no right to put herself upon us!" said the father in troubled tones. "She is as far from our daughter as heaven is from the pit. Who is she, anyway?"

"He merely introduced her as his friend Opal."

"Is there nothing else we can do?"

"We might give her our room, but it would take some time to put it in order for a guest. There would be a good many things to move—and it would be rather awkward in the morning, cots in the living room. I suppose Lynn could come in with me and you sleep on a cot!"

"Yes, that's exactly it! Do that. I don't mind."

"I suppose we'll have to," sighed the mother, "for I know Lynn would hate it having a stranger among her pretty intimate things!"

Marilyn sprang up and burst into the dining room:

"Mother! Did you think I was such a spoiled baby that I couldn't be courteous to a stranger even if she was a detestable little vamp? You're not to bother about it anymore. She'll come into my room with me of course. You didn't expect me to sail through life without any sacrifices at all did you, Motherie? Suppose I had gone to Africa as I almost did last year? Don't you fancy there'd have been some things harder than sharing my twin beds with a disagreeable stranger? Besides, remember those angels unaware that the Bible talks about. I guess this is up to me, so put away your frets and come on in. It's time we had worship and ended this day. But I guess those two self-imposed boarders of ours need a little religion first. Come on!"

She dropped a kiss on each forehead lightly and fled into the other room.

"What a girl she is!" said her father tenderly putting his hand gently on the spot she had kissed. "A great blessing in our home! Dear child!"

The mother said nothing, but her eyes were filled with a great content.

Marilyn, throwing aside her hat and appearing in the front door, called pleasantly to the two outside:

"Well, I'm ready for the music. You can come in when you wish."

They sauntered in presently, but Marilyn was already at the piano playing softly a bit from the Angel Chorus, a snatch of Handel's Largo, a Chopin Nocturne, one of Mendelssohn's songs without words. The two came in hilariously, the young man pretending to lean heavily on the girl, and finding much occasion to hold her hands, a performance to which she seemed to be not at all averse. They came and stood beside the piano.

"Now," said Opal gaily, when Marilyn came to the end of another Nocturne: "That's enough gloom. Give us a little jazz and Laurie and I'll dance awhile."

Marilyn let her hands fall with a soft crash on the keys and

looked up. Then her face broke up into a smile, as if she had
put aside an unpleasant thought and determined to be friendly:

"I'm sorry," she said firmly, "we don't play jazz, my piano
and I. I never learned to love it, and besides I'm tired. I've
been playing all day, you know. You will excuse anything
more I'm sure. And it's getting late for Sabbath Valley. Did
you have any plans for tonight?"

Opal stared, but Marilyn stared back pleasantly, and Laurie
watched them both.

"Why, no, not exactly," drawled Opal. "I thought Laurie
would be hospitable enough to look me up a place. Where is
your best hotel? Is it possible at all?"

"We haven't a sign of a hotel," said Marilyn smiling.

"Oh, horrors, nothing but a boardinghouse I suppose. Is it
far away?"

"Not even a boardinghouse."

"Oh, heavens! Well, where do you stop then?"

"We don't stop, we live," said Marilyn smiling. "I'm afraid
the only thing you can do unless you decide to go back home
tonight is to share my room with me—I have twin beds, you
know, and can make you quite comfortable. I often have a
college friend to stay with me for a few weeks."

Opal stared round-eyed. This was a college girl then,
hidden away in a hole like this. Not even an extra spare room
in the house!

"Oh, my gracious!" she responded bluntly. "I'm not used to
rooming with someone, but it's very kind of you I'm sure."

Marilyn's cheeks grew red and her eyes flashed but she
whirled back to her keyboard and began to play, this time a
sweet old hymn, and while she was playing and before the
two strangers had thought of anything to say, Mr. Severn
came in with the Book in his hand, followed by his wife, who
drew a small rocker and sat down beside him.

Marilyn paused and the minister opened his Bible and
looked around on them:

"I hope you'll join us in our evening worship," he said
pleasantly to the two guests, and then while they still stared
he began to read: "Let not your heart be troubled: ye believe
in God, believe also in me," on through the beautiful chapter.

It was as Greek to the strangers, who heard and did not
comprehend, and they looked about amazed on this little

family with dreamy eyes all listening as if it meant great
treasures to them. It was as if they saw the Severns for the
first time and realized them as individuals, as a force in the
world, something complete in itself, a family that was not
doing the things they did, not having the things considered
essential to life, nor trying to go after any of the things that
life had to offer, but living their own beautiful lives in their
own way without regard to the world, and actually enjoying
it! That was the queer part about it. They were not dull nor
bored! They were happy! They could get out from an environment like this if they chose, but *they did not*. They
wanted to stay here. It was incredible!

Laurie got out his cigarette case, selected a cigarette, got
out his match box, selected a match, and all but lit it. Then
somehow there seemed to be something incongruous about
the action and he looked around. No one was seeing him but
Opal, and she was laughing at him. He flushed, put back the
match and the cigarette, and folded his arms, trying to look at
home in this strange new environment. But the girl Marilyn's
eyes were far away as if she were drinking strange knowledge
at a secret invisible source, and she seemed to have forgotten
their presence.

Then the family knelt. How odd! Knelt down, each where
he had been sitting, and the minister began to talk to God. It
did not impress the visitors as prayer. They involuntarily
looked around to see to whom he was talking. Laurie reddened
again and dropped his face into his hands. He had met Opal's
eyes and she was shaking with mirth, but somehow it affected
him rawly. Suddenly he felt impelled to get to his knees. He
seemed conspicuous reared up in a chair, and he slid noiselessly
to the floor with a wrench of the hurt ankle that caused him
to draw his brows in a frown. Opal, left alone in this room full
of devout backs, grew suddenly grave. She felt almost afraid.
She began to think of Saybrook Inn and the man lying there
stark and dead! The man she had danced with but a week
before! Dead! And for her! She cringed, and crouched down
in her chair, till her beaded frock swept the polished floor in a
little tinkley sound that seemed to echo all over the room,
and before she knew it her fear of being alone had brought
her to her knees. To be like the rest of the world—to be even
more alike than anybody else in the world, that had always

been her ambition. The motive of her life now brought her on her knees because others were there and she was afraid to sit above lest their God should come walking by and she should see Him and die! She did not know she put it that way to her soul, but she did, in the secret recesses of her inner dwelling.

Before they had scarcely got to their knees and while that awkward hush was yet upon them the room was filled with the soft sound of singing, started by the minister, perhaps, or was it his wife? It was unaccompanied, "Abide with me, Fast falls the eventide, the darkness deepens, Lord with me abide!" Even Laurie joined an erratic high tenor humming in on the last verse, and Opal shuddered as the words were sung, "Hold thou thy cross before my closing eyes, Shine through the dark and point me to the skies." Death was a horrible thing to her. She never wanted to be reminded of death. It was a long, long way off to her. She always drowned the thought in whatever amusement was at hand.

The song died away just in time or Opal might have screamed. She was easily wrought up. And then this strange anomaly of a girl, her young hostess, turned to her with a natural smile just as if nothing extraordinary had been going on and said:

"Now, shall we say good night and go upstairs? I know you must be tired after your long ride, and I know Father has had a hard day and would like to get the house settled for the night."

Opal arose with a wild idea of screaming and running away, but she caught the twinkle of Laurie's eyes and knew he was laughing at her. So she relaxed into her habitual languor, and turning haughtily requested:

"Would you send your maid to the cyar for my bag, please?"

Before anyone could respond the minister stepped to the door with a courteous "Certainly," and presently returned with a great blue leather affair with silver mountings, and himself carried it up the stairs.

At the head of the stairs Marilyn met him, and put her head on his shoulder hiding her face in his coat, and murmured, "Oh, Daddy!"

Severn smoothed her soft hair and murmured gently:

"There, there, little girl! Pray! *Pray!* Our Father knows what's best!" but neither of them were referring to the matter of the unwelcome guests.

Mrs. Severn was solicitious about asking if there was anything the guest would like, a glass of milk, or some fruit? And Opal declined curtly, made a little moue at Shafton and followed up the stairs.

"Well!" she said rudely, as she entered the lovely room and stared around, "so this is your room!" Then she walked straight to the wall on the other side of the room where hung a framed photograph of Mark at twelve years old; Mark, with all the promise of his princely bearing already upon him.

"So this is the prefect icicle of a stunning young prince that was down on the lawn, is it? I thought there was some reason for your frantic indifference to men. Is his name Billy or Mark? Laurie said it was either Billy or Mark. He wasn't sure which."

Chapter 14

Mark Carter and Billy as they rode silently down the little street toward Aunt Saxon's cottage did not speak. They did not need to speak, these two. They had utmost confidence in one another, they were both troubled, and had no solution to offer for the difficulty. That was enough to seal any wise mouth. Only at the door as Billy climbed out Mark leaned toward him and said in a low growl:

"You're all right, kid! You're the best friend a man ever had! I appreciate what you did!"

"Aw!" squirmed Billy, pulling down his cap, "that's aw'right! See you t'morra', Cart! S'long!" And Billy stalked slowly down the street remembering for the first time that he had his aunt yet to reckon with.

With the man's way of taking the bull by the horns he stormed in:

"Aw, gee! I'm tired! Now, I 'spose you'll bawl me out fer a nour, an' I couldn't help it! You always jump on me worst when I ain't to blame!"

Aunt Saxon turned her pink damp face toward the prodigal and broke into a plaintive little smile:

"Why, Willie, is that you? I'm real glad you've come. I've kept supper waiting. We've got cold pressed chicken, and I stirred up some waffles. I thought you'd like something hot."

Billy stared, but the reaction was too much. In order to keep the sudden tears back he roared out crossly:

"Well, I ain't hungry. You hadn't oughtta have waited. Pressed chicken, did ya say? Aw, *gee!* Just when I ain't hungry! Ef that ain't *luck!* An' waffles! You oughtta known better! But bring 'em on. I'll try what I can do," and he flung himself down in his chair at the table and rested a torn elbow on the clean cloth, and his weary head on a grimy hand. And then when she put the food before him, without even suggesting that he go first and wash, he became suddenly conscious of his disheveled condition and went and washed his hands and face *without being sent!* Then he returned and did large justice to the meal, his aunt eyeing furtively with watery smiles, and a sigh of relief now and then. At last she ventured a word by way of conversation:

"How is the man on the mountain?" Billy looked up sharply, startled out of his usual stolidity with which he had learned from early youth to mask all interest or emotion from an officious and curious world.

Miss Saxon smiled:

"Mrs. Carter told me how you and Mark went to help a man on the mountain. It was nice of you, Billy."

"Oh! *That!*" said Billy scornfully, rallying to screen his agitation. "Oh, he's better. He got up and went home. Oh, it wasn't nothing. I just went and helped Cart. Sorry not to get back to Sunday school, Saxy, but I didn't think 'twould take so long."

After that most unusual explanation, conversation languished, while Billy consumed the final waffle, after which he remarked gravely that if she didn't mind he'd go to bed. He paused at the foot of the stair with a new thoughtfulness to ask if she wanted any wood brought in for morning, and she cried all the time she was washing up the few dishes at his consideration of her. Perhaps, as Mrs. Severn had told her, there was going to come a change and Billy was really growing more manly.

Billy, as he made his brief preparation for bed, told himself that he couldn't sleep, he had too much to worry about and dope out, but his head had no more than touched the pillow till he was dead to the world. Whatever came on the morrow, whatever had happened the day before, Billy had to sleep it out before he was fit to think. And Billy slept.

But up the street in the Carter house a light burned late in Mark's window, and Mark himself, his mother soothed and comforted and sent to sleep, sat up in his big leather chair that his mother had given him on the last birthday before he left home, and stared at the wall opposite where hung the picture of a little girl in a white dress with floating hair and starry eyes. In his face there grew a yearning and a hopelessness that was beyond anything to describe. It was like a face that is suffering pain of fire and studying to be brave, yet burns and suffers and is not consumed. That was the look in Mark Carter's eyes and around his finely chiseled lips. Once, when he was in that mood traveling on a railway carriage, a woman across the aisle had called her husband's attention to him. "Look at that man!" she said. "He looks like a lost soul!"

For a long time he sat and stared at the picture, without a motion of his body, or without even the flicker of an eyelash, as if he were set there to see the panorama of his thoughts pass before him and see them through to the bitter end. His eyes were deep and gray. In boyhood they had held a wistful expectation of enchanting things and doing great deeds of valor. They were eyes that dream, and believe, and are happy even suffering, so faith remain and love be not denied. But faith had been struck a deadly blow in these eyes now, and love had been cast away. The eyes looked old and tired and unbelieving, yet still searching, searching, though seeing dimly, and yet more dim every day, searching for the dreams of childhood and knowing they would never come again. Feeling sure that they might not come again because he had shut the door against them with his own hand, and by his

own act cut the bridge on which they might have crossed
from heaven to him.

A chastened face, humbled by suffering when alone, but
proud and unyielding still before others. Mark Carter looking
over his past knew just where he had started down this road
of pain, just where he had made the first mistake, sinned the
first sin, chosen pride instead of humility, the devil instead of
God. And tonight Mark Carter sat and faced the immediate
future and saw what was before him. As if a painted map lay
out there on the wall before him, he saw the fire through
which he must pass, and the way it would scorch the faces of
those he loved, and his soul cried out in anguish at the sight.
Back, back over his past life he tramped again and again.
Days when he and Lynn and her father and mother had gone
off on little excursions, with a lunch and a dog and a book,
and all the world of nature as their playground. A little
thought, a trifling word that had been spoken, some bit of
beauty at which they looked, an ant they watched struggling
with a crumb too heavy for it, a cluster of golden leaves or the
scarlet berries of the squaw vine among the moss. How the
memories made his heart ache as he thought them out of the
past.

And the books they had read aloud, sometimes the minister, sometimes his wife doing the reading, but always he was
counted into the little circle as if they were a family. He had
come to look upon them as his second father and mother. His
own father he had never known.

His eyes sought the bookcase near at hand. There they
were, some of them birthday gifts and Christmases, and he
had liked nothing better than a new book which he always
carried over to be read in the company. Oh, those years! How
the books marked their going! Even way back in his little
boyhood! *Hans Brinker or the Silver Skates*. He touched its
worn blue back and silver letters scarcely discernible *The
Call of the Wild*. How he had thrilled to the sorrows of that
dog! And how many life lessons had been wrapped up in the
creature's experience! How had he drifted so far away from it
all? How could he have done it? No one had pushed him, he
had gone himself. He knew the very moment when after days
of agony he had made the awful decision, scarcely believing
himself that he meant to stick by it; hoping against hope that

some great miracle would come to pass that should change it all and put him back where he longed to be! How he had prayed and prayed in his childish faith and agony for the miracle, and—*it had not come!* God had gone back on him. He had not kept His promises! And then he had deliberately given up his faith. He could think back over all the days and weeks that led up to this. Just after the time when he had been so happy; had felt that he was growing up, and understanding so many of the great problems of life. The future looked rosy before him, because he felt that he was beginning to grasp wisdom and the sweetness of things. How little he had known of his own foolishness and sinfulness!

It was just after they had finished reading and discussing Dante's *Vision*. What a wonderful man Mr. Severn was that he had taken two children and guided them through that beautiful, fearful, wonderful story! How it had impressed him then, and stayed with him all these awful months and days since he had trodden the same fiery way!

He reached his hand out for the book, bound in dull blue cloth, the symbol of its serious import. He had not opened the book since they finished it and Mr. Severn had handed it over to him and told him to keep it, as he had another copy. He opened the book as if it had been the coffin of his beloved, and there between the dusty pages lay a bit of blue ribbon, creased with the pages, and jagged on the edges because it had been cut with a jackknife. And lying smooth upon it in a golden curve a wisp of a yellow curl, just a section of one of Marilyn's, the day she put her hair up, and did away with the curls! He had cut the ribbon from the end of a great bow that held the curls at the back of her head, and then he had laughingly insisted on a piece of the curl, and they had made a great time collecting the right amount of hair, for Marilyn insisted it must not make a rough spot for her to brush. Then he had laid it in the book, the finished book, and shut it away carefully, and gone home, and the next day—the very next day, the thing had happened!

He turned the leaves sadly:

> In midway of this our mortal life,
> I found me in a gloomy wood, astray
> Gone from the path direct.

It startled him, so well it fitted with his mood. It was himself, and yet he could remember well how he had felt for the writer when he heard it first. Terrible to sit here tonight and know it was himself all the time the tale had been about! He turned a page or two and out from the text there stood a line:

> All hope abandon, ye who enter here.

That was the matter with himself. He had abandoned all hope. Over the leaf his eye ran down the page:

> This miserable fate
> Suffer the wretched souls of those who lived
> Without praise or blame, with that ill band
> Of angels mixed, who nor rebellious proved
> Nor yet were true to God, but for themselves
> Were only.

How well he remembered the minister's little comments as he read. How the sermons had impressed themselves upon his heart as he listened, and yet here he was, himself, in hell! He turned over the pages again quickly unable to get away from the picture that grew in his mind, the vermilion towers and minarets, the crags and peaks, the "little brook, whose crimson'd wave, yet lifts my hair with horror," he could see it all as if he had lived there many years. Strange he had not thought before of the likeness of his life to this. He read again:

> O Tuscan! thou who through the city of fire
> Alive art passing.

Yes, that was it. A City of Fire. He dwelt in a City of Fire! Hell! There was a hell on earth today and mortals entered it and dwelt there. He lived in that City of Fire continually now. He expected to live there forever. He had sinned against God and his better self, and had begun his eternal life on earth. It was too late ever to turn back. "All hope abandon, ye who enter here." He had read it and defied it. He had entered knowing what he was about, and thinking, poor fool that he was, that he was doing a wise and noble thing for the sake of another.

Over in the little parsonage, the white-souled girl was walking in an earthly heaven. Ah! There was nothing, *nothing* they had in common now anymore. She lived in the City of Hope and he in the City of Fire.

He flung out the book from him and dropped his face into his hands crying softly under his breath, "Oh, Lynn, Lynn—Marilyn!"

Chapter 15

For one instant Lynn stood against the closed door, flaming with anger, her eyes flashing fire as they well knew how to flash at times. Then suddenly her lips set close in a fine control, the fire died out of her eyes, she drew a deep breath, and a quick whimsical smile lighted up her face, which nevertheless did not look in the least like one subdued:

"You know, I could get very angry at that if I chose and we'd have all kinds of a disagreeable time, but I think it would be a little pleasanter for us both if you would cut that out, don't you?" She said it in a cool little voice that sounded like one in entire command of the situation, and Opal turned around and stared at her admiringly. Then she laughed one of her wild silvery laughs that made them say she had a lutelike voice, and sauntered over toward her hostess:

"You certainly are a strange girl!" she commented. "I suppose it would be better to be friends, inasmuch as we're to be roommates. Will you smoke with me?" and out from the depths of a beaded affair that was a part of her frock and yet looked more like a bag than a pocket, she drew forth a gold cigarette case and held it out.

Marilyn controlled the growing contempt in her face and answered with spirit:

"No, I don't smoke. And you won't smoke either—*not in here!* I'm sorry to seem inhospitable, but we don't do things like that around here, and if you have to smoke you'll have to go outdoors."

"Oh, really?" Opal arched her already permanently arched, plucked brows and laughed again. "Well, you certainly have lots of pep. I believe I'm going to like you. Let's sit down and you tell me about yourself."

"Why don't *you* tell me about *yourself?*" hedged Marilyn relaxing into a chair and leaving the deep leather one for her guest. "I'm really a very simple affair, just a country girl very glad to get home after four years at college. There's nothing complex and nothing to tell, I assure you."

"You're entirely too sophisticated for all that simplicity," declared Opal. "I suppose it's college that has given you so much poise. But why aren't you impressed with Laurie? Simply *everybody* is impressed with Laurie! I don't believe you even know who he is!"

Lynn laughed:

"How should I? And what difference would it make anyway? As for being impressed, he gave me the impression of a very badly spoiled boy out trying to have his own way, and making a great fuss because he couldn't get it."

"And you didn't know that his father is William J. Shafton, the multimillionaire?" Opal brought the words out like little sharp points that seemed to glitter affluently as she spoke them.

"No," said Marilyn, "I didn't know. But it doesn't matter. We hadn't anything better to offer him than we've given, and I don't know why I should have been impressed by that. A man is what he is, isn't he? Not what his father is. He isn't your—*brother*—is he? I was over at the church when you arrived and didn't hear the introductions. I didn't even get your name."

Opal laughed uproariously as if the subject were overwhelmingly amusing.

"No," she said recovering, "I'm just Opal. Fire Opal they call me sometimes, and Opalescence. That's Laurie's name for me, although lately he's taken to calling me effervescence.

No, he's not my brother, little simple lady, he's just one of my friends. Now don't look shocked. I'm a naughty married lady run off on a spree for a little fun." Marilyn regarded her thoughtfully.

"Now stop looking at me with those solemn eyes! Tell me what you were thinking about me! I'd lots rather hear it. It would be something original, I'm sure. You're nothing if not original!"

"I was just wondering why," said Marilyn still thoughtfully.

"Why what?"

"*Why*. Why you did it. Why you wanted to be that kind of a married woman when the real kind is so much more beautiful and satisfactory."

"What do you know about it?" blazed Opal. "You've never been married, have you?"

"My mother has had such a wonderful life with my father— and my father with my mother!"

Opal stared at her amazed for an instant, then shrugged her shoulders lightly:

"Oh, *that!*" she said and laughed disagreeably. "If one wants to be a saint, perhaps, but there aren't many *men*-saints I can tell you! You haven't seen my husband or you wouldn't talk like that! Imagine living a saintly life with Ed Verrons! But, my dear, wait till you're married! You won't talk that rubbish anymore!"

"I shall never marry unless I can," said Lynn decidedly. "It would be terrible to marry someone I could not love and trust!"

"Oh, love!" said Opal contemptuously. "You can love anyone you want to for a little while. Love doesn't last. It's just a play you soon get tired to death of. But if that's the way you feel don't pin your trust and your love as you call it to that princely icicle we saw down on the lawn. He's seen more of the world than you know. I saw it in his eyes. There! Now don't set your eyes to blazing again. I won't mention him anymore tonight. And don't worry about me, I'm going to be good and run back tomorrow morning in time to meet my dear old hubby in the evening when he gets back from a week's fishing in the Adirondacks, and he'll never guess what a frolic I've had. But you certainly amuse me with your indifference. Wait till Laurie gets in some of his work on you.

can see he's crazy already about you, and if I don't decide to
arry him off with me in the morning I'll miss my guess if he
loesn't show you how altogether charming the son of William
. Shafton can be. He never failed to have a girl fall for him
et, not one that he *went* after, and he's been after a good
nany girls, I can tell you."

Lynn arose suddenly, her chin a bit high, a light of
letermination in her eyes. She felt herself growing angry
gain:

"Come and look at my view of the moon on the valley," she
aid suddenly, pulling aside the soft scrim curtain and letting
n a flood of moonlight. "Here, I'll turn out the light so you
an see better. Isn't that beautiful?"

She switched off the lights and the stranger drew near
pathetically, gazing out into the beauty of the moonlight as it
ouched the houses half hidden in the trees and vines, and
looded the valley stretching far away to the feet of the tall
lark mountains.

"I hate mountains!" shuddered Opal. "They make me
fraid! I almost ran over a precipice when I was coming here
esterday. If I have to go back that same way I shall take
.aurie, or if he won't go I'll cajole that stunning prince of
ours if you don't mind. I loathe being alone. That's why I
an down here to see Laurie!"

But Lynn had switched on the lights and turned from the
vindow. Her face was cold and her voice hard:

"Suppose we go to bed," she said. "Will you have the bed
ext the window or the door? And what shall I get for you?
Iave you everything? See, here is the bathroom. Father and
Mother had it built for me for my birthday. And the furniture
s some of mother's grandmother's. They had it done over for
ne."

"It's really a dandy room!" said Opal admiringly. "I hadn't
xpected to find anything like this," she added without
eeming to know she was patronizing. "You are the only
hild, aren't you? Your father and mother just dote on you
oo. That must be nice. We had a whole houseful at home,
hree girls and two boys, and after Father lost his money and
iad to go to a sanitarium we had frightful times, never any
noney to buy anything, the girls always fighting over who
hould have silk stockings, and Mother crying every night

when we learned to smoke. Of course Mother was old
fashioned. I hated to have her weeping around all the time
but all our set smoked and what could I do? So I just took th
first good chance to get married and got out of it all. And E
isn't so bad. Lots of men are worse. And he gives me all th
money I want. One thing the girls don't have to fight over sil
stockings and silk petticoats anymore. I send them all the
want. And I manage to get my good times in now and the
too. But tell me, what in the world do you do in this sleep
little town? Don't you get bored to death? I should thin
you'd get your father to move to the city. There must b
plenty of churches where a good-looking minister like you
father could get a much bigger salary than out in the countr
like this. When I get back to New York I'll send for you t
visit me and show you a real good time. I suppose you'v
never been to cabarets and eaten theater suppers, and seen
real New York good time. Why, last winter I had an affair tha
was talked of in the papers for days. I had the whole lowe
floor decorated as a wood, you know, with real trees set up
and mossy banks, and a brook running through it all. It too
days for the plumbers to get the fittings in, and then they pu
stones in the bottom, and gold fish, and planted violets o
the banks and all kinds of ferns and lilies of the valley
everywhere there were flowers blossoming so the guest
could pick as many as they wanted. The stream was dee
enough to float little canoes, and they stopped in grottoes fo
champagne, and when they came to a shallow place they ha
to get out and take off their shoes and stockings and wade i
the brook. On the opposite bank a maid was waiting wit
towels. The ladies sat down on the bank and their escorts ha
to wipe their feet and help them on with their shoes an
stockings again, and you ought to have heard the shouts of
laughter! It certainly was a great time! Upstairs in the ball
room we had garden walks all about, with all kinds of flower
growing, and real birds flying around, and the walls wer
simply covered with American beauty roses and wonderfu
climbers, in such bowers that the air was heavy with per
fume. The flowers alone cost thousands— What's the matter
Did you hear something fall? You startled me, jumping lik
that! You're nervous aren't you? Don't you think music make
people nervous?"

Marilyn smiled pathetically, and dropped back to the edge of her bed:

"Pardon me," she said, "I was just in one of my tempers again. I get them a lot but I'm trying to control them. I happened to think of the little babies I saw in the tenement districts when I was in New York last. Did you ever go there? They wear one little garment, and totter around in the cold street trying to play, with no stockings, and shoes out at the toes. Sometimes they haven't enough to eat, and their mothers are so wretchedly poor and sorrowful!"

"Mercy!" shuddered Opal. "How morbid you are! What ever did you go to a place like that for? I always keep as far away from unpleasant things as I can. I cross the street if I see a blind beggar ahead. I just loathe misery! But however did you happen to think of them when I was telling you about my beautiful ballroom decorations?"

Lynn twinkled:

"I guess you wouldn't understand me," she said slowly, "but I was thinking of all the good those thousands of dollars would have done if they had been spent on babies and not on flowers."

"Gracious!" said Opal. "I *hate* babies! Ed is crazy about them, and would like to have the house full, but I gave him to understand what I thought about that before we were married."

"I *love* babies," said Marilyn. "They want me to go this fall and do some work in that settlement, and I'm considering it. If it only weren't for leaving Father and Mother again—but I do love the babies and the little children. I want to gather them all and do so many things for them. You know they are all God's babies, and it seems pitiful for them to have to be in such a dreadful world as some of them have!"

"Oh, *God!*" shuddered Opal quite openly now. "Don't talk about God! I *hate* God! He's just killed one of my best men friends! I wish you wouldn't talk about God!"

Marilyn looked at her sadly, contemplatively, and then twitched her mouth into a little smile:

"We're not getting on very well, are we? I don't like your costly entertainments, and you don't like my best Friend! I'm sorry. I must seem a little prude to you I'm afraid, but really,

God is not what you think. You wouldn't hate Him, you would love Him—if you *knew* Him."

"Fancy knowing *God*—as you would your other friends! How *dreadful!* Let's go to bed!"

Opal began to get out her lovely brushes and toilet paraphernalia and Lynn let down her wonderful golden mane and began to brush it, looking exquisite in a little blue dimity kimono delicately edged with Valenciennes. Opal made herself radiant in a rose-chiffon and old-point negligee and went through numerous gyrations relating to the complexion, complaining meanwhile of the lack of a maid.

But after the lights were out, and Lynn kneeling silently by her bed in the moonlight, Opal lay on the other bed and watched her wonderingly, and when a few minutes later, Marilyn rose softly and crept into bed as quietly as possible lest she disturb her guest, Opal spoke:

"I wonder what you would do if a man—the man you liked best in all the world—had got killed doing something to please you. It makes you go *crazy* when you think of it— someone you've danced with lying dead that way all alone. I wonder what *you'd do!*"

Lynn brought her mind back from her own sorrows and prayers with a jerk to the problem of this strange guest. She did not answer for a moment, then she said very slowly:

"I think—I don't know—but I *think* I should go right to God and ask Him what to do. I think nobody else could show what ought to be done. There wouldn't be anything else to do!"

"Oh, *murder!*" said Opal turning over in bed quickly, and hiding her face in the pillow, and there was in the end of her breath just the suggestion of a shriek of fear.

But far, far into the night Marilyn lay on her sleepless pillow, her heart crying out to God: "Oh, save Mark! Take care of Mark! Show him the way back again!"

Afar in the great city a message stole on a wire through the night, and presently the great presses were hot with its import, printing thousands and thousands of extras for early morning consumption, with headlines in enormous letters across the front page:

LAURENCE SHAFTON,
SON OF WILLIAM J. SHAFTON,
KIDNAPPED!

Mrs. Shafton is lying in nervous collapse as the result of threats from kidnappers who boldly called her up on the phone and demanded a king's ransom, threatening death to the son if the plot was revealed before ten o'clock this morning. The faithful mother gathered her treasures which included the famous Shafton emeralds, and a string of pearls worth a hundred thousand dollars, and let them down from her window as directed, and then fainted, knowing nothing more till her maid, hearing her fall, rushed into the room and found her unconscious. When roused she became hysterical and told what had happened. Then remembering the threat of death for telling ahead of time she became crazy with grief, and it was almost impossible to soothe her. The maid called her family physician, explaining all she knew, and the matter was at once put into the hands of capable detectives who are doing all they know how to locate the missing son, who has been gone only since Saturday evening; and also to find the missing jewels and other property, and it is hoped that before evening the young man will be found.

Meantime, Laurence Shafton slept soundly and late in the minister's study, and knew nothing of the turmoil and sorrow of his doting family.

Chapter 16

Though Mark had scarcely slept at all the night before he was on hand long before the city-bred youth was awake, taking apart the big machine that stood in front of the parsonage.

Like a skillful physician he tested its various valves and compartments, went over its engine carefully, and came at last to the seat of the trouble which the minister had diagnosed the night before.

Lynn with dark circles under her eyes had wakened early and slipped down to the kitchen to help her mother and the little maid of all work who lived down the street and was a member of the Sunday school and an important part of the family. It was Naomi who discovered the young mechanic at the front door. There was not much that Naomi did not see. She announced his presence to Marilyn as she was filling the saltcellars for breakfast. Marilyn looked up startled, and met her mother's eyes full of comfort and reassurance. Somehow when Mark came quietly about in that helpful way of his it was impossible not to have the old confidence in him, the old assurance that all would soon be right, the old explanation that Mark was always doing something quietly for others and never taking care for himself. Marilyn let her lips relax into a smile and went about less heavy of heart. Surely, surely, somehow, Mark would clear himself of these awful things that were being said about him. Surely the day would bring forth a revelation. And Mark's action last night when he refused to speak with her, refused to let her touch his arm, and called himself unworthy was all for her sake; all because he did not want her name sullied with a breath of the scandal that belonged to him. Mark would be that way. He would protect her always, even though he did not belong to her, even though he were not her friend.

She was almost cheerful again, when at last the dallying guests appeared for a late breakfast. Mark was still working at the car, filing something with long steady grinding noises. She had seen him twice from the window, but she did not venture out. Mark had not wished her to speak to him, she would not go against his wish—at least not now—not until the guests were out of the way. That awful girl should have no further opportunity to say things to her about Mark. She would keep out of his way until they were gone. Oh, pray that the car would be fixed and they pass on their way at once! Later, if there were opportunity, she would find a way to tell Mark that he should not refuse her friendship. What was friendship it it could not stand the strain of falsehood and gossip, and even scandal if necessary? She was not ashamed to let Mark know she would be his friend forever. There was nothing unmaidenly in that. Mark would understand her. Mark had always understood her. And so she cheered her heavy heart through the breakfast hour, and the foolish jesting of the two that sounded to her anxious ears, in the language of Scripture, like the "crackling of thorns under a pot."

But at last they finished the breakfast and shoved their chairs back to go and look at the car. Mr. Severn and his wife had eaten long ago and gone about their early morning duties, and it had been Marilyn's duty to do the honors for the guests, so she drew a sigh of relief, and, evading Laurie's proffered arm slid into the pantry and let them go alone.

But when she glanced through the dining room window a few minutes later as she passed removing the dishes from the table, she saw Mark upon his knees beside the car, looking up with his winning smile and talking to Opal, who stood close beside him all attention, with her little boy attitude, and a wide childlike look in her big effective eyes. Something big and terrible seemed to seize Marilyn's heart with a viselike grip, and be choking her breath in her throat. She turned quickly, gathered up her pile of dishes and hurried into the pantry, her face white and set, and her eyes stinging with proud unshed tears.

A few minutes later, dressed in brown riding clothes exquisitely tailored, and a soft brown felt hat, she might have been seen hurrying through the back fence, if anybody had been looking that way, across the Joneses' lot to the little green stable that housed a riding horse that was hers to ride whenever she chose. She had left word with Naomi that she was going to Economy and would be back in time for lunch, and she hoped in her heart that when she returned both of their guests would have departed. It was perhaps a bit shabby of her to leave it all on her mother this way, but Mother would understand, and very likely be glad.

So Lynn mounted her little brown horse and rode by a circuitous way, across the creek, and out around the town to avoid passing her own home, and was presently on her way up to the crossroads down which Laurie Shafton had come in the dark midnight.

As she crossed the highway, she noticed the detour, and paused an instant to study the peculiar sign, and the partly cleared way around. And while she stood wondering a car came swiftly up from the Economy way past the Blue Duck Tavern. The driver bowed and smiled and she perceived it was the chief of police from Economy, a former resident of Sabbath Valley, and very much respected in the community, and with him in the front seat was another uniformed policeman!

With a sudden constriction at her heart Mark bowed and rode on. Was he going to Sabbath Valley? Was there truth in the rumor that Mark was in trouble? She looked back to see if he had turned down the highway, but he halted the car with its nose pointed Sabbath Valleyward and got out to examine the detour on the highway. She rode slowly and turned around several times, but as long as she was in sight his car remained standing pointed toward the valley.

Chapter 17

Billy awoke to the light of day with the sound of a strange car going by. The road through Sabbath Valley was not much frequented, and Billy knew every car that usually traveled that way. They were mostly Economy and Monopoly people, and as there happened to be a mountain trolley between the two towns higher up making a circuit to touch at Brooktown, people seldom came this way. Therefore at the unusual sound Billy was on the alert at once. One movement brought him upright with his feet upon the floor blinking toward his window, a second carried him to shelter behind the curtain where he could see the stranger go by.

Billy had reduced the science of dressing to a fine degree. He could climb into the limited number of summer garments in less time than any boy in the community, and when he saw that the car had halted just above the house and that the driver was interviewing Jim Rafferty, he reached for a handful of garments, and began to climb, keeping one eye out the window for developments. Was that or was it not the chief's car out there? If it was what did it want?

Billy was in socks, trousers, and shirt by the time the car began to puff again for starting, and he stove his feet into his old shoes and dove downstairs three steps at a stride and out the door where he suddenly became a casual observer of the day.

"Hullo, Billy! That you?" accosted the chief driving slowly down the street. "Say, Billy, you haven't seen Mark Carter, have you? They said he had gone down to the blacksmith's to get something fixed for a car. I thought perhaps you'd seen him go by."

Billy shook his head lazily:

"Nope," he said, "I've been busy this morning. He mighta gone by."

"Well, I'll just drive down and see!" The car started on and turned into the lane that led to the blacksmith shop.

Billy dove into the house, made short work of his ablutions, gave his hair a brief lick with the brush, collected his cap and sweater, bolted the plate of breakfast Aunt Saxon had left on the back of the stove when she went away for her regular Monday's wash, and was ready behind the lilac bush with old trusty, down on his knees oiling her a bit, when the chief drove back with Mark Carter in the backseat looking strangely white and haughty, but talking affably with the chief.

His heart sank. Somehow he knew something was wrong with Mark. Mark was in his old clothes with several pieces of iron in his hand as if he hadn't taken time to lay them down. Billy remained in hiding and watched while the chief's car stopped at Carter's and Mark got out. The car waited several minutes, and then Mark came out with his good clothes on and his best hat, and got into the car and they drove off, Mark looking stern and white. Billy shot out from his hiding and mounting his steed flew down the road, keeping well behind the maples and hedges, and when the chief's car stopped in front of the parsonage he dismounted and stepped inside Joneses' drive to listen. Mark got out, sprang up the steps, touched the bell, and said to someone who appeared at the door, "Mr. Shafton, I'm sorry, but I'll not be able to get those bearings fixed up today. The blacksmith doesn't seem to have anything that will do. I find I have to go over to Economy on business, and I'll look around there and see if anybody has any. I expect to be back by twelve o'clock, and will you tell the lady that I will be ready to start at half past if that will suit her. I am sure we shall have plenty of time to get *her* to Beechwood by five or sooner. If anything occurs to keep me from going I'll telephone you in an hour, so that she can make other arrangements. Thank you, Mr. Shafton. Sorry I couldn't fix you up right away, but I'll look after the lady for you." Mark hurried back to the car again and they drove off.

Billy escorted the department of justice distantly, as far as the crossing at the highway, from which eminence he watched until he saw that they stopped at the Blue Duck Tavern for a few minutes, after which they went on toward Economy; then he inspected the recent clearing of his detour, obviously by the chief, and hurried down the highway toward the railroad crossing at Pleasant View. It was almost train time, and he had a hunch that there might be something interesting around that hidden telephone. If he only had had more time he might have arranged to tap the wire and listen in without having to go so near, but he must do the best he could.

When he reached a point on the highway where Pleasant View station was easily discernible he dismounted, parked his wheel among the huckleberries, and slid into the green of the valley. Stealing cautiously to the scene of the Saturday night holdup he finally succeeded in locating the hidden telephone, and creeping into a well-screened spot not far away arranged himself comfortably to wait till the trains came. He argued that Pat would likely come down to report or get orders about the same time as before, and so in the stillness of the morning he lay on the ground and waited. He could hear a song sparrow high up on the telegraph wire, sing out its wild sweet lonely strain: sweet—sweetsweet sweet—sweet-sweet—sweetsweet—and a hum of bees in the wild grape that trailed over the sassafras trees. Beside him a little wood spider stole noiselessly on her busy way. But his heart was heavy with new burdens and he could not take his usual rhapsodic joy in the things of Nature. What was happening to Mark and what could he do about it? Perhaps Mark would have been better off if he had left him in the old house on Stark Mountain. The chief couldn't have found him then and the kidnappers would have kept him safe for a good many days till they got some money. But there wouldn't have *been* any money! For Mark wasn't the right man! And the kidnappers would have found it out pretty soon and *what* would they have done to Mark? Killed him perhaps so they wouldn't get into any more trouble! There was no telling! And time would have gone on and nobody would have known what had become of Mark. And the murder trial—if it was really a murder—would come off and they couldn't find Mark, and of course they would think Mark had killed the man and then run away. And Mark would never be able to come home again! No, he was glad Mark was out and safe and free from dope. At least Mark would know what to do to save himself. Or would he? Billy suddenly had his doubts. Would Mark take care of himself, just himself, or not? Mark was always looking after other people, but he had somehow always let people say and do what they would with him. Aw, gee! Now Mark wouldn't let them locate a thing like a murder on him, would he? And there was Miss Lynn! And Mark's mother! Mark oughtta think of them. Well, maybe he wouldn't realize how much they did care. Billy had a sudden revelation that maybe that was half the matter, Mark didn't know how much any of them cared. Back in his mind there was an uncomfortable memory of Aunt Saxon's pink damp features and anxious eyes and a possible application of the same principle to his own life, as in the case of Judas. But he wasn't considering himself now. There might come a time when he would have to change his tactics with regard to Aunt Saxon somewhat. She certainly had been a good sport last night. But this wasn't the time to consider that. He had a great deal more important matters to think of now. He had to find out how he could make it perfectly plain to the world that Mark Carter had not shot a man after twelve o'clock Saturday night at the Blue Duck Tavern. And as yet he didn't see any way without incriminating himself as a kidnapper. This cut deep because in the strict sense of the word he was not a kidnapper, because he hadn't meant to be a kidnapper. He had only meant to play a joke on the kidnappers, and at worst his only really intended fault had been the putting up of that detour on the highway. But he had an uncomfortable conviction that he wouldn't be able to make the chief and the constable, and some of those people over at Economy courthouse see it that way. As matters stood he was safe if he kept his mouth shut. Nobody knew but Mark, and he didn't know the details. Besides, Mark would never tell. Mark would even go to trial for murder before he would let himself out by telling on Billy. Billy knew that as well as he knew that the old mountain on whose feet he lay stretched now would stand up there for ages and always keep his secret for him. Mark was that way. That was why it made it worse for Billy. Judas again! Billy was surprised to find how much Judas blood there seemed to be in him. He lay there and despised himself without being able to help himself out or think of anything he could do. And then quite suddenly as he was going over the whole circumstance from the time he first listened to Pat's message into the moss of the mountain, until now, the name Shafton came to him. Laurence Shafton. Shafton, son of William J., of Gates and Shafton. Those were the words the telephone had squeaked out quite plainly. And Shafton. Mr. Shafton. That was the name Mark had called the guy with the car at the parsonage. Mr. Shafton. The same guy, of course. Bah! What a mess he had made of it all! Got Mark kidnapped, landed that sissy guy on the Severns for no knowing how long, and perhaps helped to tangle Mark up in a murder case. Aw, gee! There's the train! What could he do? That rich guy! Well, there wasn't anything to that. He would get out as soon as Mark got his car fixed up and never know he had been kidnapped. And what was he, Billy, waiting here for anyway? Just a chance! Just to see whether Pat and Sam had found out yet that their quarry had vanished. Just to wonder what had become of Link and Shorty.

The trains came and went, and the hush settled down once more at the station. From where he lay, hidden under a ledge, with a thick growth of laurel and sumac between him and the world, Billy could not see the station platform, and had no means of telling whether Pat was about or not.

He had lain still a long time and was beginning to think that his trip had been in vain, when he heard a soft crackling of the twigs above him, a heavy tread crashing through the bushes, a puffing snorting breath from the porpoiselike Pat, and he held his own breath and lay very still. Suppose Pat should take a new trail and discover his hiding place? His heart pounded with great dull thuds. But Pat slid heavily down to the little clearing below him, fumbled a moment with his key, and then in a gruff guarded voice called:

"Hullo! Hullo! Sam? That you? Yes, aw'right! Yes, aw'right! How's things? What? Hell's to pay? Whaddaya mean hell? Ain't you gonta put it over? After all my trouble you ain't a gonta let that million slip through? What? Oh! Who? The valet? He's beat it, has he? Whaddaya mean? *He* took 'em. *He* took the pearls an' diamonds? Well, em'ruls then! What's tha diffrunce? *We* ain't gottum have we? Oh, bonds too! Well, whattya gonta do about it? Move him? What, the rich guy? Move him where? *Why?* We ain'ta gonta run no more risks. Link an' Shorty are sore 'za pup, when they come. I don't think they'll stan' for it. Well, where'll ya move him? Who? Shorty? Oh, Link? Both? Well, I ain't seen 'em. I tol' 'em to keep good an' far away from me. I don't build on loosin' this job just now, see? What? It's in the papers a'ready? You don't say! Well, who you figger done that? That valet? Well, where's the harm? Can't you work it all the better? We got the guy, ain't we? *He* ain't gottim that's certain. We c'n deliver the goods, so we get the reward. How much reward they offerin'? You don't say! Well, I should say, get in yer work soon 'fore we get caught. Aw'right! I'm with ya. Well, s'long! I'll be down here at nine sharp. Take a trip to China with ya next week ef ya pull it off. Aw'right! Goobby!" and Pat hung up and puffed his way up the hill again, leaving Billy drenched with perspiration and filled with vague plans, and deep anxiety. He had got a clue but what good was it? How could he work it to the salvation of Mark? He could easily put the sissy over at the parsonage wise, do him a good turn, save his dad some money, but what good would that do Mark? Mark needed to establish an alibi, he could see that with half an eye, but how would anything Billy knew help that along unless—unless he told on himself? For a moment a long trail of circumstances that would surely follow such a sacrificial ordinance appeared before him and burned into his soul, most prominent among them being Aunt Saxon, hard worked and damp pink-eyed, crying her heart out for the boy she had tried faithfully to bring up. And Miss Lynn. How sad her eyes would grow if Billy had to be tried and sentenced to prison. Not that Billy was afraid to go to prison, in fact the thought of it as an experience was rather exhilarating than not, but he was afraid to have those two know he had gone, afraid of their eyes, their sad eyes! Yes, and he was afraid of the thought of his own ingratitude, for down deep in his heart he could see a long line of things Aunt Saxon had done for him that she hadn't been obliged to do. Going without a new winter coat to get him an overcoat. His old one was warm, but his arms were out of it too far and he wouldn't wear it. Sitting up nights the time he drank swamp water and had the fever! That was fierce! How he did rag her! And how patiently she bore it! The scare she had when the dog bit him! As if a little dog bite was anything! Doggone it, why were women such fools!

And now this! Billy sat up with a jerk and shook himself free from the dead moss and leaves, wending his way sulkily across to where he had left his wheel, and pondering, pondering. Shafton! There ought to be something there to work on, but there wasn't!

Meantime Marilyn rode hard down the way to Economy, not slowing her pony till they reached the outskirts of Economy. Her mind was in such a tumult that she felt as if she were being whirled on with circumstances without having a will to choose one thing from another. Mark! The unwelcome guests! Mark and Opal! Mark and Cherry! Cherry! The chief of police! Mark! And yes, Cherry! She was on her way to see Cherry! But what was she going to do when she got there, and how was she to excuse her strange visit after almost five years since she had seen the child? If there was truth in the rumor that she was connected with a shooting affair at the Blue Duck, and especially if there was truth in the charge that Mark had been going with her, would it not seem strange—perhaps be misconstrued by Cherry? By her family? They had all known of her own intimacy with Mark in the past. She shrank from the idea. Yet Marilyn Severn had not been brought up to regard public opinion when it was a question of doing something that ought to be done. The only question was, was it really something that ought to be done or was she letting Billy influence her unduly? Billy was shrewd. He knew Mark. He knew a lot more than he ever told. What did Billy know? How she wished she had asked her father's advice before coming, and yet, if she had, he might have been unduly influenced by dreading to have her put herself in the position of prying into the matter.

As she rode and pondered she came near to the little house on the village street where Cherry lived, a house set out plumb with the sidewalk, and a little gate at the side to go round to the back door where the family lived, the front room being the tailor shop. As she drew near she looked up and was sure she saw Cherry in a short narrow skirt and an old middy blouse scurrying through the gate to the back door, and her heart thumped so hard she was almost tempted to ride on to the store first before making her call. But something in her that always held her to a task until it was completed forced her to dismount and knock at the door.

It seemed long to wait with her heart thumping so, and why did it thump? She found herself praying, "Oh, God, show me what to say!" and then the door was open a crack and a sharp wizened face with a striking resemblance to Cherry's bold little beauty, was thrust at her. It must be Cherry's mother. Of course it was!

"Mr. Fenner ain't in the shop!" said the woman. "He can't do nothin' today. He's sick!"

Marilyn smiled:

"But I wanted to see Cherry," she said. "Aren't you her mother? Don't you remember me? I'm Marilyn Severn, her old music teacher. Is Cherry in?"

A frightened look passed over the woman's face as she scanned the sweet face before her, and then a wily expression darted into her eyes:

"Oh," she said with a forced smirk, "yes, Miss Marilyn. Excuse me fer not recognizing you. You've grown a lot. Why, no, Cherry ain't at home this morning. She'll be awful sorry not to see you. She thought a lot of you, she did. She got on so well with you in her music too. I says to her the other day, I says, Cherry, I hear Miss Marilyn is home again, you'll have to take up yer music again, and she says yes, she guessed she would. She'll be around someday to see you. Sorry I can't ask you in, but Mr. Fenner's pretty sick. Oh, just the grippe, I guess. He'll soon be all right."

She began to realize that the woman was in a hurry to get rid of her and she hastened away, relieved yet puzzled at the whole affair. She rode down into the village mechanically and bought a spool of silk and the coffee strainer which had been her legitimate errand to the village, and turning back had scarcely passed the last house before she saw the chief's car coming toward her, and Mark, his face white and haggard, looking out from the backseat. He drew back as he recognized her, and tried to hide, and she rode on with only a passing bow which comprehended the whole car; but she was aware of Mark's eyes upon her, steadily, watching her. She would have known he was watching her from the darkness of the backseat if her own eyes had been shut. What was it all about and what were they doing to Mark?

Chapter 18

The last house in the village on the road to Economy was the Harricutts'. It was built of gray cement blocks that the elder had taken for a bad debt, and had neither vine nor blossom to soften its grimness. Its windows were supplied with green holland shades, and its front yard was efficiently manned with plum trees and a peach, while the backyard was given over to vegetables. Elder Harricutt walked to Economy every day to his office in the Economy bank. He said it kept him in good condition physically. His wife was small and prim with little quick prying eyes and a false front that had a tendency to go askew. She wore bonnets with strings and her false teeth didn't quite fit; they clicked as she talked. She kept a watch over the road at all times and very little ever got by her unnoticed.

In wholesome contrast next door was the trim little white cottage where Tom McMertrie and his mother Christie lived, smothered in vines and ablaze with geraniums all down the front walk. And below that, almost facing the graveyard was a little green shingled bungalow. Mary Rafferty kept her yard aglow with phlox, verbenas, and pansies, and reveled in vines and flowering shrubs.

These two women were wonderful friends, though forty years marched between them. Mary's hair was black as a crow's wing above her great pansy-blue eyes with their long curling lashes, while Christie's hair was sandy-silver and her tongue full of brrrs. They had opposite pantry windows on the neighboring sides of their houses, where they often talked of a morning while Christie molded her sweet loaves of bread or mixed scones and Mary made tarts and pies and cake for Jim's supper. Somehow without much being said about it they formed a combination against their hard little knot of a neighbor behind the holland shades.

The first house on the side street that ran at right angles to the main thoroughfare, just below Rafferty's, was Duncannon's. A picket fence at the side let into the vegetable gardens of the three, and the quiet little Mrs. Duncannon with the rippley brown hair and soft brown eyes often slipped through and made a morning call under cover of the kindly pole beans that hid her entrances and exits perfectly from any green holland-shaded windows that might be open that way. Jane Duncannon formed a third in this little combination.

On the Monday morning following the session meeting Mary Rafferty and Chrstie McMertrie were at their respective pantry windows flinging together some toothsome delicacies for the evening meal, that all might move smoothly during the busy day.

A neat line of flopping clothes glimmered in each backyard over the trim green that stretched across in front of the back door, and the irons were on in both kitchens preparing for a finish as soon as a piece should show signs of drying.

"Hev ye haird whut the extra session meetin' was called for, Mary?" asked the older woman looking up from her mixing bowl. "Tom went to the mill to tak the place of the noight watchman. His feyther's dyin' ye ken, and Tom's not come by yet. I thot ye might hev haird."

Mary lifted her eyes with troubled glance:

"Not yet," she said, "but I'm thinking of running over to Duncannon's as soon as I get these pies in the oven. The

clothes won't be dry for a while, an' I'll take my pan of peas t
shell. She'll know of course. Maybe it's nothing much—but
Jim said they held up Mark Carter and made him come in. I
was ten minutes of ten before he got away! You don't suppose
anybody's taken the gossip to the session do you?"

"There's one we know well would be full cawpable of the
same," affirmed Christie patting her biscuits into place and
tucking the bread cloth deftly over them, "but I'd be sorry t
see a meenister an' a session as wud be held up by one poor
whimperin' little elder of the like of him."

"Mr. Severn won't, I'm sure o' that!" said Mary trustingly,
"but there comes Mrs. Duncannon now. I'll run over and see
what's in the wind."

Mrs. Duncannon had grown a smile on her gentle face that
was like as two peas to her husband's wide kindly grin, but
there was no smile on her face this morning as she greeted
her two friends, and dropped into a chair by the door o
Christie's immaculate kitchen, and her soft brown eyes were
snapping: She had an air of carrying kindly mysterious
explosives:

"Did ye hear that the old ferret held up Mark Carter last
night and as good as called him a murderer in the face of the
whole session?" she asked breathlessly.

"And whut said our meenister to thot?" inquired Christie.

Jane Duncannon flashed her a twinkle of appreciation:

"He just clapped the senior elder in the chair as neat as a
pin in a pincushion an' moved an expression of confidence
utmost confidence was the word!"

"Mmmmmmmm! I thot as much!" commented Christie
"The blessed mon!"

"Oh, I'm so glad!" sighed Mary Rafferty sinking into a
chair. "Jim thinks the sun rises and sets in Mark Carter. They
were kids together you know. He says people don't know
Mark. And he said if they turned Mark down at the church
now, if they didn't stand by him in his trouble, he had no
more use for their religion!"

"Don't you believe it, Mary Rafferty! Jim Rafferty loves the
very ground the meenister walks on!"

"What was that?" exclaimed Jane Duncannon running to
the side window. "A strange car! Mary, come here! Is that the
chief of police from Economy?"

Mary darted to the window followed by the elder woman:

"Yes, it is!" she exclaimed drawing back aghast. "You *don't* suppose he's going to Carter's? He *wouldn't* do that would he?"

"He huz to do his dooty, doesn't he?" mused Christie. "But thot's not sayin' he *loikes* it, child!"

"Well, he might find a way not to frighten his mother!"

Mrs. Duncannon stretched her neck to see if he was really stopping at the parsonage, and Christie murmured: "Perhaps he will."

The little group lingered a moment, till Mary bethought her of her pies in the oven and the three drifted thriftily back to their morning tasks, albeit with mind and heart down in the village.

Presently on the glad morning air sounded again the chug chug of the motor, bringing them sharply back to their windows. Yes, there was the chief's car again. And Mark Carter with white haggard face sat in the backseat! Apprehension flew to the soul of each loyal woman.

But before the sound of the chief's motor bearing Mark Carter Economyward had passed out of hearing, Jane Duncannon in a neat brown dress with a little round brown-ribboned hat set trimly on her rippley hair, and a little round basket on her arm covered daintily with a white napkin, was nipping out her tidy front gate between the sunflowers and asters and tripping down Maple Street as if it had been on her mind to go ever since Saturday night.

Even before Mary Rafferty had turned from her Nottingham laced parlor window and gone with swift steps to her kitchen door Christie McMertrie stood on her back step with her sunbonnet on and a glass of jelly wrapped in tissue paper in her hand:

"She's glimpsed 'em," she whispered briefly, with a nod toward the holland shades, "an' she's up in her side bedroom puttin' on her Sunday bunnit. She'll be oot the door in another two meenits, the little black crow! If we bide in the fields we can mak Carters' back stoop afore she gets much past the tchurch!"

Mary Rafferty caught up her pan of peas, dashed them into a basket that hung on the wall by the door, and bare-headed as she was hastened out through the garden after her friend for all the world as if she were going to pick more peas. Down the green lane between the bean poles they hurried through the picket gate, pushing aside the big gray Duncannon cat who basked in the sun under a pink hollyhock with a Duncannon smile on its gray whiskers like the rest of the family.

"Jane! Jane Duncannon!" called Christie McMertrie. But the hollow echoes in the tidy kitchen flung back emptily, and the plate of steaming cinnamon buns on the white scrubbed table spoke as plainly as words could have done that no one was at home.

"She's gone!"

The two hurried around the house, through the front gate, across the street with a quick glance up and down to be sure that the Petrie babies playing horse in the next yard were their only observers, and then ducking under the bars of the fence they scuttled down a slope, crossed a trickle of a brook that hurried creekward, and up the opposite bank. Behind Little's barn they paused to glance back. Someone was coming out the Harricutt door, someone wearing a bonnet and a black veil. They hurried on. There were two more fences separating the meadows. Mary went over and Christie between. They made quick work of the rest of the way and crept panting through the hedge at the back of Carter's just as Jane Duncannon swung open the little gate in front with a glimpse back up the street in triumph and a breath of relief that she had won. By only so much as a lift of her lashes and a lighting of her soft brown eyes did she recognize and incorporate the other two in her errand, and together the three entered the Carter house by the side entrance, with a neighborly tap and a call: "Miz Carter, you home?"

Quick nervous steps overhead, a muffled voice calling catchily, "Yes, I'm coming, just set down, won't you?" and they dropped into three dining room chairs and drew breath, mopping their warm faces with their handkerchiefs and trying to adjust their minds to the next move.

Their hostess gave them no time to prepare a program. She came hurriedly downstairs, obviously anxious, openly with every nerve on the qui vive, and they saw at once that she had been crying. Her hair was damp about her forehead as if from hasty ablution. She looked from one to another of her callers with a frightened glance that went beyond them as if looking for others to come, as she paused in the doorway puzzled.

"This is a s'prise party, Miz Carter," began Jane Duncannon laughing. "We all brought our work along and can't stay but a minute, but we got an idea an' couldn't keep it till Ladies' Aid. You got a minute to spare? Go get your knitting and set down. *Now!* It's Miz Severn's birthday next Sat'day an' we thought 'twould be nice to get her a present. What do you think about it?"

Mrs. Carter who had stood tensely in the doorway, her fingers whitely gripping the woodwork, her face growing whiter every minute, suddenly relaxed with relief in every line of her body, and bloomed into a smile:

"Oh, why, *is* it? Of course! What'll it be? Why couldn't we finish that sunburst bed quilt we started last year while she was away? If we all get at it I think we could finish. There's some real fast quilters in the Aid. Wait, till I get my apples to pare. I promised Mark I'd have applesauce for lunch!"

A quick glance went from eye to eye and a look of relief settled down on the little company. She *expected Mark home for lunch* then!

They were in full tide of talk about the quilting pattern when a knock came on the front door, and Mary Rafferty jumped up and ran to open it. They heard the Harricutt voice, clear, sharp, incisive:

"I came to sympathize—!" And then as Mary swung her face into the sunlight the voice came suddenly up as against a stone wall with a gasp and "Oh, it's *you!* Where's Mrs. Carter? I wish to see Mrs. Carter."

"She's right back in the dining room, Miz Harricutt. Come on back. We're talking over how to celebrate Miz Severn's birthday. Do you like a straight quilting or diamond, Miz Harricutt. It's for the sunburst coverlet, you know!"

"The sunburst coverlet!" exclaimed Mrs. Harricutt irately, as though somehow it were an indecent subject at such a time as this, but she followed Mary back to the dining room with a sniff of curiosity. She fairly gasped when she saw Mrs. Carter with her small sensitive face bright with smiles:

"Just take that chair by the window, Mrs. Harricutt," she said affably, "and *excuse me* fer not getting up. I've got to get

these apples on the fire, for I promised Mark some applesauce for lunch, and he likes it stone cold."

Mrs. Harricutt pricked up her ears:

"Oh, Mark is coming home for *lunch* then!" Her voice was
cold, sharp, like a steel knife dipped in lemon juice. There
was a bit of a curl on the tip of it that made one wince as it
went through the soul. Little Mrs. Carter flushed painfully
under her sensitive skin, up to the roots of her light hair. She
had been pretty in her girlhood, and Mark had her coloring
in a stronger way.

"Oh, yes, he's coming home for lunch," she answered
brightly, glad of this much assurance. "And he has to have it
early because he has to drive that strange young woman from
the parsonage back somewhere down in New Jersey. She
came alone by herself yesterday, but the mountain passes sort
of scairt her, and she asked Mark to drive back with her."

"Oh!" There was a challenge in the tone that called the red
to Mrs. Carter's cheek again, but Christie McMertrie's soft
burring tongue slid in smoothly:

"What wad ye think o' the briar pattern around the edge? I
know it's some worruk, but it's a bonnie border to lie under,
an' it's not so tedious when there's plenty o' folks to tak a
hand."

They carried the topic along with a whirl then and Mrs.
Harricutt had no more chance to harry her hostess. Then
suddenly Mary arose in a panic:

"I left my pies in the oven!" she cried. "They'll be burned
to a crisp. I must go. Miz Harricutt, are you going along
now? I'll walk with you. I want to ask you how you made that
plum jam you gave me a taste of the other day. Jim thinks it is
something rare, and I'll have to be making some or he'll
never be satisfied, that is if you don't mind—" And before
Mrs. Carter realized what was happening Mary had mar-
shaled the Harricutt vulture down the street, and was questioning eagerly about measures of sugar and plums and lemon
peel and nuts.

"Now," said Christie setting down her jelly glass that she
had been holding all this time, "we'll be ganging awa. There's
a big jar of raspberry jam for the laddie with the bright smile,
an' you think it over and run up and say which pattern you
think is bonniest."

"It was just beautiful of you all to come," said little Mrs. Carter looking from one to another in painful gratitude—"why it's been just *dear* of you to run in this way."

"Yes, a regular party!" said Jane Duncannon squeezing her hand with understanding. "See, Mary has left her peas. You'd best put them on to boil for Mark. He'll be coming back pretty soon. Come, Christie, wumman, it's time we was back at our worruk!" and they hurried through the hedge and across the meadows to their homes once more, but as they entered the Duncannon gate they marked Billy Gaston, head down, pedaling along over on Maple Street, his jaws keeping rhythmic time with his feet.

One hour later the smooth chug of a car that was not altogether unfamiliar to their ears brought those four women eagerly to their respective windows, and as the old clock chimed the hour of noon they beheld Mark Carter driving calmly down the street toward his own home in his own car. *His own car!* And Billy Gaston lounging lazily by his side chewing rhythmically.

Mark's car! Mark! Billy! *Ah, Billy!* Three of them mused with a note of triumph in their eyes.

And Mrs. Harricutt as she rolled her Sunday bonnet strings mused:

"Now, how in the world did that Mark Carter get his own car down to Economy when he went up with the chief? He had it down here this morning, I know, for I saw him riding round. And that little imp of a Billy! I wonder why he always tags him round! Miss Saxon ought to be warned about that! I'll have to do it! But how in the world did Mark get his car?"

Billy enjoyed his lunch that day, a bit of cold chicken and bread, two juicy red-cheeked apples, and an unknown quantity of sugary doughnuts from the stone crock in the pantry. He sat on the side step munching the last doughnut he felt he could possibly swallow. Mark was home and all was well. Himself had seen the impressive glance that passed between Mark and the chief at parting. The chief trusted Mark that was plain. Billy felt reassured. He reflected that that guy Judas had been precipitate about hanging himself. If he had only waited and *done* a little something about it there might have been a different ending to the story. It was sort of up to Judas anyway, having been the cause of the trouble.

With this virtuous conclusion Billy wiped the sugar from his mouth, mounted his wheel and went forth to browse in familiar and much neglected pastures.

He eyed the Carter house as he slid by. Mrs. Carter was placidly shaking out the tablecloth on the side porch. Mark had eaten his applesauce and gone. He passed Brown's, Todd's, Bateses' chasing a white hen that had somehow escaped her confines, but in front of Joneses' he suddenly became aware of the blue car that stood in front of the parsonage. It had come to life and was throbbing. It was backing toward him and going to turn around. On the sidewalk leaning on a cane stood the obnoxious stranger for whose presence in Sabbath Valley he, Billy Gaston, was responsible. He lounged at ease with a smile on his ugly mug and acted as if he lived there! There was nothing about his appearance to suggest *his* near departure. His disabled car still stood silent and helpless beside the curb. Aw, *gee!*

Billy swerved to the other side of the road to avoid the blue car at a hairbreadth, but as it turned he looked up impudently to behold the strange girl with the flour on her face and the green baseball bats in her ears smiling up into the face of Mark Carter, who was driving. Billy nearly fell off his wheel and under the car, but recovered his balance in time to swerve out of the way without apparently having been observed by either Mark or the lady, and shot like a streak down the road. Beyond the church he drew a wide curve and turned in at the graveyard, casting a quick furtive eye toward the parsonage, where he was glad not to discover even the flutter of a garment to show that Lynn Severn was about. That guy was there, but Miss Lynn was not chasing him. That was as it should be. He breathed a sigh from his heavy heart and stole sadly back to the old mossy stone where so many of his life problems had been thought out. Still, that guy *was there! He* had the advantage! And Mark and that lady! Bah! He sat down to meditate on Judas and his sins. It seemed that life was just about as disappointing as it could be! His rough young hand leaned hard against the grimy old stone till the half worn lettering hurt his flesh and he shifted his position and lifted his hand. There on the palm were the quaint old letters, imprinted in the flesh, "Blessed are the dead—" Gosh yes! *Weren't* they? Judas had been right after all. "Aw, gee!" he said aloud. "Whatta fool I bin!" He glanced down at the stone as he rubbed the imprint from the fleshy part of his hand. The rest of the text caught his eye. "Blessed are the dead that die in the Lord!" There was a catch in that of course. It wasn't blessed if you didn't *die in the Lord*. "In the Lord" meant that you didn't do anything Judaslike. He understood. The people who didn't die in the Lord weren't blessed. They didn't go to heaven, whatever heaven was. They went to *hell*. Heaven had never seemed very attractive to Billy when he thought of it casually, and he had taken it generally for granted that he being a boy was naturally destined for the other place. In fact until he knew Lynn Severn he had always told himself calmly that he *expected* to go to hell sometime, it had seemed the manly thing to do. Most men to his mind were preparing for hell. It seemed the masculine place of final destiny. Heaven was for women. He had ventured some of this philosophy on his aunt once in a particularly strenuous time when she had told him that he couldn't expect the reward of the righteous if he continued in his present ways, but she had been so horrified, and wept so long and bitterly that he hadn't ever had the nerve to try it again. And since Marilyn Severn had been his teacher he had known days when he would almost be willing to go to heaven—for her sake. He had also suspected, at times, that Mr. Severn was fully as much of a man as Mark Carter, although Mark was *his own*, and if Mark decided to go to hell Billy felt there could be no other destiny for himself.

But now, face-to-face with realities, Billy suddenly began to realize what hell was going to be like. Billy felt hell surrounding him. Flames could not beat the reproach that now flared him in the face and stung him to the quick with his own sinfulness. He, Billy Gaston, captain of the Sabbath Valley baseball team, prospective captain of the Sabbath Valley football team, champion runner, and high jumper, champion swimmer and boxer of the boys' league of Monopoly County, friend and often tolerated companion of Mark Carter the great, trusted favorite of his beloved and saintly Sunday school teacher, was in *hell!* He could never more hold up his head and walk proud of himself. He was in hell at fourteen for life, and by his own act! And gosh hang it! Hell didn't look so attractive in the near vision stretching out that way through

life, and *then some*, as it had before he faced it. He'd rather
walk through fire somewhere and stand some chance of
getting done with it sometime. "Aw, gee! Gosh! Whatta fool I
bin!"

And then he set himself to see just what he had done,
while the high walls of sin seemed to rise closer about him,
and his face burned with the heat of the pit into which he had
put himself.

There was that guy Shafton—sissyman! He had put him in
the parsonage along with his beloved teacher! If he only
hadn't taken that ten dollars or listened to that devil of a Pat,
he wouldn't have put up that detour and Shafton would have
gone on his way. What difference if he had got kidnapped?
His folks wouldda bailed him out with their old jewels and
things. Whaddid anybody want of jewels for anyway? Just
nasty little bits of stone and glass! Mark had seen the guy
there in church. Mark didn't like it. He knew by the set of
Mark's mouth. Of course Mark went with Cherry sometimes,
but then that was different! Lynn was—well, Lynn was Miss
Marilyn! That was all there was about it.

And, if he hadn't put up that detour, Mark would have
gone home that night before twelve and his mother would
have known he was home, and likely other people would
have seen him, and been able to prove he wasn't out shooting
anybody, and then they wouldn't have told all those awful
things about him. Of course now Mark was safe, *of course*,
but then it wasn't good to have things like that said about
Mark. It was fierce to have a thing like that session meeting
to remember! He wanted to kill that old ferret of a Harricutt
whenever he thought about it. Then he would be a murderer,
and be hanged, and he wouldn't care if he did mebbe. *Aw,
gee!*

A meadowlark suddenly pierced the sky with its wild sweet
note high in the air somewhere, and Billy wondered with a
sick thud of his soul how larks dared to sing in a world like
this where one could upset a whole circle of friends by a
single little turn of finance that he hadn't meant anything
wrong by at all. The bees droned around the honeysuckle
that billowed over the little iron fence about a family burying
lot, and once Lynn Severn's laugh—not her regular laugh,
but a kind of a company polite one—echoed lightly across to

his ears and his face dropped into his hands. He almost groaned. Billy Gaston was at the lowest ebb he had ever been in his young life, and his conscience, a thing he hadn't suspected he had, and wouldn't have owned if he had, had risen up within him to accuse him, and there seemed no way on earth to get rid of it. A conscience wasn't a *manly* thing according to his code, yet here he was, he Billy Gaston, with a conscience!

It was ghastly!

Chapter 19

Laurie Shafton had caught Lynn as she came down the stairs with a bit of sewing in her hand to give Naomi a direction from her mother, and had begged her to come out on the porch and talk to him. He pleaded that he was lonesome, and that it was her duty as hostess to amuse him for a while.

Lynn had no relish for talking with the guest. Her heart was too sore to care to talk with anyone. But her innate courtesy and natural gentleness finally yielded to his pleading, for Laurie had put on a humility that was almost becoming, and made her seem really rude to refuse.

She made him sit down in the hammock at the far end, however, and insisted on herself taking the little rocker quite near the front door. She knew her father would soon be returning from some parish calls and would relieve her, so she settled herself with the bit of linen she was hemstitching and prepared to make the best of it.

"It's a shame my car is out of commission yet," began Laurie settling back in the hammock and by some strange miracle refraining from lighting a cigarette. It wouldn't have entered his head that Lynn would have minded. He didn't know any girls objected to smoking. But this girl interested him strangely. He wasn't at all sure but it was a case of love at first sight. He had always been looking for that to happen to him. He hoped it had. It would be such a delightful experience. He had tried most of the other kinds.

"Yes, it is too bad for you to be held up in your journey this way," sympathized Lynn heartily, "but Father says the blacksmith is going to fix you up by tomorrow he hopes. Those bearings will likely come tonight."

"Oh, but it has been a dandy experience. I'm certainly glad it happened. Think what I should have missed all my life, not knowing *you!*"

He paused and looked soulfully at Lynn waiting for an appreciative glance from her fully occupied eyes, but Lynn seemed to have missed the point entirely:

"I should think you might have well afforded to lose the experience of being held up in a dull little town that couldn't possibly be of the slightest interest to you," she said dryly, with the obvious idea of making talk.

"Oh, but I think it is charming," he said lightly! "I hadn't an idea there was such a place in the world as this. It's ideal, don't you know, so secluded and absolutely restful. I'm having a dandy time, and you people have been just wonderful to me. I think I shall come back often if you'll let me."

"I can't imagine your enjoying it," said Lynn looking at him keenly. "It must be so utterly apart from your customary life. It must seem quite crude and almost uncivilized to you."

"That's just it, it's so charmingly quaint. I'm bored to death with life as I'm used to it. I'm always seeking for a new sensation, and I seem to have lighted on it here all unexpectedly. I certainly hope my car will be fixed by morning. If it isn't I'll telegraph for my man and have him bring down some bearings in one of the other cars and fix me up. I'm determined to take you around a bit and have you show me the country. I know it would be great under your guidance."

"Thank you," said Lynn coolly, "but I haven't much time for pleasuring just now, and you will be wanting to go on your way—"

He flushed with annoyance. He was not accustomed to being baffled in this way by any girl, but he had sense enough to know that only by patience and humility could he win any notice from her.

"Oh, I shall want to linger a bit and let this doctor finish up this ankle of mine. It isn't fair to go away to another doctor before I'm on my feet again."

He thought she looked annoyed, but she did not answer.

"Did you ever ride in a racer?" he asked suddenly. "I'll teach you to drive. Would you like that?"

"Thank you," she said pleasantly, "but that wouldn't be necessary, I know how to drive."

He almost thought there was a twinkle of mischief in her eye:

"You know how to drive! But you haven't a car! Oh, I suppose that young Carter taught you to drive his," he said with chagrin. He was growing angry. He began to suspect her of playing with him. After all, even if she was engaged to that chap, he had gone off with Opal quite willingly it would appear. Why should he and she not have a little fling?

"No," said Marilyn, "Mr. Carter did not have a car until he went away from Sabbath Valley. I learned while I was in college."

"Oh, you've been to college!" the young man sat up with interest. "I thought there was something too sophisticated about you to have come out of a place like this. You had a car while you were in college I suppose."

Lynn's eyes were dancing:

"Why didn't you say 'dump' like this? That's what your tone said," she laughed, "and only a minute ago you were saying how charming it was. No, I had no car in college, I was—" But he interrupted her eagerly:

"Now, you are misunderstanding me on purpose," he declared in a hurt tone. "I think this is an ideal spot off in the hills this way, the quaintest little utopia in the world, but of course you know you haven't the air of one who had never been out of the hills, and the sweet sheltered atmosphere of this village. Tell me, when and where did you drive a car, and I'll see if I can't give you one better for a joy ride."

Lynn looked up placidly and smiled:

"In New York," she said quietly, "at the beginning of the war, and afterward in France."

Laurie Shafton sat up excitedly, the color flushing into his handsome face:

"Were you in France?" he said admiringly. "Well, I might

have known. I saw there was something different about you. Red Cross, I suppose?"

"No," said Lynn, "Salvation Army. My father has been a friend of the commander's all his life. She knew that we believed in all their principles. There were only a very few outsiders, those whom they knew well, allowed to go with them. I was one."

"Well," said Laurie, eyeing her almost embarrassedly, "you girls made a great name for yourselves with your doughnuts and your pies. The only thing I had against you was that you didn't treat us officers always the way we ought to have been treated. But I suppose there were individual exceptions. I went into a hut one night and tried to get some cigarettes and they wouldn't let me have any."

"No, we didn't sell cigarettes," said Lynn with satisfaction. "That wasn't what we were there for. We had a few for the wounded and dying who were used to them and needed them of course, but we didn't sell them."

"And then I tried to get some doughnuts and coffee, but would you believe it, they wouldn't let me have any till all the fellows in line had been served. They said I had to take my turn! They were quite insulting about it! Of course they did good, but they ought to have been made to understand that they couldn't treat United States officers that way!"

"Why not? Were you any better than any of the soldiers?" she asked eyeing him calmly, and somehow he seemed to feel smaller than his normal estimate of himself.

"An *officer?*" he said with a contemptuous haughty light in his eye.

"What is an officer but the servant of his men?" asked Lynn. "Would you *want* to eat before them when they had stood hours in line waiting? They who had all the hard work and none of the honors?"

Laurie's cheeks were flushed and his eyes angry:

"That's rot!" he said rudely. "Where did you get it? The officers were picked from the cream of the land. They represent the great nation. An insult to them is an insult to the nation!"

Lynn began to smile impudently—and her eyes were dancing again.

"I beg your pardon, Mr. Shafton, you must not forget I was

there. I knew both officers and men. I admit that some of the officers were princely, fit men to represent a great Christian nation, but some of them again were well—the scum of the earth, rather than the cream. Mr. Shafton, it does not make a man better than his fellows to be an officer, and it does not make him fit to be an officer just because his father is able to buy him a commission."

Laurie flushed angrily again:

"My father did not buy me a commission!" he said indignantly. "I went to a training camp and won it."

"I beg your pardon, Mr. Shafton, I meant nothing personal, but I certainly had no use for an officer who came bustling in on those long lines of weary soul-sick boys just back from the front, and perhaps off again that night, and tried to get ahead of them in line. However, let's talk of something else. Were you ever up around Dead Man's Curve? What division were you in?"

Laurie let his anger die out and answered her questions. For a few minutes they held quite an animated conversation about France and the various phases of the war. Laurie had been in air service. One could see just how handsome he must have looked in his uniform. One would know also that he would be brave and reckless. It was written all over his face and in his very attitude. He showed her his service medal.

"Mark was taken prisoner by the Germans," she said sadly as she handed it back, her eyes dreamy and faraway, then suddenly seeming to realize that she had spoken her thoughts aloud she flushed and hurried on to other experiences during the war, but she talked abstractedly, as one whose thoughts had suddenly been diverted. The young man watched her baffled:

"You seem so aloof," he said all at once watching her as she sewed away on the bit of linen. "You seem almost as if you—well—*despised* me. Excuse me if I say that it's a rather new experience. People in my world don't act that way to me, really they don't. And you don't even know who I am nor anything about me. Do you think that's quite fair?"

Lynn looked at him with suddenly arrested attention:

"I'm sorry," she said, "I didn't mean to be rude. But possibly you've come to the heart of the matter. I am not of your world. You know there's a great deal in not being able to get another's point of view. I hope I haven't done you an injustice. I haven't meant to. But you're wrong in saying I don't know who you are or anything about you. You are the son of William J. Shafton—the only son, isn't that so? Then you are the one I mean. There can't be any mistake. And I do know something about you. In fact I've been very angry at you, and wished I might meet you and tell you what I thought of you."

"You don't say!" said Laurie getting up excitedly and moving over to a chair next to hers regardless of his lame ankle. "This certainly is interesting! What the deuce have I been doing to get myself in your bad graces? I better repent at once before I hear what it is?"

"You are the one who owns the block of warehouses downtown and won't sell at any price to give the little children in all that region a place to get a bit of fresh air, the grass, and a view of the sky. You are the one who won't pull down your old buildings and try new and improved ways of housing the poor around there so that they can grow up decently clean and healthy and have a little chance in this world. Just because you can't have as many apartments and get as much money from your investment you let the little children crowd together in rooms that aren't fit for the pigs to live in, they are so dark and airless, and crowded already. Oh, I know you keep within the law! You just skin through without breaking it, but you won't help a little bit, you won't even let your property help if someone else is willing to take the bother! Oh, I've been so boiling at you ever since I heard your name that I could hardly keep my tongue still, to think of that great beautiful car out there and how much it must have cost, and to hear you speak of one of your other cars as if you had millions of them, and to think of little Carmela living down in the basement room of number eighteen in your block, growing whiter and whiter every day, with her great blue eyes and her soft fine wavy hair, and that hungry eager look in her face. And her mother, sewing, sewing, all day long at the little cellar window, and going blind because you won't put in a bigger one; sewing on coarse dark vests, putting in pockets and buttonholes for a living for her and Carmela, and you grinding her down and running around in cars like that and taking it out of little Carmela, and little Carmela's mother! Oh! How can I help feeling aloof from a person like that?"

Laurie sat up astonished watching her:

"Why, my dear girl!" he exclaimed. "Do you know what you're talking about? Do you realize that it would take a mint of money to do all the fool things that these silly reformers are always putting up to you? My lawyer looks after all those matters. Of course I know nothing about it!"

"Well, you *ought* to know," said Lynn excitedly. "Does the money belong to your lawyer? Isn't it yours to be responsible for? Well, then if you are stealing some of it out of little Carmela and a lot of other little children and their mothers and fathers oughtn't you to know? Is your lawyer going to take responsibility about it in the kingdom of heaven I should like to know? Can he stand up in the judgment day and exempt you by saying that he had to do the best he could for your property because you required it of him? Excuse me for getting so excited, but I love little Carmela. I went to see her a great deal last winter when I was in New York taking my senior year at the university. And I can't help telling you the truth about it. I don't suppose you'll do anything about it, but at least you ought to know! And *I'm not your dear girl, either!*"

Marilyn rose suddenly from her chair, and stood facing him with blazing eyes and cheeks that were aflame. It was a revelation to the worldly wise young man that a saint so sweet could blossom suddenly into a beautiful and furious woman. It seemed unreal to find this wonderful, unique, excitable young woman with ideas in such a quiet secluded spot of the earth. Decidedly she had ideas.

"Excuse me," he said, and rose also, an almost deprecatory air upon him, "I assure you I meant nothing out of the way, Miss Severn. I certainly respect and honor you. And really, I had no idea of all this about my property. I've never paid much heed to my property except to spend the income of course. It wasn't required of me. I must look into this matter. If I find it as you think—that is if there is no mistake, I will see what I can do to remedy it. In any case we will look after little Carmela. I'll settle some money on her mother, wouldn't

that be the best way? I can't think things are as bad as you
say—"

"Will you really do something about it?" asked Lynn
earnestly. "Will you go up to New York and see for yourself?
Will you go around in *every room* of your buildings and get
acquainted with those people and find out just what the
conditions are?"

"Why—I—" he began uncertainly.

"Oh, I thought you couldn't stand that test! That would be
too much bother— You would rather—"

"No, wait! I didn't say I wouldn't. Here! I'll go if you'll go
with me and show me what you mean and what you want
done. Come. I'll take you at your word. If you really want all
those things come on and show me just what to do. I'm game.
I'll do it. I'll do it whether it needs doing or not, *just for you*.
Will you take me up?"

"Of course," said Lynn quickly, "I'll go with you and show
you. I expect to be in New York next month helping at the
Salvation Home while one of their workers is away on her
vacation. I'll show you all over the district as many times as
you need to go, if it's not too hot for you to come back to the
city so early."

He looked at her sharply. There was a covert sneer in her
last words that angered him, and he was half inclined to
refuse the whole thing, but somehow there was something in
this strange new type of girl that fascinated him. Now that
she had the university and the war and the world for a
background, she puzzled and fascinated him more than ever.
Half surprised at his own interest he bowed with a new kind
of dignity over his habitual light manner:

"I shall be delighted, Miss Severn. It will not be too hot for
me if it is not too hot for you. I shall be at your service, and I
hope you will discover that there is one officer who knows
how to obey."

She looked at him half surprised, half troubled and then
answered simply:

"Thank you. I'm afraid I've done you an injustice. I'm
afraid I didn't think you would be game enough to do it. I
hope I haven't been too rude. But you see I feel deeply about
it and sometimes I forget myself."

"I am sure I deserve all you have said," said Laurie as

gravely as his light nature could manage, "but there is one thing that puzzles me deeply. I wish you would enlighten me. All this won't do *you* any good. It isn't for *you* at all. *Why* do you care?"

Marilyn brought her lovely eyes to dwell on his face for a moment thoughtfully, a shy beautiful tenderness softening every line of her eager young face:

"It's because—" she began diffidently. "It's because they all are God's children—and I love *Him* better than anything else in life!"

The swift color made her face lovely as she spoke, and with the words she turned away and went quickly into the house. The young man looked after her and dared not follow. He had never had a shock like that in his life. Girls had talked about everything under heaven to him at one time or another, but they had never mentioned God except profanely.

Marilyn went swiftly up to her room and knelt down by her bed, burying her hot cheeks in the cool pillow and tried to pray. She was glad, glad that she had spoken for her poor city children, glad that there was a prospect of help perhaps; but beside and beyond it all her heart was crying out for another matter that was namelessly tugging away at the very foundations of her soul. Why, oh, *why* had Mark gone away with that girl? He must have seen what she was! He must have known that it was unnecessary! He must have known how it would hurt his friends, and that the man she came to see could have gone as well as he and better. Why did he go? She would not, she could not believe anything wrong of Mark. Yet *why did he go?*

Chapter 20

Billy had no appetite for the nice supper that Aunt Saxon had ready when he came dejectedly home that night. He had passed the parsonage and seen through the dining room window that the rich guy was sitting at the supper table opposite Marilyn laughing and talking with her and his soul was sick within him. That was his doing! Nobody else but himself to blame!

Aunt Saxon had apple dumplings with plenty of "goo," black with cinnamon just the way he loved it, but he only minced at the first helping and scarcely tasted the second. He chopped a great many kindling after supper, and filled the woodbox, and thoughtfully wound the clock. Then instead of going out with his usual "I gotta beat it!" he sat languidly on the doorstep in the dusk, and when she anxiously questioned if he were sick he said crossly:

"Aw, gee! Can't ya let a fella *alone!* I'm all in, can't ya *see it?* I'm gonta bed!" and knowing he had said the most alarming thing in the whole category he slammed upstairs to his own room and flung himself across his bed.

Aunt Saxon filled with vague fears crept softly up after him, tapping at his locked door:

"Willie, what is the matter? Just tell Auntie where the pain is and I'll get you some medicine that will fix you all up by morning. I'll get you a hot water bag!"

"DON'T WANT NO HOT WATER BAGS!" roared the sore-hearted Billy. "Can't ya lemme *alone?*"

Silence a moment while Aunt Saxon pondered tearfully and sighfully, then:

"Willie, is it the toothache?"

"NoooOH!" roared Billy.

A pause, then:

"Billy, you've had a fall off that wheel and hurt yer head or cut yer knee, I know, I've always thought you'd do that, that old wheel! You oughtta have a new one. But I'll bring the arnica and bathe it. And we'll paint it with iodine—where was it, Willie? Yer knee?"

Billy's shoes came to the floor with a bang:

"Aw, gee! Can't ya keep yer mouth shut an' let a fella have a little sleep. It ain't *nowhere!* It ain't *nothin'* an' I didn't have no fall an' I don't want no new bicycle. D'ye hear? I don't want nothin' 'cept just to be let alone. I wantta go ta sleep. Ain't I ben tellin' ya fer the last half hour? It ain't *sinful* fer a fella to wantta take a little sleep is it when he's been up half the night before taking care of a fella on the mountain? But if

I ain't allowed, why then I'll get up an' go out somewheres. I know plenty of places where they'll lemme sleep—"

"Oh, *Wil-lee!*" sobbed Aunt Saxon. "That's all right, dear! Just you lie right down in your bed and take a good sleep. I didn't understand. Auntie didn't understand. All right, Willie. I'll keep it real still. Now you lie down, won't you? You will, won't you? You'll really lie down and sleep, won't you, Willie?"

"Didn't I say I would?" snapped Willie shamedly, and subsided on his bed again while Aunt Saxon stole painfully, noiselessly over the creak in the stair, closed the house for the night and crept tearfully to her own bed, where she lay for hours silently wiping the steady trickle of hopeless tears. Oh, Willie, Willie! And she had had such hopes!

But Billy lay staring wide-eyed at the open square of his window that showed the little village nestling among the trees dotted here and there with friendly winking lights, the great looming mountains in the distance, and Stark Mountain, farthest and blackest of them all. He shut his eyes and tried to blot it out, but it seemed to loom through his very eyelids and mock him. He seemed to see Mark, his idol, carried between those other three dark figures into the blackness of that haunted house. He seemed to see him lying helpless, bound, on the musty bed in the deserted room, Mark, his beloved Mark. Mark, who had carried him on his shoulder as a tiny child, who had ridden him on his back, and taught him to swim and pitch ball and box. Mark, who let him go where even the big boys were not allowed to accompany him, and who never told on him or treated him mean nor went back on him in any way! Mark! *He* had been the means of putting Mark in that helpless position, while circumstances which he was now quite sure the devil had been specially preparing, wove a tangled maze about the young man's feet from which there seemed no way of extrication.

Billy shut his eyes and tried to sleep but sleep would not come. He began to doubt if he would ever sleep again. He lay listening to the evening noises of the village. He heard Jim Rafferty's voice going by to the night shift, and Tom McMertrie. They were laughing softly and once he thought he heard the name "Old Haircut." The Tully baby across the street had colic and cried like murder. Murder! *Murder!* Now why did he have to think of *that* word of all words? Murder?

Well, it was crying like it wanted to murder somebody. He wished he was a baby himself so he could cry. He'd cry harder'n that. Little's dog was barking again. He'd been barking all day long. It was probably at that strange guy at the parsonage. Little's dog never did like strangers. That creak was Barneses' gate with the iron weight hitched on the chain to make it shut, and somebody laughed away up the street! He thought it must be about three in the morning! And then he must have dozed off for a little, for when he woke with a start it was very still and dark, as if the moon had gone away, had been and gone again, and he heard a cautious little mouse gnawing at the baseboard in his room, gnawing and stopping and gnawing again, then whisking over the lath like fingers running a scale on the piano. He had watched Miss Lynn do it once on the organ.

He opened his eyes and looked hard at the window. The dim outline of Stark Mountain off in the distance began to grow into form, and what was that? A speck of light? It must be his eyes. He rubbed them sleepily and looked again. Yes, a light. Alert at once with the alertness that comes to all boys at the sound of a fire bell or some such alarm, he slid from his bed noiselessly and stole to the window. It was gone! Ah, gee! He had been alseep and dreamed it. No, there it was again, or was it?

Blackness all before his eyes, with a luminous sky dimly about the irregular mountaintop fringed with trees. This was foolish. He felt chilly and crept back to bed, but could not keep his eyes from the dark spot against the sky. He tried to close the lids and go to sleep, but they insisted on flying open and watching. And then came what he had been watching for. Three winks, and stop, three winks, stop, and one long flash. Then all was dark. And though he watched till the church clock struck three he saw no more.

But the old torment came back. Mark and Cherry and Lynn. The guy at the parsonage and the girl with the floured face and baseball bats in her ears! Aw, gee! He must have a fever! It was hours since the clock had struck three. It must be nearly four, and then it would soon be light and he could get up. There seemed to be a light somewhere down the street through the trees. Not the street lamp either. Somebody sick likely. Hark! What was that? He wished he hadn't undressed. He sat up in bed and listened. The purr of a car!

Someone was stealing Mark's car! Mark was away and everybody knew it. Nobody in Sabbath Valley would steal, except, perhaps over at the plush mill. There were new people there— Was that Mark's car? *Some car!*

With a motion like a cat he sprang into the necessary garment which nestled limply on the floor by the bed, and was at the window in a trice. A drop like a cat to the shed roof, down the rain waterspout to the ground, a stealthy step to the back shed where old trusty leaned, and he was away down the road a speck in the dark, and just in time to see the dim black vision of a car speeding with muffled engine down the road toward the church. It was too dark to say it was Mark's car. He had no way but to follow.

Panting and puffing, pedaling with all his might, straining his eyes to see through the dark the car that was flying along without lights, his hair sticking endwise, his sleepy hungry face peering wanly through the dark, he plodded after. Over the highway! He slowed down and wasn't quite sure till he heard the chug of the engine ahead, and a few seconds later a red light bloomed out behind and he drew a new breath and pedaled on again, his heart throbbing wildly, the collar of his pajamas sticking up wildly like his hair, and one pajama leg showing whitely below his trouser like a tattered banner. The pedals cut his bare feet, and he shivered though he was drenched with perspiration, but he leaned far over his handlebars and pedaled on.

Down past the Blue Duck Tavern, and on into the village of Economy the car went, not rapidly now as though it were running away, but slower, and steadier like a car on legitimate business and gravely with a necessary object in view. Billy's heart began to quake. Not for nothing had he learned to read by signs and actions at the feet of the master Mark. An inner well-developed sense began to tell him the truth.

The car stopped in front of the chief's house, and a horn sounded softly once. Billy dismounted hastily and vanished into the shadows. A light appeared in the upper window of the house and all was still. Presently the light upstairs went out, the front door opened showing a dimmer light farther in, and showing the outline of the chief in flannel shirt and trousers. He came down the walk and spoke with the man in the car, and the car started again and turned in at the chief's driveway, going back to the garage.

Billy left his wheel against a hedge and hiked noiselessly
after, slinking behind the garage door till the driver came out.
It was Mark!

He went down the drive, met the chief at the gate and they
went silently down the dark street, their rubber heels making
no noise on the pavement. Economy was asleep and no wiser,
but Billy's heart was breaking. He watched the two and
followed afar till they turned down the side street which he
feared. He stole after and saw them enter the brick building
that harbored the county jail. He waited with shaking limbs
and bleeding heart, waited, hoping, fearing, dreading, but not
for long. The chief came out alone! It was as he had feared.

Then as if the very devil himself pursued him, Billy turned
and fled, retrieving his bicycle and whirled away noiselessly
down the road, caring not where he was going, ready to hang
himself, wild with despair and self-condemnation.

The dark lay over the valley like a velvet mantle black and
soft with white wreaths of mist like a lady's veil flung aside
and blown to the breeze, but Billy saw naught but red
winking lights and a jail, grim and red in the midnight, and
his friend's white face passing in beneath the arched door.
The bang of that door as it shut was echoing in his soul.

He passed the Fenner cottage. There were lights and
moving about, but he paid no heed. He passed the Blue
Duck Tavern, and saw the light in the kitchen where the cook
was beginning the day's work just as the rest of the house had
been given over to sleep. There was the smell of bacon on
the air. Someone was going away on the milk train likely. He
thought it out dully as he passed with the sick reeling motion
of a rider whose life has suddenly grown worthless to him.
Over bottles and nails, and bumping over humps old trusty
carried him, down the hill to Sabbath Valley, past the graveyard where the old stones peered eerily up from the dark
mounds like wakened curious sleepers, past the church in the
gray of the morning with a pinkness in the sky behind. Lynn
lying in a sleepless bed listening to every sound for Mark's
car to return, and recognizing Billy's back wheel squeak. On
down the familiar street, glad of the thick maples to hide
him, hunching up the pajama leg that would wave below in
the rapidly increasing light, not looking toward the Carters',
plodding on, old trusty on the back porch; shinning up the

waterspout, tiptoeing over the shed roof, a quick spring in his
own window and he was safe in his bed again staring at the
red morning light shining weirdly, cheerily on his wall and
the rooster crowing lustily below his window. Drat that
rooster! What did it want to make that noise for? Wasn't there
a rooster in that Bible story? Oh, no, that was Peter perhaps.
He turned hastily from the subject and gave his attention to
his toilet. Aunt Saxon was squeaking past his door, stopping
to listen:

"Willie?"

"Well." In a low growl, not encouragingly.

"Oh, Willie, you up? You better?"

"Nothin' the matter with me."

"Oh—"

"Breakfast ready?"

"Oh, yes, Willie! I'm so glad you're feeling better." She
squeaked on down the stairs sniffing as if from recent tears!
Doggone those tears! Those everlasting tears! Why didn't a
woman know! Now, what did he have to do next? Do! Yes, he
must do something. He couldn't just sit here, could he? What
about Stark Mountain and the winking light? What about that
sissy guy making up to Miss Lynn? If only Mark were here
now he would tell him everything. Yes, he would. Mark
would understand. But Mark was in that unspeakable place!
Would Mark find a way to get out? He felt convinced he
could, but *would* he? From the set of his shoulders Billy had
a strong conviction that Mark would not. Mark seemed to be
going there for a purpose. Would the purpose be complete
during the day sometime and would Mark return? Billy must
do something before night. He wished it might be to smash
the face of that guy Shafton. Assuredly he must do something. But first he must eat his breakfast. He didn't want to,
but he had to. Aunt Saxon would raise a riot if he didn't.
Well, there was ham. He could smell it. Ham for breakfast
Aw, gee! Saxy was getting extravagant. Somehow pretty soon
if he didn't hang himself he must find a way to brighten up
Saxy and pay her back for all those pink tears.

And over on Stark Mountain as the morning dawned a
heavy foot climbed the haunted stairs and a bloodshot eye
framed itself at the little half-moon in the front window that
looked out over Lone Valley toward Economy, and down over

Sabbath Valley toward Monopoly commanding a strategic position in the whole wild lovely region.

Down in the cellar where the rats had hitherto held sway a soft chip, chip, chipping sound went steadily forward hour by hour, with spaces between and chip, chip, chipping again, a new kind of rat burrowing into the earth, over close to the edge of the long deserted scanty coal pile. While up under the dusty beams in a dark corner various old parcels were stowed away awaiting a later burial. From the peep-hole where the eye commanded the situation a small black speck went whirling along the road to Monopoly which might be a boy on a bicycle, but no one came toward Stark Mountain on that bright sunny morning to disturb the quiet worker in the dark cellar.

Billy was on his way to Monopoly, his aunt appeased for the time being, with the distinct purpose of buying the morning paper. Not that he was given to literature, or perused the daily news as a habit, but an idea had struck him. There might be a way of finding out about Mark without letting anyone know how he was finding out. It might be in the paper. Down at Monopoly no one would notice if he bought a county paper, and he could stop in the woods and read it.

But when he reached the newsstand he saw a pile of New York papers lying right in front, and the great black headlines caught his eye:

FATE OF LAURENCE SHAFTON
STILL UNKNOWN

Son of multimillionaire of New York City who was kidnapped on Saturday night on his way from New York to a weekend house party at Beechwood, N.J., not yet heard from. No clue to his whereabouts. Detectives out with bloodhounds searching country. Mother in a state of collapse. It is feared the bandits have fulfilled their threats and killed him. Father frantically offering any reward for news of son!

Billy read no further. He clapped down a nickel and stuffed the paper indifferently into his pocket, almost forgetting in his disgust to purchase the county news. "Aw, gee!" he said to himself. "More o' that Judas stuff. I gotta get rid o' them thirty pieces!"

He stepped back and bought a county paper, stood idly looking over its pages a moment with the letters swimming before his eyes, at last discovering the column where the Economy "murder" was discussed, and without reading it stuffed it in the pocket of the other side and rode away into the sunlight. Murder! It was called murder! Then Dolph must be dead! The plot thickened! Dead! Murder! Who killed him? Surely he wasn't responsible for that at least! He was out on the road with Mark when it happened. *He* hadn't done anything which in the remotest way had to do with the killing, he thanked his lucky stars for that. And Mark. But who did it? Cherry? She might be a reason for what Mark did last night.

At a turn in the road where a little grove began he got off his wheel and seeking a sheltered spot dropped down under a tree to read his papers. His quick eye searched through the county paper first for the sensational account of the murder, and a gray look settled over his pug countenance as he read. So might a mother have regarded her child in deep trouble, or a lover his beloved. Billy's spirit was bowed to the depths. When he had devoured every word he flung the paper aside wrathfully, and sat up with a kind of hopeless gesture of his hard young hands. "Aw, gee!" he said aloud, and suddenly he felt a great wet blob rolling down his freckled cheek. He smashed it across into his hair with a quick slash of his dirty hand as if it had been a mosquito annoying him, and lest the other eye might be meditating a like trick he gave that a vicious dab and hauled out the other paper, more as a matter of form than because he had a deep interest in it. All through the description of those wonderful Shafton jewels, and the mystery that surrounded the disappearance of the popular young man, Billy could see the word murder dancing like little black devils in and out among the letters. The paragraph about Mrs. Shafton's collapse held him briefly:

"Aw, gee!" He could see pink tears everywhere. He supposed he ought to do something about that. For all the world like Aunt Saxon! He seemed to sense her youth through the printed words as he had once sensed Mrs. Carter's. He saw her back in school, pretty and little. Rich women were always pretty and little to his mind, pretty and little and helpless and always crying. It was then that the thought was born that made him look off to the hills and ponder with drawn brows and anxious mien. He took it back to his home with him and sat moodily staring at the lilac bushes, and gave Aunt Saxon another bad day wondering what had come to Willie. She would actually have been glad to hear him say: "I gotta beat it! I gotta date with tha fellas!"

That evening the rumor crept back to Sabbath Valley from who knows where that Dolph was dead and Mark Carter had run away!

Chapter 21

Tuesday morning Lynn slipped down to Carter's with a little cake she had made all white frosting and sprinkles of nuts. Her face was white but brave with a smile, and she said her mother wanted to know how Mrs. Carter's neuralgia was getting on.

But Mrs. Carter was the only one in the village perhaps who had not heard the rumor, and she was gracious and pleased and said she wished Mark was home, he loved nut cake so much.

"You knew he was called back to New York suddenly last night didn't you?" she said. "He felt real sorry to leave so soon, but his partner wired him there was something he must see to himself, and he just took his car and went right away as soon as he got back from taking that girl home. He hoped he'd get back again soon though. Say, who was that girl? Wasn't she kind of nervy to ask Mark to take her home? Seems somehow girls are getting a little forward these days. I know you'd never do a thing like that with a perfect stranger, Marilyn."

The girl only stayed a few minutes, and went home with a braver heart. At least Mark was protecting his mother. He had not changed entirely. He wouldn't let her suffer! But what was he doing? Oughtn't he to be told what rumors were going around about him? But how could it be done? Her father? Perhaps. She shrank from that, Mark had so withdrawn from them, he might take it as an interference. Billy? Ah, yes, Billy!

But Billy did not appear anywhere, and when she got back she found that Shafton's car had been finished and was ready to drive, and he wanted her to take a little spin with him to try it, he said. He warily invited her mother to go along, for he saw by her face that she was going to decline, and the mother watching her daughter's white face said: "Yes, Marilyn, we will go. It will do you good. You have been housed up here ever since you came home." And there was nothing for the girl to do but succumb or seem exceedingly rude. She was not by nature rude, so she went.

As they drove by the Saxon cottage Billy was just coming out, and he stared glumly at the three and hardly acknowledged Marilyn's greeting. He stared after them scowling.

"Hell!" said Billy aloud, regardless of Aunt Saxon at the front window. "Yes! *Hell!*" and he realized the meaning of his epithet far better than the young man he was staring after had the first night he had used it in Sabbath Valley.

"What was that you said, Willie?" called Aunt Saxon's anxious voice.

"Aw, nothing!" said Billy, and slammed out the gate, his wheel by his side. *Now!* Something had to be done. He couldn't have *that* going on. He was hurt at Mrs. Severn. She ought to take better care of her daughter! In sullen despair he mounted and rode away to work out his problem. It was certain he couldn't do anything with Saxy sniveling round. And *something had to be done!*

Billy managed to get around the country quite a little that morning. He rode up to Economy and learned that Mr. Fenner, the tailor, was sick, had been taken two nights ago, was delirious and had to have two men to hold him down. He thought everybody was an enemy and tried to choke them all. He rode past the jail but saw nothing though he circled the block three times. The chief stood out in front talking with three strange men. Billy sized them up for detectives. When there was nothing further to be gained in Economy he turned his steed toward Pleasant Valley and took in a little

underground telephone communication between a very badly
scared Pat and a very angry Sam at some unknown point at
the end of the wire. It was then, lying hidden in the thick
undergrowth, that a possible solution of his difficulties occurred to him, a form of noble self-sacrifice that might in part
do penance for his guilt. Folded safely in his inner pocket was
the thirty pieces of silver, the blood money, the price of Mark
Carter's freedom and good name. If he had not taken that he
might have fixed this Pat so he would be a witness to Mark's
alibi. But according to the code he had been taught it would
not be honorable to squeal on somebody whose money he
had taken. It wasn't square. It wasn't honorable. It was yella,
and yella he would not be if the sky fell. It was all the religion
he had as yet, not to be yella. It stood for all the fineness of
his soul. But he had reasoned within himself that if in some
way he could get that money back to Pat, then he would be
free from obligation. Then he could somehow manage to put
Pat where he would have to tell the right thing to save Mark.
Just how it could be done he wasn't sure, but that was
another question.

When Pat had trundled away to the train he rolled himself
out from ambush and went on his way across Lone Valley by a
little tree-shaded path he knew that cut straight over to Stark
Mountain.

Not a ripple of a leaf showed above him as he passed
straight up the mountain to the old house, for the watchful
eye looking out to see. Billy was a great deal like an Indian in
his goings and comings, and Billy was wary. Had he not seen
the winking light? Billy was taking no chances. Smoothly
folded in his hip pocket he carried a leaf of the New York
paper wherein was offered a large reward for information
concerning jewels and bonds and other property taken from
the Shafton country home on pretense of setting free the son.
Also there was a stupendous reward offered for information
concerning the son, and Billy's big thought as he crept along
under the trees with all the stealth of a wild thing, was that
here was another thirty pieces of silver multiplied many
times, and *he wasn't going to take it!* He *could,* but he
wouldn't! He was going to give these folks the information
they wanted, but he wasn't going to get the benefit of it. That
was going to be his punishment. He had been in hell long

enough, and he was going to try to pull himself out of it by his good works. And he would do it in such a way that there wouldn't be any chance of the reward being pressed upon him. He would just fix it so that nobody would particularly know he had anything to do with the clews. That was Billy all over. He never did a thing halfway. But first he must find out if there was anybody about the old house. He couldn't get away from those three winks he had seen.

So, feeling almost relieved for a moment, Billy left his wheel on guard and crept around to his usual approach at the back before he came out in the open. And then he crept cautiously to the cellar window where he had first entered the house. He gripped Pat's old gun with one hand in his pocket, and slid along like a young snake, taking precaution not to appear before the cellar window lest his shadow should fall inside. He flattened himself at last upon the grass a noticeless heap of gray khaki trousers and brown flannel shirt close against the house. One would have to lean far out of a window to see him, and there he lay and listened a while. And presently from the depths beyond that grated window he heard a little scratch, scratch, scratch, tap, tap, tap, scratch, tap, scratch, tap, steadily, on for some time like his heart-beats, till he wasn't sure he was hearing it at all, and thought it might be the blood pounding through his ears, so strange and uncanny it seemed. Then, all at once there came a puff, as if a long breath had been drawn, like one lifting a heavy weight and then a dull thud. A brief silence and more scratching in soft earth now.

He listened for perhaps an hour, and once a footstep grated on the cement floor, and coals rattled down as if they were disturbed. Once too a soft chirrup from up above like the call of a wood bird, only strangely human and the sounds in the cellar ceased altogether, till another weird note sounded and they began again.

When he was satisfied with his investigations he began slowly to back away from his position, lifting each atom of muscle slowly one at a time till his going must have been something like the motion picture of a bud unfolding, and yet as silent as the flower grows he faded away from that cellar window back into the green and no one was the wiser. An hour later the watchful eye at the little half-moon opening in

the shutter might have seen a little black speck like a
spider whizzing along on the highroad and turning down
toward Sabbath Valley, but it never would have looked as if it
came from Stark Mountain, for it was headed straight from
Lone Valley. Billy was going home to get cleaned up and
make a visit to the parsonage. If that guy was still there he'd
see how quick he would leave! If there wasn't one way to
make him go there was another, and Billy felt that he held
the trick.

But as fate would have it Billy did not have to get cleaned
up, for Miss Severn stood on the front porch looking off
toward the mountains with that wistful expression of hers that
made him want to laugh and cry and run errands for her
anywhere just to serve her and make her smile, and she
waved her hand at Billy, and ran down to the gate to speak to
him.

"Billy, I want to ask you— If you were to see Mark Carter—
of course you mightn't, but then you might—you'll let him
know that we are of course his friends, and that anything he
wants done, if he'll just let us know—"

"Sure!" said Billy lighting off his wheel with a downward
glance at his dirty self, all leaves and dust and grime. "Sure,
he'd know that anyhow."

"Well, Billy, I know he would, but I mean, I thought
perhaps you might find something we *could do*, something
maybe without letting him know. He's very proud about
asking any help, you know, and he wouldn't want to bother
us. You may discover something he—needs—or wants done—
while—he is away—and maybe we could help him out.
Father or Mother or I. You'll remember, won't you, Billy?"

"Sure!" said Billy again feeling the warm glow of her
friendliness and loyalty to Mark, and digging his toes into the
turf embarrassedly. Then he looked up casually as he was
about to leave:

"Say is there a guy here named Shafton? Man from n'York?"

"Why, yes," said Lynn looking at him curiously. "Did you
want to see him?"

"Well, if he's round I might. I got a message for him."

She looked at him keenly:

"You haven't *seen* Mark today, have you, Billy?"

"Aw, naw, 'taint from him," he grinned reassuringly. "He's

away just now. But I might see him soon, ya know, ur hear from him."

Lynn's face cleared. "Yes, of course. His mother told me he was suddenly called back to New York."

"Yep. That's right!" said Billy as if he knew all about it, and pulled off his old cap with a glorious wave as she turned to call the stranger.

Billy dropped his wheel at the curb and approached the steps as he saw Shafton coming slowly out leaning on a cane. He rustled the folded newspaper out from his pocket with one hand and shook it open as only a boy's sleight of hand can do, wafting it in front of the astonished Laurie, and saying with an impudent swag:

"Say, z'your name Shafton? Well, *see that?* Why don't you beat it home? Your ma is about t'croke, an' yer dad has put up about all his dough, an' you better rustle back to where you come from an' tell 'em not to b'leeve all the bunk that's handed out to 'em! Good night! They must need a nurse!"

Laurie paused in the act of lighting one of his interminable cigarettes with which he supplied the lack of a stronger stimulant, and stared at the boy curiously, then stared at the paper he held in his hand with the flaring headlines, and reaching out his hand for it began to laugh:

"Well, upon my word, kid, where'd you get this? If that isn't a joke! I wonder if Opal's seen it. Miss Severn, come here! See what a joke! I'm kidnapped! Did you ever hear the like? Look at the flowery sentences. It's almost like reading one's own obituary, isn't it?"

Marilyn, glancing over his shoulder at the headlines, took in the import of it instantly. "I should think you'd want to telephone your mother at once. How she must have suffered!" she said.

Laurie somewhat sobered agreed that it would be a good idea:

"The mater's a good old scout," he said lightly. "She's always helping me out of scrapes, but this is one too many to give up her emeralds, the Shafton emeralds! Gosh but Dad will be mad about them! And, oh, say, call that boy back will you? I want to give him a dollar!"

But Billy had faded down the road with mortal indignation in his breast. To think of giving up a ten-thousand-dollar

reward and having a dollar flung at you! It seemed to
measure the very depth of the shame to which he had
descended.

The Severns came a few paces out of their indifference to
this self-imposed guest and gathered around the sheet of
newspaper while Laurie held an intensive conversation with
his family beginning with several servants who were too
excited at first to identify his voice.

But at last he hung up the receiver and turned toward
them:

"Well, I guess there's nothing for it but for me to pull out.
The mater doesn't think she'll be satisfied till she has her
hands on me. Besides, I've got to get things started about
those jewels. Dad and Mother are too excited to know what
they're about. I declare, it's like being dead and seeing how
they feel about it."

There was a boyish eager look about the young man's face
that made him for the first time seem rather lovable, Mrs.
Severn thought. The mother in her rose to appreciation.
Lynn was so glad that he was going away that she was almost
friendly during lunch. And when the young man was about to
depart he went to Mr. Severn's study and wrote a check for
five hundred dollars:

"Just in appreciation of your kindness," he said as he held
it out to the minister.

The minister looked amused but did not offer to take it:

"That's all right," he said pleasantly, "we don't keep boarders you know. You were welcome to what we could give you."

"But, my dear sir, I couldn't think of not remunerating
you," declared Laurie.

"And I couldn't think of taking it," smiled the minister.

"Well, then take it for your poor people," he insisted.

"From what Lynn tells me you have more of those than we
have," answered the minister.

The young man looked annoyed:

"Well, then take it for something for your church, another
bell or something, anything you're interested in."

"I can give you an address of a young missionary out West
who is having a hard time of it, and has a very needy parish,"
said the minister taking out his fountain pen and writing the
address on a card, "but I should prefer that you would send it

to him yourself. He wouldn't take it from me, but if you'd send it he'll write and tell you what he does with it, and he'll tell me too, so it will give pleasure all around. He's a game young chap, and he's given his life. You couldn't help but like him."

Laurie had to be content with this, though he felt annoyed at having to write a letter to a missionary. He felt he shouldn't know how to address him.

"I'll send it tonight when I get home," he declared, "or no, I'll send it now," and he sat down at the minister's desk, and scribbled a note. It read: "Your friend Severn won't take anything himself for kindness to me, so he's letting me send you this for your work. Here's wishing you good luck." This he signed and handed to the minister with a relieved air as if to say: "There! That's that!"

"You see," said Laurie getting up and taking his hat again, "I want to come back here again and see your daughter. I may as well tell you I'm crazy about your daughter."

"I see," said the minister gravely, albeit with a twinkle in his eye. "The fact is I'm somewhat crazy about her myself. But in all kindness I may as well tell you that you'll be wasting your time. She isn't your kind, you know."

"Oh, well," said Laurie with an assured shrug, "that's all right if I don't mind, isn't it?"

"Well, no," said the minister smiling broadly now, "you forget that she might mind, you know."

"I don't get you," said Laurie looking puzzled as he fitted on his immaculate driving glove. "She might mind, what do you mean?"

"I mean that my daughter minds very much indeed whether her men friends ask in a certain tone of voice for something to *drink* at midnight, and use language such as you used when you first arrived here, smoke continual cigarettes, and have friends like the young woman who visited you last Sunday."

"Oh, I see!" laughed Laurie thoroughly amused. "Well, after all, one doesn't have to keep on doing all those things, you know—if it were worth one's while to change them."

"I'm afraid," said the minister still amused, "that it would have to be worth your while to change before she would even consider you as a possibility. She happens to have a few ideas about what it takes to make a man, her ideal man, you know."

Laurie smiled gaily:

"Perhaps I can change those ideas."

"Help yourself, young man. You'll find it a task, I assure you."

"Well, I'm coming back anyway."

"We shall welcome you," said the minister politely, but not at all gladly, and Laurie departed without his usual complacency, assuring the minister that he had found Sabbath Valley the garden spot of the world and meant to return soon and often.

Billy watched him from the graveyard enclosure whither he had retired to write a letter, and he made a face and wasted a gesture of defiance after his departing car. So much Billy felt he had accomplished toward reparation. He was now attempting a third act.

On the smooth end of the old stone he had a newspaper spread, and upon that a sheet of letter paper which he had extracted from Aunt Saxon's ancient box in the old secretary in the corner of the kitchen. Kneeling beside the stone he carefully inscribed the following words:

Yoors to cummand,
    B. Gaston.

He folded the paper with his smudgy fingers, and stuffed it into a soiled envelope on which he wrote Mark's name, and as he had seen Lynn write down in the corner of a note that he had taken to Monopoly for her, "Kindness of Billy," so he wrote "Kindnus of Cheef." Then he mounted his wheel and rode to Economy. After some apparently aimless riding he brought up at the back of the chief's garage where he applied a canny eye to a crack and ascertained just how many and what cars were inside. He then rode straight to the bank where he was pretty sure the chief would be standing near the steps at this hour. Waiting a time of leisure he handed him the envelope:

"Say, Chief, c'n I trouble you to d'liver that?"

The chief looked at the envelope and then at Billy and opened his lips to speak, but Billy forestalled him:

"I know you don't know where he is at all now, Chief, o'course, but I just thought you might happen to meet up with him sometime soon. That's all right, Chief. Thank ya." Billy ended with a knowing wink.

The chief turned the envelope over, noted that it was unsealed, grinned back and put it in his pocket. They had been good friends, these two, for several years, ever since Billy had been caught bearing the penalty for another boy's misdemeanor.

"That's all right, Billy," said the chief affably, "I won't forget it—if I see him! Seen anything more of those automobile thieves?"

"Nope," said Billy sadly, "but I gotta line on 'em. 'F I find anythin' more I'll callyaup!"

"Do!" said the chief cordially, and the interview was closed.

Billy bought some cakes at the bakery with ten cents he had earned running an errand from the grocery that morning, and departed on important business. He had definitely decided to give up his thirty pieces of silver. No more blood money for him. His world was upside down and all he loved were suffering, and all because he had been mercenary. The only way to put things right was to get rid of any gain that might accrue to himself. Then he would be in a position to do something. And Pat was his first object now. He meant to give back the money to Pat! He had thought it all out, and he meant to waste no time in getting things straight.

He went to the Economy Post Office and on the back of a circular that he found in the wastebasket he wrote another note:

Pat. This is blood money an' I can't kep it. I didunt no when I undertuk the job wot kind of a job it was. Thers only one way fur yoo to kep yur hid saf, an that is to tel the trooth abot wot hapuned. If yoo ar wiling to tel the trooth put a leter heer sayin so. If yoo dont I am havin' you watshed an you will los yoor job an likely be hanged. We are arumd so be keerful. This ain't yella. This is rite.

THE KID.

It was a long job and he was tired when it was finished, for his days at school had been full of so many other things

besides lessons that literary efforts were always strenuous for
him. When he had finished he went out and carried three
parcels for the meat market, receiving in return thirty cents,
which exactly made up the sum he had spent from his tainted
money. With this wrapped bunglingly in his note he proceeded
to ambush near Pleasant Valley. He had other fish to fry, but
not till dark. Meantime, if that underground telephone was
being used at other times in the day he wanted to know
it.

He placed the note and money obviously before the little
hidden telephone from which he had cleared the leaves and
rubbish that hid it, and then retired to cover where he
settled himself comfortably. He knew Pat would be busy till
the two evening trains had arrived; after that if he did not
come there would likely be no calls before morning again,
and he could go on his way. With a pleasant snack of sugar
cookies and cream puffs he lay back and closed his eyes, glad
of this brief respite from his life of care and perplexity. Of
course he couldn't get away from his thoughts, but what a
pleasant place this was, with the scent of sassafras and
wintergreen all around him, and the meadowlark high in the
air somewhere. There were bees in the wild honeysuckle not
far away. He could hear their lazy drone. It would be nice to
be a bee and fly, fly away from everything. Did bees care
about things? Did they have troubles, and love folks and lose
'em? When a bee died did the other bees care? Aw, gee!
Mark in—j— *No!* He wouldn't say it! Mark was in New York!
Yes, of course he was. I twould all come right someday. He
would catch those crooks and put 'em in jail—no, first he'd
use 'em to clear Mark. When he got done here he was going
up to watch the old house and find out about that noise, and
he'd see whether Link and Shorty would put anything more
over! Link and Shorty and Pat, and that sissy Shafton and
Sam, whoever Sam was! They were all his enemies! If Mark
were only here how they would go to that old haunted house
together and work this thing out. He ought to have told Mark
everything. Fool! Just to save his own hide! Just to keep Mark
from blaming him! Well, he was done saving himself or
getting ill-gotten gains. Him for honesty for the rest of his
life.

The bees droned on and the lark grew fainter and fainter.

Billy's eyes drooped closer shut, his long curling lashes lay on his freckled cheeks the way they lay sometimes when Aunt Saxon came to watch him. That adorable sweep of lash that all mothers of boys know, that air of dignity and innocence that makes you forget the day and its doings and undoings and think only, this is a man child, a wonderful creature of God, beloved and strong, a gift of heaven, a wonder in daytime, a creature to be afraid of sometimes, but weak in sleep, *adorable!*

Billy slept.

The afternoon train lumbered in with two freight cars behind, and a lot of crates and boxes to manipulate, but Billy slept. The five o'clock train slid in and the evening express with its toll of guests for the lake hotel who hustled off wearily, cheerily, and on to the little lake train that stood with an expectant insolent air like a necessary evil waiting for a tip. The two trains champed and puffed and finally scampered away, leaving echoes all along the valley, and a red stream of sun down the track behind them from a sky aflame in the west preparing for a brilliant sunset. The red fingers of the sun touched the freckles on Billy's cheek lightly as if to warn him that the time had come. The shutters slammed on at the little station. The agent climbed the hill to his shack among the pines. Pat came out the door and stood on the platform looking down the valley, waiting for the agent to get out of sight.

And Billy slept on!

Chapter 22

Three days later a pall hung over Sabbath Valley. The coroner's inquest had brought in a verdict of murder, and the day of the hearing had been set. Mark Carter was to be tried for murder—was *wanted* for murder as Elder Harricutt put it. It was out now and everybody knew it but Mrs. Carter, who

went serenely on her way getting her regular letters from
Mark postmarked New York and telling of little happenings
that were vague but pleasant and sounded so like Mark, so
comforting and sonlike. So strangely tender and comforting
and more in detail than Mark's letters had been wont to be.
She thought to herself that he was growing up at last. He
spoke of a time when he and she would have a nice home
together somewhere, some new place where he would get
into business and make a lot of money. Would she like that?
And once he told her he was afraid he hadn't been a very
good son to her, but sometime he would try to make it up to
her, and she cried over that letter for sheer joy. But all the
rest of the town knew that Mark was suspected of murder,
and most of them thought he had run away and nobody could
find him. The county papers hinted that there were to be
strange revelations when the time of the trial came, but
nothing definite seemed to come out from day to day more
than had been said at first, and there was a strange lack of any
mention of Mark in connection with it after the first day.

Lynn Severn went about the house quiet and white, her
face looking like an angel's prayer, one continual petition, but
she was sweet and patient, and ready to do anything for
anybody. Work seemed to be her only respite from the
gnawing horror of her thoughts. To know that the whole
village believed that Mark, her lifelong playmate, had been
guilty of a crime so heinous was so appalling that sometimes
she just stood at the window and laughed out into the
sunshine at the crazy idea of it. It simply could not be. Mark,
who had always been so gentle and tender for every living
thing, so chivalrous, so ready to help! To think of Mark killing
anyone! And yet, they might have needed killing. At least, of
course she didn't mean that, but there were circumstances
under which she could imagine almost anyone doing a deed—
well what was the use, there was no way to excuse or explain
a thing she didn't understand, and she could just do nothing
but not believe any of it until she knew. She would trust in
God, and yes, she would trust in Mark as she always had
done, at least until she had his own word that he was not
trustable. That haughty withdrawing of himself on Sunday
night and his "I am not worthy" meant nothing to her now
when it came trailing across her consciousness. It only seemed

one more proof of his tender conscience, his care for her reputation. He had known then what they were saying about him, he must have known the day before that there was something that put him in a position so that he felt it was not good for her reputation to be his friend. He had withdrawn to protect her. That was the way she explained it to her heart, while yet beneath it all was the deep down hurt that he had not trusted her, and let her be his friend in trouble as well as when all was well.

She had written him a little note, not too intimate, just as a sister might have written, expressing her deep trust, and her sincere desire to stand by and help in any time of need. In it she begged him to think her worthy of sharing his trouble as she used to share his happiness, and to know always that she was his friend whatever came. She had read it over and over to be sure she was not overstepping her womanly right to say these things, and had prayed about it a great deal. But when it came to sending it she did not know his New York address. He had been strangely silent during the last few months and had not written her. She did not want to ask his mother. So she planned to find it out through Billy. But Billy did not come. It had been two days since Billy had been around, or was it three? She was standing at the window looking down the road toward the Saxon cottage and wondered if she wanted to go down and hunt for Billy when she saw Miss Saxon coming up the street and turning in at the gate, and her face looked wan and crumpled like an old rose that had been crushed and left on the parlor floor all night.

She turned from the window and hurried down:

"Miss Marilyn," Aunt Saxon greeted her with a gush of tears, "I don't know what to do. Billy's away! He hasn't been home for three days and three nights! His bed ain't been touched. He never did that before except that last time when he stayed out to help Mark Carter that time on the mountain with that sick man, and I can't think what's the matter. I went to Miz Carter's, but she ain't seen him, and she says Mark's up to his business in New York, so Billy can't be with him, and I just know he's kilt, Miss Marilyn. I just know he's kilt. I dreamt of a shroud night before last and I can't help thinkin' he's *kilt!*" and the tears poured down the tired little face pitifully.

Marilyn drew her tenderly into the house and made her sit down by the cool window, brought a palm leaf fan and a footstool, and told Naomi to make some iced orangeade. Then she called her mother and went and sat down by the poor little creature who now that somebody else was going to do something about it had subsided into her chair with relief born of exhaustion. She had not slept for three nights and two of those days she had washed all day.

"Now, Miss Saxon, dear, you're not to worry," said the girl taking the fan, and waving it gently back and forth, touching the work-worn hand tenderly with her other hand. "Billy is not dead, I'm sure! Oh, I'm quite sure! I think somehow it would be hard to kill Billy. He has ways of keeping alive that most of us don't enjoy. He is strong and young and sharp as a needle. No one can put anything over on Billy, and I have somehow a feeling, Miss Saxon, that Billy is off somewhere doing something very important for somebody. He is that way, you know. He does nice unusual things that nobody else would think of doing, and I just expect you'll find out someday that Billy has been doing one of those. There's that man on the mountain, for instance. He might be still very sick, and it would be just like Billy to stay and see to him. Maybe there isn't anybody else around to do it, and now that Mark has gone he would feel responsible about it. Of course he ought to have told you before he went, but he wouldn't likely have expected to stay long, and then boys don't think. They don't realize how hard it is not to understand!"

"Thas'so, Miss Marilyn," sniffed Miss Saxon. "He don't hardly ever think. But he mighta phomed."

"Well, it isn't likely they have phones on the mountain, and you haven't any, have you? How could he?"

"He mighta phomed to you."

"Yes, he might, but you know how boys are, he wouldn't want to bother anybody. And if the man was in a lonely cabin somewhere he couldn't get to a phone."

"Thas'so too. Oh, Miss Marilyn, you always do think up comfort. You're just like your ma and pa. But Billy, he's been so kinda peaked lately, so sorta gentle, and then again sorta crazy like, just like his mother useta be 'fore her husband left her. I couldn't help worryin'."

"Well, now Miss Saxon, I'll inquire around all I can without rousing any suspicion. You know Billy would hate that."

"Oh, I know he would," flushed the little woman nervously.

"So I'll just ask the boys if they know where he is and where they saw him last, and don't you worry. I'll tell them I have a message for him, you know, and you just stop crying and rest easy and don't tell a soul yet till I look around. Here comes Mother. She'll help you better than I can."

Mrs. Severn in a cool white dimity came quietly into the room, bringing a restful calm with her, and while Lynn was out on her errand of mercy she slipped a strong arm around the other woman's waist and had her down on her knees in the alcove behind the curtains, and had committed the whole matter to a loving heavenly Father—Billy, and the tired little Aunt, and all the little details of life that harrow so on a burdened soul—and somehow when they rose the day was cooler, and life looked more possible to poor Aunt Saxon.

Presently came Lynn, brightly. She had seen the boys. They had met Billy in Economy day before yesterday. He had said he had a job, he didn't know how long it would last, and he might not be able to come to baseball practice. He told them who to put in his place till he got back.

"There, now, Miss Saxon, you go home and lie down and take a good sleep. You've put this whole thing in the hands of the Lord, now don't take it out again. Just trust Him. Billy'll come back safe and sound, and there'll be some good reason for it," said Mrs. Severn. And Aunt Saxon, smiling wistfully, shyly apologetic for her foolishness, greatly cheered and comforted, went. But Lynn went up to her little white room and prayed earnestly, adding Billy to her prayer for Mark. Where was Billy Gaston?

When Miss Saxon went home she found a letter in the letter box out by the gate addressed to Billy. This set her heart to palpitating again and she almost lost her faith in prayer and took to her own worries once more. But she carried the letter in and held it up to the window, trying her best to make out anything written therein. She justified this to her conscience by saying that it might give a clue to Billy's whereabouts. Billy never got letters. Maybe, it might be from his long lost father, though they had all reason to believe him dead. Or maybe—Oh, what if Albert Gaston had come back and kidnapped Billy! The thought was too awful. She dropped right down in the kitchen where she stood by the old patchwork rocking chair that always stood handy in the window when she wanted to peel potatoes, and prayed: "Oh, God, don't let it be! Don't bring that bad man back to this world again! Take care of my Billy and bring him back to me, Amen!" Over and over again she prayed, and it seemed to comfort her. Then she rose, and put the teakettle on and carefully steamed open the letter. She had not lost all hope when she took time to steam it open in place of tearing it, for she was still worse afraid that Billy might return and scold her for meddling with his precious letter, than she was afraid he would not return. While the steam was gathering she tried to justify herself in Billy's eyes for opening it at all. After her prayer it seemed a sort of desecration. So the kettle had almost boiled away before she mustered courage to hold the envelope over the steam, and while she did this she noticed for the first time significantly that the postmark was New York. Perhaps it was from Mark. Then Billy was not with Mark! But perhaps the letter would tell.

So she opened the flap very carefully, and pulled out the single sheet of paper, stepping nearer the window to read it in the late afternoon light. It read: "Dear Kid, shut your mouth and saw wood. Buddy." That was all.

Aunt Saxon lifted frightened eyes and stared at the lilac bush outside the window, the waterspout where Billy often shinned up and down, the old apple tree that he would climb before he was large enough to be trusted, and then she read the letter again. But it meant nothing to her. It seemed a horrible riddle. She took a pencil and a scrap of paper and quickly transcribed the mysterious words, omitting not even the punctuation, and then hurriedly returned the letter to its envelope, clapped the flap down and held it tight. When it was dry she put the letter up in plain sight on the top of the old secretary where Billy could find it at once when he came in. She was taking no chances on Billy finding her opening his mail. It never had happened before, because Billy never had had a letter before, except notices about baseball and athletic association, but she meant it never should happen. She knew instinctively that if it ever did she would lose Billy, if not immediately, then surely eventually, for Billy resented above all things interference. Then Aunt Saxon sat down to study the transcription. But after a long and thorough perusal she folded it carefully and pinned it in her bosom. But she went more cheerily down to the market to get something for supper. Billy might come any time now. His letter was here, and he would surely come home to get his letter.

Down at the store she met Marilyn, who told her she looked better already, and the poor soul, never able to hold her tongue, had to tell the girl about the letter.

"He's had a letter," she said brightening, "about a job I guess. It was there when I got back. It's sawing wood. The letter doesn't have any head. It just says about sawing wood. I s'pose that's where he is, but he ought to have let me know. He was afraid I'd make a fuss about it, I always do. I'm afraid of those big saws they use. He's so careless. But he was set on a grown-up job. I couldn't get him to paste labels on cans at the factory, he said it was too much of a kid game."

"Oh," said Marilyn, wondering. "Sawing wood. Well, that's where he is of course, and it's good healthy work. I wouldn't worry. Billy is pretty careful, I think. He'll take care of himself."

But to herself on the way home she said: "How queer for Billy to go off sawing wood just now! It doesn't seem like him. They can't be so hard up. There must be something behind it all. I hope I didn't start anything asking him to stick by Mark! Oh, *where* is Mark?"

That afternoon Marilyn took a horseback ride, and touched all the points she knew where there might be likely to be woodsawing going on, but no Billy was on the job anywhere.

As she rode home through Economy she saw Mrs. Fenner scuttling down a side street from the jail, and hurrying into her own side gate like a little frightened lizard.

Marilyn came back home heartsick and sad, and took refuge in the church and her bells. At least she could call to Billy across the hills somewhere by playing the songs he loved the best. And perhaps their echoes would somehow cross the miles to Mark too, by that strange mysterious power that spirit can reach to spirit across space or years or even estrangement, and draw the thoughts irresistibly. So she sat at the organ and played her heart out, ringing all the old sweet songs that Mark used to love when the bells first were

new and she was learning to play them; "Highland Laddie,"
"Bonnie Bonnie Warld," "Mavourneen," "Kentucky Home,"
songs that she had kept fresh in her heart and sometimes
played for Billy now and then. And then the old hymns. Did
they echo far enough to reach him where he had gone, Mark
sitting alone in his inferno? Billy holding his breath and
trying to find a way out of his? Did they hear those bells
calling?

> O God, our help in ages past,
>   Our hope for years to come!
> Our refuge from the stormy blast,
>   And our eternal home!

The soul of the girl in the little dusky church went up in a
prayer with the bells.

> Before the hills in order stood,
>   Or earth received her frame,
> From everlasting Thou art God!
>   A thousand years the same!

Every mortal in the village knew the words, and in kitchens now, preparing savory suppers, or down in the mills and
factories, or out on the street coming home, they were
humming them, or repeating them over in their hearts. The
bells did not ring the melody alone. The message was well
known and came to every heart. Mark and Billy knew them
too. Perhaps by telepathy the tune would travel to their
minds and bring their words along:

> Under the shadow of Thy wings
>   Thy saints have dwelt secure,
> Sufficient is Thine arm alone,
>   And Thy defense is sure!

The bells ceased ringing and the vibration slowly died
away, hill answering to hill, in waves of softly fading sound,
while the people went to their suppers with a light of blessing
and uplift on their faces. But in the darkened church, Marilyn,
with her fingers on the keys and her face down upon her

hands was praying, praying that God would shelter Mark and
Billy.

Chapter 23

High in the tree over Billy's head a little chipmunk whisked
with a nut in his mouth. He selected a comfortable rocking
branch, unfurled his tail for a wind shield at his back, and sat
up to his supper table as it were with the nut in his two
hands. Something unusual caught his attention as he was
about to attack the nutshell, and he cocked his little striped
head around, up, and down, and took in Billy. Then a
squirrel smile overspread his furry face and a twinkle seemed
to come in his eye. With a wink down toward Billy he went to
work. Crack, crack, crack! The shell was open. Crack! And a
large section fell, whirling spinning down, straight down. The
squirrel paused in his nibbling and cocked an eye again with
that mischievous twinkle as if he enjoyed the joke, watching
the light bit of shell in its swift descent, plump on the end of
Billy's nose. It couldn't have hit straighter if Chippie had
been pitcher for the Sabbath Valley baseball team.

Billy opened his eyes with a start and a scowl, and there
before him, glaring like a wild beast, thick lips agape showing
gnarled yellow teeth, wicked eyes, red glittering and murder-
ous, was Pat, ugly, formidable, and threatening!

"Come outta there you little varmint you!" roared Pat.
"Come out and I'll skin the nasty yella hide off'n ya. I gotcha
good and hard now right where I wantcha an' ye won't—"

Bang! Click! BANG!

Billy had been lying among the thick undergrowth, flat on
his back, his left arm flung above his head, but his right arm
was thrust out from his body under a thick clump of laurel,
and his right hand held the gun ready for any emergency
when he inadvertently went to sleep. The gun was pointed

down the valley along the ground and his fingers wrapped
knowingly, lovingly around the weapon. He had so long
wanted to own one of his own. That gun was not included in
the blood money and was not to be returned. It was a
perquisite of war.

Billy was all there always, and even awakening suddenly
from much needed sleep he was on the job. One glance at
Pat's devilish face and his fingers automatically pulled the
trigger. The report roared out along the valley like a volley
from a regiment.

Billy hardly felt the rebound of the weapon before he
realized that Patrick was no more between his vision and the
sun's last rays. Patrick was legging it down the valley with all
the strength he had left, and taking no time to look back.
Billy had presence of mind to let off another volley before he
rose to investigate; but there was nothing left of Pat but a
ruffled path in the undergrowth and a waving branch or two
he had turned aside in his going. So that was that! Doggone
it, why did he have to go to sleep? If he had only been ready
he could have managed this affair so much better for his own
ends. He wanted a heart-to-heart talk with Pat while he had
him good and frightened, and now it was too late. He must
get back to the other job. He shinned up a tree and observed
the broad shoulders of Pat wallowing up the bank over by the
railroad. He was going back to the station. It was as well. He
might see him again tomorrow perhaps, for Pat he must have
as evidence. And besides, Pat might read the note and
conclude to come back and answer it.

Billy parted the bushes to see if Pat had taken the money
and note with him, and lo, here was the rude mountain
telephone box wide open with the bunch of keys in the lock
just as Pat must have left it when he discovered the paper
and money, or perhaps Pat had been going to report to Sam
what had happened, who knew? You see Billy knew nothing
of his little red and brown striped partner up in the tree who
had dropped a nut to warn him of danger, and did not realize
that Chippie had also startled Pat, and set him looking among
the bushes for the sources of the sound.

But Billy knew how to take advantage of a situation if he
didn't know what made it, and in a trice he was down on his
knees with the crude receiver in his hands. It was too late to

ride down to the Blue Duck and telephone, but here was a telephone come to him, and now was a chance to try if it was a telephone at all, or only a private wire run secretly. He waited breathless with the long hum of wires in his ears, and then a quick click and "Number please." Billy could hardly command his voice but he murmured "Economy thirteen" in a low growl, his hard young hands shaking with excitement. "Your letter please!" Billy looked wildly at the rough box but could see no sign of number. "Why, it's the station, doncha know? What's thamatterwithya?" His spirits were rising. "Jay" stated the operator patiently. "Well, jay then," said Billy, "WhaddoIcare?" "Just-a-minute-please," and suddenly the chief's voice boomed out reassuringly. Billy cast a furtive eye back of him in the dusk and fell to his business with relief.

"Say, Chief, that you? This's Bill! Say, Chief, I wantcha he'p right away pretty quick! Got a line on those guys! You bring three men an' ge'down on the Lone Valley Road below Stark Mountain an' keep yer eye peeled t'ward the hanted house. Savvy? Yes, old hanted house, you know. You wait there till I signal. Yes, flash! Listen, one wink if you go to right, two come up straight, and three to the left. If it's only one repeated several times, you spread all round. Yep. I'm goin' up there right now. No, Chief, I wouldn't call ye 'f I didn't think 'twas pretty sure. Yep! I think they'll come out soon's it gets real dark. Yep, I think they ben there all day. I ain't sure, but I think. You won't fail me, will you, Chief? No, sure! I'll stick by. Be sure to bring three men, there's two of 'em, I ain't rightly sure but three. I jus' stirred another up. Whatssay? No, I'm 'lone! Aw, I'm aw'right! Sure. I'll be careful. Whatssay? Where? Oh, I'm at a hole in the ground. Yes, down below Pleasant Valley station. Some telephone! I'll show it to you t'morra! S'long, Chief, I gotta go! It's gettin' dark, goobbye!"

Billy gave hurried glances about and rustled under the branches like a snake over to where old trusty lay. In ten minutes more he was worming his way up the side of Stark Mountain, while Pat was fortifying himself well within the little station, behind tables and desks for the night, and scanning the valley from the dusty windowpanes.

Billy parked his wheel in its usual place and continued up the hill to the opening at the back, then stood long listening. Once he thought he heard something drop inside the kitchen door, but no sound followed it and he concluded it had been a rat. Halfway between himself and the back door something gleamed faintly in the starlight. He didn't remember to have seen anything there before. He stole cautiously over, moving so slowly that he could not even hear himself. He paused beside the gleam and examined. It was an empty flask still redolent. Ummm! Booze! Billy wasn't surprised. Of course they would try to get something to while away their seclusion until they dared venture forth with their booty. He continued his cautious passage toward the house and then began to encircle it, keeping close to the wall and feeling his way along, for the moon would be late and small that night and he must work entirely by starlight. It was his intention after going around the house to enter and reconnoiter in his stocking feet. As he neared the front of the house he dropped both hands to his sweater pockets, the revolver in his right hand with its two precious cartridges, the flashlight which he had taken care to renew in Economy in his left hand, fingers ready to use either instantly. He turned the corner and stole on toward the front door, still noiseless as a mouse would go, his rubber sneakers touching like velvet in the grass.

He was only two feet from the front stoop when he became aware of danger, something, a familiar scent, a breathlessness, and then a sudden stir. A dark thing ahead and the feeling of something coming behind. Billy, as if a football signal had been given, grew calm and alert. Instantly both arms flashed up, and down the mountain shot two long yellow winks of light, and simultaneously two sharp reports of a gun, followed almost instantly by another shot, more sinister in sound, and Billy's right arm dropped limply by his side, while a sick wave of pain passed over him.

But he could not stop for that. He remembered the day when Mark had been coaching the football team and had told them that they must not stop for *anything* when they were in action. If they thought their legs were broken, or they were mortally wounded and dying, they must not even think of it. Football was the one thing, and they were to forget they were dead and go ahead with every whiff of punch there was in them, blind or lame, or dead even, because when they were playing, football was the only thing that counted. And if they were sick or wounded or bleeding let the wound or the

sickness take care of itself. *They* were *playing football!* So
Billy felt now.

He hurled himself viciously at the dark shadow ahead,
which he mentally registered as Link because he seemed
long to tackle, and then kicked behind at the thing that came
after, and struggled manfully with a throttling hand on his
throat till a wad of vile cloth was forced into his mouth—and
just as he had a half nelson on Shorty, too! If he could have
got Shorty down and stood on him he might have beaten off
Link until Chief got there. Where was Chief? Where was the
gun? Where was he? His head was swimming. Was it his
head he had hit against the wall, or did he bang Shorty's?
How it resounded! There were winding stairs in his head and
he seemed to be climbing them, up, up, up, till he dropped
in a heap on the floor, a hard floor all dust, and the dust came
into his nostrils. He was choking with that rag! Why couldn't
he pull it out? What was cutting his wrists when he tried to
raise his hand? And what was that queer pain in his shoulder?

There were shouts outside. How did he get inside? Was
that more shooting? Perhaps he had found his gun after all.
Perhaps he was shooting the men before the chief got there,
and that was bad, because he didn't feel competent to judge
about a thing as serious as shooting with that dirty rag in his
mouth. He must get rid of it somehow. Doggone it! He had
somehow got his hands all tangled up in cords, and he must
get them out no matter if they did cut. He had to give the
chief a signal.

He struggled again with all his might, and something
somewhere gave way. He wasn't sure what, but he seemed to
be sinking down, perhaps downstairs or down the mountain,
somehow so it was down where the chief—where Mark! The
light in his brain went out and he lay as one dead in the great
dusty front bedroom where a man who had sinned, hanged
himself once because he couldn't bear his conscience any
longer.

And outside in the front door yard five men struggled in
the dark, with curses, and shots, and twice one almost
escaped, for Link was desperate, having a record behind him
that would be enough for ten men to run away from.

But after the two were bound and secured in the car down
at the foot of the mountain, the chief lingered, and looking up

said in a low tone to one of his men: "I wonder where that boy is!"

"Oh, he's all right," said his assistant easily, "he's off on another piece of business by this time, Chief. He likes to seem mysterious. It's just his way. Say, Chief, we gotta get back if we wantta meet that train down at Unity t'night."

That was true too, and most important, so the chief with a worried glance toward the dark mountain turned his car and hurried his captives away. Now that they were where he could get a glance at them in the dim light of the car, he felt pretty sure they were a couple of "birds" he had been looking for for quite a while. If that was so he must reward Billy somehow. That boy was a little wonder. He would make a detective someday. It wouldn't be a bad idea to take him on in a quiet sort of way and train him. He might be a great help. He mustn't forget this night's work. And what was that the kid had said about a secret underground wire? He must look into it as soon as this murder trial was off the docket. That murder trial worried him. He didn't like the turn things were taking.

Chapter 24

In the gray of the morning Billy came to himself and stared around in the stuffy grimness everywhere. The gag was still in his mouth. He put up his hand involuntarily and pulled it out, and then remembered that his hands had been tied. Then he must have succeeded in breaking the cord! The other hand was still encumbered and his feet were tied together, but it happened that the well hand was the freed one, and so after a hard struggle he succeeded in getting out of the tangle of knots and upon his feet. He worked cautiously because he wasn't sure how much of what he remembered was dream and how much was reality. The two men might be in the house yet, very likely were, asleep somewhere. He must steal down and get away before they awoke.

There was something warm and sticky on the floor and it had got on his clothes, but he took no notice of it at first. He wondered what that sick pain in his shoulder was, but he had not time to stop and see now or even to think about it. He must call the chief before the men were awake. So he managed to get upon his feet and steady himself against the wall, for he felt dizzy and faint when he tried to walk. But he managed to get into the hall, and peer into each room, and more and more as he went he felt he was alone in the house. Then he had failed and the men were gone! Aw, gee! Pat too! What a fool he had been, thinking he could manage the affair! He ought to have taken the chief into his confidence and let him come along. Aw, gee!

Down in the kitchen he found a pail of water and a cup. He drank thirstily. His head felt hot and the veins in his neck throbbed. There seemed to be a lump on his forehead. He bathed his face and head. How good it felt! Then he found a whiskey bottle on the table half full. This after carefully smelling he poured over his bruised wrists, sopping it on his head and forehead, and finally pouring some down his shoulder that pained so, and all that he did was done blindly, like one in a dream; just an involuntary searching for means to go on and fulfill his purpose.

After another drink of water he seemed to be able to think more clearly. That tapping in the cellar yesterday! What had that been? He must look and see. Yes, that was really what he had come about. Perhaps the men were down there yet hidden away. He opened the cellar door and listened. Doggone it, where was that gun of his? But the flashlight! Yes, the flashlight!

He shot the light ahead of him as he went down, moving as in a dream, but keeping true to type, cautious, careful, stealthy. At last he was down. No one there! He turned the little flash into every nook and cranny, not excepting the ledges above the cellar wall whereon the floor beams rested. Once he came on a tin box long and flat and new looking. It seemed strange to meet it here. There was no dust upon it. He poked it down with his torch and it sprawled open at his feet. Papers, long folded papers printed with writing in

between, like bonds or deeds or something. He stooped and
waved the flash above them and caught the name Shafton in
one. It was an insurance paper, house and furniture. He felt
too stupid to quite understand, but it grew into his consciousness that these were the things he was looking for. He
gathered them up, stuffing them carefully inside his blouse.
They would be safe there. Then he turned to go upstairs, but
stumbled over a pile of coal out in the floor and fell. It gave
him a sick sensation to fall. It almost seemed that he couldn't
get up again, but now he had found the papers he must. He
crawled to his knees, and felt around, then turned his light
on. This was strange! A heap of coal out in the middle of the
floor, almost a foot from the rest! A rusty shovel lay beside it,
a chisel, and a big stone. Ah! The tapping! He got up
forgetting his pain and began to kick away the coal, turning
the flashlight down. Yes, there was a crack in the cement, a
loose piece. He could almost lift it with his foot. He pried at
it with the toe of his shoe, and then lifted it with much effort
out of the way. It was quite a big piece, more than a foot in
diameter! The ground was soft underneath as if it had been
recently worked over. He stooped and plunged the fingers of
his good hand in and felt around, laying the light on the floor
so it would shed a glare over the spot where he worked. He
could feel down several inches. There seemed to be something soft like cloth or leather. He pulled at it and finally
brought it up. A leather bag girt about with a thong of
leather. He picked the knot and turned the flash in. It sent
forth a million green lights. There seemed also to be a rope of
white glistening things that reminded him of Saxy's tears.
That brought a pang. Saxy would be crying! He must remember that and do something about it. He must have been away
a long time and perhaps those men would be coming back.
But it wouldn't do to leave these things here. They were the
Shafton jewels. What anybody wanted of a lot of shiny little
stones like that and a rope of tears! But then if they did they
did, and they were theirs and they oughtta have 'em. This
was the thing he had come to do. Get those jewels and
papers back! Make up as far as he could for what he had
done! And he must do it now quick before he got sick. He felt
he was getting sick and he mustn't think about it or he would
turn into Aunt Saxon. That was the queerest thing, back in

his mind he felt this *was* Aunt Saxon down here in the haunted cellar playing with green stones and ropes of tears, and he must hurry quick before she found him and told him he couldn't finish what he had to do.

He did the work thoroughly, feeling down in the hole again, but found nothing more. Then he stuffed the bag inside his blouse and buttoned up his sweater with his well hand and somehow got up the stairs. The arm pained him a lot, and he found his sweater was wet. So he took his handkerchief and tied it tight around the place that hurt the most, holding one end in his teeth to make the knot firm.

The sun blinded him as he stumbled down the back steps and went to get his wheel, but somehow he managed it, plunging through the brakes and tangles, and back to the road.

It ran in his brain where the Shaftons lived out in the country on the Jersey Shore. He had a mental picture in the back of his mind how to get there. He knew that when he struck the highroad there was nothing to do but keep straight on till he crossed the state line and then he would find it somehow, although it was miles away. If he had been himself he would have known it was an impossible journey in his present condition, but he wasn't thinking of impossibilities. He had to do it, didn't he? He, Billy, had set out to make reparation for the confusion he had wrought in his small world, and he meant to do so, though all hell should rise against him. Hell! That was it. He could see the flames in hot little spots where the morning sun struck. He could hear the bells striking the hour in the world he used to know that was not for him anymore. He zigzagged along the road in a crazy way, and strange to say he met nobody he knew, for it was early. Ten minutes after he passed the crossroads Elder Harricutt went across the highway toward Economy to his day's work, and he would have loved to have seen Billy, and his rusty old wheel, staggering along in that crazy way and smelling of whiskey like a whole moonshiner, fairly reeking with whiskey as he joggled down the road, and a queer little tinkle now and then just inside his blouse as if he carried loaded dice. Oh, he would have loved to have caught Billy shooting crap!

But he was too late, and Billy swam on, the sun growing

hotter on his aching head, the light more blinding to his
bloodshot eyes, the lump bigger and bluer on his grimy
forehead.

About ten o'clock a car came by, slowed down, the driver
watching Billy, though Billy took no note of him. Billy was
looking on the ground dreaming he was searching for the
state line. He had a crazy notion it oughtta be there somewhere.

The man in the car stopped and called to him:

"How about putting your wheel in the backseat and letting
me give you a lift? You look pretty tired."

Billy lifted bleared eyes and stopped pedaling, almost
falling off his wheel, but recovering himself with a wrench of
pain and sliding off.

"Aw'right!" said Billy. "Thanks!"

"You look all in, son," said the man kindly.

"Yep," said Billy laconically, "'yam! Been up all night. Care
'f I sleep?"

"Help yourself," said the man, giving a lift with the wheel,
and putting it in behind.

Billy curled down in the backseat without further ceremony.

"Where are you going, son?"

Billy named the country seat of the Shaftons, having no
idea how far away it was. The man gave a whistle.

"What! On that wheel? Well, go to sleep, son. I'm going
there myself, so don't worry. I'll wake you up when you get
there."

So Billy slept through the first long journey he had taken
since he came to live with Aunt Saxon, slept profoundly with
an oblivion that almost amounted to coma. Sometimes the
man, looking back, was tempted to stop and see if the boy
was yet alive, but a light touch on the hot forehead showed
him that life was not extinct, and they whirled on.

Three hours later Billy was awakened by a sharp shake of
his sore shoulder and a stinging pain that shot through him
like fire. Fire! Fire! He was on fire! That was how he felt as
he opened his eyes and glared at the stranger.

"Aw, lookout there, whatterya doin'?" he blazed. "Whadda
ya think I am? A football? Don't touch me. I'll get out. This
the place? Thanks fer tha ride, I was all in. Say, d'ya know a
guy by the name of Shafton?"

"Shafton?" asked the man astonished. "Are you going to Shafton's?"

"Sure," said Billy, "anything wrong about that? Where does he hang out?" The look of Billy, and more than all the smell of him made it quite apparent to the casual observer that he had been drinking, and the man eyed him compassionately. Poor little fool! He's beginning young. What on earth does he want at Shafton's?

"I s'pose you've come down after the reward," grinned the man. "I could have saved you the trouble if you'd told me. The kidnapped son has got home. They are not in need of further information."

Billy gave him a superior leer with one eye closed:

"You may not know all there is to know about that," he said impudently. "Where did you say he lived?"

The man shrugged his shoulders indifferently.

"Suit yourself," he said, "I doubt if they'll see you. They have had nothing but a stream of vagrants for two days and they're about sick of it. They live on the next estate and the gateway is right around that corner."

"I ain't no vagrant," glared Billy, and limped away with old trusty under his left arm.

No one molested him as he walked in the arched and ivied gateway, for the gatekeeper was off on a little private errand of his own at a place where prohibition had not yet penetrated. Billy felt too heavy and dizzy to mount his wheel, but he leaned on the saddle as he walked and tried to get things straight in his head. He oughtn't to have gone to sleep, that's what he oughtn't. But this job would soon be over and then he would hike it for home. Gee! Wouldn't home feel good! And Aunt Saxon would bathe his head with witch hazel and make cold things for him to drink! Aw, gee!

The pedigreed dogs of which the place boasted a number came suddenly down upon him in a great flare of noise, but dogs were always his friends, why should he worry? A pity he couldn't stop to make friends with them just now. Some dogs! Here, pup! Gee! What a dog to own! The dogs whined and fawned upon him. Pedigree or no pedigree, rags and whiskey and dirt notwithstanding, they knew a man when they saw one, and Billy hadn't batted an eyelid when they tried their worst tramp barks on him. They wagged their silky tails and tumbled over each other to get first place to him, and so escorted proudly he dropped old trusty by a clump of imported rhododendrons and limped up the marble steps to the wide vistas of circular piazzas that stretched to seemingly infinite distances, and wondered if he should ever find the front door.

An imposing butler appeared with a silver tray, and stood aghast.

"Shafton live here?" inquired Billy trying to look business-like. "Like to see him er the missus a minute," he added as the frowning vision bowed. The butler politely but firmly told him that the master and mistress had other business and no desire to see him. The young gentleman had come home, and the reward had been withdrawn. If it was about the reward he had come he could go down to the village and find the detective. The house people didn't want to interview any more callers.

"Well, say," said Billy disgusted, "after I've come all this way too! You go tell 'er I've brought her jewels! You go tell 'er I've *gottum here!*"

The butler opened the door a little wider: he suggested that seeing was believing.

"Not on yer tintype!" snapped Billy. "I show 'em to nobody an' I give 'em to nobody but the owner! Where's the young fella? He knows me. Tell 'im I brang his ma's string o' beads an' things."

Billy was weary. His head was spinning round. His temper was rising.

"Aw, you make me tired! Get out of my way!" He lowered his head and made a football dive with his head in the region of the dignified butler's stomach, and before that dignitary had recovered his poise Billy with two collies joyously escorting him, stood blinking in wonder over the great beautiful living room, for all the world as pretty as the church at home, only stranger, with things around that he couldn't make out the use of.

"Where'ur they at? Where are the folks?" he shouted back to the butler who was coming after him with menace in his eye.

"What is the matter, Morris? What is all this noise about?" came a lady's voice in pettish tones from up above somewhere. "Didn't I tell you that I wouldn't see another one of those dreadful people today?"

Billy located her smooth old childish face at once and strode to the foot of the stairs peering up at the lady, white with pain from his contact with the butler, but alert now to the task before him:

"Say, Miz Shaf't'n, I got yer jools, would ya mind takin' 'em right now? 'Cause I'm all in an' I wantta get home."

His head was going around now like a merry-go-round, but he steadied himself by the bannister.

"Why, what do you mean?" asked the lady descending a step or two, a vison of marcelled white hair, violet and lace negligee, and well preserved features. "You've got them *here*? Let me see them."

"He's been drinking, Sarah, can't you smell it?" said a man's voice higher up, "Come away and let Morris deal with him. Really, Sarah, we'll have to go away if this keeps up."

"Say, you guy up there, just shut yer trap a minute won't a! Here, Miz Shaf't'n, are these here yours?"

Billy struggled with the neck of his blouse and brought forth the leather bag, gripped the knot fiercely in his teeth, an his fingers in the bag as he held it in his mouth, his lamed rm hanging at his side, and drew forth the magnificent pearls.

"William! My pearls!" shrieked the lady.

The gentleman came down incredulous, and looked over her shoulder.

"I believe they are, Sarah," he said.

Billy leered feverishly up at him, and produced a sheaf of papers, seemingly burrowing somewhere in his internal regions to bring them forth.

"And here, d'these b'long?"

The master of the house gripped them.

"Sarah! The bonds! And the South American shares!" They were too busy to notice Billy who stood swaying by the newel post, his duty done now, the dogs grouped about him.

"Say, c'n I get me a drink?" he asked of the butler, who hovered near uncertain what to be doing now that the tide was turned:

The lady looked up.

"Morris!"

He scarcely heard the lady's words but almost immediately
a tall slim glass of frosty drink, that smelled of wild grapes,
tasted of oranges, and cooled him down to the soul again, was
put into his hand and he gulped it greedily.

"Where did you say you found these, young man?" The
gentleman eyed him sternly, and Billy's old spirit flamed up:

"I didn't say," said Billy.

"But you know we've got to have all the evidence before
we can give the reward!"

"Aw, cut it out! I don't want no reward. Wouldn't take it if
you give it to me! I just wanta get home. Say, you gotta
telephone?"

"Why certainly." This was the most astonishing burglar!

"Well, where is't? Lemme call long distance on it? I ain't
got the tin now, but I'll pay ya when I git back home!"

"Why, the idea! Take him to the telephone, Morris. Right
there! This one—"

But Billy had sighted one on a mahogany desk near at hand
and he toppled to the edge of the chair that stood before it.
He took down the receiver in a shaky hand, calling long
distance.

"This Long Distance? Well, gimme Economy thirteen."

The Shaftons for the instant were busy looking over the
papers, identifying each jewel, wondering if any were missing. They did not notice Billy till a gruff young voice rang out
with a pathetic tremble in it: "That you, Chief? This is Billy.
Say, c'n I bother you to phone to Miss Severn an' ast her to
tell m'yant I'm aw'right? Yes, tell her I'll be home soon now
an' I'll explain. And, Chief, I'm mighty sorry those two guys
got away, but I couldn't help it. We'll get 'em yet. Hope you
didn't wait long. Tell you more when I see ya. S'long—"

The boyish voice trailed off into silence as the receiver fell
with a crash to the polished desk, and Billy slipped off the
chair and lay in a huddled heap on the costly rug.

"Oh, mercy!" cried the lady. "Is he drunk or what?"

"Come away, Sarah, let Morris deal—"

"But he's sick, I believe, William. Look how white he is. I
believe he is dead! William, he may have come a long way in
the heat! He may have had a sunstroke! Morris, send for a
doctor quick! And—call the ambulance too! You better telephone the hospital. We can't have him here! William, look

here, what's this on his sleeve? Blood? Oh, *William!* And we didn't give him any reward!"

And so, while the days hastened on Billy lay between clean white sheets on a bed of pain in a private ward of a wonderful memorial hospital put up by the Shaftons in honor of a child that died. Tossing and moaning, and dreaming of unquenchable fire, always trying to climb out of the hot crater that held him, and never getting quite to the top, always knowing there was something he must do, yet never quite finding out what it was. And back in Sabbath Valley Aunt Saxon prayed and cried and waited and took heart of cheer from the message the chief had sent to Lynn. And quietly the day approached for the trial of Mark Carter, but his mother did not yet know.

Chapter 25

Mrs. Gibson, the wife of the comparatively new elder of the Sabbath Valley church, was a semi-invalid. That is she wasn't able to do her own work and kept "help." The help was a lady of ample proportions whose husband had died and whose fortunes were depleted. She consented to assist Mrs. Gibson provided she were considered one of the family, and she presented a continual front of offense so that the favored family must walk most circumspectly if they would not have her retire to her room with hurt feelings and leave them to shift for themselves.

On the morning of the trial she settled herself at her side of the breakfast table, after a number of excursions to the kitchen for things she had forgotten, the cream, the coffee, and the brown bread, of which Mr. Gibson was very fond. She was prepared to enjoy her own breakfast. Mr. Gibson generally managed to bolt his while these excursions of memory were being carried on and escape the morning news, but Mrs. Gibson, well knowing which side her bread was buttered, and not knowing where she could get another housekeeper, usually managed to sit it out.

"Well, this is a great day for Sabbath Valley," said Mrs. Frost mournfully, spreading an ample slice of bread deep with butter, and balancing it on the uplifted fingers of one hand while she stirred the remainder of the cream into her coffee with one of the best silver spoons. She was wide and bulgy and her chair always seemed inadequate when she settled thus for nourishment.

"A great day," she repeated sadly, taking an audible sip of her coffee.

"A great day?" repeated little Mrs. Gibson with a puzzled air, quickly recalling her abstracted thoughts.

"Yes. Nobody ever thought anybody in Sabbath Valley would ever be tried for murder!"

"Oh!" said Mrs. Gibson sharply, drawing back her chair as if she were in a hurry and rolling up her napkin quickly.

"Yes, poor Mark Carter! I remember his sweet little face and his long yellow curls and his baby smile as if it were yesterday!" narrowing her eyes and harrowing her voice, "I wonder if his poor mother knows yet."

"I should hope not!" said Mrs. Gibson rising precipitately and wandering over to the window where hung a gilded canary cage. "Mrs. Frost, did you remember to give the canary some seed and fresh water?"

"Yes, I b'lieve so," responded the fat lady, "but you can't keep her from knowing it always. What'll you do when he's *hung?* Don't you think it would be easier for her to get used to it little by little?"

"Mrs. Frost, if you were a dog would you rather have your tail cut off all at once, or little by little?" said Mrs. Gibson mischievously.

"I shouldn't like to have it cut off at all I'm quite sure," said Mrs. Frost frostily.

"Well, perhaps Mrs. Carter might feel that way too," said the lady bending over a rose geranium and pinching a leaf to smell.

"I don't understand you," said Mrs. Frost from her coffee cup. "Oh, you mean that perhaps Mark may not be convicted? Why, my dear lady, there isn't a chance at all, not a chance in the world for Mark, and while I'm real sorry I can't say I'd approve. Think of how he's carried on, going with that little huzzy of a Cherry. Mrs. Harricutt says she saw him have her out riding in his automobile one day!"

"Oh, *Mrs. Harricutt!*" said Mrs. Gibson impatiently. "Mrs. Frost, let's find something pleasanter to talk about. It's a wonderful morning. The air's like wine. I wonder if I couldn't take a little walk. I mean to ask the doctor."

"My dear woman," said Frost patronizingly, "you can't get away from the unpleasant things in this world by just not talking about them!"

"It seems not," said the Gibson lady patiently, and wandered out on the porch.

Down the street Marilyn lingered by her mother's chair:

"Are you—going to Economy today, Mother?"

"Yes, dear, your father and I are both going. Did you—think you ought—wanted to—go, dear?"

"Oh, I should *hate it!*" cried Lynn flinging out her hands with a terrible little gesture of despair, "but I wanted to go just to stand by Mark. I shall be there anyway, wherever I am. I shall see everything and feel everything in my heart I know. But in the night it came to me that someone ought to stay with Mrs. Carter!"

"Yes, dear! I had hoped you would think of that. I didn't want to mention it because I wanted you to follow your own heart's leading, but I think she needs you. If you could keep her from finding out until it was over—"

"But suppose—"

"Yes, dear, it is possible. I've thought of that, and if it comes there will be a way I'm sure, but until it does—*then* suppose—"

"Yes, Mother, I'll go and make her have one happy day first anyway. If any of those old vultures come around I'll play the piano or scream all the while they are there and keep them from telling her a thing!"

"I think, dear, the old vultures will all be in Economy today."

"All except Mrs. Frost, Mother dear. She can't get away. But she can always run across the street to borrow a cup of soda."

So Lynn knelt for a moment in her quiet room, then came

down, kissed her mother and father with a face of brave
serenity, and went down the maple-shaded street with her
silk workbag in her hand. And none too soon. As she tapped
at the door of the Carter house she saw Mrs. Frost ambling
purposefully out of the Gibson gate with a teacup in her
hand.

"Oh, hurry upstairs and stay there a minute till I get rid of
Mrs. Frost," Lynn whispered smiling as her hostess let her
in. "I've come to spend the day with you, and she'll stay till
she's told you all the news and there won't be any left for
me."

Mrs. Carter, greatly delighted with Lynn's company, hurried obediently up the stairs and Lynn met the interloper,
supplied her with the cup of salt she had come for this time,
said Mrs. Carter was upstairs making the beds and she
wouldn't bother her to come down—*beds*, mind you, as if
Mark was at home of course—and Mrs. Frost went back
across the street puzzled and baffled and resolved to come
back later for an egg after that forward young daughter of the
minister was gone.

Lynn locked the front door and ran upstairs. She tolled her
hostess up to the attic to show her some ancient gowns and
poke bonnets that she hadn't seen since she was a little girl in
which she and Mark used to dress up and play history stories.

Half the morning she kept her up there looking at garments long folded away, whose wearers had slept in the
church yard many years; trinkets of other days, quaint old
pictures, photographs and daguerreotypes, and a beautiful
curl of Mark's:

"Marilyn, I'm going to give that to you," the mother said as
she saw the shining thing lying in the girl's hand. "There's no
one living to care for it after I'm gone, and you will keep it I
know till you're sure there's no one would want it I—mean—"

"I understand what you mean," said Marilyn, "I will keep
it and love it—for you—and for him. And if there is ever
anybody else that—deserves it—why I'll give it to them!"
Then they both laughed to hide the tears behind the unspo-
ken thoughts, and the mother added a little stubbed shoe and
a sheer muslin cap, all delicate embroidery and hemstitching:

"They go together," she said simply, and Lynn wrapped
them all carefully in a bit of tissue paper and laid them in her

silk bag. As she turned away she held it close to her heart while the mother closed the shutters. She shuddered to think of the place where Mark was sitting now, being tried for his life. Her heart flew over the road, entered the court, and stood close by his side, with her hand on his shoulder, and then slipped it in his. She wondered if he knew that she was praying, praying, praying for him and standing by him, taking the burden of what would have been his mother's grief if she had known, as well as the heavy burden of her own sorrow.

The air of the courtroom was heavy for the place was crowded. Almost everybody from Sabbath Valley that could come was there, for a great many people loved Mark Carter, and this seemed a time when somehow they must stand by him. People came that liked him and some that did not like him, but more that liked him and kept hoping against hope that he would not be indicted.

The hum of voices suddenly ceased as the prisoner was led in and a breath of awe passed over the place. For until that minute no one was quite sure that Mark Carter would appear. It had been rumored again and again that he had run away. Yet here he was, walking tall and straight, his fine head held high as had been his wont. "For all the world like he walked when he was usher at Mary Anne's wedding," whispered Mrs. Hulse, from Unity.

The minister and his wife kept their eyes down after the first glimpse of the white face. It seemed a desecration to look at a face that had suffered as that one had. Yet the expression upon it now was more as if it had been set for a certain purpose for this day, and did not mean to change whatever came. A hopeless, sad, persistent look, yet strong withal and with a hint of something fine and high behind it.

He did not look around as he sat down, merely nodded to a few close to him whom he recognized. A number pressed close as he passed, and touched him, as if they would impress upon him their loyalty, and it was noticeable that these were mostly of a humble class, workingmen, boys, and a few old women, people to whom he had been kind.

Mrs. Severn wrote a little note and sent it up to him, with the message, "Lynn is with your mother." Just that. No name signed. But his eyes sought hers at once and seemed to light, and soon, without any apparent movement on his part a card came back to her bearing the words: "I thank you." But he did not look that way again all day it seemed. His bearing was quiet, sad, aloof, one might almost have said disinterested.

Mark's lawyer was one whom he had picked out of the gutter and literally forced to stop drinking and get back on his job. He was a man of fine mind and deep gratitude, and was having a frantic time with his client, for Mark simply wouldn't talk:

"I wasn't there, I was on Stark Mountain, I am not guilty," he persisted, "and that is all I have to say."

"But, my dear friend, don't you realize that mere statements unadorned and uncorroborated won't get you anywhere in court?"

"All right, don't try to defend me then. Let the thing go as it will. That is all I have to say." And from this decision no one had been able to shake him. His lawyer was nearly crazy. He had raked the county for witnesses. He had dug into the annals of that night in every possible direction. He had unearthed things that it seemed no living being would have thought of, and yet he had not found the one thing of which he was in search, positive evidence that Mark Carter had been elsewhere and otherwise employed at the time of the shooting.

"Don't bother so much about it, Tony," said Mark once when they were talking it over, or the lawyer was talking it over and Mark was listening. "It doesn't matter. Nothing matters anymore!" and his voice was weary as if all hope had vanished from him.

Anthony Drew looked at him in despair:

"Sometimes I almost think you *want* to die," he said. "Do you think I shall let you go when you pulled me back from worse than death? No, Mark, old man, we're going to pull you through somehow, though I don't know how. If I were a praying man I'd say that this was the time to pray. Mark what's become of that kid you used to think so much of, that was always tagging after you? Billy—was that his name?"

A wan smile flitted across Mark's face, and a stiff little drawing of the old twinkle about eyes and lips:

"I think he'll turn up sometime."

The lawyer eyed him keenly:

"Mark, I believe you've got something up your sleeve.

believe that kid knows something and you won't let him tell. Where is he?"

"I don't know, Tony" and Mark looked at him straight with clear eyes, and the lawyer knew he was telling the truth.

Just at the last day Anthony Drew found out about the session meeting. But from Mark he got no further statement than the first one. Mark would not talk. An ordinary lawyer, one that had not been saved himself, would have given up the defense as hopeless. Anthony simply wouldn't let Mark go undefended. If there were no evidence he would make some somehow, and so he worked hoping against hope up to the very last minute. He stood now, tall, anxious, a fine face, though showing the marks of wreck behind him, dark hair silvered at the edges, fine deep lines about his eyes and brows, looking over the assembled throng with nervous hurrying eyes. At last he seemed to find what he wanted and came quickly down to where the minister sat in an obscure corner, whispering a few words with him. They went out together for a few minutes and when they came back the minister was grave and thoughtful. He himself had scoured the country round about quietly for Billy, and he was deeply puzzled. He had promised to tell what he knew.

The business of the day went forward in the usual way with all the red tape, the cool formalities, as if some trifling matter were at stake, and those who loved Mark sat with aching hearts and waited. The Severns in their corner sat for the most part with bended heads and praying hearts. The witnesses for the prosecution were most of them companions of the dead man, those who had drunk and caroused with him, frequenters of the Blue Duck, and they were herded together, an evil-looking crowd, but with erect heads and defiant attitude, the air of having donned unaccustomed garments of righteousness for the occasion, and making a great deal of it because for once everyone must see that they were in the right. They were fairly loudmouthed in their boasting about it.

There was the little old wizened up fellow that had been sitting with the drinks outside the booth the night Billy telephoned. There were the serving men who had waited on Mark and Cherry. There was the proprietor of the Blue Duck himself, who testified that Mark had often been there with Cherry, though always early in the evening. Once he had

caught him outside the window looking in at the dancers as
late as two o'clock at night, the same window from which the
shot was fired that brought Dolph to his death. They testified
that Mark had been seen with Cherry much of late driving in
his car, and that she had often been in deep converse as if
having a hot argument about something.

The feeling was tense in the courtroom. Tears were in
many eyes, hopeless tears in the eyes of those who had loved
the boy for years.

But the grilling order marched on, and witness after witness came, adding another and another little touch to the
gradually rising structure that would shut Mark Carter away
from the world that loved him and that he loved forever.

Cherry was called, a flaunting bit of a child with bobbed
golden hair and the air of a bold young seraph, her white face
bravely painted, her cherry lips cherrier even than the cherry
for which she had been named. She wore a silk coat reaching
to the bottom of her frock, which was shorter than the
shortest, and daring little high-heeled, many strapped shoes
with a myriad of bright buckles. Her hat was an insolent affair
of cherry red. She made a blinding bit of color in the dreary
courtroom. She appeared half frightened, half defiant. Her
sharp little face seemed to have lost its round curves and
childlike sweetness. She testified that she had been with
Mark on the night of the shooting, but that he had taken her
home early and she had seen no more of him that night. She
admitted that she had returned later to the Blue Duck Tavern
with Dolph and had danced late and eaten supper with him
afterwards, and that it was while they were eating that the
shot was fired and Dolph fell over on the table. No, she
didn't see any face at the window. She had covered her face
with her hands and screamed. She guessed she fainted.
Questioned further she admitted that she had had an argument with Mark earlier in the evening, but she didn't remember what it was about. They often argued. Yes, Dolph
was jealous of Mark and tried to stop her going with him. Yes,
Mark had tried to stop her going with Dolph too, but he
never acted jealous— On and on through the sorry little
details of Cherry's career. The courtroom vultures receiving it
avidly, the more refined part of the company with distaste
and disgust. Mark sat with stern white face looking straight at

Cherry all the time she was on the stand as if he dared her to say other than the truth. When she happened to look that way she gave a giggling little shudder and half turned her shoulder away, avoiding his eyes. But when she was done she had said nothing against Mark, and nothing to clear him either.

The sharp unscrupulous lawyer who acted for the prosecution had secured some fellows "of the baser sort" who testified that they had seen Mark Carter buying a gun, that they had seen him creep softly to the window, peer into the room, and take aim. They had been on their way home, had seen Mark steal along in a very suspicious manner and had followed him to find out what it meant. There were three of them, fellows whom Mark had refused to play against on a County team because they were what is called "dirty" players. There had been hot words between Mark and them once when one of them had kicked a man in the face with spiked shoes who was just about to make a goal. Mark had succeeded in winning the umpire to his point of view and the others had lost their game and incidentally some money, and they had a grudge against him. Moreover there was money in this testimony for the Blue Duck Tavern could not afford to have its habitues in the public eye, and preferred to place the blame on a man who belonged more to the conservative crowd. The Blue Duck had never quite approved of Mark, because though he came and went he never drank, and he sometimes prevented others from doing so. This was unprofitable to them. So matters stood when the noon hour came and court adjourned for lunch.

Chapter 26

And while the long morning dragged itself away in Economy listening to a tale of shame, over on the bright Jersey coast

the waves washed lazily on a silver strand reflecting the
blueness of the September sky, and soft breezes hovered
around the classic little hospital building that stood in a grove
of imported palms, and lifted its white columns picturesquely
like some old Greek temple.

There was nothing in the life he was living now to
remind Billy of either hell or Sabbath Valley, yet for long
days and weeks he had struggled through flames in a deep
dark pit lighted only by lurid glare and his soul had well
nigh gone out under the torture. Once the doctors and
nurses had stood around and waited for his last breath.
This was a marked case. The Shaftons were deeply interested
in it. The boy had mysteriously brought back all their
valuable papers and jewels that had been stolen from
them, and they were anxious to put him on his feet again.
It went sadly against the comfortable self-complacent grain
of a Shafton to feel himself under such mortal obligation
to anyone.

But Billy was tougher than anyone knew, and one night
after he had made the usual climb through the hot coals on
his bare knees to the top of the pit, and come to the place
where he always fell back, he held on a little tighter and set
his teeth a little harder, and suddenly, with a long hard pull
that took every atom of strength in his wasted young body, he
went over the top. Over the top and out into the clean open
country where he could feel the sea breeze on his hot
forehead and know that it was good. He was out of hell and
he was cooling off. The first step in the awful night that began
that night in the old haunted house on the mountain had
been won.

For three days he lay thus, cooling off and resting. He was
fed and cared for but he took no cognizance of it except to
smile weakly. Swallowing things was like breathing. You had
to do it and you didn't think about it. The fourth day he
began to know the nurses apart, and to realize he was feeling
better. As yet the past lay like a blur of pain on his mind, and
he hadn't a care about anything save just to lie and know that
it was good to smell the salt, and see the shimmer of blue
from the window. At times when he slept the sound of bells
in old hymns came to him like a dream and he smiled. But on
the fifth morning he lifted his light head uncertainly and

looked out of the window. Gee! That was pretty! And he
dropped back and slept again. When he awoke there was a
real meal for him. No more slops. Soup, and potato and bit of
bread and butter. Gee! It tasted good! He slept again and it
was morning, or was it the same morning? He didn't know.
He tried to figure back and decided he had been in that
hospital about three days, but when the next morning dawned
and he felt the life creeping back into his veins he began to
be uncertain. He asked the nurse how soon he could get up
and get dressed. She smiled in a superior way and said the
doctor hadn't said. It would likely be some time yet, he had
been pretty sick. He told her sharply he couldn't spare much
more time, and asked her where his clothes were.

She laughed and said:

"Oh, put away. You'll have some new clothes when you get
well. I heard Mrs. Shafton talking about it this morning when
she was in the office. She's coming to see you pretty soon,
and they mean to do a lot for you. You brought back her
jewels, didn't you? Well, I guess you'll get your reward all
right."

Billy looked at her blankly. Reward! Gosh! Was that reward
going to meet him again?

"Say," said he frowning, "I want my own clothes. I don't
want any new ones. I want my own! Say, I got some stuff in
my pockets I don't wantta have monkeyed with!"

"All right," she said cheerily, "they're put away safe. You
can have them when you're well." But when he asked her
suddenly what day it was she said vaguely, "Tuesday," and
went away. He was so tired then he went to sleep again and
slept till they brought his dinner, a big one, chicken and
fixings and jelly, and a dish of ice cream! Oh, gee! And then
he went to sleep again. But in the morning—how many days
was it then? He woke to sudden consciousness of what he had
to do and to sudden suspicion of the time. Billy was coming
back to his own. His wilyness had returned. He smiled at the
nurse ravishingly and asked for a newspaper, but when she
brought it he pretended to be asleep, so she laid it down and
went away softly. But he nabbed that paper with a weak hand
as soon as her back was turned and read the date! His heart
fell down with a dull thud. The third! This was the day of the
trial! It couldn't be! He read again. Was it really the day of

the trial? The paper that had the court program had been in his trousers pocket. He must have it at once. Perhaps he had made a mistake. Oh, gee! What it was to be helpless! Why, he was weaker than Aunt Saxon!

He called the nurse crossly. She bustled in and told him the doctor had just said he might sit up tomorrow if he kept on without a temperature for twenty-four hours longer. But he paid no heed to her. He demanded his clothes with a young roar of a voice that made her open her eyes. Billy had heretofore been the meekest of meek patients. She was getting the voice and manner now that he generally retained for family use. He told her there was something in the pocket he must see right away, and he made such a fuss about it that she was afraid he would bring up his temperature again and finally agreed to get the clothes if he would lie real still and rest afterward. Billy dropped his head back on the pillow and solemnly said: "Aw'right!" He had visions of going to court in blue and white striped pajamas. It could be done, but he didn't relish it. Still, if he had to—

The nurse brought his jacket and trousers. The sweater was awfully dirty she said, but she was finally prevailed upon to bring that too, and Billy obediently lay down with closed eyes and his arm stretched out comfortingly over the bundles. The nurse hovered round till he seemed to be asleep and then slipped out for a moment, and the instant her white skirt had vanished from the doorway Billy was alert. He fumbled the bundles open with nervous fingers and searched eagerly for the bit of paper. Yes, there it was and the date the third of September. Aw, gee!

He flung back the neatly tucked sheets, poked a slim white foot that didn't look like his at all into a trouser leg, paused for breath and dove the other in, struggled into his jacket and lay down again quickly under the sheet. Was that the nurse?

He had to admit that he felt queer, but it would soon pass off, and anyhow if it killed him he had to go. Aw, bah! What was a little sickness anyhow? If he stayed in the hospital any longer they'd make a baby out of him!

The nurse had not returned. He could hear the soft plunk, plunk of her rubber heels on the marble steps. She was going downstairs. Now was his time! Of course he had no shoes and stockings, but what was a little thing like that? He grasped the bundle of sweater tightly and slid out of bed. His feet felt quite inadequate. In fact he began to doubt their identity. They didn't seem to be there at all when he stood on them, but he was not to be foiled by feet. If they meant to stick by him they'd gotta obey him.

Slowly, cautiously, with his head swimming lightly on ahead of him and a queer gasp of emptiness in the region of his chest that seemed to need a great deal of breath, he managed a passage to the door, looked down the long white corridor with its open doors and cheerful voices, saw a pair of stairs to the right quite nearby, and with his steadying hands on the cool white wall slid along the short space to the top step. It seemed an undertaking to get down that first step, but when that was accomplished he was out of sight and he sat down and slid slowly the rest of the way, wondering why he felt so rotten.

At the foot of the long stairs there was a door, and strange it was made so heavy! He wondered a nurse could swing it open, just a mere girl! But he managed it at last, almost winded, and stumbled out on the portico that gave to the sea, a wide blue stretch before him. He stopped, startled, as if he had unexpectedly sighted the heavenly strand, and gazed blinking at the stretch of blue with the wide white shore and the boom of an organ following the lapping of each white crested wave. Those palm trees certainly made it look queer like Saxy's Pilgrim's Progress picture book. Then the panic for home and his business came upon him and he slid weakly down the shallow white steps, and crunched his white feet on the gravel wincing. He had just taken to the grass at the edge and was managing better than he had hoped when a neat little coupe rounded the curve of the drive, and his favorite doctor came swinging up to the steps, eyeing him keenly. Billy started to run, and fell in a crumpled heap, white and scared and crying real tears, weak, pink tears!

"Why, Billy! What are you doing here?" The stern loving voice of his favorite doctor hung over him like a knife that was going to cut him off forever from life and light and forgiveness and all that he counted dear.

But Billy stopped crying.

"Nothin," he said, "I just came out fer a walk!"

The doctor smiled.

"But I didn't tell you you might, Billy boy!"

"Had to," said Billy.

"Well, you'll find you'll have to go back again, Billy. Come!" and the doctor stooped his broad strong shoulders to pick up the boy. But Billy beat him off weakly:

"Say, now, Doc, wait a minute," he pleaded. "It's jus' this way. I simply *gotta* get back home t'day. I'm a very 'mportant witness in a murder case, see? My bes' friend in the world is bein' tried fer life, an' he ain't guilty, an I'm the only one that knows it fer sure, an' can prove it, an' I gotta be there. Why, Doc, the trial's *going on now* an' I ain't there! It ud drive me crazy to go back an' lay in that soft bed like a reg'lar sissy, an' know he's going to be condemned. I put it to you, Doc, as man to man, would you stand fer a thing like that?"

"But, Billy, suppose it should be the end of you!"

"I sh'd worry, Doc! Ef I c'n get there in time an' say what I want I ain't carin' fer anythin' more in life, I tell ye. Say, Doc, you wouldn't stop me, would ya? Ef you did I'd get thar anyhow *someway!*"

The earnestness of the eager young face, wan in its illness, the light of love in the big gray eyes, went to the doctor's heart. He gave the boy a troubled look.

"Where is it you want to go, Billy?"

"Economy, Doc. It ain't far, only two or three hours' ride. I c'n get a jitney somewheres I guess ta take me. I'll pay up ez soon as I get home. I got thirty dollars in the bank my own self."

"Economy!" said the doctor. "Impossible, Billy, it would kill you!"

"Then I'm goin' anyhow. Good-bye, Doc!" and he darted away from the astonished doctor and ran a rod or so before the doctor caught up with him and seized him firmly by his well shoulder:

"Billy, look here!" said the doctor. "If it's as bad as that I'll take you!"

"Oh, would ya, Doc? Would ya? I'll never forget it, Doc!"

"There now, Billy, never mind, son, you save your strength and let me manage this thing the right way. Couldn't I telephone and have them hold up things a few days? That can be done, you know."

"Nothin' doing, Doc, there's them that would hurry it up

all the more if they thought I was comin' back. You get in, Doc, and start her up. I c'n drive myself if you'll lend me the m'chine. P'raps you ain't got time to go off 'ith me like this."

"That's all right, Billy. You and I are going on a little excursion. But first I've got to tell the nurse, or there'll be all kind of a time. Here, you sit in the machine." The doctor picked him up and put him in and ran up the steps. Billy sat dizzily watching and wondering if he hadn't better make his escape. Perhaps the doc was just fooling him, but in a moment back he came again, with a nurse trailing behind with blankets and a bottle.

"We're going to get another car, son, this one's no good for such a trip. We'll fix it so you can lie down and save your strength for when you get there. No—son—I don't mean the ambulance," as he saw the alarm in Billy's face, "just a nice big car. That's all right, here she comes!"

The big touring car came round from the back almost immediately, and the backseat was heaped with pillows and blankets and Billy tenderly placed among them where he was glad enough to lie down—and close his eyes. It had been rather strenuous. The nurse went back for his shoes, bringing a bottle of milk and his medicine. The doctor got in the front seat and started.

"Now, son," he said, "you rest. You'll need every bit of strength when you get there if we're going to carry this thing through. You just leave this thing to me and I'll get you there in plenty of time. Don't you worry."

Billy with a smile of heavenly bliss over his newly bleached freckles settled back with dreamy eyes and watched the sea as they were passing swiftly by it, his lashes drooping lower and lower over his thin young cheeks. The doctor glancing back anxiously caught that look the mothers see in the young imps when they are asleep, and a tenderness came into his heart for the staunch loyal little sinner.

Doctor Norris was a good scout. If he had got a soft snap of a job in that Shafton hospital, it was good practice of course, and a step to really big things where he wouldn't be dependent upon rich people's whims, but still he was a good scout. He had not forgotten the days of the grasshopper, and Billy had made a great appeal to his heart. He looked at his watch, chose his roads, and put his machine at high speed. The sea receded, the Jersey pines whirled monotonously by, and by and by the hills began to crop up. Off against the horizon Stark Mountain loomed, veiled with a purple haze, and around another curve Economy appeared, startlingly out of place with its smug red brick walks and its gingerbread porches and plastered tile bungalows. Then without warning Billy sat up. How long had that young scamp been awake? Had he slept at all? He was like a man, grave and stern with business before him. The doctor almost felt shy about giving him his medicine.

"Son, you must drink that milk," he said firmly. "Nothing doing unless you drink that!" Billy drank it.

"Now where?" asked the doctor as they entered the straggling dirty little town.

"That red brick building down the next block," pointed Billy, his face white with excitement, his eyes burning like two dark blue coals.

The big car drew up at the curb, and no one there to notice, for everybody was inside. The place was jammed to the door.

Cherry had come back late after lunch, her hat awry and signs of tears on her painted face. Her eyes were more obviously frightened and she whispered a message which was taken up to Mark. Mark lifted a haggard face to hear it, asked a question, bowed his head, and continued listening to the cross-examination of a man who said he had heard him threaten to kill Dolph the week before the murder down at Hagg's Mills. When the witness was dismissed Mark whispered a word to his lawyer, the lawyer spoke to the judge and the judge announced that the prisoner wished to speak. Every eye was turned toward Mark as he rose and gave a sweeping glance around the room, his eyes lingering for just a shadow of an instant wistfully on the faces of the minister and his wife, then on again as if they had seen no one, and round to the judge's face.

It was just at this instant that Billy burst into the room and wedged his way fiercely between elbows, using his old football methods, head down and elbows out, and stood a moment breathless, taking it all in.

Then Mark spoke:

"Your Honor, I wish to plead guilty to the charge!"

A great sigh like a sob broke over the hush in the court-room and many people half rose to their feet as if in protest, but Billy made a dive up the aisle, self and sickness forgotten, regardless of courts or law or anything, and stood between the judge and Mark:

"It ain't so, an' I can prove it!" he shouted at the top of his lungs.

The prosecuting attorney rose to a point of order like a bulldog snapping at his prey, the sergeant at arms rushed around like corn popping off in a corn popper, but Anthony Drew whispered a word to the judge, and after order was restored Billy was called to the witness stand to tell his story.

Doctor Norris, standing squeezed at the back of the room looking for his quondam patient, recognized with a thrill the new Billy standing unafraid before all these people and speaking out his story in a clear direct way. Billy had ethere-alized during his illness. If Aunt Saxon had been there—she was washing for Gibsons that day and having her troubles with Mrs. Frost—she would scarcely have known him. His features had grown delicate and there was something strong and sweet about his mouth that surely never had been there before. But the same old forceful boy speech wherewith he had subdued enemies on the athletic field, bullied Aunt Saxon, and put one over on Pat at the station, was still his own. He told the truth briefly and to the point, not omitting his own wrongdoing in every particular, and he swayed that crowd as a great orator might have been proud to sway a congregation. They laughed till they cried and cried till they laughed again at Billy's quaint phrases, and they enjoyed the detour— Oh, how they enjoyed that detour! Even the judge had twinkles in his eyes.

For the first time since the trial began Mark was sitting up proudly, a warm look of vivid interest in his face, the cold mask gone. His eyes dwelt upon Billy with a look almost fatherly, at least brotherly. It was a startling contrast to what he had been all day. This was a different man.

Suddenly from the corner of the prosecution the low growl which had been gradually rising like a young storm, broke, and the prosecuting attorney arose and lifted his voice above all others:

"I protest, Your Honor, against this witness. He has mentioned no less than five different lies which he has told, and has narrated a number of episodes in which he deliberately broke the law. Is it or is it not a misdemeanor for anyone to meddle with our highroads in the manner that has just been described? By his own confession this young man is disqualified for a witness! By his own confession he is a lawbreaker and a liar!"

"Aw, gee!" broke forth Billy furiously. "Didn't I tell ya I come here to tell the truth n' get it off'n my chest?"

Someone put a strong hand on Billy and silenced him, and someone else rose to protest against the protestor, and the air grew tense with excitement once more.

The prosecution declared that Billy was in league with Mark, that everybody knew he trailed him everywhere, therefore his testimony was worthless. He was probably bribed; there was nothing, absolutely nothing in the story the boy had told to prove anything.

Billy was growing whiter and angrier, his eyes flashing, his fists clenched. His testimony was not going to be accepted after all! It had been vain to bear the shame himself. Nothing, *nothing* that he could do would blot out the trouble because he had unfitted himself to blot it out. It had to be a witness who told the truth who would be believed. It had to be one with a good record to take away the shame! That was something like what Miss Marilyn said in Sunday school once, that only Jesus Christ could take the place of a sinner and make it right about our sinning because He had never sinned. It had sounded like rot when she said it, but he began to understand what she meant now. Yes, that was it. Only God's Son could do that and he, Billy Gaston, had tried to do it himself!

The courtroom seemed to be very dark now. His head was whirling away and getting beyond his control. When he looked up he seemed to see it on the other side of the room. He did not recognize the two men in handcuffs that the chief was bringing into the room. He did not hear what the judge was saying. He had slumped in a little heap on the witness stand with his eyes closed, and his hands groping together. He thought that he was praying to God's Son to come and help Mark because he had failed. *He* wasn't good enough and he *had failed!*

The doctor had come with a bound up the aisle and was

kneeling with Billy in his arms. Mark was leaning over the rail with a white anxious face. The minister was trying to make a way through the crowd, and the sergeant at arms was pushing the crowd back, and making a space about the unconscious boy. Someone opened a window. The chief and one of his men brought a cot. There was a pillow from the car, and there was that medicine again—bringing him back— just as he thought he had made God hear— Oh, *why* did they bother him?

Suddenly down by the door a diversion occurred. Someone had entered with wild burning eyes dressed in a curious assortment of garments. They were trying to put him out, but he persisted.

The word was brought up: "Someone has a very important piece of evidence which he wishes to present."

Billy's gray eyes opened as the man mounted to the witness stand. He was lying on the cot at one side and his gaze rested on the new witness, dazedly at first, and then with growing comprehension. Old Ike Fenner, the tailor, Cherry Fenner's father! Mark was looking at Billy and had not noticed.

But the man began to speak in a high shrill voice:

"I came to say that I'm the man that killed Dolph Haskins! Mark Carter had nothin' to do with it. I done it! I *meant* to kill him because he ruined the life of my little girl. *My baby!*"

There was a sudden catch in his voice like a great sob, and he clutched at the rail as if he were going to fall, but he went on, his eyes burning like coals:

"I shot him with Tom Petrie's gun that I found atop o' the door, an' I put it back where I found it. You take my fingerprints and compare 'em with the marks on the gun an' the windersill. You ask Sandy Robison! He seen me do it. You ask Cherry! She seen me too. She was facin' the winder eatin' her supper with that devil, and I shot him and she seen me! *I* did it—"

His voice trailed off. He swayed and got down from the stand, groping his way as if he could not see. The crowd gave way with a curious shudder looking into his wild burning eyes as he passed. A girl's scream back by the door rang through the court. The man moaned, put out his hands and fell forward. Kindly hands reached to catch him. The doctor left Billy and came to help.

They carried him outside and laid him on the grass in front of the courthouse. The doctor used every restorative he had with him. Men hurried to the drugstore. They tried everything, but all to no avail. Ike Fenner the tailor was dead! He had gone to stand before a higher court!

When it was all over, the fingerprints and the red tape, and the case had been dismissed, Mark came to Billy where he was lying in the big car waiting, with his eyes closed to keep back weak tears that would slip out now and then. He knelt beside the boy and touched his hand, the hand that looked so thin and weak and so little like Billy's:

"Kid," he said gently, "kid, you've been a wonder! It was really you that saved me, buddy! *My buddy!*"

Billy's tears welled over at the tone, the words, the proud intimate name, but he shook his head slowly, sadly.

"No," he said; "no, it wasn't me. I tried, but I wasn't fit! It had to be *Him*. I didn't understand! They wouldn't believe me. But *He* came as soon as I ast!"

Mark looked at the doctor.

"Is he wandering a little?" he asked in a low tone.

"I shouldn't wonder. He's been through enough to make anyone wander. Here, son, take this."

Billy smiled and obediently accepted his medicine. Mark held his hand all the way home. He knew that Mark didn't understand but he was too tired to tell him now. Sometime he would explain. Or perhaps Miss Lynn would explain it for him. He was going home, home to Saxy and Sabbath Valley and the bells, and Mark was free! He hadn't saved him, but Mark was free!

It was like a royal passage through the village as they came into Sabbath Valley, for everybody came out to wave at Mark and Billy. Even Mrs. Harricutt watched grimly from behind her holland shades. But Billy was too weak to notice much, except to sense it distantly, and Mark would only lift his hat and bow gravely, quietly, as if it didn't matter, just as he used to do when they carried him round on their shoulders after a football game, and he tried to get down and hide. Why did Mark still have that sad look in his eyes? Billy was too tired to think it out. He was glad when they reached Aunt Saxon's

door and Mark picked him up as he used to do when he was
just a little kid, and carried him up to his room. Carried him
up and undressed him, while Saxy heard the story from the
doctor's lips, and laughed and cried and laughed again. The
nervy little kid! He would always be a little kid to Saxy, no
matter what he did.

He turned over in his own bed, *his bed*, and smelled the
sweet breath of the honeysuckle coming in at the window,
heard the thrushes singing their evening song up the street.
The sea had been great, but, oh, you Sabbath Valley! Out
there was the waterspout, and someday he would be strong
enough to shin down it, and up it again. He would play
football this fall, and run Mark's car! Mark, grave, gentle,
quiet, sitting beside him till he got asleep, and his mother
not knowing, down the street, and Miss Lynn—

"Mark—you'll tell Miss Marilyn about it all?" He opened
his eyes to murmur lazily, and Mark promised still gravely.

He shut his eyes and drifted away. What was that the chief
had told him down at Economy in the car? Something about
three strange detectives stepping off the train one day and
nabbing Pat? And Pat was up at Sing Sing finishing his term.
Was that straight or only a dream? And anyhow he didn't
care. He was home again, home—*and forgiven!*

Night settled sweetly down upon Sabbath Valley, hiding
the brilliant autumn tinting of the street. Lynn had made a
maple nut cake and set the table for two before she left the
Carters', for her mother had slipped out of the courtroom and
telephoned her, and a fire was blazing in the little parlor with
the lace curtains and asters in every vase all gala for the
returning son. The mother and son sat long before the fire,
talking, pleasant converse, about the time when Mark would
send for her to come and live with him, but not a word was
said about the day. He saw that his friends had helped to save
his mother this one great sorrow that she could not have
borne, and he was grateful.

Marilyn, up at the parsonage, with a great thankfulness
upon her, went about with smiling face. The burden seemed
to have lifted and she was glad.

But that night at midnight there came the doctor from
Economy driving hard and stopping at the parsonage. Cherry

Fenner was dying and wanted to see Miss Marilyn. Would she come?

Chapter 27

Cherry's little bedroom under the roof was bright with the confusion of cheap finery scattered everywhere and swept aside at the sudden entrance of the death angel. A neighbor had done her best to push away the crude implements of complexion that were littering the cheap oak bureau top, and the doctor's case and bottles and glasses crowded out the giddy little accessories of beauty that Cherry had collected. Two chairs piled high with draggled finery, soiled work aprons, and dresses made a forlorn and miscellaneous disorder in one corner, and the closet door sagged open with visions of more clothing hung many deep upon the few hooks.

Mrs. Fenner stood at the head of the bed wringing her hands and moaning uncontrolledly, and Cherry, little Cherry, lay whitely against the pillow, the color all gone from her ghastly pretty little face, that had lately hid its ravished health and beauty behind a camouflage of paint. There were deep dark circles under the limpid eyes that now were full of mortal pain, and pitiful lines around the cherry mouth that had been wont to laugh so saucily.

The doctor stood by the window with the attitude of grave waiting. The helpful neighbor lingered in the doorway, holding her elbows and taking minute note of Marilyn's dress. This might be a sad time, but one had to live afterward, and it wasn't every day you got to see a simple little frock with an air like the one the minister's daughter wore. She studied it from neck to hem and couldn't see what in the world there was about it anyway to make her look so dressed up. Not a scratch of trimming, not even a collar, and yet she could look like that! Mercy! Was that what education and going to college did for folks?

The light of a single unshaded electric bulb shone startlingly down to the bed, making plain the shadow of death even to an inexperienced eye.

Marilyn knelt beside the bed and took Cherry's cold little hand in her own warm one. The waxen eyelids fluttered open, and a dart of something between fright and pain went over her weird little face.

"Can I do anything for you, Cherry?" Marilyn's voice was tender, pitiful.

"It's *too late*," whispered the girl in a fierce little whisper. "Send 'em out— I—wantta—tell—you—someth—" The voice trailed away weakly. The doctor stepped over and gave her a spoonful of something, motioned her mother and the neighbor away, tiptoeing out himself and closing the door. The mother was sobbing wildly. The doctor's voice could be heard quieting her coldly:

The girl on the bed frowned and gathered effort to speak:

"Mark Carter—didn't mean no harm—goin'—with me!" she broke out, her breath coming in grasps. "He was tryin' —to stop me—goin'—with—*Dolph!*" The eyes closed wearily. The lips were white as chalk. She seemed to have stopped breathing!

"It's all right—Cherry—" Marilyn breathed softly. "It's all right—I understand! Don't think any more about it!"

The eyes opened fiercely again, a faint determination shadowed round the little mouth:

"You gotta know!" she broke forth again with effort. "He was good to me—when I was a little kid, and when he found I was in trouble—" the breath came pitifully in gasps—"he— offered—to—*marry me!*"

Marilyn's fingers trembled but she held the little cold hand warmly and tried to keep back the tears that trembled in her eyes.

"He—didn't—*want to*—! He—just—*done it to be kind!* But I—couldn't—see—it— That's—what we—*argued*—" Her voice grew fainter again. Marilyn with gentle controlled voice pressed the little cold hand again:

"Never mind, Cherry dear—it's all right!"

Cherry's eyes opened with renewed effort, anxiously:

"You won't—blame—Mark? He never—did—nothin'—wrong! He's—*your*—friend!"

"No, Cherry! It's all right!"

The girl seemed to have lost consciousness again, and Marilyn wondered if she ought not to call the doctor, but suddenly Cherry screamed out:

"There he is again! He's *come for me!* Oh—I'm—a—gon'ta—*die!* An' I'm *afrrr-aid!*"

Cherry clutched at Marilyn's arm, and looked up with far-off gaze in which terror seemed frozen.

The minister's daughter leaned farther over and gathered the fragile form of the sick girl in her arms tenderly, speaking in a soothing voice:

"Listen, Cherry. Don't be afraid. Jesus is here. He'll go with you!"

"But I'm afraid of Jesus!" the sharp little voice pierced out with a shudder. "I haven't been—*good!*"

"Then tell Him you are sorry. You *are* sorry, aren't you?"

"Oh, *yes!*" the weak voice moaned. "I—never—*meant*—no—harm! I only—wanted—a little—good time!"

The eyes had closed again and she was almost gone. The doctor had come in and he now gave her another spoonful of medicine. Marilyn knew the time was short.

"Listen, Cherry, say these words after me!" Cherry's eyes opened again and fastened on her face, eagerly:

"Jesus, I'm sorry!"

"Jesus—I'm—sor-ry!" repeated the weak voice in almost a whisper.

"Please forgive me," said Marilyn slowly, distinctly.

"Please—for—give—" the slow voice repeated.

"And save me."

"—save—" the voice was scarcely audible.

The doctor came and stood close by the bed, looking down keenly, but Cherry roused once more and looked at them, her sharp little voice stabbing out into the silence piercingly,

"Is that—*all?*"

"That is all," said Marilyn with a ring in her voice, "Jesus died to take care of all the rest! You can just rest on Him!"

"*Oh-h!*" The agony went out of the pinched little face, a half smile dawned and she sank into rest.

As Marilyn went home in the dawn with the morning star

beginning to pale, and the birds at their early worship, something in her own heart was singing too. Above the feeling of awe over standing at the brink of the river and seeing a little soul go wavering out, above even the wonder that she had been called to point the way, there sang in her soul a song of jubilation that Mark was exonerated from shame and disgrace. Whatever others thought, whatever she personally would always have believed, it still was great that God had given her this to make her know that her inner vision about it had been right. Perhaps sometime, in the days that were to come, Mark would tell her about it, but there was time enough for that. Mark would perhaps come to see her this morning. She somehow felt sure that at least he would come to say he was glad she had stayed with his mother. It was like Mark to do that. He never let any little thing that was done for him or his pass unnoticed.

But the morning passed and Mark did not come. The only place that Mark went was to see Billy.

"Billy, old man," he said, sitting down by the edge of the bed where Billy was drowsing the early morning away, just feeling the bed, and sensing Saxy down there making chicken broth, and knowing that the young robins in the apple tree under the window were grown up and flown away. "Billy, I can't keep my promise to you after all. I've got to go away. Sorry, kid, but she'll come to see you and I want you to tell her for me all about it. I'm not forgetting it, kid, either, and you'll know, all the rest of my life, *you and I are buddies!* Savvy, kid?"

Billy looked at Mark with big understanding eyes. There was sadness and hunger and great self-control in that still white face that he worshiped so devotedly. All was not well with his hero yet. It came to him vaguely that perhaps Mark too had even yet something to learn, the kind of thing that was only learned by going through fire. He struggled for words to express himself, but all he could find were:

"I say, Mark, why'n't'tya get it off'n yer chest? It's *great!*"

Perhaps there wouldn't have been another human in Sabbath Valley, except perhaps it might have been Marilyn who would have understood that by this low growled suggestion Billy was offering confession of sin as a remedy for his friend's ailment of soul, but Mark looked at him keenly, almost

tenderly for a long minute, and shook his head, his face
taking on a grayer, more hopeless look as he said:

"I can't, kid. It's *too late!*"

Billy closed his eyes for a moment. He felt it wasn't quite
square to see into his friend's soul that way when he was off
his guard, but he understood. He had passed that way
himself. It came to him that nothing he could say would make
any difference. He would have liked to tell of his own
experience in the courtroom and how he had suddenly known
that all his efforts to right his wrong had been failures, that
there was only One who could do it, but there were no words
in a boy's vocabulary to say a thing like that. It sounded
unreal. It had to be *felt*, and he found his heart kept saying
over and over as he lay there waiting with closed eyes for
Mark to speak: "Oh, God! Why'n'tchoo show him Yerself?
Why'n'tchoo show him Yerself?" He wondered if Miss Lynn
couldn't have shown Mark if he had only gone and talked it
over with her. But Mark said it was too late. "Well, why'n'tchoo
show him Yerself, then? Why'n'tchoo show him Yerself,
God—*please!*"

Mark got up with a long sigh.

"Well, s'long, kid, till I see you again. And I won't forget,
kid, you know I won't forget! And, kid, I'm leaving my gun
with you. I know you'll take good care of it and not let it do
any damage. You might need it you know to take care of your
aunt or—or—Miss Severn—or—!"

"Sure!" said Billy with shining eyes clasping the weapon
that had been Mark's proud possession for several years. "Aw,
gee! Ya hadn't oughtta give me this! You might need it
yourself."

"No, kid, I'd rather feel that you have it. I want to leave
someone here to kind of take my place—watching—you
know. There'll be times—"

"Sure!" said Billy, a kind of glory overspreading his thin
eager face. "Aw, gee! Mark!"

And long after Mark had gone, and the sound of his
purring engine had died away in the distance, Billy lay back
with the weapon clasped to his heart, and a weird kind of
ryhthm repeating itself over and over somewhere in his spirit:
"Why'n'tchoo show him Yerself, God? Why'n'tchoo show him
Yerself? You will! I'll bet You *will!* yet!"

And was that anything like the prayer of faith translated into theological language?

Aunt Saxon went up tiptoe with the broth and thought he was asleep and tiptoed down again to keep it warm awhile. But Billy lay there and felt like Elisha after the mantle of the prophet Elijah had fallen upon him. It gave him a grand solemn feeling, God and he were somehow taking Mark's place till Mark got ready to come back and do it himself. He was to take care of Sabbath Valley as far as in him lay, but more particularly of Miss Marilyn Severn.

And then suddenly, without warning, Miss Marilyn herself went away, to New York she said, for a few weeks, she wasn't sure just how long. But there was something sad in her voice as she said it, and something pathetic about the look she wore that made him sure she was not going to the part of New York where Mark Carter lived.

Billy accepted it with a sigh. Things were getting pretty dry around Sabbath Valley for him. He didn't seem to get his pep back as fast as he had expected. For one thing he worried a good deal, and for another the doctor wouldn't let him play baseball nor ride a bicycle yet for quite awhile. He had to go around and act just like a "gurrull!" Aw, gee! Sometimes he was even glad to have Mary Little come across the street with her picture puzzles and stay with him awhile. She was real good company. He hadn't ever dreamed before that girls could be as interesting. Of course, Miss Marilyn had to be a girl once, but then she was Miss Marilyn. That was different.

Then too, Billy hadn't quite forgotten that first morning that Saxy got her arms around him and cried over him glad tears, bright sweet tears that wet his face and made him feel like crying happy tears too. And the sudden surprising desire he felt to hug her with his well arm, and how she fell over on the bed and got to laughing because he pulled her hair down in his awkwardness, and pulled her collar crooked. Aw, gee! She was just Aunt Saxy and he had been rotten to her a lot of times. But now it was different. Somehow Saxy and he were more pals, or was it that he was the man now taking care of Saxy and not the little boy being taken care of himself? Somehow during those weeks he had been gone Saxy had cried out the pink tears, and was growing smiles, and home was kinda nice after all. But he missed the bells. And nights before he got into bed he got to kneeling down regularly, and saying softly inside his heart: "Aw, gee, God, please why'n'tcha make Mark understand, an' why'n'tcha bring 'em both home?"

Chapter 28

Marilyn had not been in New York but a week before she met Opal. She was waiting to cross Fifth Avenue, and someone leaned out of a big limousine that paused for the congestion in traffic and cried:

"Why, if that isn't Miss Severn from Sabbath Valley. Get in please, I want to see you."

And Lynn, much against her will, was persuaded to get in, more because she was holding up traffic than because the woman in the limousine insisted:

"I'll take you where you want to go," she said in answer to Lynn's protests, and they rolled away up the great avenue with the moving throng.

"I'm dying to know what it is you're making Laurie Shafton do," said Opal eagerly. "I never saw him so much interested in anything in my life. Or is it you he's interested in? Why, he can't talk of anything else, and he's almost stopped going to the Club or any of the house parties. Everybody thinks he's perfectly crazy. He won't drink anymore either. He's made himself quite *notorious*. I believe I heard someone say the other day they hadn't even seen him smoking for a whole week. You certainly are a wonder."

"You're quite mistaken," said Lynn, much amused, "I had nothing to do with Mr. Shafton's present interest, except as I happened to be the one to introduce him to it. I haven't seen him but twice since I came to New York, and then only to take him around among my babies at the settlement and once over to the Orphans' Home, where I've been helping out while an old friend of mine with whom I worked in France is away with her sick sister."

"For mercy sake! You don't mean that Laurie consented to go among the poor? I heard he'd given a lot of money to fix up some buildings, but then all the best men are doing things like that now. It's quite the fad. But to go himself and see the wretched little things. Ugh! I don't see how he could. He must be quite crazy about you I'm sure if he did all that for you."

"Oh, he seemed to want to see them," said Lynn lightly, "and he suggested many of the improvements that he is making himself. They tell me he has proved a great helper, he is on hand at all hours superintending the building himself, and everybody is delighted with him!"

"Mmmm!" commented Opal looking at Marilyn through the fringes of her eyes. "You really are a wonder. And now that you are in New York I'm going to introduce you to our crowd. When can you come? Let's see. Tomorrow is Sunday. Will you spend the evening with me tomorrow? I'll certainly show you a good time. We're going to motor to—"

But Lynn was shaking her head decidedly:

"I couldn't possibly spare a minute, thank you. I'm only out on an errand now. I'm needed every instant at the home!"

"For mercy sake! Hire someone to take your place then. I want you. You'll be quite a sensation, I assure you. Don't worry about clothes, if you haven't anything along. You can wear one of my evening dresses. We're almost of a size."

"No," said Lynn smiling. "It simply isn't possible. And anyway, don't you remember Sabbath Valley? I don't go out to play Sunday nights, you know."

"Oh, but this is New York! You can't bring Sabbath Valley notions to New York."

Lynn smiled again:

"You can if they are a part of you," she said. "Come in and see how nicely I'm fixed."

Opal looked up at the beautiful building before which they were stopping.

"Why, where is this?" she asked astonished, "I thought you were down in the slums somewhere."

"This is a home for little orphan children kept up by the Salvation Army. Come in a minute and see it."

Following a whim of curiosity Opal came in, and was led down a long hall to a great room where were a hundred tiny children sitting on little chairs in a big circle playing kindergarten games. The children were dressed in neat pretty frocks such as any beloved children would wear, with bright hair ribbons and neckties, and each with an individuality of its own. The room was sunny and bright, with a great playhouse at one end, with real windows and furniture in it and all sorts of toboggan slides and swings and kiddy cars and everything to delight the soul of a child. On a wide space between two windows painted on the plaster in soft wonderful coloring blended into the gray tint of the wall, there glowed a life-size painting of the Christ surrounded by little children, climbing upon His knees and listening to Him as He smiled and talked to them.

Opal paused in the doorway and looked at the picture first, shyly, shamedly, as though it were no place for her to enter, then curiously at the little children, with a kind of wistful yearning, as if here was something she had missed of her own fault. Lynn called out a charming baby and made her shake hands and bow and say a few lisping smiling words. Opal turned to Lynn with a strangely subdued look and spoke in a moved tone:

"I guess you're right," she said, "you wouldn't fit at my company. You're different! But some day I'm coming after you and bring you home all by yourself for a little while. I want to find out what it is you have that I need."

Then she turned with swift steps and went down the hall and out the door to her waiting limousine, and Lynn smiled wonderingly as she saw her whirled away into the world again.

Lynn had not seen Mark.

Laurie Shafton had called upon her many times since those two trips they had taken around the settlements and looking over his condemned property, but she had been busy, or out somewhere on her errands of mercy, so that Laurie had got very little satisfaction for his trouble.

But Mark had seen Lynn once, just once, and that the first time she had gone with Laurie Shafton, as they were getting out of his car in front of one of his buildings. Mark had slipped into a doorway out of sight and watched them, and after they passed into the building had gone on, his face whiter and sadder than before. That was all.

Marilyn was to spend only a month in New York, as at first planned, but the month lengthened into six weeks before the friend whose place she was taking was able to return, and two days before Marilyn was expecting to start home there came a telephone message from her mother:

"Lynn, dear, Mrs. Carter is very low, dying, we think, and we must find Mark at once! There is not a minute to lose if he wants to see her alive. It is a serious condition brought on by excitement. Mrs. Harricutt went there to call yesterday while everybody else was at Ladies' Aid. And Lynn, *she told her about Mark!* Now, Lynn, can you get somebody to go with you and find Mark right away? Get him to come home at once? Here is the last address he gave, but they have no telephone and we dare not wait for a telegram. See what you can do quickly!"

It was four o'clock in the afternoon when this message came. Lynn put on a uniform of dark blue serge and a poke bonnet that was at her disposal whenever she had need of protection, and hurried out.

She found the address after some trouble, but was told that the young gentleman was out. No one seemed to know when he would return.

Two or three other lodgers gathered curiously, one suggesting a restaurant where he might be found, another a club where he sometimes went and a third laughed and called out from halfway up the stairs:

"You'll find him at the cabaret around the corner by ten o'clock tonight if you don't find him sooner. He's always there when he's in town."

Sick at heart Lynn went on her way trying carefully each place that had been suggested but finding no trace of him. She met with only deference for her uniform wherever she went, and without the slightest fear she traveled through streets at night that she would scarcely have liked to pass alone in the daytime in her ordinary garb. But all the time her heart was praying that she might find Mark before it was too late. She tried every little clue that was given her, hoping against hope that she would not have to search for her old friend in a cabaret such as she knew that place around the corner must be. But it was almost ten o'clock and she had not found Mark. She went back to the first address once more, but he had not come, and so she finally turned her steps toward the cabaret.

Sadly, with her heart beating wildly, hoping, yet fearing to find him, she paused just inside the doors and looked around, trying to get used to the glare and blare, the jazz and the smoke, and the strange lax garb, and to differentiate the individuals from the crowd.

Food and drink, smoke and song, wine and dance, flesh and odd perfumes! Her soul sank within her, and she turned bewildered to a servitor at the door.

"I wonder, is there any way to find a special person here? I have a very important message."

The man bent his head deferentially as though to one from another world, "Who did you want, Miss?"

"Mr. Mark Carter," said Marilyn, feeling the color rise in her cheeks at letting even this waiter see that she expected to find Mark Carter here.

The man looked up puzzled. He was rather new at the place. He summoned another passing one of his kind:

"Carter, Carter?" the man said thoughtfully. "Oh, yes, he's the guy that never drinks! He's over there at the table in the far corner with the little dancer lady—" The waiter pointed and Lynn looked. "Would you like me to call him, Miss?" Lynn reflected quickly. Perhaps he might try to evade her. She must run no risks.

"Thank you, I will go to him," she said, and straight through the maze of candle-lighted tables, and whirling dancers, in her quiet holy garb, she threaded her way hastily, as one might have walked over quicksands, with her eye fixed upon Mark.

She came and stood beside him before he looked up and saw her, and then he lifted his eyes from the face of the girl with whom he was talking, and rose suddenly to his feet, his face gone white as death, his eyes dark with disapproval and humiliation.

"Marilyn!" His voice was shaking. He knew her instantly in spite of poke bonnet and uniform. She was the one thought present with him all the while, perhaps for years wherever he had been. But he did not look glad to see her. Instead it was as if his soul shrank shamedly from her clear eyes as she looked at him.

Marilyn had not known what she was going to say to him when she found him. She did not stop to think now.

"Mark, your mother wants you. She is dying! You must come quick or she will be gone!"

Afterward she repeated over the words to herself again and again as one might do penance, blaming herself that she had not softened it, made it more easy for him to bear. Yet at the time it seemed the only thing there was to say, at such a time, in such a place. But at the stricken look upon his face her heart grew tender. "Come," she said compassionately. "We will go!"

They went out into the night and it was as if they had suddenly changed places, as if she were the protector and he the led. She guided him the quickest way. There was only a chance that they might catch the midnight train, but there was that chance. Into the subway she dived, he following, and breathless, they brought up at the Pennsylvania Station at their train gate as it was being closed, and hurried through.

All through that agonized night they spoke but few words, those two who had been so much to each other through long happy years.

"But you are not going too?" he spoke suddenly roused from his daze as the train started.

"Yes, I am going too, of course, Mark," she said.

He bowed his head and almost groaned:

"I am not worthy, Marilyn!"

"That—has nothing to do with it!" said Marilyn sadly. "It never will have anything to do with it! It never did!"

Mark looked at her, with harrowed eyes, and dropped his gaze. So he sat, hour after hour, as the train rushed along through the night. And Marilyn, with head slightly bent and meek face, beneath the poke bonnet with its crimson band, was praying as she rode. Praying in other words the prayer that Billy murmured beside his bed every night.

But Billy was not lying in his bed that night, sleeping the sleep of the just. He was up and on the job. He was sitting in the Carter kitchen keeping up the fires, making a cup of tea for the nurse and the doctor, running the endless little errands, up to the parsonage for another hot water bag, down

to the drugstore for more aromatic spirits of ammonia, fixing
a newspaper shade to dull the light in the hall, and praying,
all the time praying: "Oh, God, ain'tcha gonta leave her stay
till Mark gets here? Ain'tcha gonta send Mark quick? You
know best I 'spose, but ain'tcha *gonta?*" And then, "Aw, gee! I
wisht Miss Lynn was here!"

In the chill before the dawning the two stepped down from
the train at a little flag station three miles from Sabbath
Valley on the upper road that ran along the ridge. They had
prevailed upon the conductor to let them off there. Mark had
roused enough for that. And now that they were out in the
open country he seemed to come to himself. He took care of
Lynn, making her take his arm, guiding her into the smooth
places, helping her over rough places. He asked a few
questions too. How did she know of his mother's condition?
How long had she been this way? Had she any idea that his
mother's heart was affected? Did she have a shock?

Lynn did not tell all she knew. It was hard enough without
that. He need not know that it was the knowledge of his
disgrace that had brought her to the brink of death.

So, walking and talking almost as in the old days, they
passed into Sabbath Valley and down the street, and Christie
McMertrie, listening perhaps for this very thing, crept from
her bed in her long flannel nightgown, and big ruffled night-
cap, and looked out the window to see them go by. "Bless
them!" she breathed and crept back to her bed again. She
had nursed all day, and all the night before, and would have
been there too tonight, only Mary Rafferty took things in her
own hands and had her go to bed, herself taking charge. Mrs.
Duncannon was there too. There really was no need of her,
but Christie could not sleep, and after they passed she rose
and dressed and slipped down the street with a hot porridge
that had been cooking on the stove all night, and the makings
of a good breakfast in her basket on her arm.

Mark Carter reached home in time to take his mother in
his arms and bid her good-bye. That was all. She roused at
his voice and touch, and reached out her little pretty hands
toward him. He took her in his big strong arms and held her,
kissed her with tender lips and she drew a beautiful smile of
perfect content and slipped away, with the graying golden
hair straying out over Mark's sleeve to the pillow in a long

curl, and a quiver of her last smile on the pretty curve of her lips, as if this was all that she had waited for, the little pretty girl that had gone to school so long ago with golden hair and a smile. Billy, standing awed in the doorway whither he had come to say there was more hot water ready, caught the vision of her face, remembered those school days, and felt a strange constriction in his throat. Some day Saxy would have to go like that, and would show the little girl in her face too, and he maybe would have to hold her so and think of how cross he had been. Aw, gee! Whattaqueer thing life was anyhow! Well, hadn't his prayer been answered? Didn't Mark get here in time? Well, anyhow it was likely better for Mrs. Carter to go. But it was rotten for Mark. Aw, gee! *Mark!* Was *this* the way he had to learn it? Aw, gee! Well, God would have to show him. *He* couldn't dope it out anyhow.

During the days that followed Mark hardly stirred from the side of the pretty little clay that had been his mother except when they forced him for a little while. An hour before the service he knelt alone beside the casket, and the door opened and Marilyn came softly in, closing it behind her. She walked over to Mark and laid her hand on his hand that rested over his mother's among the flowers, and she knelt beside him and spoke softly:

"Oh, God, help Mark to find the light!"

Then the soul of Mark Carter was shaken to the depths and suddenly his self-control which had been so great was broken. His strong shoulders began to shake with sobs, silent, hard sobs of a man who knows he has sinned, and tears, scalding tears from the depths of his self-contained nature.

Marilyn reached her arm out across his shoulders as a mother would try to protect a child, and lifted her face against his, wet with tears, and kissed him on his forehead. Then she left him and went quietly out.

"Well," said Mrs. Harricutt with satisfaction as she walked home after the funeral with Christie McMertrie, "I'm glad to see that Mark Carter has a little proper feeling at last. If he'd showed it sooner his ma mighta ben in the land of the living yet."

Christie's stern face grew sterner as she set her teeth and

bit her tongue before replying. Then she said with more brrrr than usual in her speech:

"Martha Harricutt, there's na land that's sa livin' as tha land where Mark Carter's mither has ganged tae, but there's them that has mair blame to bear fer her gaein' than her bonny big son, I'm thinkin', an' there's them in this town that agrees with me too, I know full well."

Down in front of the parsonage the minister had his arm around Mark Carter's shoulders and was urging him:

"Son, come in. We want you. Mother wants you, I want you. Marilyn wants you. Come, son, come!"

But Mark steadily refused, his eyes downcast, his face sad, withdrawn:

"Mr. Severn, I'll come tomorrow. I can't come tonight. I must go home and think!"

"And you will promise me you will not leave without coming, Mark?" asked the minister sadly when he saw that it was no use.

"Yes, I will promise!" Mark wrung the minister's hand in a warm grip that said many things he could not speak, and then he passed on to his lonely home. But it was not entirely empty. Billy was there, humbly, silently, with dog-true eyes, and a grown-up patient look on his tired young face. He had the coffeepot on the stove and hot sausages cooking on the stove, and a lot of Saxy's doughnuts and a pie on the table. Billy stayed all night with Mark. He knew Saxy would understand.

Chapter 29

In the middle of the night the fire bell rang out wildly. Three minutes later Mark and Billy were flying down the street, with Tom McMertrie and Jim Rafferty close after and a host of other tried and true, with the minister on the other side of the street. The fire company of Sabbath Valley held a proud record, and the minister was an active member of it.

The fire was up in the plush mill and had already spread to a row of shackley tenements that the owners of the mills had put up to house the foreign labor that they had put in. They called them apartment houses, but they were so much on the order of the city tenements of several years back that it made Lynn's heart ache when she went there to see a little sick child one day. Right in the midst of God's trees and mountains, a man *for money* had built a deathtrap, tall, and grim and dark, with small rooms and tiny windows, built it with timbers too small for safety, and windows too few for ventilation, and here an increasing number of families were herded, in spite of the complaints of the town.

"I ben thenkin' it would coom," said Tom as he took long strides. "It's the apartmints fer sure, Jimmy. We better beat it. There'll be only a meenit er so to get the children oot, before the whole thing's smoke!"

They were all there, the doctor, the blacksmith, the postmaster, the men from the mills, and the banks, and the stores. Economy heard the bells—for Marilyn had hurried to the church and added the fire chime to the call—and came over with their little chemical engine. Monopoly heard and hurried their brand-new hook and ladder up the valley road, but the fire had been eating long in the heart of the plush mill and laughed at their puny streams of water forced up from the creek below, laughed at the chemicals flung in its face like drops of rain on a sizzling red-hot stove. It licked its lips over the edge of the cliff on which it was built, and cracked its jaws as it devoured the mill, window by window, section by section, leaping across with an angry red tongue to the first tall building by its side.

The fire had worked cunningly, for it had crept out of sight to the lower floors all along the row, and unseen, unknown, had bitten a hold on each of those doomed buildings till when the men arrived it went roaring ghoulishly up the high narrow stairs cutting off all escape from above, and making entrance below impossible. Up at the windows the doomed people stood, crying, praying, wringing their hands, and some losing their heads and trying to jump out.

The firemen were brave, and worked wonders. They flung

up ladders in the face of the flames. They risked their lives
every step they took, and brought out one after another,
working steadily, grimly, rapidly. And none was braver
among them all than Mark Carter and the minister, each
working on the very top of a tall treacherous ladder, in the
face of constant danger, bringing out one after another until
the last.

The next house to the mill had caved in, and Mark had
come down just in time with an old woman who was bedrid-
den and had been forgotten. The workers had paused an
instant as the horrible sound of falling timbers rent through
the other noises of that horrible night, and then hurried to
increase their vigilance. There were people in the top floor of
the next house and it would go next. Then the word went
forth that no more must go up the ladder. The roof was about
to fall in, and a young mother shrieked, "My baby! My baby!
She's up in the bed. I thought Bob had her, but he couldn't
get up!" Mark Carter looked at her sharply. "Which window?" he asked, and was up the ladder before detaining
hands could reach him, and Billy, sliding under the arm of
the fire chief, swung up just behind.

The crowd watched breathless as they mounted round after
round, Aunt Saxon standing with a shawl over her head and
gasping aloud, "Oh, *Willie!*" and then standing still in fear
and pride, the tears streaming down a smiling countenance
on which the red glare of the fire shone. The ladder was set
crazily against the flaming window and swayed with their
weight. Every step seemed as if it would topple the building,
yet the ladder held, and Mark sprang through the blazing
window out of sight. It seemed an eternity till he returned
bring a tiny bundle with him, and handing it out to Billy
waiting below.

The boy received as it had been a holy honor, that little
bundle of humanity handed through the fire, and came
solemnly down amid the breathless gaze of the crowd, but
when they looked to the top again Mark had disappeared!

A murmur of horror went round the throng, for the flames
were licking and snapping, and the roof seemed to vibrate
and quiver like a human thing. Then before anyone could
stop him or even saw what he was going to do, the minister

sprang forward up the ladder like a cat, two rounds at a time—three! He dashed through the fire and was gone!

For an instant it seemed that the people would go mad with the horror of it. *Those two!* Even the fire chief paused and seemed petrified. It was Billy who sensed the thing to do.

"Getcher canvas man? Are ya' asleep?"

And instantly a great piece of canvas was spread and lifted. But the building tottered, the flames ate on, and the window seemed entirely enveloped. The moment lasted too long for the hearts that waited. A groan rent the air. Then suddenly a breath seemed to part the flames and they saw the minister coming forward with Mark in his arms!

It was just at this instant that Lynn came flying down the street. She had kept the bells going till she knew all the help had come from a distance, and now she was coming to see if there was anything else for her to do. There before her she saw her father standing in that awful setting of fire, with Mark limp and lifeless in his arms! Then the flames licked up and covered the opening once more. *Oh, God!* Were they *both gone?*

Only for an instant more the suspense lasted, and then the cataclysm of fire came. The roof fell carrying with it the floors as it went, down, down, down, shuddering like a human thing as it went, the rain of fire pouring up and around in great blistering flakes and scorching the onlookers and lighting their livid faces as they stood transfixed with horror at the sight.

The canvas fluttered uselessly down and fire showered thick upon it. Timbers and beams crumbled like paper things and were no more. The whole flimsy structure had caved in!

Paralyzed with terror and sorrow the firemen stood gazing, and suddenly a boy's voice rang out: "Aw, gee! Git to work there! Whatterya doin'? Playin' dominoes? Turn that hose over there! That's where they fell. Say, you, Jim, get that fire hook and lift that beam! *Aw, gee!* Ya ain't gonta let 'em *die*, are ya? *Them two!*"

Billy had seized a heavy hose and was turning it on a central spot and Jim Rafferty caught the idea and turned his stream that way, and into the fire went the brave men, one and another, instantly, cheerfully, devotedly, the men who

loved the two men in there. They would all die together. The
fire chief stood close to Billy, and shouted his directions, and
Billy worked with the tallest of them, black, hoarse and
weary.

It seemed ages. It was hours. It was a miracle! But they got
those two men out alive! Blackened and bruised and broken,
burned almost beyond recognition, but they were alive. They
found them lying close to the front wall, their faces together,
Mark's body covered by the minister's.

Tender hands brought them forth and carried them gently
on stretchers out from the circle of danger and noise and
smoke. Eagerly they were ministered to, with oil and old
linen and stimulants. There were doctors from Economy and
one from Monopoly besides the Sabbath Valley doctor, who
was like a brother to the minister and had known Mark since
he was born. They worked as if their lives depended upon it,
till all that loving skill could do was done.

Billy, his eyelashes and brows gone, half his hair singed off,
one eye swollen shut and great blisters on his hands and
arms, sat huddled and shivering on the ground between the
two stretchers. The fire was still going on but he was "all in."
The only thing left he could do was to bow his bruised face on
his trembling knees and pray:

"*Oh, God,* ain't You gonta let 'em live—*please!*"

They carried Mark to the Saxon cottage and laid him on
Billy's bed. There was no lack of nurses. Aunt Saxon and
Christie McMertrie, the Duncannons and Mary Rafferty, Jim
too, and Tom. It seemed that everybody claimed the honors.
The minister was across the street in the Little house. They
dared not move him farther. Of the two the case of the
minister was the most hopeless. He had borne the burden of
the fall. He had been struck by the falling timbers, his body
had been a cover for the younger man. In every way the
minister had not saved himself.

The days that followed were full of anxiety. There were a
few others more or less injured in the fire, for there had been
fearless work, and no one had spared himself. But the two
who hung at the point of death for so long were laid on the
hearts of the people, because they were dear to almost
everyone.

Little neighborhood prayer meetings sprang up quietly

here and there, beginning at Duncannons. The neighbor on
either side would come in and they would just drop down
and pray for the minister, and for "that other dear brave
brother." Then the Littles heard of it and called in a few
friends. One night when both sufferers were at the crisis and
there seemed little hope for the minister, Christie McMertrie
called in the Raffertys and they were just on the point of
kneeling down when Mrs. Harricutt came to the door. She
had been crying. She said she and her husband hadn't slept a
wink the night before, they were so anxious for the minister.
Christie looked at her severely, but remembering the com-
mands about loving and forgiving, relented:

"Wull, then, come on ben an' pray. Tom, you go call her
husband! This is na time fer holdin' grudges. But mind,
wumman, if ye coom heer to pray ye must pray with as
mooch fervor for the healin' o' *Mark Carter* as ye do fer the
meenister! He's beloved of the Lord too, an' the meenister
nigh give his life for him."

And Mrs. Harricutt put up her apron to her eyes and
entered the little haircloth parlor, while Tom, with a wry face,
went after the elder. The elder proved that underneath all his
narrowness and prejudice he had a grain of the real truth, for
he prayed with fervor that the Lord would cleanse their
hearts from all prejudice and open their minds to see with
heavenly vision that they might have power in prayer for the
healing of the two men.

So, through the whole little village breaches were healed,
and a more loving feeling prevailed because the bond of
anxiety and love held them all together and drew them
nearer to their God.

At last the day came when Mark, struggling up out of the
fiery pit of pain, was able to remember.

Pain, fire, flame, choking gases, smoke, remorse, despair!
It was all vague at first, but out of it came the memory slowly.
There had been a fire. He had gone back up the ladder after
Mrs. Blimm's baby. He remembered groping for the child in
the smoke-filled room, and bringing it blindly through the
hall and back to the window where the ladder was, but that
room had all been in flames. He had wished for a wet cloth
across his face. He could feel again the licking of the fire as
he passed the doorway. A great weight had been on his chest.

His heart seemed bursting. His head had reeled, and he had
come to the window just in time. Someone had taken the
child—was it Billy? or he would have fallen. He *did* fall. The
memory pieced itself out bit by bit. He remembered thinking
that he had entered the City of Fire literally at last, "the
minarets" already he seemed to descry "gleaming vermilion
as if they from the fire had issued." It was curious how those
old words from Dante had clung in his memory. "Eternal fire
that inward burns." He thought he was feeling now in his
body what his soul had experienced for long months past. It
was the natural ending, the thing he had known he was
coming to all along, the road of remorse and despair. A fire
that goes no more out! And this would last forever now!
Then, someone, some strong arm had lifted him—God's air
swept in—and for an instant there seemed hope. But only
that little breath of respite and there came a cry like myriads
of lost souls. They were falling, falling, down through fire,
with fire above, below, around, everywhere. Down, down—
an abysmal eternity of fire, till his seared soul writhed from
his tortured body, and stood aside looking on at himself.

There, there he lay, the Mark Carter that had started with
life so fair, friends, prospects, so proud that he was a man,
that he could conquer and be brave—so blest with opening
life, and heaven's high call! And then—in one day—he had
sinned and lost it all, and there he lay, a white upturned face.
That was himself, lying there with face illumined by the fire,
and men would call him dead! But he would not be dead! He
would be living on with that inward fire, gnawing at his
vitals, telling him continually what he might have been, and
showing him what high heaven was that he had had, and
lost. He saw it now. He had deliberately thrown away that
heaven that had been his. He saw that hell because he made
it so, it was not God that put him there, but he had chosen
there to go. And still the fire burned on and scorched his
poor soul back into the body to be tortured more. The long
weeks upon that bed seemed like an infinite space of burning
rosy, oily flames poured upward from a lake of fire, down
through which he had been falling in constant and increasing
agony.

And now at last he seemed to be flung upon this peaceful
shore where things were cool and soothing for a brief respite,

that he might look off at where he had been floating on
that molten lake of fire, and understand it all before he was
flung back. And it was all so very real. With his eyes still
closed he could hear the rushing of the flames that still
seemed ascending in columns out a little way from shore, he
could see through his eyelids the rosy hue of livid waters—of
course it was all a hallucination, and he was coming to
himself, but he had a feeling that when he was fully awake it
would be even more terrible than now. Two grim figures,
Remorse and Despair, seemed waiting at either hand above
his bed to companion him again when he could get more
strength to recognize them. And so he lay thus between life
and death, and faced what he had done. Hours and hours he
faced it, when they knew not if he was conscious yet, going
over and over again those sins which he knew had been the
beginning of all his walk away from Hope. On through the
night and into the next morning he lay thus, sometimes
drowsing, but most of the time alert and silent.

It was a bright and sparkling morning. There was a tang of
winter in the air. The leaves were gone from the apple trees
at the window and the bare branches tapped against the
waterspout like children playing with a rattle. A dog barked
joyously, and a boy on the street shouted out to another—*Oh,
to be a boy once more!* And suddenly Mark knew Billy was
sitting there. He opened his eyes and smiled: There were
bandages around his face, but he smiled stiffly, and Billy
knew he was smiling.

"Kid," he said hoarsely from out the bandages, "this is
God's world." It seemed to be a great thought that he had
been all this time grasping, and had to utter.

"Sure!" said Billy in a low happy growl.

A long time after this, it might have been the next day, he
wasn't sure, or perhaps only a few minutes, he came at
another truth:

"Kid, you can't get away from God—even when you try."

"I'll say not," said Billy.

"But—when you've sinned—" speculatively.

"You gotta get it off yer chest."

"You mean—confess?"

"Sure thing. Miss Lynn tells us in Sunday school about a
fella in the Bible got downta eatin' with the pigs in a far

country, an' when he come to himself he thought about his father's servants, an' he said 'I'll get up and beat it home an' say I'm sorry!' "

"I know," said Mark, and was still the rest of the day. But the next morning he asked the doctor how soon he might get up. This was the first real indication that Mark was on the mend, and the doctor smiled with satisfaction. He meant to take off some of the bandages that morning.

That afternoon with his head unswathed, Mark began to ask questions. Before that he had seemed to take everything for granted:

"Billy, where's the minister?" For Billy had never left his idol's side except when Aunt Saxon needed him to help.

"Oh, he's up to tha parsonage," responded Billy carelessly.

"But why hasn't he been to see me, kid?"

"Why—he—hasn't been feelin' very good." Billy's voice was brisk as if it wasn't a matter of much moment.

Mark turned his thoughtful gray eyes steadily on Billy:

"Now, look here, kid, I'm well, and there's no further need to camouflage. Billy, is the minister dead?"

"Not on yer tintype, he ain't dead!"

"Well, is he hurt?"

"Well, _some_," Billy admitted cheerfully.

"Kid, look me in the eye."

Billy raised a saucy eye as well masked as Mark's own could be on occasion.

"Kid, how much is he hurt! _Tell me the truth!_ If you don't I'll get right up and go and see."

"I'll tell the world, you won't!" said Billy rising lazily and taking a gentle menacing step toward the bed.

"Kid!"

"Well—he's some hurt—but he's getting along fine now. He'll be aw'right."

"How'd he get hurt?"

"Oh, the fire, same's you."

"How?" insisted Mark.

"Oh, he went up again after a fella when it was too late—"

"Billy, was it me?"

"Uh huh!" nodded Billy.

Mark was so still that Billy was frightened. When he looked up worried he saw that a great tear had escaped out from under the lashes which were growing nicely now, and had rolled down Mark's cheek. *Mark crying!*

In consternation Billy knelt beside the bed:

"Aw, gee! Mark, now don't you feel like that. He's gettin' all right now they hope, an' gee! He was *great!* You oughtta seen him!"

"Tell me about it," said Mark huskily.

"He just ran up that there ladder when it was shaking like a leaf, an' the wall beginning to buckle under it, an' he picked you up. Fer a minute there the flames kinda blew back, and we seen ya both, and then the roof caved, an' you all went down. But when we gotcha out he was layin' right atop of ya, 'ith his arms spread out, trying t' cover ya! Gee, it was *great!* Everybody was just as still, like he was preachin'!"

After a long time Mark said:

"Billy, did you ever hear the words, 'Greater love hath no man than this, that a man lay down his life for his friend'?"

"Yep," said Billy, "that's in the Bible I think, if 'taint in Shakespeare. Miss Lynn said it over last Sunday. She says a lot of things from Shakespeare sometimes, and I kinda get 'em mixed."

But Mark did not talk anymore that day. He had a great deal to think about.

But so did Billy, for looking out the window in the direction of the parsonage he had sighted the big Shafton car stopping before the door that morning. "Aw, gee!" he said. "That sissy guy again? Now, how'm I gonta get rid of him this time? Gee! Just when Mark's gettin' well too! If life ain't just *one thing after another!*"

Chapter 30

It was a bright frosty morning in the edge of winter when at last they let Mark go to see the minister, and Billy took care that no hint of the Shafton car should reach his knowledge. Slowly, gravely he escorted Mark down the street and up the parsonage steps.

The minister was lying on a couch in the living room and there was a low chair drawn up nearby with a book open at the place, and a bit of fluffy sewing on the low table beside it. Mark looked hungrily about for the owner of the gold thimble, but there was no sign of either Mrs. Severn or Marilyn about.

There was a bandage over the minister's eyes. They hadn't told Mark about that yet.

The minister held out a groping hand with his old sweet smile and hearty welcoming voice:

"Well, son, you've come at last! Beat me to it, didn't you? I'm glad. That was fair. Young blood, you know."

Mark knelt down by the couch with his old friend's hand held fast: Billy had faded into the landscape out on the front steps somewhere, and was even now settling down for an extended wait. If this interview went well he might hope to get a little rest and catch up on sports sometime soon. It all depended on this.

Mark put up his other hand and touched the bandage:

"Father!" he said. "Father!" and broke down "Father, I have sinned—" he said brokenly.

The minister's arm went lovingly up across the young man's shoulders:

"Son, have you told your heavenly Father that?" he asked gently.

"I've tried," said Mark. "I'm not sure that He heard."

"Oh, He *heard*," said the minister with a ring of joy in his voice. "While you were a great way off He came to meet you, son."

"You don't know yet," said Mark lifting a white sad face.

"If you've told Him I'll trust you, son. It's up to you whether you tell me or not."

"It is your right to know, sir. I want you to know. I cannot rest again until you do."

"Then tell." The minister's hand folded down tenderly over the boy's, and so kneeling beside the couch Mark told his story:

"I must begin by telling you that I have always loved Marilyn."

"I know," said the minister, with a pressure on the hand he covered.

"One day I heard someone telling Mrs. Severn that I was not good enough for her."

"I know," said the minister again.

"You know?" said Mark in surprise.

"Yes, go on."

"I went away and thought it over. I felt as if I would die. I was mad and hurt clear through, but after I thought it over I saw that all she had said was true. I wasn't good enough. There was a great deal of pride mixed with it all of course, I've seen that since, but I wasn't good enough. Nobody was. Lynn is *wonderful!* But I was just a common, insignificant nobody, not fit to be her mate. I knew it! I could see just how things were going too. I saw you didn't realize it, you nor Mrs. Severn. I knew Marilyn cared, but I thought she didn't realize it either, and I saw it was up to me. If she wasn't to have to suffer by being parted from me when she grew older, I must teach her not to care before she knew she cared. For days I turned it over in my mind. Many nights I lay awake all night or walked out on the hills, threshing it all over again. And I saw another thing. I saw that if it was so hard for me then when I was not much more than a kid it would be harder for her if I let her grow up caring, and then we had to be parted, so I decided to make the break. The day I made the decision I went off in the hills and stayed all day thinking it out. And then I looked up in the sky and told God I was done with Him. I had prayed and prayed that He would make a way out of this trouble for me, and He hadn't done anything about it, and I felt that He was against me too. So when I had done that I felt utterly reckless. I didn't care what happened to me, and I decided to go to the bad as fast as I could. I felt it would be the best way too to make Marilyn get over being fond of me. So I went down to Monopoly that night and looked up a fellow that had been coaching the teams for a while and was put out by the association because he was rotten. He had always made a fuss over me, wanted to make a big player out of me, and I knew he would be glad to see me.

"He was. He took me out to supper that night and gave me liquor to drink. You know I had never touched a drop. Never had intended to as long as I lived. But when he offered it to me I took it down as if I had been used to it. I didn't care. I wanted to do all the wrong I could.

"I drank again and again, and I must have got pretty drunk. I remember the crowd laughed at me a great deal. And they brought some girls around. It makes me sick to think of it now. We went to a place and danced. I didn't know how, but I danced anyway. And there was more drinking. I don't remember things very distinctly. I did whatever the coach said, and he had been going a pretty good pace himself. That night—" His voice choked with shame and it seemed as though he could not go on—but the minister's clasp was steady and the boy gathered courage and went on— "That night—we—went—to a house of shame!"

He dropped his head and groaned. The minister did not attempt to break the pause that followed. He knew the struggle that was going on in the bitterness of the young man's soul. He maintained that steady handclasp:

"In the morning—when I came to myself—" he went on, "I know what I had done. I had cut myself off forever from all that made life worthwhile. I would never be worthy again to even speak to you all whom I loved so much. I would never be able to look myself in the face again even. I was ashamed. I had given up God and love, and everything worthwhile.

"That was when I went away to New York. Mother tried to stop me, but I would go. I tried when I got to New York to plunge into a wild life, but it didn't attract me. I had to force myself. Besides, I had resolved that whatever came, wherever I went I would not drink and would *keep clean*. I thought that by so doing I might in time at least win back my self-respect. Later I conceived the idea of trying to save others from a life of shame. I did succeed in helping some to better ways I think, both men and girls. But I only won a worse reputation at home for it, and I'm not sure I did much good. I only know I walked in hell from morning to night, and in time I came to dwell among lost souls. It seemed the only place that I belonged.

"You remember when you read us Dante 'Thou who through the City of Fire alive art passing'? You used to preach in church about beginning the eternal life now, and making a little heaven below, I'm sure that is as true of hell. I began my eternal life five years ago, but it was in hell, and I shall go on living in that fire of torture forever, apart from all I love. I tried to get out by doing good to others, but it was of no avail. I thought never to tell you this, but something made me, after you—you gave your life for me!"

"And had you forgotten," said the minister tenderly, "that the blood of Jesus Christ His Son cleanseth us from all sin? And that He said, 'Come now and let us reason together: though your sins be as scarlet they shall be as white as snow'?"

"I gave up all right to that when I gave up God on the mountain."

"But God did not give up you," said the minister. "Do you think a true father would cast out a child because it got angry and shook its fist in his face? You will find Him again when you search for Him with all your heart. You have told Him you were sorry, and He has promised to forgive. You can't save yourself, but He can save you. Now, son, go and tell Marilyn everything."

"Do you mean it—*Father?*"

"I mean it—*Son*. The doctor is coming by and by to take off these bandages, and I want the first thing that my eyes rest upon after my dear wife's face, to be the faces of you two. My beloved children."

Sabbath Valley lay tucked warm and white beneath a blanket of snow. All the week it had been coming down, down, in great white flakes of especially sorted sizes, filling the air mightily with winter clean and deep. Here in the fastnesses of the hills it seemed that the treasure troves of the sky had been opened to make all beautiful and quiet while winter passed that way. Lone Valley was almost obliterated, pierced with sharp pine trees in bunches here and there, like a flock of pins in a pincushion, and the hills rose gently on either side like a vast amphitheater done in white and peopled thick with trees in heavy white furs.

The highway was almost impassable for a day or two, but the state snowplow passed over as soon as the snow stopped falling, and left a white pavement with white walls either side. The tunnel through the mountains was only a black dot in the vast whiteness, and Pleasant View Station wore a heavy cap of snow dripping down in lavish fringes edged with icicles. The agent's little shanty up the mountain was buried out of sight behind a snowdrift and had to be dug out from the back, and no lake train ran anymore. The express was five hours late. Stark Mountain loomed white against the sky. And over in Sabbath Valley the night it stopped snowing all the villagers were out shoveling their walks and calling glad nothings back and forth as they flung the white stardust from their shovels, and little children came out with rubber boots and warm leggings and wallowed in the beauty. The milkman got out an old sleigh and strung a line of bells around his horse. The boys and girls hurried up the mountain to their slide with homemade sleds and laughing voices, and the moon came up looking sweetly from a sudden clearing sky.

Over in the church the windows shone with light, and the bells were ringing out the old sweet songs the villagers loved. Marilyn was at the organ and Mark by her side. In the body of the church willing hands were working, setting up the tall hemlocks that Tom and Jim had brought in from the mountain, till the little church was fragrant and literally lined with lacey beauty, reminding one of ancient worship in the woods. Holly wreaths were hanging in the windows everywhere, and ropes of ground pine and laurel festooned from every pillar and corner and peak of roof.

Laurie Shafton had sent a great coffer of wonderful roses, and the country girls were handling them with awe, banking them round the pulpit, and trailing them over the rail of the little choirloft, wonderful roses from another world, the world that Marilyn Severn might have married into if she had chosen. And there sat Marilyn as indifferent as if they were dandelions, praising the *trees* that had been set up, delighting in their slender tops that rose like miniature spires all round the wall, drawing in the sweetness of their winter spicy breath, and never saying a word about the roses. "Roses? Oh, yes, they look all right, girls, just put them wherever you fancy. I'll be suited. But aren't those trees too beautiful for words?"

When the work was done they trooped out noisily into the moonlight, bright like day only with a beauty that was almost unearthly in its radiance. The others went on down the street calling gay words back and forth, but Mark and Marilyn lingered, bearing a wreath of laurel, and stepping deep into the whiteness went over to the white piled mound where they had laid Mrs. Carter's body to rest and Mark stooped down and pressed the wreath down into the snow upon the top:

"Dear little Mother," he said brokenly, "she loved pretty things and I meant to give her so many of them sometime to make up—"

"But she'll be glad—" said Marilyn softly. "We loved each other very much!"

"Yes, she'll be glad!" he answered. "She often tried to find out why I never went to the parsonage anymore. Poor little mother! That was her deepest disappointment! Yes, she'll be glad!"

When morning came it seemed as though the very glory of God was spread forth on Sabbath Valley for display. There it lay, a shining gem of a little white town, in the white velvet cup of the valley, dazzling and resplendent, the hills rising round about reflecting more brightness and etched with fringes of fine branches each burdened with a line of heavy furry white. Against the clear blue sky the bell tower rose, and from its arches the bells rang forth a wedding song. Marilyn in her white robes, with a long white veil of rare old lace handed down through the generations, falling down the back and fastened about her forehead, and with a slim little rope of pearls, also an heirloom, was ringing her own wedding bells, with Mark by her side, while the villagers gathered outside the door waiting for the wedding march to begin before they came in.

The minister and his wife stood back in his little study behind the pulpit, watching their two with loving eyes, and down by the front door stood Billy in a new suit with his hair very wet and licked back from an almost crimson countenance, waiting the word to fling open the door and let the congregation in.

"*Tum*, diddy*dum*—Diddy*dum*—diddy*dum*—Diddy*dum*— diddy*dum*—Diddy*dum*—*dum*—*dum*—Dum—Dum—Dum!" began the organ and Billy flung the portals wide and stood

aside on the steps to let the throng pass in, his eyes shining
as if they would say, "Aw, gee! Ain't this great?"

And just at that moment, wallowing through the snow, with
the air of having come from the North Pole there arrived a
great car and drew up to the door, and Laurie Shafton
jumped anxiously out and flung open the door for his passengers.

"Aw, gee! That fish! Whadde wantta come here for? The
great *chump!* Don't he knew he ain't *in it?*"

Billy watched in lofty scorn from his high step and decided
to hurry in and not have to show any honors to that sissy guy.

Then out from the car issued Opal, done in furs from brow
to shoe and looking eagerly about her, and following her a big
handsome sporty man almost twice her age, looking curiously
interested, as if he had come to a shrine to worship, Opal's
husband. Billy stared, and then remembering that the wedding
march was almost over and that he might be missing something:

"Aw, gee! Whadduw I care? He ain't little apples now,
anyhow. He couldn'ta bought her with *barrels* of roses, an' he
knows it too, the poor stiff. He must be a pretty good scout
after all, takin' his medicine straight!"

Then Billy slid in and the quiet little ceremony began.

The organ hushed into nothing. Marilyn arose, took Mark's
arm, and together they stepped down and stood in front of
the minister, who had come down the steps of the pulpit and
was awaiting them, with Marilyn's mother sitting only a step
away on the front seat.

It was all so quiet and homey, without fuss or marching or
any such thing, and when the ceremony was over the bride
and groom turned about in front of the bank of hemlock and
roses and their friends swarmed up to congratulate them.
Then everybody went into the parsonage, where the ladies of
the church had prepared a real country wedding breakfast
with Christmas turkey and fixings for a foundation and going
on from that. It wasn't every day in the year that Sabbath
Valley got its minister's daughter married, and what if the
parsonage *was* small and only fifty could sit down at once,
everybody was patient, and it was all the more fun!

The three guests from out of town, self-imposed, looked on
with wonder and interest. It was a revelation. Marilyn looked
up and found big Ed Verrons frankly staring at her, a puzzled

pleased expression on his large coarse face. She was half annoyed and wondered why they had come to spoil this perfect day. Then suddenly the big man stepped across the little living room and spoke:

"Mrs. Carter, we came over today because Opal said you had something that would help us begin over again and make life more of a success. I want to thank you for having this chance to see a little bit of heaven on earth before I die."

Later, when the city guests were fed and comforted perhaps, and had climbed back into the big car, Billy stood on the front porch with a third helping of ice cream and watched them back, and turn, and wallow away into the deep white world, and his heart was touched with pity:

"Aw, gee! The poor fish! I 'spose it *is* hard lines! And then it was sorta my faultchu know," and he turned with a joyful sigh that they were gone, and went in to look again at Mary Louise Little, and see what it was about her in that new blue challis that made her look so sorta nice today.

Novels of Enduring Romance and Inspiration by

GRACE LIVINGSTON HILL

☐	23558	**CHRISTMAS BRIDE #62**	$2.50
☐	20286	**MAN OF THE DESERT #63**	$2.25
☐	24736	**AN UNWILLING GUEST #65**	$2.50
☐	26364	**THE GIRL FROM MONTANA #66**	$2.75
☐	24876	**A DAILY RATE #67**	$2.50
☐	26437	**THE STORY OF A WHIM #68**	$2.75
☐	26389	**ACCORDING TO THE PATTERN #69**	$2.75
☐	25253	**IN THE WAY #70**	$2.95
☐	25459	**EXIT BETTY #71**	$2.50
☐	25573	**THE WHITE LADY #72**	$2.95
☐	25733	**NOT UNDER THE LAW #73**	$2.95
☐	25806	**LO, MICHAEL #74**	$2.95
☐	25930	**THE WITNESS #75**	$2.95
☐	26104	**THE CITY OF FIRE #76**	$2.95

Prices and availability subject to change without notice.

Buy them at your local bookstore or use this handy coupon for ordering:

Bantam Books, Inc., Dept. GLH, 414 East Golf Road, Des Plaines, Ill. 60016

Please send me the books I have checked above. I am enclosing $_____
(please add $1.50 to cover postage and handling). Send check or money order
—no cash or C.O.D.'s please.

Mr/Mrs/Miss_____

Address_____

City _____ State/Zip _____

GLH—11/86

Please allow four to six weeks for delivery. This offer expires 5/87.

CLASSICS BOOK ON SIGNING
By Elaine Costello

Dr. Elaine Costello, educator and author, has been an innovator in the field of deafness for more than twenty years. She is currently the director and editor in chief of the Gallaudet College Press at Gallaudet College in Washington, D.C., the world's only liberal arts college for the deaf.

☐ **SIGNING: HOW TO SPEAK WITH YOUR HANDS (34250-9 • $10.95)**
American Sign Language is a wonderful silent language of hands, face and body that is rich with nuance, emotion and grace—a marvelous mode of communication that encourages self-expression and creativity as it serves the essential, everyday functions of a living language. This totally new, comprehensive guide contains all the basic vocabulary and linguistic information that families, individuals and professionals need to communicate effectively with deaf children and adults. Over 150,000 copies have already been sold of this indispensable guide to ASL.

☐ **RELIGIOUS SIGNING (34244-4 • $9.95)**
RELIGIOUS SIGNING is the first and only interdenominational guide to religious sign language. This totally new guide contains all the vocabulary and information you need to communicate effectively in most religious settings:

- From Alleluia to Zizith, more than 500 signs and their specific meanings.
- Large, clear upper-torso illustrations that show the corresponding movements of hands, body and face.
- A special section on signing favorite verses, prayers and blessings.
- A complete index and cross-reference for quick access to any sign.

Look for them at your bookstore or use this coupon for ordering:

Now, the complete stories and novels about the master of detectives, Sherlock Holmes, by Sir Arthur Conan Doyle are available in paperback for the first time:

SHERLOCK HOLMES:
The Complete Novels and Stories
Volumes I & II
from Bantam Classics

☐ VOLUME I (21241-9 • $4.95):
  THE ADVENTURES OF SHERLOCK HOLMES
  THE MEMOIRS OF SHERLOCK HOLMES
  THE RETURN OF SHERLOCK HOLMES
  THE SIGN OF FOUR
  A STUDY IN SCARLET

☐ VOLUME II (21242-7 • $4.95):
  THE CASE BOOK OF SHERLOCK HOLMES
  HIS LAST BOW
  THE HOUND OF THE BASKERVILLES
  THE VALLEY OF FEAR

Both volumes are also available as a box set:

☐ VOLUMES I & II BOX SET (32825-5 • $9.90)

Look for them at your bookstore or use this coupon for ordering: